MRS NARWHAL'S DIARY

MRS NARWHAL'S DIARY

S J Norbury

2021
Louise Walters Books

Mrs Narwhal's Diary
by S J Norbury

A catalogue card for this book is available from the British Library.

Produced and published in 2021
by Louise Walters Books

ISBN 9781 916 11 23 15
eISBN 9781 916 11 23 22

Typeset in PTSerif 11pt / 14.8pt by Blot Publishing

Printed and bound by Clays Ltd, Elcograf S.p.A

louisewaltersbooks.co.uk

info@louisewaltersbooks.co.uk

Louise Walters Books
PO Box 755
Banbury
OX16 6PJ

To G, N & K, my very best beloveds,
whose glorious disinterest in this book
gave me just the space I needed to write it

16TH MAY

Despite the reassurances Ian gave me last week about the Tree House, the minute we were all up there today I was quite certain none of us would make it back down again. Not alive anyway. I barely heard a word of Hugh's speech as my ears were far too busy listening out for cracking timbers, falling family members, and other signs of imminent disaster. Rose had somehow managed to get up the ladder in the most unbelievably high heels, spiking away at all that rotten wood, though at least she doesn't weigh much. The piper meanwhile looked to be the wrong side of seventeen stone, and therefore by far the most likely of us to plummet through the floor to certain death. I put him right at the front under the gable, ostensibly for dramatic effect ("The Mist Covered Mountains of Home" echoing movingly across Grandpa Hugh's patch of green and pleasant land, etc, etc), but in reality because that's where Ian told me to put the fattest person. Did feel guilty mentally weighing everyone as we made our way up there, as it seemed so judgemental, *and* I was supposed to be thinking about Grandpa. Billy at least looked appropriately sombre, hands clasped, eyes down, but Pete kept fiddling with the bell rope, as I bribed him yesterday with the promise of doing the actual Ringing, while Rose was motionless and inscrutable behind her black glasses; she could just as easily have been asleep as overcome by emotion at this year's memorial to her father.

It's not exactly a well-known means of honouring a dead relative, is it, really? Not exactly laying flowers on a grave, raising a toast, observing a minute's silence. But that's the Narwhals for you. Why do something simple and low key when there's a perfectly good, mad, and over-elaborate alternative? Like making everyone struggle up a Tree House ladder for a full-blown ceremony in which the most recently deceased head of household is saluted by the current one with a speech, a piper, and the ringing of a great bronze bell? (Not even a legitimately procured bell either. Pinched, no less. From an orthodox church in Constantinople by an ancestral Narwhal.) And then supper in dinner dress, at which the posh tableware must be used and a goose – specifically this vast, oven-destroying bird – must be eaten.

When I tell people about the Ringing, they usually respond with delight. What a charmingly eccentric family tradition, they cry! And how wonderful that it's still going strong now, years and years (and years...) after it was begun. I tend to stay quiet at this point, as it seems rather whiny and mean-spirited to contradict them, like showing someone a photo of your jam-coated child and responding to their indulgent coos with a rant about the industrial clean-up operation that had to follow. But oh my goodness how I'd love a good rant! If the Ringing was the only Narwhal obligation I needed to fulfil, perhaps I'd manage to be more magnanimous about the efforts involved, but of course it's just the tip of the iceberg, and I'm never more aware of this than when we're in the Tree House. Because while you get the most beautiful long-distance views from up there, which everyone exclaims upon and which were, no doubt, the reason the Tree House was built originally, the immediate vista is stuffed to bursting with things which I'm supposed to be looking after: dovecot (leaning at worrying angle, ash tree sprouting happily through roof); sunken pool (swamped by wild strawberries from the outside, marsh irises from the inside); grotto (used as chicken house in the 1930s, other than absence of chickens still looks like chicken house from the 1930s); pagoda (missing a leg, paint long since flaked off), glasshouse, Athena statue, war memorial... I can see all of them from up there, waving their ailments at me like a bunch of querulous old ladies, insisting that their own cracks, or ivy asphyxiation, or slumping roofs, are the most worthy of immediate attention, while I can only blink at them in anguish.

Obviously, there was no point mentioning any of these concerns about the place to anyone else up there today, as I've long learned I'm the only one who frets. The boys would look at me blankly, Hugh would be instantly irritated and I don't think Rose would have the first idea what I was talking about, let alone the interest to find out. Besides, nothing *outside* the Tree House was as pressing an issue as what was going on *inside* it – was it my imagination or were the floorboards beneath the piper's ample frame beginning to bow? Would it be quicker to call an ambulance, or just squash all the casualties in the car and take them to Hereford myself?

But in all senses of the phrase, we got away with it. Hugh said a few lovely words about Grandpa, Pete let the bell toll three times, and then the piper played. I think Grandpa would have been touched. And no one died, which was rather a bonus.

*

Supper was not a success. As always, I asked Ian to join us, and, as always, he refused, with that standard quiet indignation that makes you think you've just proffered up offence and not an invitation, so there were just the five of us. And despite our smartness (a term that could really only be applied accurately to Rose) we seemed as ever quite unable to match the table's expectations of its diners – not numerous enough or grand enough or accustomed enough to ludicrous towering candelabras, Venetian glass, and translucent porcelain to warrant the disturbance of their attic slumber, let alone their use. (This snootiness so very misjudged when you consider the near worthlessness of every single item – any real value long lost in the deep dents in the silver, the chips and superglued seams in everything else.) To be fair, Hugh and Rose seemed pretty oblivious to the demands of the tableware, but Billy, acutely aware of its alleged preciousness, approached every sip and morsel as if they were finely triggered explosive devices, while Pete entertained himself by causing me repeated bursts of panic as he "accidentally" nearly knocked over or dropped everything within his reach.

'Peter,' I hissed in his ear after a particularly close shave, 'will you *please* behave.'

'Oh, leave him be,' said Rose, unhelpfully, ruffling his hair. 'He's probably bored to tears. I know I am,' she added loudly, making it clear from the glance she gave her brother that she held him entirely responsible for this. Hugh was busy carving the goose, but it wasn't focus on his task that made him ignore her.

'In the old days,' she went on, in a cosy storytelling voice designed to draw both boys to listen, 'before your Grandpa

Hugh died, your mum and your dad and I used to have a lot of fun at the Ringings, though they were for Great Grandpa Hugh then of course. Usually we'd turn it into a bit of a party; get some friends over in the evening, put some music on outside and dance, or go skinny dipping in the lake, or – oh, so many lovely things,' she continued, setting her enormous dangly earrings swinging as she shook her head in nostalgia. 'Certainly it was never like *this.*'

She was right, of course. There'd never have been fewer than twenty round the table then (Grandpa Hugh would have been very disappointed otherwise) and had you glanced down the room you'd have seen the faces of friends in every state of animation – laughing, talking intently, listening intently, interrupting, grimacing or exclaiming at some outrage or absurdity – while the room, so cavernous and unimpressed tonight, would settle back in pleasure and satisfaction. As did Grandpa Hugh himself, liking nothing more than being surrounded by "the young", sometimes as participant but mainly as benign and proprietary observer. It was only when the space could no longer contain us – when we were no longer willing to be contained – that the nature of our enjoyment diverged from his and he'd retire to the snug peaceably with a whisky in his hand and Delilah, her head on her paws, at his feet.

For the first Ringing after he died, seven years ago now, we made the same preparations as always: same guests, same lugging boxes from the attic, same wrestling with goose. But even as I saw no reason why the outcome, a fantastic evening, shouldn't be the same as it always had been, some part of me suspected that it wouldn't be, and it wasn't. Hugh sat in his father's chair, but his gaze upon the scene before him told me quite clearly he was ill at ease. He rose abruptly and with unnecessary frequency to top up glasses, making sure to stand back as he did so, never once laying his free hand on someone's shoulder or dropping in some dry comment as he would have done as a matter of course just a year before. Had he not been at the head of the table, his discontent might have been less noticeable, perhaps mentioned only in passing by guests on their way home, but just as Grandpa Hugh's beamed benevolence had somehow urged on past gatherings, so Hugh's edginess now seemed to hold that one back, dragging at conversations, causing the usual arc of uproar to tilt into desultory appetites and early departures.

Nothing, he'd said, when I'd asked him at the end of the night what was wrong. He was just tired, he'd said. But somehow, when the next Ringing came around, I understood that it was not to be a party, and that – when Rose complained on hearing this – I was to imply that this was merely a temporary suspension due to the demands of work and young kids, whether I believed this or not. I didn't, as it happens, but it made no difference anyway; I accepted the change and got on with it. Rose, on the other hand, would not. As each subsequent year rolled by, and it became harder and harder for any of us to pretend that the Ringings would ever revert to their old shape and size and not remain as shrivelled as they'd become, she took increasingly to a sort of multi-purpose scorn (directed almost entirely towards Hugh) that achieved with great efficacy all manner of objectives except the one she cared about the most. Because although Hugh heard that the Ringings were dull and that this was his fault because *he* had grown dull, that he'd let down his ancestors and his descendants and that she herself was far too interesting and glamorous to succumb willingly to such tedium, what he didn't hear was that Rose *missed* him. Where had he gone, she was crying out, and *why*?

It's horrible to watch this pining for him, this refusal to give up. She's been banging her fists on him for seven years, and everyone would be much better off – herself particularly – if she'd just let him go.

'You wouldn't believe it to look at him now,' Rose went on, in a quieter voice, 'but your dad was the best fun of anyone.'

We all looked at Hugh, trying to superimpose a bon viveur upon the man before us. This proved difficult, as he was currently cutting a potato with a great deal more force and frowning than my cooking of it required – certainly not with the sort of carefree abandon you'd expect from a man who approved of chandelier swinging in anyone, let alone himself.

I felt a sudden surge of sadness, which I repressed, and of loyalty, which I didn't.

'We're nearly middle-aged, Rose,' I said, with a little more heat than I'd intended, 'with children, a business, *this* place. It's not that we don't have fun anymore, it's just a quieter sort. More sofa than bouncy castle, if you like.'

There was a long pause, then Rose drained her glass, set it down, and said, 'Who wants to drive my car round the paddock?' From the cool, fixed look she gave Hugh at the same time, it was clear that only the nice crispy skin of this question was for the boys. Its meat and gristle and marrow she heaved onto her brother's plate, for him alone to chew on.

The children, of course, leapt immediately to their feet, clamouring to be first to sit in the driving seat, and I allowed their pleasure to override my irritation at their aunt's blatant manipulation of them, because this – like so many of her more challenging characteristics – is just part of the percussion she needs to drown out her violins.

'Will you…?' I began, but the three of them had already bustled out of the door, leaving Hugh and me and the sudden silence.

I looked at him for a moment before breaking it. He was slumped in his chair, his right elbow resting on its arm, supporting in turn his balled fist and his head. His left hand was gently turning the stem of his wine glass round and round, and I took advantage of his absorption in this to try and suspend his familiarity and see him afresh.

He looked like a man with the world on his shoulders, which I suppose he is. What had I said to Rose? Children, a business, this place – responsibilities familiar to so many people until you factor in exactly what "this place" means. Not a nice normal house that you came upon and chose and bought and will at some point probably sell, a house for *living* in, but one that was destined for you from the day you were born. That you always knew was coming for you, bringing nothing in its wake but debt, duty, work and despair. Imagine reading a cheery description like that in the estate agent's window – wouldn't you run a mile? Is it any wonder he's not the man he used to be? What does Rose expect? Life makes its demands on you and you've just got to get on with them. That's just what you *do*.

The candlelight fluttered in one of the many exciting draughts in which this house specialises, and cast a flush of warmth over Hugh's head. Both he and Rose have the quite preposterously gorgeous Narwhal hair – thick and glossy chestnut locks. It's the sort of hair that belongs on the cover of a bodice ripper, cascading improbably to the heroine's waist or swooping sexily over her lover's eye. Rose is only too glad of hers; Hugh has always found his rather traitorous, and I have to say it did seem cruelly unsympathetic to his leaden face beneath it this evening...

I thought about suggesting a walk to cheer him up – the bluebells would be out and it was warm outside – but dismissed it. He was probably itching to go to the workshop and end the evening, so why bother to offer something I knew would be refused?

Sure enough–

'I think I'll go and do some work,' he said, with a sigh. He began to lift himself out of his chair, then paused midway as something struck him. 'You don't mind?'

'Of course not,' I said briskly, having already begun to scrape the plates. I told him I'd see him later, thinking as I did so that actually our bluebells were always late, and no one could say it was *that* warm.

17TH MAY

It was *Woman's Hour* who suggested I keep a diary. They said it was good for mental health, and I must say I did feel much less frazzled after writing everything down yesterday. The frustrations were all still there, but somehow smoothed out – as if by a really good steam iron. So I think I'll carry on with it for now. It's not often you come across a mood enhancer that's both free *and* non-alcoholic, after all. What's more it's meant I can make use of those empty scrapbooks in the library, which I've been hoping for ages to repurpose.

There are thirty or forty full ones. Hugh calls them the commonplace books, not scrapbooks, and they must contain at least a century's worth of Narwhal jottings, recipes, bon mots, calling cards, letters, poems, prayers, pressed flowers, and goodness knows what else. One of them, I remember, consists entirely of drawings of elephants. The books are beautifully bound in red Morocco, with lovely, thick pages that are a delight to write on; I could never afford to buy such a diary. I just hope it doesn't mind my scribblings on it. At least I use my best pen.

There was a dent in Hugh's pillow this morning, but that's the only way I know his head lay on it, as he hadn't come back from the workshop by the time I went to sleep, and he wasn't here when I woke up. Of all the usual things he could be avoiding – taking the boys to school, me asking him too many things too early – I suspect the major one today was his sister. I can see that a man who finds an excess adverb a little indulgent, let alone a whole conversation, would be alarmed by Rose's frothy chat – like an ascetic hotly pursued by a vast cream cake – and I do understand why it's left to me to look after her, not least because, excuse or no excuse, he does have to work. But I wouldn't be at all surprised if Rose said more in the average day than Hugh will in the rest of his life, and it took me some time this morning to accustom myself to the one after being so used to the other.

Nothing was said about last night, perhaps because Rose was far more interested in talking about the piper, allegedly called Donald, whom she somehow managed to seduce yesterday in the half hour between "Amazing Grace" and "Auld Lang Syne". This is *very* fast work, even for her.

Did I notice his hands, Rose wanted to know, and the way his hair curled under the bottom of his piper hat? I was able to say in all honesty that I hadn't, though didn't mention this was because I was too busy analysing the probable weight of his gut. Well, they were the most beautiful hands and the most wonderful curls and she couldn't wait to admire them again when she met him next weekend. Her clear excitement gave me both pleasure and anxiety.

'Rose,' I began, but she put up her hand to stop me.

'I know, I know,' she said. 'I have a history of falling for people, but this time it's *definitely* different.'

'Rose,' I said, but again with the hand.

'I know; I know I have a history of falling for people and each time saying this time it's definitely different, but this time it *really,* really is.'

I sighed. In one way, I'm most fond of her when we're alone. As soon as anyone else is present (men particularly) her attention flits to them, or not to them so much as to the presentation of herself before them. It's as if she steps onto a stage – putting her beauty through its paces, kicking up a little simper here, a little hauteur there, whatever will best beguile or impress or diminish as she desires. But somehow I've always been much more stage-hand than audience. And though this means I'm the first to be dismissed when the curtain rises, it also means I don't mind, because I get to see what the others don't: her true self, or whatever she believes to be true. There's an honour in this which I value hugely, not just because I know she must trust me, but because I need this access to her heart. I worry about her, have *always* worried about her to a greater or lesser degree – how could I not? I've known her since she was fourteen. I was part big sister, part *mother* even long before I was her brother's wife, and until I feel the worry's not needed I can only keep on at it, taking her temperature endlessly through her words, biting my lip at her chills and fevers...

I waved her off just before lunchtime, sorry to see her go but at the same time rather relieved that she'd be taking all her talking with her. I do love her, but this is the downside of being with her on my own: the woman is quite exhausting. She didn't even begin her actual goodbye until way after she'd started the engine. As she chatted on about Donald's manly legs, I found myself looking through the car windows and wondering if there was any mileage in a

Through the Keyhole spin-off involving people's vehicles rather than their houses. Rose's car couldn't belong to anyone other than Rose, full as it was of posh shopping bags with ribbon handles, a tangle of clothes, a polythene puddle of dry cleaning, a yoga mat, and a small collection of empty Evian bottles. Dear Lord, she was *still* talking: could I keep an eye out for her hairbrush, and say goodbye to the boys, and to Hugh, and she'd always fancied a tam-o'-shanter, and shit, did she have her phone? And yes, she did have her phone, and then – just as I thought she might never leave – she smiled winningly, blew me a kiss, and drove off.

I waited for a moment in the yard, listening with a great exhale of breath to the pigeons in the beech trees behind the glasshouse, then went back inside to finish off last night's clearing up.

I had a very productive afternoon. By the time I collected the boys from school the dining room was at last clear – everything washed, dried, boxed and carried back to the attic with no breakages and a mostly successful quashing of unhelpful thoughts about what a palaver the Ringing was. I'd typed up the PCC minutes, got a wash on and out, stripped the goose carcass, and spotted, scooped up, and evicted yet another toad that had found its way under the piano. (I suppose it could be the same one each time, but you'd think then he wouldn't always look so surprised?)

At supper, Pete was full of how much fun it had been driving round the paddock with Aunty Ro, and how basically he could definitely drive on the roads now.

'How old is Aunty Ro?' said Billy thoughtfully.

'Thirty-two going on sixteen,' said Hugh, glowering.

'What does that mean?' said Pete.

'She's thirty-two, Pete,' I said, feeling the surprise I

always feel that she's the age she is, not – I'm determined to believe – because she's immature, but rather in the way a parent can never quite grasp the growing up of her offspring. 'Though she seems younger because, you know, she does.'

'She's irresponsible,' said Hugh.

'Playful,' said I.

'Self-obsessed.'

'She doesn't *mean* to be...'

'Purposeless.'

'Just a bit *lost*, Hugh,' I pressed, still incredulous after so long that all his old compassion and tolerance towards his sister, the accuracy of his empathy, his ability to coax or gently chide or soothe her through the dark forests of her escapades and eccentricities, had turned to such stony disapproval. There was no point in saying this, as I've said it all before, and even though he's well aware of his change in attitude, not only does he not regret it, he sees it as long overdue. What I thought of as love (just billions of examples of this: him holding her hair back when she was sick; him drawing up a revision timetable for her, complete with cartoons and smiley faces; him marching her over to Farmer Dan's so she could confess to her "liberation" of his cows and help him bring them back; and above all how he tended to her when their mother died) he now sees stubbornly as indulgence. He's exchanged pity for punishment, humour for harshness, and what I see as the cost of this – the wounded withdrawal of Rose's trust and adoration – he doesn't seem to see as a cost at all.

Poor, poor Rose. She can't understand why he changed, and I can't understand why she can't understand. You need at least a bit of buoyancy in yourself to help keep others afloat, and Hugh lost his when the house and all its burdens landed upon him. It was suddenly hard enough to keep his own head above water, let alone anyone else's, and why – really – couldn't she look after herself? She had a nice little London flat and plenty of money; in Hugh's newly narrowed eyes she had more than enough for self-sufficiency. Envy and resentment have plugged his heart so comprehensively she'd have to have a knife at her throat before he heard her needs now, let alone responded to them. Anything less – mere misery, for example – sounds to him like whining, like Marie Antoinette's complaints about her pinching shoes.

'Well, I like her,' said Peter then.

'Yeah. *I* like her,' said Billy.

'I'm glad to hear it,' I said, giving them both a kiss on the head, 'because she likes you very much too.'

Hugh and I did the washing-up in a not unpleasant silence, my brain picking over the day and the people within it, while I couldn't tell you what Hugh's brain was doing. Then, as usual, we said good night to the boys and went into the snug to watch a bit of what we're into on the telly. It's a drama about international heroin smuggling at the moment. We're on episode two, and the jury's still out as to whether Hugh likes it or not. The protagonist's girlfriend seems to smile at all times, regardless of whether she's happy, distraught, battling a masked intruder, or lost in the throes of passion, and Hugh keeps shouting, '*Stop fucking smiling!*' every time she comes on. But this doesn't necessarily mean he's not enjoying it. I sometimes think he's at his happiest, as we all are to a certain extent, when bawling our discontent at people who can't hear us.

19TH MAY

There was real warmth in the sun yesterday, and I felt as I always do at this time of year: an absolute compulsion to be outside amongst the blossom and all the tender greens, praising the wanted ones and threatening the others. Just you wait, you little bastards, I said to the fresh young couch grass springing up between the roses; this is the year I'm going to get you. And you, ground elder, and you, brambles pushing through the columns of the folly. So cheerful was I that when I saw Charles I's head had fallen off his plinth on the west wall of the house (royalist ancestral Hugh), I didn't flap or tut, but merely popped him in my wheelbarrow to put in the scullery with Richard III's for Ian to stick back when money and time permits.

Maybe one day, I thought wildly, we'd be able to get a gardener and I'd have the sort of help that meant I wasn't fire-fighting all the time but making real progress, and I spent a bit of time stroking my old plans, finding them untouched and perfect beneath the dust sheets that had long covered them over in my mind.

The first project would always be to introduce some much needed coherence to the grounds, as hardly anything makes sense where it is. Take the wisteria tunnel. You'd expect what the gardening magazines call "a feature" at the end of it, and there is one – the war memorial – but plonked behind that, not even directly behind it but just slightly off eyeline, is the fountain. And there's no point turning round for a more pleasing vista at the other end, because there's a hawthorn hedge *right* there across it, sealing it off so effectively you can't really call it a tunnel but what – a sort of blocked off tube? I can only think the land beyond got sold, and instead of doing something sensible like diverting the wisteria, or taking it down, they just bunged up a boundary hedge and went inside for tea.

So bizarre is most of it (there's a rotting twelve-foot totem pole in the middle of the orchard, for goodness' sake) that I often find myself asking the ancestral Hughs: what *were* you thinking? Did you just wander out on a Sunday afternoon with your wife and a vague idea, close your eyes, point and build? Did you not plan? *Why* did you not plan? Did you not care, or did you just not *see* the oddness of it all? Each generation, I always think, was as determined to put their own stamp on the place as they were to leave respectfully untouched the contributions of the generation before, four hundred years of Narwhal whim and fancy blithely indulged, with not so much as a thought for those of us at the end of the line who have to look after it all with only a fraction of their time and finances.

I say that, but really, what do I know? Maybe it isn't every longstanding family that's like this, just the Narwhals. I've got nothing to compare them with as they're the only ones I've met.

The house is even worse than the garden. It might be depressing outside, but – if you're sensible – you're at least relatively safe, whereas all manner of perils lurk indoors. You might open a window one summer morning to watch the whole casement fall from your fingertips into the currant bushes below (me), or find the lower part of your left leg has disappeared through a floorboard (Billy), or that you poke an intriguing bulge in your ceiling with the end of your fishing rod and release a great torrent of water over your head (Peter). It really is quite stressful. Particularly because, with no money for proper repairs, the Heath Robinson patching up is possibly more of a risk to our lives than the problems it tries to resolve. Not that anyone else seems bothered by this. The boys, in fact, see it as an actual plus, and have developed the half-tiptoe/half-dare approach to their surroundings that children playing in bomb sites do. They have developed an exacting instinct for risk, the line between frisson and actual danger precisely understood and relinquished for no man, certainly not their mother, who has given up trying to get them to redefine it. Not only will they not keep clear of the Acrow prop that has held up a section of the main staircase for the past four years, for example, but endlessly exploit it, as climbing frame, ship's mast, and stake to which can be tied hapless teddies, Lego men, and aunts when in the mood.

The one mercy, that I return to over and over again for the shudder of gratitude it gives me, is that the house is so much smaller than it originally was. Dear Bigwig Hugh (this epithet due to the exuberant hairpiece he sports in his portrait, at which I often blow a kiss as I pass) knocked down two thirds of the building circa 1750. Half-crazed by his wife's flagrant infidelities, his intent was to curb them by destroying forty-odd rooms in which they could occur. Though this logic could not have been more cockeyed – not least because Arabella was well-known throughout the land to prefer the vigour of al fresco sex – incredibly, Bigwig's aim was achieved. Arabella was awed into faithfulness. What jewels or posies, what sweet seductions could ever compete with half a house torn down for the love of her? She and Bigwig were inseparable ever after, and I have a great deal less house to worry about than I might have done, though as with everything else here, it's only outsiders who are struck by the contradictions of the building that remains. Its grandeur is way too big for it, giving the place the sort of valiant, vulnerable, slightly ludicrous air of a dowager duchess stuck in traffic.

But, as I say, I was immune to all anxieties while in the garden yesterday, happily (and sacrilegiously, obviously) driving an imaginary JCB, knocking things down here, ripping things up there, and having such a lovely time that, when six o'clock came, I made a couple of celebratory gin and tonics and took them out to the workshop to see Hugh.

He had just finished with Mrs Yarwood, and I knew straightaway that he was in a very particular state of mind as a result.

His upholstery customers generally fall into two broad camps. The first, and by far the biggest, consists of those who seem to give him work almost against their will, needing it done but resentfully so, either openly challenging the cost, the process, the time it will take, or doing it through insinuation, so that – no matter how beautiful a job he's done – neither party can ever take pleasure from this: the customer because they're certain, even though they can't see how, that they haven't got what they wanted or paid for, and Hugh because he knows this, and infers from it that his best will never be good enough.

When he's completed a job for a member of this group, it's important that he and I avoid a conversation that runs something like this: I compliment him warmly, and genuinely, on his workmanship. He gets irritated, as it's not upholstery he should be doing, he always says (and how many times does he have to tell me), but his furniture making. I say stoutly that I'm sure it's only a matter of time before people buy his furniture. He says I know you don't believe that. I think about the good people around, most of whom would pass out if an Ikea flatpack entered their homes, let alone tables of reclaimed oak with lime green resin inserts and scaffolding legs, and I say well, would you ever try making something a bit different? He says, defiantly, no. We stare at each other in mute despair.

But when a customer belongs to the second group – those who have total faith not only in Hugh's craftsmanship, but crucially in his aesthetic skills too, and who give him the double luxury of a free rein and a large budget – the finishing of their project produces in him a sort of twitchy excitement, like a runner waiting to start a race, and this is exactly what he was like last night. Though he clearly felt pride in what he'd done for Mrs Yarwood (a Victorian button-backed chair, now resplendent in the sort of teal velvet you'd plead to have a ball gown made out of, never mind the lack of balls at which to wear it, with the buttons themselves pops of gorgeousness in ochre silk), this was only – as it always is in these circumstances – a stepping stone to the real reason for his happy agitation, a surge of self-belief and optimism that seemed to set the grubby workshop alight.

These times are like comets, or fireworks – as glorious as they are short-lived – so I take care to savour them. We drained our drinks and went back to the house and opened a bottle of wine, and Hugh said what about some scrambled eggs in the garden, that he'd make them, and I said great, just as I would have done if it was broiled sheep's eyes he was offering, so long as I got to watch him striding round the kitchen, talking about an exhibition he was thinking about going to, and did I want to come, while he cracked the eggs one-handed and set the butter bubbling.

When everything was ready he called Pete and Billy, and we all went outside and sat on the terrace to eat, the boys extrapolating from this relaxing of usual midweek supper rules the likelihood of further leniency. Consequently, their bottoms remained upon their chairs for only the absolute minimum time possible, springing up with the rest of them the minute they'd laid down their knives and forks to tear off across the lawn, confident that calls for bath or bedtime would not be soon forthcoming.

We watched them for a moment with that sort of fond, loving amusement you think parenthood is full of until you actually become a parent. Then Hugh stood up, took a deep breath and let out a massive lion-like roar that set both boys squealing with terrified delight long before he'd reached them and actually pounced.

I don't know if all mothers are the same, but I find I count the times that Hugh plays with the boys – like pennies in a "well-balanced childhood" pot. This is probably in part because they don't happen often (Hugh being most comfortable with the children when they're not there) and are therefore precious. Not that the boys see the same value in these interactions as I do. Having mostly grown up without it, they neither look for his attention nor rise to meet it when it appears, but, rather as I do when Hugh's in a good mood, just enjoy it while it lasts. It's only me who does the counting.

I looked at the three of them, Hugh now on his back as each boy in turn jumped on him and was first tickled mercilessly then thrown off, and felt the rightness of my absence. This wasn't a scene for me to take part in, but to observe: a father with his cubs, tumbling with a roughness I always think excessive but have learned is somehow not, even when it ends in injury, which just then it did, Billy howling my cue to intervene. When it turned out that the wound was too small to warrant the tears, and that tiredness rather than pain was no doubt the real reason for them, I packed both boys upstairs to bed, deaf to Peter's outraged indignation at this. When they were both tucked up, I went back downstairs, hoping Hugh's cheerfulness had not burned itself out while I'd been away.

It hadn't, I realised, as soon as I heard he'd put his nineties playlist on in the kitchen, loudly, and was singing along to it, badly.

'Dead?' he said when he saw me.

'They will be any minute,' I replied.

'Let's go back outside then,' he said. 'That wine's not going to drink itself.'

The first bottle certainly didn't, and neither did the second, and with each glass that we emptied Hugh grew more and more expansive, waving his hands around and making all sorts of increasingly improbable plans that seemed like utter genius to both of us at the time – opening a shop for his furniture, growing some turkeys for Christmas – and I thought warmly what a wonderfully creative man I'd married, and Hugh said what a wonderfully supportive wife I was. And when he said he was sorry about the money and that he'd do whatever it took to make some more, I fell over myself telling him it didn't matter, and we'd sort it out together, and though things get a bit hazy after that I do remember the tone of it all – each of us heaping praise onto the other, fiercely claiming blame for ourselves...

I can only assume from the fact that we both woke up in the middle of the night to find ourselves stiff and freezing on the grass that either it had seemed like a brilliant idea to go to sleep there, or it had just happened; but either way it was clear from the way we wrapped our own silence about us as we crept upstairs that we'd left all the evening's goodwill behind us on the lawn. And although this morning's routine appeared superficially identical to every other morning, there was a strange sheepishness hanging between Hugh and me. You could see it in the tiny sidesteps between bedroom and bathroom, a fine shellac sheen on our exchanges, an avoidance of gaze, and – perhaps most of all – our refusal even once to acknowledge the monstrous hangovers that so exactly symbolised our shame. Ashamed of *what*, though, I tried to work out through the throbbing of my head as I went downstairs to get breakfast ready. The outpouring of devotion we preferred to keep sealed? No. That might have been true once, but it didn't sound right now. But if not that, then what?

If my pounding headache wasn't enough reason for me to discontinue my thoughts on this, the trip to school was. I would have given my right arm for peace and quiet, but it was Billy's turn in the front seat, which opportunity he took to empty his pencil case onto his lap and provide me with a detailed provenance of every item. The football rubber came from so-and-so, and he got the ink eraser as a swap for a smelly pen – did I remember the smelly pen – Mum, Mum, do you remember the smelly pen? Not the watermelon one because that one came from Sophie, but the orange one that was in that shop at the seaside that you got me because Pete had an ice cream but I don't like ice creams so you said you'd get me the orange smelly pen? Mum?

Meanwhile Pete had his earphones in and was singing something that may or may not have been a recording of a cat having its claws pulled out one by one, and it struck me how exquisite is the punishment that children deliver to their hungover parents.

Got back to find a very stiff message on the answer machine from one of the fabric suppliers saying no, they could not fulfil our order until our overdue account had been paid, so I had to tell Hugh, who I knew needed the fabric to get started on Mrs Willis. He looked at me, so instantly incensed that it was almost as if he'd just been waiting for the opportunity to be so, and yelled, '*Why is there never any fucking money?*' And I was able then to answer the question I'd put to myself first thing this morning; the reason we'd felt ashamed about last night was not because we'd articulated our intimacy, but because without the drunkenness we weren't sure there was any intimacy there at all.

20th May

Very glad that today was the day I'd promised to help dear friend Rachel cut out some flowerbeds, as I woke up feeling rather low, and couldn't seem to shift it. Unhelpful thoughts about Hugh, or Hugh and me, kept floating to the surface. If you live a certain way for long enough you stop really thinking about it, and if the life you're living is not ideal this is useful, this not thinking. You don't want to hear little voices telling you to look at the things you don't want to look at. You don't want to hear them saying that, actually, a bearable life is not enough. A bearable marriage is not OK. That bearing is *not* OK. What use are such thoughts to me? I needed someone to help me pull myself back together, cheer me up, and who better than Rachel? There's no drama the woman can't diminish; you don't even need to talk to her about it – five minutes in her presence and it just quietly melts away.

I always think of the track to her farm as a sort of intensive course in animal husbandry. You're started off gently, through a field or two of cows, who take little notice of you, then as you get closer to the house you come to the horses, who like to trot along the fence in line with the car. About this time you hear dogs barking, followed shortly afterwards by the dogs themselves – very waggy, quite shouty, of breeds and number that seem to vary substantially on each visit. They escort the car, oblivious to the high chance of being run over in their enthusiasm to lick, fatally maim, or possibly just greet you (they like to keep it a surprise) until the final few yards to the back door, where all manner of farmyard fauna bursts upon the senses. A couple more horses nod at you from their stables, and you may – depending on the weather – spot two or three cats lazing on bales in the open barn, sharing this spot with any one or more of the following: lambs, puppies in whelping box, small girls cleaning tack, ducks, and chickens with or without their full complement of legs.

You open the car door to the rich, deep brown smell of mud, together with the onslaught of the dogs, while Rachel appears out of some outbuilding to yell so mightily at the dogs that all licking and maiming is immediately halted, and you are instantly aware that here is a woman very much in command of her dominion.

Had a quick chat while I got my wellies on – how had I got on with the book she'd lent me (bugger, I'd forgotten to bring it back), how had she got on with the cat's abscess (squeezed that morning, results unclear) – then went straight round the back of the house to the garden, where the first thing I saw was her four veg beds, which had been obliterated by such an avalanche of manure that the chicken wire surrounding them, carefully erected by Rachel last year, was entirely crushed. Thought wistfully how glad I'd be if an avalanche of anything obliterated our own veg patch, but remembered just in time that she loves her veg. What on earth happened? I said. It turned out that Mark, her husband, was the culprit. He'd asked if she wanted any cow muck on her beds and Rachel, touched at this thoughtfulness, had said yes please and gone off to start supper, only to hear the Matbro starting up and to return to the garden to find the avalanche. Any excuse, she said crossly, to use a bloody machine rather than a garden fork like the rest of us.

You see, I told myself then, you *see*? And the next thing I knew I was telling her about Hugh, and Hugh and me. But the version I told her was full of eye rolls, and light exasperation, and each time she laughed she ratified it further into fact. And I found myself remembering what we all know – that time is relative. Seven years when you're busy with children and work and everything else could *easily* be described as a blip, as *more* than worthy of bearing.

With only a brief pause to flick away three dog turds, we began cutting out the turf, and I was immediately reminded of the phenomenal strength differential between Rachel and me. For every square of grass I removed, she managed three – flinging them aside like feathers, as no doubt she does with sacks of Happy Hoof and bullocks' testicles – but this didn't bother either of us as it was the chat more than the work that we were there for, after all.

We covered the usual topics – children, school, events ahead and behind – and in one way this was a simple exchange of information, but in another it was like we were each shaking out our work for the other to study, professional to professional, the patterns of much less interest than the means of their making, the hows and whys of the warp and weft, as I guess all good friendships are.

All too soon the flowerbeds were finished and it was time to go. Rachel offered a cup of tea but I refused it, partly because we were both conscious of To Do lists tapping at us, and partly because – now fortified and focused – I wanted to get home and put this to good use while it was still fresh. Before I went it was important, however, to ask about her horses as they are her main love, and this was the very least courtesy she deserved from me after the help she had (probably entirely unknowingly) provided. Even though I do try to remember all horsey terminology, I see her not quite frequently enough for it to stick, and the gift of my questioning is therefore rather like handing over a bottle of wine that no one can get the cork out of. How are the horses? I ask. Ponies, says Rachel. Yes, ponies? Well, Mabel's got a sore on her hock. Which one's Mabel again? The bay. Oh. Which is bay again? Brown. Oh yes, the brown one. What's a hock? Thank God she's such a trusty subscriber to it being the thought that counts...

I stopped impulsively at the garage on the way home to splash out on a strawberry Cornetto for Hugh, which I took to him in the workshop the moment I got back. 'Thought you might like this,' I said, holding it out to him with a big smile.

He took it at once, as I knew his sweet tooth would make him, and had already got the wrapper off and taken his first bite before he thanked me.

'What's the special occasion?' he asked, mouth full.

'I don't know,' I said with a shrug from the door. 'Just the general joys of life?'

'Of course,' said Hugh, nodding wryly. 'Those. I always forget.'

He grinned at me then. It was more with his mouth than his eyes, but still strong enough to linger with me as I crossed the yard back to the house.

You see, I told myself. You *see?*

26TH MAY

Received phone call from Rose saying the weekend with Donald had proved a disaster. Did I know his name wasn't even really Donald, but Martin?

'And I had such high hopes for the sex,' she went on. 'It was so promising at the Ringing – you can usually tell – but give him a bed and a whole night rather than a quickie up against the dovecot and turns out his MO is not at all what I thought it was. Lots of hair stroking and sighing and smiling, you know that sort? A "tender lover",' she said, the phrase passed down the line by the tip of its tail, like a decapitated mouse.

I found myself feeling rather sorry for Martin. 'Might you give it a bit more of a go than just one weekend?' I asked. 'It sounds as if he really likes you.'

'I don't want to be liked by him,' she said. 'There's no point in pretending – it's a waste of everyone's time. And besides, I need to steer clear of men for a while if I'm going to pursue my yoga.'

My yoga, I heard with a sinking sense in my stomach. What else have we had recently – my cooking, my jewellery, my clothes design – all claimed as true vocations then abruptly discarded. It's always been as if she's standing anxiously on a cold pavement in a bad neighbourhood at night, peering at the flow of oncoming traffic, mistaking each set of headlights for the cab that *must* be coming to take her safely home…

'Right,' I said, because you mustn't mention any of this to her. 'Right. Your yoga.'

'Yes,' she said. 'In fact, I've just booked a place on this fantastic retreat in Santorini – incredibly booked up, but I know a girl who got me in. Tantric and shamanic. Five star. Run by the absolute leader in the field. It's going to be amazing. It's going to change *everything*.'

'Right,' I said, thinking I must stop saying *right*. 'When are you going?'

'Tomorrow.'

I could only tell her I hoped it would be wonderful, which I meant, but did not for one second believe.

Having wheedled a deposit out of Mrs Willis for her sofa, we were able to get her fabric in, and she turned up this afternoon to discuss it. According to the usual (and, if I'm honest, rather resented) distribution of labour between Hugh and me, Hugh disappeared five minutes before she was due to arrive and I was left with the delicate task of managing Mrs Willis's (considerable) expectations. She had wanted a fabric in keeping with her Very Large Elizabethan Residence and had chosen a design so stiff with stags, oaks, unicorns and eagles that Elizabeth I herself, I said obsequiously, would have been proud to have it.

'I should think so at that price,' said Mrs Willis tartly. 'Now the stags *must* be positioned centrally on the back cushions, Mrs Narwhal, and those little dogs – I hope they're whippets? – can go on the armrests. No armrest covers, thank you. We are close enough to bankruptcy with just the re-covering.'

It's always at this point in conversations with such customers that I think three things:

- How nice it would be to sell golf balls or milk or something else cheap and easy.
- Why, if you want to keep costs down on the re-upholstery of a sofa for your Very Large Elizabethan/Georgian/Victorian residence, must we get the blame for the price when you have chosen a fabric at £80+ per metre?
- What would your face look like, do you think, if I told you to shove your dog-wee-stained, woodworm-ridden sofa up your arse?

Hugh appeared out of the undergrowth (surely he wasn't actually *hiding* from her?) just as her Range Rover turned onto the lane, and listened grimly as I catalogued her demands. When I'd finished, he asked if I'd told her to shove her sofa up her arse. I said no, but that I'd very much wanted to, and we spent a few minutes in the sort of sniggery bitching that I always enjoy at the time, then rather regret. It's nice to build a cosy nest for ourselves, but not when we've nicked all the sticks from someone else's, even an utter cow like Mrs Willis.

Just spent half an hour googling tantric and shamanic yoga – still clueless.

1ST JUNE

Overslept, which put me in a spin, as not only would we probably be late for school but also it was Jo's day today and I knew immediately I wouldn't have time to do any cleaning before she came to clean, the consequences of which were unlikely to be positive.

At rest, Jo's face looks like she's just about to punch you, let alone when she's annoyed. Which she often is – usually with her husband (useless wanker) or her kids (useless wankers). I have to say, all that fury is wonderful in one way for a cleaner – any dirt that sees her coming throws itself instantly into her mop bucket in terror – but on the other hand it makes me so *jangly*, always certain that today is the day I'll commit some hideous misdemeanour and get flattened by full-throttle wrath. Which is probably why I've been such a coward and have not yet been able to bring myself to tell her that we really can't afford her and are going to have to let her go. Each time she comes I gird my loins, but then she'll tell me how one of the useless wankers has been particularly useless over some tiny domestic transgression (not wiping the nozzle of the toothpaste after every use is one that sticks particularly in mind) and I'll think, dear Lord, this is a woman who'd rip my head off for not taking the fluff out of the tumble dryer; if I told her we had to let her go she'd make the Four Horsemen of the Apocalypse look like pre-teens from the Pony Club.

Things I have learned not to do with Jo:

- Ask her to clean anything other than what she wishes to clean.
- Ask her to consider alternative days or times for cleaning appointments.
- Offer any sort of refreshment.
- Open any sort of conversation.
- Approach her from behind.

As long as I stay out of her way, and keep eye contact to a minimum, we mostly get along, but it does help if the loos, at least, are given a quick once over before she arrives. As she became aware that not even this had been done this morning, her irritation began to show itself in increased banging about of buckets and cupboard doors, so that an unsuspecting visitor might think an angry rhinoceros was loose somewhere inside the house, and my own nerves were so on edge that I jumped when the phone rang.

It was Mrs Willis, I just about managed to hear over the roar of the hoover. She was having a dinner party next week at which there would be some Very Important People and her sofa must be ready by then, as she had waited an age already and she therefore also expected it to be delivered back to her free of charge. I was the epitome of courtesy and helpfulness, and even managed to avoid pointing out to her that the delay was due to the six weeks it had taken her to choose her fabric, and not our inefficiency. She grunted triumphantly and rang off, presumably in a hurry to return to her torture of small children or other favoured pastimes.

As I put the phone down, Greer popped into my head, summoned there no doubt by Jo and Mrs Willis, as archetypes so often are by their paler imitations. She would have eaten both of them for breakfast, neatly, quietly, napkin on her lap... How would our lives be different, I asked myself for the hundredth time, if she'd survived as long as everyone naturally assumed she would? She'd still be living here, I'm absolutely certain, and not with the tremulous bewilderment of your standard widow either. Her faculties would be as hard as her calf muscles, the missiles of age and ill health and solitude ricocheting off them, the mere thought of her son and me moving in quite absurd. Which means – what? – we'd still be in London, Hugh still happy at Vaughan's? Or a cottage somewhere, maybe. Or something more modern, and manageable, close enough to this place to acknowledge our duty, but far enough (I'm ashamed to say) to eke out its fulfilment. Maybe I'd be doing my gardening, in normal gardens, and being *paid*...

No matter how delicious these dreams, I wouldn't for one moment want them realised if the price was having Greer back. Not unless by some miracle her entire personality had been transformed. Any damage she did to Hugh has long been dwarfed by that of his inheritance, but Rose is a different matter altogether – she might as well have "made by bad mothering" stamped on her forehead – and I can never forgive Greer for that.

Usually, when you meet someone for the first time, the wish of both parties is to impart the information that they are not an axe murderer and are at least moderately pleased to make your acquaintance. This was emphatically not the case when I met Greer; not from her side anyway. We'd come up for Phil and Sarah's wedding, and I was standing nervously with Hugh in the hall when I heard her.

'Is that you, Hugh?' were her first words, her vowels arriving a good few seconds before the rest of her. There was no change in tone once she actually appeared, no indication whatsoever that either of us – even Hugh – was anything other than an unwelcome interruption to her day. 'We've lunched already,' was all she said by way of a greeting. In one hand she carried a brace of pheasants, and in the other a cleaver, both of which accompanied her person as timidly as the pearls around her neck. All I could think, as Hugh introduced us, was that I'd never come across anyone as... as *impenetrable* as Greer before. I'd hoped on the journey up to make a good impression – this was clearly laughable. It was as if she was incapable of accepting any impression at all. I gave her my broadest smile and watched it bounce off her hairspray and the hoods of her eyes. Had she been a statue I doubt even the pigeons would have dared sit on her.

No. I'm sorry. I never thought I'd say such a dreadful thing about anyone, but Greer? I much prefer her dead than alive.

6TH JUNE

It was the June Jamboree in the village hall last night, much improved from previous years by the fact that someone has been brave enough to make the change everyone's secretly wanted forever. When it was time for the auction you could feel the room set its shoulders stoically as always, but the minute Geoff said he was going to sell things off in groups and not individually there was such a burst of happy relief you knew how grateful everyone was. Last year I counted twenty-seven items, all homemade or homegrown – jams, pies, cakes, chutneys, clutches of carrots and cucumbers and bags of broad beans – sold one by one, never for more than £2; the only people not wishing for an early grave after approximately three minutes of this those competitive matrons desperate to learn if their coffee-and-walnut would raise more for the church than their neighbour's.

To have returned to us so unexpectedly the hour we would all have dutifully sacrificed added a certain giddiness to the atmosphere both inside – the banter pressing right up to the bone – and outside, where the climbing frame was quite alive with frenzied, overtired children.

We had Phil and Sarah on our table, which enabled us to catch up in the usual fashion – Sarah and I through regular conversation, Phil and Hugh through the happy exchange of insults about each other's hair, age and weight. Farmer Dan, on Hugh's right, seemed to spend most of the evening either collecting food from the buffet table, piling it up with the sort of conscientious greed that comes over those ever driven to squeeze a bargain from a fixed ticket price, or eating it.

That's how he was introduced to me by Hugh at the first Jamboree I attended – not Dan Coates, but Farmer Dan. There was also Digger Joe and Sam the Van; these names offered up with such nonchalance that I felt touched by the welcome of their familiarity. This feeling only deepened as the conversations went on and I understood how long they'd known Hugh. They teased him about youthful misdemeanours, his hippy stage, filling his nappy in Joe's digger while on Joe's lap, their affection clear in their efforts to embarrass him, Hugh's in his mock indignant refusal to let them succeed.

None of this took place at our table, of course. In those days there was indeed an "our" table, just as there was an "our" pew in the church, emitting a force field of exclusion as powerful as it was invisible, which Greer sanctioned, but reversed. 'We need to be thoughtful,' she'd said quietly as she steered me to the front pew that first Christmas. 'People don't appreciate change. They wouldn't like us to sit elsewhere – it would cause awkwardness,' she went on, in the carefully hushed tones she'd use to alert me to a large piece of spinach between my teeth.

Our table at the Jamboree was for the Narwhals, their guests, the vicar, and no one else. There Greer sat that first year, erect, watchful, like a buzzard at the top of a telegraph pole. When Hugh and I returned with our pudding, we found Rose – just fifteen and still all angles – leaning across her mother and saying heatedly to the Rev. David Thorneycroft, 'Yes, but what about bishops? When can we be bishops? Archbishops? You're nowhere *near* yet.'

Dave (christened "Call me Dave" by Greer) looked at Rose with amused bewilderment, too young a vicar to be shocked by such teenage attacks, but too old to take them seriously.

'These things don't happen overnight, you know,' he said.

'You've had years,' Rose snapped back. 'How much longer do you need?'

'Over the top you go, David,' said Grandpa Hugh, leaning back and folding his arms in merriment. 'Good luck!'

Dave seemed to consider his options. Then he interlaced his hands on the table and said, 'Perhaps you're thinking of entering the Church yourself, Rose?'

Rose ignored her father's delighted guffaw.

'"What do you want to be when you grow up, little girl?"' she said. 'Is that the best you can do?'

'No, no, no, of course not,' said Dave. 'I just wondered if your interest was personal, that's all.'

'It doesn't have to be about *me* to be important,' said Rose.

Grandpa Hugh leaned towards Dave and said in a stage whisper, 'It'll be the sisterhood, bet you.'

'And so what if it is?' said Rose, properly angry now. 'So what if—'

'David,' Greer interrupted calmly, reaching for the jug beside her, 'more water?'

And that was all it took to silence Rose – her great castle toppled as if by a single sigh. She sat back amongst the rubble, stunned, crushed by the ease of her defeat, while Hugh and I exchanged stern glances, as there was nothing else we could do. We were too late to support her cause – in her crumpled state she'd spot the pity in it straightaway…

Joan Cook sat in Rose's spot at "our" table last night. There hasn't been a Narwhal there since Grandpa Hugh died, but whether that's coincidence or not I honestly couldn't say. All I do know is that both lots of my potato salad went, each bowl as clean as a whistle. (Can conclude definitively therefore that spring onions were the problem last year.)

It was dusk when we walked back – the beautiful, soft, fragrant one I think we'd anticipated when we'd decided not to drive – but the boys were scratchy, the exhaustion they'd kept at bay on the climbing frame now claiming them with a vengeance. You would have thought the mile of lane between the village hall and home was a vast Arctic waste, banked up not with great clouds of cow parsley but hard-packed drifts of snow, through which we had cruelly forced them to trudge. They whined, they fought, they caught my hands and dragged on them, pushing and pushing for the snarl that would release the tears that – with their beds a thousand leagues away – were their nearest means of relief.

I was determined to avoid this, reaching ever deeper into my bag of tricks, but they threw everything (let's count our steps, let's sing a song, even sweets when we got back) so petulantly aside that before I knew it I was indeed snarling, and they were indeed crying, and I too was thinking wildly that with the huskies and the sledges nowhere in sight, how would we *ever* get home?

I forced my amends by hugging them roughly, and though this worked in the sense that my compassion for them came back, in another sense it didn't. My frustration, outraged at this thwarting, looked around angrily for an alternative outlet, and found it. In Hugh.

Though we'd started off walking together, he'd drifted ahead when the whining started, and was now a good way in front of us, his long and easy stride – something I've always liked so much about him – now infuriating, as if it belonged to me and he'd pinched it just when I wanted it.

I opened my mouth, then shut it again. What would he see if I called him? His wife crouching awkwardly on the tarmac in the gloom, a weeping child clutched fiercely in each arm. A hard little knot of snot and wails and recrimination which, no matter how fun the Jamboree, or how beguiling the June night, he'd look upon grim-lipped.

No, thank you, I thought primly. We can manage quite well without you, if that's the way you're going to be about it, and the heat of this thought fired up my veins enough to get the boys competently home. But by the time I'd got them into bed, and had locked up, and put the dishwasher on, and got out the breakfast things, I was bone-tired and irritable, any chance of me managing this completely doomed when I went into the bedroom to find that not only had I forgotten to re-make the bed after stripping it that morning, but that although the clean sheets were waiting, Hugh – brushing his teeth in the bathroom – had ignored them *and* strewn his clothes all over the top of them.

When exactly did he become so selfish? I asked myself, though of course I knew when. In the old days, comparisons with my friends' boyfriends showed him as remarkably solicitous, and sweetly, almost naively so, as is often the case with self-taught skills. His father had nothing to teach him in this regard, after all. But now. Now...

I had my back to him when he came into the bedroom, but I heard the pause I'd wanted as he took in his clothes dumped by the door, the slap of the sheets as I over-shook them. This brought with it a sort of vertigo – an exhilaration I feared as much as I relished – but there wasn't time to contemplate this soberly because Hugh spoke and we were off.

'What's the problem?' he said coldly.

'No problem, Hugh. Don't you concern yourself. I'll just make the bed, and look after the children, and the customers, and Rose, and all the rest of it. It's completely fine.'

What are you *doing*? I said to myself. You sound pathetic. This isn't the way it goes. *Stop* it.

'Straight in with the sarcasm,' he said. 'Nice. Mature.'

'That's what people do when they're pissed off, Hugh,' I said, jabbing the bottom sheet under the mattress. 'When they've had enough of their husbands living on an entirely separate, selfish planet, where children don't need to be got into bed, and sheets don't need to be changed, or Mrs Willis sucked up to, and it's OK to leave stuff everywhere.'

I knew very well that this was the verbal equivalent of picking up whatever random objects I could lay my hands on and chucking them at him, and I mistook the split second of silence that followed as his response to a direct hit. But...

'Oh, *I'm* on a selfish planet,' he said, in a slow tone of faux realisation, 'sitting on my arse while you work your fingers to the bone. Pottering about in the garden, chatting with my sister... No *wonder* you're annoyed.'

I looked round at this in amazement – not the better to see him so much as the image that hung between us. In many ways, your own existence is a lot more vulnerable than your other possessions. The person who wouldn't dream of touching your biro without permission is more than happy to manhandle your life with impunity – a judgement here, a criticism there. Whether spoken or not, we all do it to other people and therefore must conclude that it's done to us, but when the version of yourself you're shown is so cruelly opposed to your own, and the very one that would most upset you; when, only days before, your accuser – albeit with a bottle of wine inside him – was praising your support and your selflessness...

'If my life is so easy, then why the hell am I so resentful of yours?' I shouted. 'Nice and quiet in the workshop, no one bothering you, meals waiting on the table, this place kept in check. You're the sun around which we have no choice but to revolve. *Your* work, *your* moods, *your* wills and won'ts.'

Hugh shook his head with a sour little smile. 'Tell you what. *You* get a job,' he said, thrusting his arms into the air as if flinging a great boulder towards me, 'and I'll take on the incredible load of your life.'

I took a deep breath and tried to collect myself. 'Hugh,' I said quietly, 'this is crazy. I've tried to get work, you know I have, and it's not really... You're just– just so *unhappy*.'

I'd genuinely hoped to douse his anger with this appeal, but I'd forgotten in the moment that – just as with his sister – you do not ever, ever, tell Hugh that he's sad.

'It's *you* who's clearly unhappy,' he yelled, 'not me. What's this been about other than that you're pissed off and miserable? That's such a fucking female thing to do, twisting it round. Like the nagging and the whining and the banging on. Is it any surprise to you, really, that I'm in the workshop as much as I am?' He pushed his neck slowly forwards then, which told some ancient part of me to beware of what was coming. 'The one thing I was certain of – that you'd never turn into a fucking old nag. Your average middle-aged bitch. And here we are.'

That did it. I found myself turning away from him and walking out into the corridor, hurling nothing in my wake: no tears, no slammed door, no last word. I headed instinctively for Rose's room. I shut the curtains, got undressed in the dark, slipped silently into her bed and lay very still.

It took a long time for the shock to ebb away enough for me to see the debris left behind it on the shore. I picked over it gingerly, not at all sure what I was going to find, as we'd never had that sort of row before. 'Never go to sleep on an argument,' I found first. Well, I wasn't going back in there and I very much doubted Hugh would come to me, so that was that. 'I didn't mean what I said,' came next – wasn't that what they always said in the films? The only words I'd really meant were those I'd said at the end; the ones before that were just the poorly-designed prototypes that had to precede them. But what about Hugh? You fucking old nag. *You fucking old nag.* With his head bent forward. 'I'm sorry I called you a fucking old nag. I didn't mean it.' Nope – I couldn't hear it.

It was only as the things in Rose's room began to reveal themselves that I realised I still had my eyes open. The ancient oak wardrobe, the basin with the wonky cold tap, the pink wicker nursing chair – they were all familiar, but not from the angle I was at. And this jolting of a well-known room brought back for a moment the feeling I'd get when ill in bed as a child, when the disconnection came not from the perspective but the time – daylight whitening curtains that should have been black, the sounds of traffic, and footsteps (some of them children's) on pavements that should have been silent. I'd feel outside of life, but not unpleasantly so – not excluded so much as consoled by my absence, as if it had been granted by a very special permission slip.

It was probably because of this that my eyes were so ready to prickle with self-pity when they landed on the photo that stood on Rose's bedside table. Regardless of the fact I could only see the shape of the frame, I knew every detail of the picture inside it.

We'd got Ravi to take our wedding photos because we didn't want formal and we didn't want expensive and Ravi was enthusiastically neither. And of all the billions that it felt like he took on the day, this was the one we liked best, surprised at this because Hugh and I aren't looking at the camera, or even at each other. He is behind me, his arms around me, and mine are over his. We're laughing heartily at someone – I've never known who – off to our right, and just visible in the background is Delilah, tail mid-wag, ears back, eyes eagerly awaiting the disembodied arm that's reaching out to stroke her.

It's a ridiculous picture in so many ways – Greer would have instantly passed over it – but *everything* is held within it. You look at Hugh and me and know at once that we see our love as the trusty sort that can sustain without ostentation – like joists, or roots, or the ten thousand hours of practice unseen in the smile of the pianist as she walks onto the stage. There too is the busy, gregarious, slightly scatty life we think we're embarking on, the sparkling stream on which we'll sail our beautiful pea-green boat...

It's not that we didn't argue then, but more that our hearts were never really in it. Hugh never seemed to be angry *with* me, only *at* me when he needed somewhere to put the frustration of a bad day, so that it was the sort of easi-peel attack that could be removed and discarded without leaving a trace. And whenever I felt the beginnings of irritation – as I did clearing bits of salmon out of the dishwasher when he'd tried to poach one in there, or when my good black tights had been sacrificed to some project he was doing – he'd only be half-sorry because I was only half-cross, appeased by his jokes and his coaxing long before any apology reached his lips.

You will *not* cry, I said to myself. And I tried to put myself in the shoes of all those women who worked harder than me, bore more than me, complained less than me; you owe them, I said to myself. Pull your bloody socks up.

But, *such a female thing to do. Banging on.*

They were the last words in my head when I finally fell asleep.

I emerged from Rose's room this morning as I might from a bunker after a night of air raids, wary of stumbling into sheered-off walls or vast smoking craters. My ears were ringing and it was rather a surprise to find myself physically intact. He'd *wanted* to hurt me – that was the worst of it. Not accidentally, but with careful aim and aggression. Never before had he done that, and never – I realised then – had I felt this roar of adrenaline in response. *You fucking old nag.* Are you sorry, Hugh? I thought with fierce heat, pausing at the top of the stairs. A wife I am, a punchbag I am not. Are you sorry?

There was a split second, as I came into the kitchen,

when I saw Hugh before he saw me. The kettle was on and he was standing in front of it, waiting for it to boil, but with his head down and his arms braced so hard against the counter it looked as if he was about to try and push it through the wall. A lump came, unhelpfully, into my throat; now was *not* the time for sympathy. As soon as he caught sight of me, though, he straightened and turned to face me.

'I'm sorry,' he said. 'I'm sorry. I shouldn't have said those things. It was wrong and it was unfair and it was cruel.'

I stared at him. Here was the apology I'd wanted – as genuine as I could possibly have hoped for – but it was also odd. There was a stiff formality to both his stance and his words, so that I felt somehow more distanced than clasped. But he misinterpreted my silence as a demand for deeper remorse.

'I take it all back,' he said. 'Every word. I need to pull myself together – be more thoughtful, help you. All the things you said,' he added, offering his palm to me in emphasis. Only he looked more like a waiter showing a customer to their chair. Why wasn't anything he said or did reaching me as he'd intended? But if I wanted to make things right I had to ignore the manner and try to focus on the message, its sincerity, its appeal.

I cleared my throat. 'Thank you,' I said. 'I'm grateful. I do my best, you know. I don't think I nag.'

'I know. And you don't nag.'

'OK,' I said. 'So.' It all felt like a small plaster on a massive oozing wound. 'Good.' But I didn't have the first clue how to sew it up. 'Thank you.'

And that was that. There was no hug or joke or any other seal on this brief exchange. We merely nodded at each other with pressed lips as the kettle started to boil. Hugh made us both a coffee in silence, rubbed my arm briefly, and went off to the workshop, leaving me to try and untangle what had – or rather hadn't – just happened. I believed his apology, I did, but I also thought he didn't mean his regret as much as he was trying to. He wanted to be more sorry than he was. Which meant what, exactly? That he hadn't really faced, let alone resolved, whatever it was that had caused his outburst last night? I knew only one thing with certainty. No matter how hard he'd tried to persuade himself and me of his contrition, it hadn't worked. There was more trouble coming, I was sure of it.

The day ahead looked at me balefully and I thought I'd better get out of the house; I needed to do a shop anyway. Unsurprisingly, being allowed on screens on Sunday mornings, neither of the boys wanted to come with me, so I set off on my own, turning the radio on as soon as I got into the car.

I'd taken the shopping list off the fridge but didn't look at it until I'd reached the supermarket car park, at which point I discovered the entire family had contributed something. In tiny neat handwriting, Billy had put "more choclat biskits". Hugh wanted "different but normal" cheese, whatever that was, and some oatcakes. Pete had listed three items: "fire liquid, magneezium ribbon, and double albatrosses".

I felt my spirits begin to lift.

Most of the family's requests went unfulfilled. The biscuits and the oatcakes weren't a problem, but the available cheeses were either different *or* normal, and there didn't seem to be any shelf space at all dedicated to probably dangerous chemicals sought by terrorists and small boys (although I did manage, after triumphant translation, to get some double A batteries).

I always think people underestimate supermarkets. Looked at in one way, they are such accurate embodiments of the plodding monotony of life that they could have been specifically designed as such – installations by some award-winning artist in aggressive spectacles. Up and down the aisles we trudge, reaching dull-eyed for Easter eggs and Christmas cakes, strawberries and swedes, so bovine that if we're even aware of the Big Business manipulations we're obeying, we don't care. We don't want to disrupt or challenge; we're *grateful* for the automatic steering, no matter how sinister, as it means we don't have to drive. But, mostly, I'm a cheerful sort of person and so mostly I don't see the herd-like lumpenness of common purpose and behaviour but the individuality it throws so effectively into relief. There is Sue, one of the order picking ladies, who tends to narrate her work as she goes along (oranges… oranges… no… let's go for… oh, it's Jaffas not those), and Stan, who shops every day as it's important to get out, and the tiny, toned woman who always seems to want the tomatoes when I do, and the tattooed biker who told me what star anise is for. Sandwiched between the uniformity of the strip lighting and the beige speckled floor are all kinds of conversations that have enlightened me on all kinds of things: that there's a wine offer coming next week, that you can donate your hair to make wigs for cancer sufferers, that Plato said after democracy comes chaos, that I've put my stuff in someone else's trolley by mistake, and how to make your own Christmas wreath, or cook kale, or get the best revenge on an ex.

I had a slightly stern word with Louise at the checkout, as her wrist was still bandaged and she still hasn't had it properly looked at. 'Who's after the oatcakes?' she wanted to know, changing the subject. 'That's not usual for you.' Told her they were for Hugh, and that it would give the faceless customer profilers something to think about. (That's me living on the edge – confusing the supermarket algorithms with some unexpected oatcakes in the otherwise utterly predictable Narwhal trolley. They'll probably have to be completely rewritten now.)

Very glad to have bumped into Jemima, the foodie mum from school, only as I was leaving and all my stuff was hidden away in bags. She doesn't usually visit the supermarket – the farm shop being much more her natural territory – but when she does she will only have a basket, in which are carefully placed the sort of impossibly exotic and on-trend ingredients that would cause the algorithm computer to spontaneously combust if they went through the checkout in my trolley. Last time I saw her it was in the freezer section (I can only think she must have been passing through in order to cool down after her Pilates session) and she tapped on my shoulder just as I was reaching for some frozen Yorkshire puddings. You can't try and escape a catch like that. I did think about it – oh, I was just getting them for a friend; oh, I've suddenly gone blind and am just trying to find the quinoa – but actually it's far better to come clean and confess that I'm a lazy Sunday roast cook. Which I did. She was very sweet about it, and tried very hard to reassure me with her own culinary short cuts, lowering her voice to admit that sometimes, when she was really pressed, she used a stock cube rather than making her own stock...

After all this, I returned home feeling much better than I had when I'd left. Hugh had apologised. He hadn't meant what he said last night. We *could* put the whole thing behind us, I decided, as I heaved the bags out of the boot. One hundred per cent. And when I walked into the kitchen to find him sitting at the table talking animatedly with a man I'd never seen before, I only felt further reassured. Everything was clearly fine.

Hugh gave me a remarkably cheery hello and introduced the stranger as Tony, a stonemason, who'd just agreed to take on the spare workshop. This must be why, I thought at first as I shook Tony's hand, Hugh was looking so pleased. We'd almost given up on letting out the second workshop, and the prospect of a tenant at last, or rather the rent he would bring with him, would have lifted the most downcast heart. But there was more to it than that, I realised, exploring this stonemason with my eyes.

He must have been in his mid-fifties, with such big, boldly drawn features that Hugh's in contrast looked almost fragile, over-expressive, young. His grip was callused and warm. He was somehow exactly what he was, like the oldest boulder on the beach, the one you'd make for straightaway with your picnic because its lee was by far the broadest and best against the wind and sand. Hugh liked him – that was why he was smiling. I could see why.

I offered tea, but Hugh said they were just off to the pub to celebrate. I must have looked expectant then (and no surprise because we *never* go to the pub, with nice stonemasons or anyone), because, 'Do you want to come?' asked Hugh. He was putting his wallet in his back pocket, picking up his keys so that they rattled, moving like a man on a mission. Avoiding my eyes.

Tony looked from one of us to the other. 'The more the merrier as far as I'm concerned,' he said.

Hugh said nothing. Seemed keen to check his phone.

'It's fine, Tony, thank you,' I said, trying not to sound sniffy. 'I've got plenty to get on with here anyway. It was really lovely to meet you. So glad about the workshop.'

Tony gave me a friendly, concurring nod, then smiled in readiness at Hugh.

'Let's go, then,' said Hugh. 'They might still have some seats outside. See you later,' he added over his shoulder as they went out.

I'd planned a chicken for lunch, and stood looking at it in the fridge for a moment. Sod you, Hugh, I thought. We could all have gone to the pub, a bit of a treat, help make things right after last night, but apparently no. Not invited. I continued to knead my resentment at this for so long that the fridge buzzer went off, so I closed the door, opened it again, and focused on the chicken. There were two options as I saw it. I could cook it, with usual Sunday lunch trimmings, as planned. Pros: Hugh wouldn't get to eat any because he'd be in the pub, and that would serve him right. Cons: I'd still have to cook the wretched thing. Or we could have packet pizzas instead. Pros: vast amounts of time freed up; wouldn't seem petty in depriving Hugh of his roast. Cons: wouldn't get to deprive Hugh of his roast.

Shame at this conniving made me go for the second option but have the chicken in the evening instead, the perfect choice as far as the boys were concerned. We ate the pizzas with our fingers on the terrace, while I tried not to notice the holes in the Tree House roof or that fallen willow in the lake, but focus on the conversation, which followed its usual bewildering path of non sequiturs. If there is in fact a link between the likelihood of alien invasion and what farts are for I am a long way from discovering it.

Then I took the boys down to the village hall for an hour to help with the clearing up and to collect my bowls, and we'd only been back five minutes when I heard the front door slam and Hugh walked a little blearily into the kitchen.

'Dad's drunk!' said Pete.

Hugh blinked at him. 'Dad is not drunk,' he said. 'It's called relaxed.'

'Dad's relaxed!' said Pete.

Billy said nothing, but watched with a small, attentive frown as Hugh made his way to the sofa and sat down heavily upon it, laying his arms along its back and closing his eyes.

'Why don't you two go outside and let Dad have a rest?' I said carefully.

'Wait!' said Hugh, raising both arms in half-order/half-invitation. 'Hug.'

The boys made their way obediently to the sofa and sat down on either side of him. His summons lent the scene a slight awkwardness, as if he were not their father but an aged and bewhiskered aunt or other semi-stranger. Hugh himself was not remotely aware of this – pulling them towards him and kissing them noisily on the tops of their heads as he tends to do on those rare occasions when he's feeling affectionate. The boys submitted to his embrace.

Billy wrinkled his nose. 'You smell of beer,' he said.

'And you,' said Hugh, sniffing him loudly, 'smell like pants and boy and pizza.'

Billy gave the shy smile of someone who's less mollified than they want to appear and wriggled his shoulders a little.

'That's it now,' I said. 'Come on – out you go. If you're lucky I'll bring you a biscuit in a bit.' I opened the French windows and shooed them out, rather glad to see Billy break into a run only a couple of seconds after his brother.

I turned my attention to Hugh. He'd closed his eyes again and had his legs up on the footstool. He looked so peaceful, and had circumstances been different I might have left him to it. Instead I moved round to stand in front of him, and found myself crossing my arms.

'How did you get home?' I said.

'Tony dropped me back,' he mumbled. 'Van's at the pub.'

'You had a good time, then.'

He was too drunk to pick up on my tone, just yawned and stretched, linking his hands behind his head. 'I did,' he said. 'Nice to be out. Nice bloke.'

'Why didn't you want us to come with you, Hugh?'

For a horrible moment, as he frowned at me in surprise, I thought he was going to deny my accusation. As someone I couldn't ever love would have done. Just like Rose, Hugh always chooses honesty when he sees the opportunity to lie, no matter the cost to himself. It's a characteristic I cherish in them both and would mourn hugely if it vanished. So when he inhaled deeply, and rubbed the back of his head with his linked hands, relief was the first thing I felt.

'I don't know,' he said eventually. 'I'm sorry. I just... To get away?'

'And did it work? Do you feel better?' I said, unable to prevent a sigh as I sat down opposite him. Because even if he knew the answer was no, and said so, and understood with this admission how stubborn his unhappiness actually was, it wouldn't change a thing.

He didn't speak for the longest time. He swung his legs off the footstool onto the floor and leant heavily on his thighs, moving one hand over the other as if washing them carefully. He looked down, then up at me, then down and up again.

'You're a wonderful woman, did you know that?' he said, smiling wanly.

'You always say that when you're drunk,' I said. 'It's when you're sober the problems start.'

He nodded. 'I'm liking the booze too much.'

It was true. It had slipped under my radar, but now I thought about it – all that clinking in the supermarket trolley and the recycling bin... It wasn't a glass or two every evening anymore; how much was it? A bottle? More? Falling asleep on the sofa, his snoring–

'A bit, yes.'

'I do like it.'

'Yes.'

I was conscious I wasn't saying much and I wasn't moving either, sitting very still and keeping my eyes upon him in a way that was more than waiting. After suffering this scrutiny for a minute or two, with more rubbing of his hands and glancing up and down at me, Hugh at last lifted his gaze to mine and held it.

'I'm going to sell the top field,' he said, suddenly sober.

My mouth dropped open. It was the very last thing I expected him to say – not just then, but ever. For the Narwhals, selling anything has always been taboo. Things *in* the family home are bad enough, but the land that surrounds it is practically sacred. How this belief has survived intact when the farms, the cottages, almost all of the original estate has in fact long gone is beyond me; perhaps, with so little left, Hugh feels its preservation is more important than ever? The last crust in a once abundant larder? I don't know. All I do know is that for him the sale of that field would be a final resort, considered only once everything else – every item in every room, not one but both of his kidneys – had been considered first. And what's more, it was the ultimate lose-lose decision, not just for him but for all of us. Because no matter how great the price the field went for, or what reprieve it gave us, it spelt nothing but shame for Hugh and therefore a darkening and lengthening of the shadow he already cast upon the rest of us.

I looked at him. There it all was on his face, that shame and bitter self-reproach, as if he didn't feel enough of a failure already, as if the field was already sold. No wonder he was drinking so much. No wonder he'd lashed out at me last night.

'But the second workshop,' I said. 'The rent?'

'It's not enough,' he said. 'Nowhere near. Have you seen the south chimney? Really looked at it? If that comes down, half the roof will come down with it. The van's got an oil leak I can't fix, the tyres are bald, my compressor's just packed up… If I can't work we're even more screwed than we are now. I've got to get cash,' he said, spreading his fingers so wide the tendons jumped out from the back of his hands.

He lowered his head. His hair, cruelly insensitive as ever, looked magnificent. He'd never mentioned the state of the chimney to me before but I wasn't surprised he was aware of it, his discussion of problems being in inverse proportion to his anxiety about them. It's why I try so hard to manage as many as I can on my own.

'How far have you got?' I said. 'I expect Dan would bite your arm off for it?'

Hugh shook his head slowly, not in contradiction but rather acknowledgement of Dan's eagerness to get his mitts on that field. 'Haggling,' he said wearily. 'He'd like the shirt off my back as well as the land.'

Part of me wanted very much to take Hugh's hand at this point, but the other part – doubtful of how well this would be received – won.

'I'm so sorry, Hugh,' I said. 'I know how much you don't want to do this. I wish I could think of a way you won't already have thought of...' He sat back when I started to speak and now had his face propped up, most of his fingers over his mouth, his eyes upon me in a way I couldn't quite read. There was no comfort I could give him, no "it's only land," or chirpy "needs must". Not when this was worse than both kidneys. So, 'It'll get better, Hugh,' I said. 'I know it will. Something will turn up. Maybe sooner rather than later even – you never know.'

He said nothing to this, just moved his eyes slowly over my face in the sort of solemn contemplation that precedes a weighty decision of some kind. I knew what it was – whether or not he could bear to do us both the kindness of allowing a little hope on the scene. He surprised me then. He leaned forward, took my face gently in his hands and kissed me. Out of pity? Gratitude? Love? I honestly couldn't say. After that he stood and went quietly from the room.

8TH JUNE

I am a cheerful person. In my school reports they often called me "sunny", and I got to be board monitor, and look after anyone new. And just in case I was ever in any doubt, my dear dad called me Sunshine right up to the day he died. "Where's my Sunshine?", "Come on, Sunshine!" Cheerful is good; cheerful makes people happy. Makes *me* happy. I'd like to say too that there's a strength, a sort of self-reliance in this best foot forward approach, though I know it's seen as old-fashioned now. But really, is it so stupid to focus on the good stuff and just push through the bad? Particularly when there are so many ticks in my Lucky Life questionnaire. Everyone healthy, a roof over our heads (if not a particularly secure one), no horrors of war or famine or persecution or any of the other myriad sufferings that millions endure on a daily basis. An ideal life is not, should never be, a right, after all.

That's not to say you shouldn't strive to improve your lot, but usually there's only so much you can do. Particularly when other people are the overriding problem. "You can't change anyone else," my mother always said, inadvertently providing me with the best possible advice for a life with Hugh, "only yourself." All his unhappiness could be summed up with a single sentence: he works every hour at a job he hates, to sustain a house he didn't choose, and insists there's no escape from either. Any attempts to question this seem to appal him, like attacks on the very heart of his integrity. So what can I do but get on? Work around him. Keep my chin high. Be happy. Absolutely. It's the least, or the most, doesn't matter which, that I can do.

9TH JUNE

Discovered toad under piano again. Took him outside, then returned to the piano area in the hall and got on all fours to try and work out how he's getting in. Had I known this would reveal so much unwelcome information I would certainly have left well alone. Things I discovered:

- The flagstones, usually relatively dry at this time of year, were wet enough to leave damp patches on the knees of my jeans.
- The veneer around the piano pedals is peeling off.
- When I crawled the most direct path between the piano and the outside wall I arrived at the coffer chest. When I looked under this, I saw there was an air brick (good), but that it was mostly covered up with soil from the outside (bad). There was also a suspiciously toad-sized hole in its bottom left hand corner.
- It quickly became apparent that other animals had also made use of this members-only entrance; the back of the coffer chest was thick with evidence (if not actual presence) of woodlice, beetles, some sort of desiccated pupa and various other unidentifiable invertebrates.

It must have been the first or second time Hugh brought me here that he asked casually how I felt about wildlife. A whole host of rural retreat, brochure-style images had rushed at once into my townie head: hedgehogs nuzzling through autumn leaves, deer drinking from a lake edge in early morning mist, dormice asleep in their little grass nests – and oh yes, I'd enthusiastically replied, I *love* wildlife. But of course he wasn't referring to these sorts of photogenic, resolutely outdoor creatures, but the rather less appealing ones that prefer to be inside, with us, like the mice that will often scurry along the bottom of the panelling while we're watching telly, or those spiders that seem to find themselves in open view quite by mistake, the panic this clearly produces in them in comic contravention of their superlative hideousness and size. Then there are the snails in the folds of the curtains and any number of ladybirds, asleep in great scarlet clusters in the corners of the bedrooms in the winter, patrolling the windowsills in the summer... I do seem to spend a great deal of time either letting things out or trying vainly to stop them getting in.

I rummaged in the rag drawer and found a bit of ripped pillowcase which I stuffed into the hole of the air brick, and added *dig soil away from air brick* to my To Do list. I've got four pages' worth at the moment, with only the very easy jobs, like *clean out boys' ears*, crossed out. It therefore seemed sensible to forget about the damp for the moment.

Hugh is fine, and I am fine.

12th June

Had a relatively quiet morning, so asked Ian if he was free to come and have a proper look at the Tree House with me. As I see it, there are only two possible solutions: either we find some carpenters so thrilled to take on the renovation project they offer to do it for free, or we wait for the gods to remove the problem by sending a good heavy storm to knock the wretched thing down once and for all. I presented these options to Ian, who looked nonplussed at the former and so horrified by the latter that I wondered, for a moment, if I'd said what I thought I'd said or rather that I'd confessed to garrotting the children in the night.

I shouldn't have been surprised at this reaction, though, as his knowledge of Narwhal history is surpassed only by his monumental devotion to it. He has never been employed permanently by us – his father was the last of the Stantons to be so tied – but he has inherited his fierce loyalty to all things Narwhal, past and present, and so suggesting we allow the Tree House to be torn down in a storm really *is* like saying I've murdered my children, as far as Ian is concerned.

It can be so humbling, this unquestioning reverence for a house he may know intimately but under whose roof he has never once slept. But when you put Hugh and Rose into the equation, whose incumbency here you'd assume would bring with it the patent on familial pride and not – as seems bewilderingly to be the case – shrugged acceptance, Ian's attitude actually *embarrasses* me. On their behalf. They don't seem to acknowledge his respect. It just came with the house, to be lived with, like the stained glass scenes in the windows, and the secrets tucked inside the acanthus leaves carved on the staircase, and the fireplace in the drawing room that I know is special somehow though have never learned quite why.

I'm still outraged by this after all these years, still waving the banner for Ian's right to recognition despite realising very early on that the greatest opponent to my campaign was the man himself. There was an exact moment when I knew.

Hugh and Rose were sitting at the kitchen table trying to plan Grandpa's funeral while I tried to be helpful with half a brain on baby Billy on my hip, and the other half on Peter pressing Play-Doh deep into the cracks between the flagstones on the floor. Ian was also there, as he'd been tasked with organising parking for the wake. He was standing, very still, near the French windows.

Funeral preparations are always stressful, but the Narwhals make sure theirs trump anyone else's in this regard by imposing an extra tier of demand and ritual for the bereaved to fulfil; it had been exactly the same when Greer died. A horse-drawn hearse. Bells. "Your finest casket", lead-lined. Five shillings for every family in the village. Hugh's calculator was practically steaming with the size of the figures he put into it, each one inducing a little more anxiety so that the total seemed to teeter alarmingly.

'I just don't see how we're going to afford it,' said Hugh, shaking his head. 'Even without the shillings.'

'Then make it cheaper,' said Rose, whose face alone among the adults present showed none of the tension apparent on her brother's. She spoke witheringly, as if long bored of waiting for him at the conclusion he was only just approaching. 'Mum's dead, Dad's dead, it's our turn now. We can do what we like.'

As Hugh met her gaze, I paid attention. At some point in the days since their father had died, already yellowing when Delilah led me to him in the bed in which he'd been born, Hugh and Rose had found themselves split asunder. No trial of time or space or heart or mind had ever succeeded in this before, but the death of their father had clearly unsheathed a sharper blade. And not only were they apart but becoming more so every minute, each interaction feeding their divergence just as it had once fed their intimacy, like a couple of magnets with the poles of one now reversed. We all saw it, though none of us could have guessed then how enduring it would turn out to be.

'It's not as straightforward as that, and you know it,' Hugh said. 'There are obligations.'

Rose stared at him in genuine puzzlement. 'Since when did you care about obligations?'

'When do you think?' said Hugh, equally baffled.

That was it, right there. The crux of it all. How each sibling saw Hugh's heirdom. For Hugh, it was ancient, humourless, intransigent. A list of blood-written laws to be rigidly obeyed. For Rose it was a mere transfer of property; duty and obedience being optional extras. And each was incredulous at the views of the other; the naiveté of them, the *waste*.

'Look,' I said quickly, 'let's not get into a row about it now. Hugh, you and I can have a look at the figures later –

I don't want to hold Ian up. I know he's very kindly going to help with the parking, but, actually, I've been thinking, as he's so... if he would like more *involvement*? Perhaps do a reading, or sit with us, or something to reflect, to *honour* all he's done for this family?' Such a silence fell upon the room that Peter was startled from his Play-Doh, as if by a loud bang. 'What?' I said, looking at each face in turn. 'Wouldn't that be a good idea? Ian?' I turned to him as I said this, but he was frowning with great concentration through the window – as if a unicorn had suddenly appeared in the middle of the lawn. 'Ian?' I said again. 'Would you like to? Something? Anything?'

He pulled his eyes reluctantly away from the unicorn and rested them instead somewhere on my hairline. 'It's as it should be,' he said. 'I'll be needed for the parking.'

'Oh, I'm sure we could find a way round that,' I said. 'Hugh? Rose? Don't you think?'

Hugh looked over at Ian. Before he even formed the question which followed, I knew, from the weary half mast of his eyebrows, his long familiarity with the answer, and that he was requesting it only for my benefit.

'Ian. Would you like a role at the funeral?' Despite his air of resignation, I had to admit there was still real sincerity in his tone. 'You know there's a place for you at all these things – just waiting for you to want it.'

But– 'I'll be needed for the parking, thank you all the same,' said Ian, with a short sniff.

As Hugh gave me a "You see?" glance, I frowned, considering whether or not to push one last time. It had never occurred to me that Ian wouldn't be pleased by the offer. It was as if I'd flung open the door of a caged bird to find it saying politely but resolutely that it was quite happy where it was. I felt a flush of confusion, frustration and embarrassment, the latter partly for Ian (I never meant to make things awkward for him) and partly for me (my grand gesture, made in such good faith, shown up as ignorant at best and patronising at worst).

What path to take with him going forward? I've never really been able to decide. I *do* wave the banner for him, like inviting him to eat with us after every Ringing, or making a fuss of his birthday, but knowing full well how much he'd prefer I didn't does rather nibble away at my militancy... And there's always the sneaking suspicion that he has the last laugh anyway, camouflaged in the background, conducting his guerrilla war while I march with my trumpets and redcoats...

Back at the Tree House I gave a deep sigh. It *is* wonderful that Ian is so protective of everything; it was he, for example, who stopped a sixteen-year-old Hugh from covering the eighteenth century Chinese wallpaper in his room with wads of ruinous Blu Tack and posters of young ladies in very un-eighteenth century string bikinis. But it can also be irritating in the way that pride without any of the ties of ownership – creation, purchase, inheritance, responsibility – so often is. Particularly to someone who, on bad days, feels as if she was slightly tricked into the latter, blindly skipping up the aisle. Who might, on bad days, reinvent that pivotal church scene to one without a bride.

We started at the top and worked our way down, noting all defects and (in my case, at least) trying not to cry. Most of the wooden tiles were either missing or rotten. The beam from which the bell was suspended was actually not too bad, but the posts supporting the beam were. So were the two more exposed walls. Only two panes of glass out of the six windows were intact, and three little oak saplings had taken root in the south corner – the squirrels' preferred spot judging from the acorn husks and nearby pile of poo. Somebody had nested in the chimney, and ivy had spread so enthusiastically around the door-frame that it was now impossible either to open or close the door.

I looked at Ian and puffed out my cheeks and raised my eyebrows. 'Yes,' he said cautiously, 'yes, bit of work maybe. Bit of work.'

I rummaged furiously through my brain trying to think of some way of achieving this "bit of work" that did not involve money, or speaking to Hugh, which left me with only one idea – presumably provided by the film I watched with the boys yesterday. Perhaps, I thought, our squirrels could be trained as Willy Wonka had managed to train his. If they could sort the good and bad nuts so efficiently, would basic carpentry be such a leap?

13TH JUNE

I phoned Rose this morning to see how Santorini had gone, and also to try and pick her brains about the Tree House. I'd done some mental preparation regarding the former before dialling. There was no point trying to guess what stage she'd reached on her yoga enthusiasm trajectory, as I've learned from those of her past passions that although their shape is always the same, the forces that drive them are not. It's never been a simple matter of time; Marxism lasted only a month or two, for example, while veganism went on for a good couple of years. It's true that people can influence her sometimes; not all people, of course – in all the world she's really only ever been able to hear Greer, Hugh and Nick – but none of them has been involved where the yoga's concerned, one being dead, one not knowing (as I was careful not to tell him) and one long amputated from her life, so there were no clues there.

It's not about obstacles; or failure either. Or even success – she dropped her jewellery design just days after receiving her first big commission, my relieved congratulations (because surely this was The One) shrugged off her shoulders like the jacket of a misguided gallant.

No. There was no predicting what I'd get when she answered. All I could do was hold my hands out and hope for the best. But as it turned out, I didn't get any of the Roses I'd prepared for. What I got was the very rare, lesser spotted, shivery one that you have to crouch down – oh so gently – to see.

She was dreadfully low. She said she'd been expelled from the yoga retreat for getting drunk and sleeping with a waiter, and that ever since she'd stayed pretty much all day every day in her flat, eating pickled onion Monster Munch and watching bad daytime TV. I don't know what I'm *for*, she said, and I don't know what I want; and I was quite undone by her flash of self-knowledge, as you might be by an apology more fulsome than you ever thought you'd get.

I did the only thing I can ever think of doing under these circumstances and told her to pack her biggest bag and come and stay immediately. Hugh won't be pleased, but he'll have to lump it, I'm afraid.

The wanting to look after Rose felt so fiery that I decided to make use of it to call Mrs Willis to prod her for the balance she owes us. She puffed impatiently and said really, it was extremely inconvenient as she was terribly busy, and anyway she hadn't even had a proper invoice from us and she wouldn't be paying a penny until she had. Oh, that *is* strange, Mrs Willis, I said, as we posted it out before we delivered the sofa. Well, she said (as if I were a person of very limited mental capacity), you'd better send another one, hadn't you? Goodbye.

How is it possible, I ask myself with incredulity and not a little awe, that people can be so spectacularly vile? And why do so many of them seem to find their way to us for their upholstery needs? It has occurred to me in the past that we ourselves make them that way to a certain extent. I do try to keep the customers away from Hugh, but sometimes there's a question that only he can answer and I'll have to call him from the workshop. Out he'll come, suspicious and glowering in greeting, while I become increasingly twittery to compensate, and sometimes a customer who has been perfectly nice up to that point will begin to frown, sniffing deceit or desperation somewhere, like you do when a shop assistant is over-effusive about an outfit you're trying on. Which makes me more unctuous than ever, and Hugh more monosyllabic, and before we know it the customer is narrowing her eyes and muttering about how it's all totting up to a lot more than she thought.

Hugh has never been someone who could boast of customer-facing skills on his CV. While no one would dream of accusing him of being a people pleaser, you'd think that the wish to secure (much-needed) sales would squeeze a little rudimentary courtesy out of him, but not so. I wonder about this sometimes – his inability to bow his head by so much as a millimetre, regardless of the benefits. It looks so much like arrogance at first; then I think perhaps it's more an artist's impatience with all aspects of his work other than its creation. That's certainly how they seemed to define it when he was working at Vaughan's, guarding the space between their star designer and their clients in a way that made each party feel protected from the other, and grateful for it.

But Narwhal Upholstery is not Vaughan Design, and sorry though I genuinely am to say it, there's just no room for artistes here. Not in deepest Herefordshire, not in upholstery, not in a husband and wife team, and particularly not when the most ravening claim on the income sought is the artist's own ancient, crumbling, insatiable estate.

Hugh hasn't said anything else about the field, but I know he hasn't got any further with selling it because the other day I bumped into Farmer Dan, who seemed very keen to sidle up and tell me the many ways in which the land was practically worthless.

So I've decided to try and get a job. Lord knows who will have me (as the twelve-year-old at the temp agency last winter was only too quick to tell me), but it's worth a try. It won't make much of a dent in our money worries but, as I find I say daily about one thing or another, it's better than a kick in the teeth.

14TH JUNE

Pete said at breakfast that he thinks he might need glasses. I asked him if his eyes hurt when he looked at the board at school, and he said, 'Only when I've got both eyes open.' I was completely mystified by this reply (does he wink his way through his lessons? Is he mainly asleep?) but I do try to avoid asking for clarifications from Pete when possible. Not only do his responses tend to confuse things further, but he's so at ease within the bewildering tangle of his neural pathways and so insistent on their obvious logic that one's own sanity is very swiftly brought into question – by both parties. After a moment's consideration, therefore, I told him we'd book him in with an optician and wisely said no more about it.

Tony arrived mid-morning with a transit full of his stonemason stuff and was greeted like an old friend by Hugh. Went to give them a hand unpacking but couldn't even move, let alone lift, the first three boxes, so asked instead did they want a cup of tea? They both did, but before I went off to make it I thought I'd better check what flavour Tony wanted as perhaps, being a craftsman sort of person, he might not want builders' but something a bit fancier (simultaneously worrying that I didn't think we actually had anything fancier). This was far more of a significant question than Tony could possibly have known, as Hugh has a sliding scale of disapproval for non-builder teas: from a slight frown for Lapsang to utter contempt for anything with berries or infusion on the packet. Was the beautiful friendship that was developing between them about to be shattered by a request for a cup of camomile?

But Tony is a builders' man, thank the Lord. I fetched tea for all three of us, and sat outside with Tony and Hugh in the sun, thinking that now might be an excellent opportunity to find out a bit more about our new tenant. It turns out he's married, sadly. I don't mean sadly in that the marriage is sad, although for all I know it may be, but in the sense that single men are like BOGOFs at the supermarket – it's good to stock up with them even if you can't think of an immediate use for them – and if he's taken, I've got to put him back on the shelf. I'm rather sorry about this, as the man is clearly a catch for anyone who has the sense to spot it.

His pleasures in life are simple, as of course they would be. He loves his work, and a decent pint, and wildlife – the watching of and, it turned out, the killing of – fishing being his great love. I glanced at Hugh as Tony said this, curious to see his reaction. He's never been as ostentatious in his support of animal rights as his sister, but he abhors cruelty all the same, with his most acute condemnation reserved for those who kill for their own amusement. I saw him hear Tony's words and consider them, and found myself unsurprised to see that not only had they not diminished his liking for this man but actually heightened it. Because for Tony, the killing of a trout was as much about his respect for it as the patience he paid out to catch one, and the nod he gave its escape if he failed.

'It's wrong to return it to the water,' he said. 'And it's wrong not to eat what you've caught.'

I got distracted by the silence that settled over the three of us then, thinking how peaceful it was. Had Tony turned around and told Hugh and me that he'd known each of us since birth, I don't think either of us would have batted an eyelid. Nor been anything but delighted at the news.

But I was brought back to myself with a jolt, when I realised Hugh had just offered up our lake for Tony's use. Oh, dear Diary, the lake! Another massive ancestral Hugh plate I'm not spinning successfully, overgrown as it is with reeds and rushes, and studded with footballs/rugby balls/Frisbees/tennis balls in various states of decay. I instantly began the urgent task of lowering Tony's expectations, just as you would if a surprise guest asked to use the back loo, but too late. He and Hugh had already sprung up to go and see it, as deaf to my protestations as the boys are whenever I tell them no, that enormous parcel is nothing interesting, no, not a toy, no – just some things for Dad's work – Dad's work, no – *not a toy* – OK, go on, if you must, open it anyway...

With both of them gone, and Rose not coming till later, I decided with a sigh I should really go and have a look at the vegetable patch. I strongly suspected it would have been conducting a secret campaign of world domination since I'd last been there, and this was exactly what I found. The rocket had bolted, as had the rhubarb, and I think I've missed the broad beans too as the ones I tried were very tough. I pulled up a large potato plant hoping vainly to find a mass of beautiful new potatoes, but there were only two – about the size of walnuts and covered in black scabs. What *am* I doing wrong, apart from not weeding or watering, or actually visiting at all? Every year it's the same. The only success stories are the nettles and the docks and the wretched courgettes, which were already romping happily out of bounds onto the gravel and which I can see I will yet again be picking for the entire summer and trying to insert surreptitiously in all manner of unsuitable dishes, such as fish pie.

I do try; or keep meaning to. There just always seems to be something more pressing to do. But then I look at all the bounty that nature keeps on (and on...) providing and feel absolutely *racked* with guilt for not showing my respect and gratitude for it through harvesting, as Tony does with his trout. Oh, the Tyranny of Veg! The fruit isn't so bad, as the birds often get to the cherries and the damsons before they're ripe, so that even as I make a show of cursing their greed I'm piteously thankful for every last beak – saved as I am from four months locked in the kitchen, making bad jam and worse chutney.

I'm pretty sure that even the most ardent veg growers have moments like this. You start to see a panicked look in their eyes around this time of year as their own gardens go into overdrive and they try desperately to offload things. It's like when you spot a chugger ahead on the street – it's *imperative* to avoid eye contact or else before you know it you'll have three bags of stringy runner beans thrust into your hands, which you'll put in a corner of the kitchen and pretend to forget about until they go mouldy and you can scuttle out with them under cover of darkness while your husband isn't looking and tuck them into the compost heap.

I stared at the veg patch gloomily as the courgettes called out to me in all their fat, glossy greenness, the gifts of earth and sun and rain practically bursting through their skins. Ended up picking an armful of the wretched things as I simply couldn't bear the guilt of leaving them there. Put them in the corner of the kitchen while I thought what to do with them...

Rose arrived just before I had to leave to pick up the boys from school, so I got her to come with me to surprise them. She was wearing what looked like a silk nightie, with a pair of silver trainers, and those massive dark glasses again. Both forearms were encircled with so many bangles, clickety clackety-ing whenever she moved, that it was a bit like sitting next to a loom. I didn't want to ask her How *are* you? as it's only ten minutes to school, so just said I was so glad she'd come up and that she must stay as long as she likes. She didn't say anything to this, but grasped my hand and held onto it so tightly that I didn't feel I could release it, and instead had to adjust my driving so as to stay in third gear at all times.

The boys were beside themselves to see her. Billy flung himself at her, and Pete said, 'Hello, Aunty Rose,' which is pretty effusive for him. As for the rest of the mums waiting for their own kids, they were agog. Lipstick is considered pretty radical at pickup in this part of the world, so Rose – all five feet, ten inches of her, with jangly bangles and silky nightie (with, I noticed, impressed, absolutely nothing on underneath) – was as rare and fascinating a sight as if Aphrodite herself had just got out of my Skoda. This attention cheered her up no end, and she scooped both boys to her unfettered boobs and kissed them theatrically.

'Darlings,' she said breathily, as if she hadn't seen them for years, 'what a joy to see you. You are *enormous*! Tell me *everything*!' Which they competed to do all the way home.

P.S. Tony stuck his head round the kitchen door later to say he was off, then fixed his eyes on the log pile of courgettes in the corner. I spotted this instantly, and asked – as lightly as I could – did he like courgettes and would he like to take any home? Well, only if you can spare them, he said. The innocent!

17TH JUNE

I have to say I'm rather confused (and, if I'm honest, suspicious) to find we've had just the most lovely couple of days. The weather has been glorious, so Hugh has made a water slide out of a large piece of builders' plastic sheeting which he's laid down the bank into the lake and which the boys have been enjoying from the moment they return from school until bedtime. The hairs on their little skinny legs have been completely rubbed off by the friction and their swimming trunks are basically ruined, but this seems a small price to pay for their delight in the sort of wholesome activity (like climbing trees, building dens or cavorting with badgers) that the responsible parent considers the apotheosis of child play but which the offspring themselves so often disdain.

Rose, meanwhile, has rediscovered her grandmother's piano after years of disinterest, and seems to have regained her Grade 8 proficiency in no time at all. Having endured nothing but "Chopsticks" and thudding one-fingered renditions of "Silent Night" at the hands of the boys, the poor piano seems to positively thrill at her touch, like a long-celibate spinster seduced at last. I'm grateful for this on so many levels, first of which is the relief at the piano's use. It's a bit like the courgettes; I can't help but think that things which have no purpose have no value, and if they have no value I want rid of them, but then the guilt of the waste and the ingratitude stops me, and the item itself is inevitably saved from eviction. So when the piano is given a new lease of life, I'm jubilant; almost hopeful, in fact, that every other obsolete object with which this house is crammed – the half-sewn tapestries and stuffed squirrels, the top hats and fish kettles and soup tureens the size of Shetland ponies – will soon be resurrected to usefulness too.

I pay attention when Rose plays, wondering if it's proving therapeutic for her. I've listened for a pattern that might justify this hope, a slow and steady lifting in the mood of the pieces she plays, but even though I've found none, I still think the piano is helping her. There's been no mention of the conversation she and I had on the phone when I told her to come and stay, or of her fleeing London, so that I think her playing is a letting of emotion, if not quite its understanding. I keep an eye on her though, make sure that – from time to time – I contrive a quiet space between us in which she can talk to me if she wants to. Just in case.

Hugh, too, is cheerier at the moment – due, I think, to the companionship of Tony. Does the proximity of a successful craftsman lift his respect for his own trade? Or maybe just help him bear his hatred of it? I have no idea. They take their breaks together, and if ever I'm outside at the time, I hardly ever see them talking. Whatever it is that flows from Tony to Hugh doesn't seem to need any vehicle. It comes with the mutual nod to another man's intimacy with tools, half-hums to a dusty radio, and the quiet bringing forth of hand-shaped things.

I did consider being sad that the boys and I, his loving family, are apparently incapable of improving his mood one jot (feel often in fact that we actually make it worse), but decided instead just to be glad that *someone* can reach those parts of Hugh that other people can't, and that that someone was a kind and decent man and not the more reckless sort of rescuer that middle-aged men can be known to choose. Because we're all benefitting. There was no fuss when I said Rose was coming to stay, no grumpy questions as to why and how long for. And the water slide was his idea – not pulled out of him but offered voluntarily. Everything is *lighter* somehow.

There was a moment yesterday evening, in fact, when I was quite convinced I was dreaming. Through the French windows drifted the delicious scent of jasmine and the happy shouts of the boys on the water slide. Gin and tonic in one hand, Hugh led his sister to the piano stool with the other, smiled at her, and began the bottom half of a duet that Rose instantly recognised and joined, while I could only grasp the nearby banister to ready myself for an imminent stroke at the shock of the Happy Scene. There were too many incongruities to absorb at once: Hugh and Rose together, and smilingly so; the laughter of the children completely unpunctured by screams of pain or anguish; and, from the silky feel of the banister, I could only assume that Jo had managed to conquer the ingrained boy hand stickiness on the woodwork – presumably with a combination of raw aggression and some sort of radioactive acid.

It was all too precious and too strange to trust somehow, so I went back to the kitchen to get on with the salad, dimly aware that you shouldn't be seeking solace *from* nice things but *in* them. But the vigorous spinning of the wet lettuce was useful here – like two brisk fingers pinching out a badly-placed bud – and I was pretty much myself again by supper.

21ST JUNE

I didn't go straight home after dropping the boys at school this morning. I went to the far side of town on a superfluous errand, so that I could say in truth when I went to Mrs Willis's that I was "just passing". I knocked robustly on the door, took a deep breath, and squared my shoulders, ready to employ whatever force was necessary to wrestle our money out of her, only to find the door opened by a small pale man I'd never seen before but whose weary look of resigned defeat identified him immediately as Mr Willis.

I felt a rush of sympathy, then guilt at having to ask this poor man for some money (hadn't he suffered enough?), but he couldn't have been lovelier about it. He took me into the kitchen so that he could get his cheque book, saying how much the sofa had already been admired and how comfortable it was, and how sorry he was that we'd had to send two invoices (*two* – hah! – the lying old witch!). He held out the cheque and I had to resist a huge urge to close his hands around it and shout Run! Run while you can! I said instead how much Hugh had enjoyed working on their sofa and how beautiful it looked in their hall, a little white lie the very least I could do.

I drove straight to the bank to deposit the cheque as we are on the very knife edge of our overdraft, and, besides, I couldn't bear to look at poor Mr Willis's wobbly signature a moment longer than necessary. There was quite a queue, but I didn't mind too much, as I fell into an interesting conversation with the lady behind me. It began with the usual chat about the weather (I did so despise this traditional British opener when younger, but have learned that it is a very useful social snack – just enough to respectfully acknowledge the existence of a nearby fellow human, but leaving plenty of room either to proceed to a conversational main course, or metaphorically pat one's stomach with apologetic excuses and move on), then progressed to her running that very smart lingerie boutique on Whitburn Street. You should come and have a look, she said, as I'd rather feared, our bank balance prohibiting my entrance to *any* retail establishment with even a whiff of boutique. Then she looked very pointedly at each of my boobs in turn and said, 'You're a 30C, right?'

I was dumbstruck.

I'm impressed enough by other people's skills, but when they're so embedded as to be instinctive, needing no other tool than the person's brain (it's a very good thing I never had a boyfriend into astronomy, as he'd have had me bedded and wedded before he could say Cassiopeia) I am as overawed as a small child shown a magic trick. It's possible I should get out more.

I told the lady that while I was quite dazzled by her expertise, it was with great regret I had to confess that no, actually I was a 32B, to which she nodded slowly and asked when had I last been fitted for a bra? I thought for a bit, then told her I couldn't remember when I'd last purchased a bra, let alone been fitted for one, at which she looked triumphant and said she'd put a tenner on my being a 30C.

Curiouser and curiouser... When I reached Rebecca at the counter, I found myself asking her if she'd ever been fitted for a bra? Oh God, yes, she said, with a horrified expression, as though I'd asked if pain relief was a good idea during childbirth; you should get measured at *least* every six months. I realised I'd fallen into another black hole of ignorance about things all women should know – like Spandex and the miracles of Febreze – and wondered how many more I have yet to encounter?

Got home to find a big soily bag of elderly spring greens on the doorstep (*damn* you, mystery glut offloader) and Rose sunbathing naked in full view of the yard, with the postman shortly to arrive. I found myself cross. I have very positive opinions about nudity in general, but I do think it's unfair to spring it on people who might not feel the same way, particularly elderly postmen with a history of angina.

22ND JUNE

The boob and bra information I received yesterday led me to the full-length mirror as I got dressed this morning. I do this only glancingly with all my clothes on, let alone in my underwear, as there is only one test my reflection needs to pass: cleanliness. I do realise that other women differ in this, Rose being a perfect example, and every now and then in my life I've decided to make more of an effort. I'll splash out on a new hair clip, put on some mascara, or even do some exercises for a while in the hope that these nods to fashion and firmed buttocks will soon become habit. But it's futile. I'd have more luck changing the Earth's orbit, or training Peter to use his laundry basket. I just don't understand a lot of it. Rose used to wear a top that utterly bewildered me – a polo-neck jumper with no arms. I'd stare and stare at it, trying to comprehend its logic. Jumper is to keep warm – sensible. Sleeveless items are to keep cool – sensible. But in the same clothe?

I'm old enough now to accept defeat, and even to shrug off the raised eyebrows or comments that might have persuaded a younger me to persevere. Ian can look me up and down as sadly as he wants – I will never reach the pressed and tweedy perfections of Greer, and have no wish to. Clean and temperature-controlled is more than enough for me.

It took some frowning this morning therefore to focus

on the reflection in the mirror. I heaved my bra straps up and down and could see, from the bouncing this produced, that perhaps I *did* need a better fit. And perhaps the colour of the bra (unintentional grey), and its bit of fuzzy thread where the tiny bow (its only concession to prettiness) had fallen off, meant it fell below even my subterranean levels of acceptability.

And what of the rest of it? The body itself? Well, definitely in good working order. It didn't creak or hurt when I did things. There were wobbly bits, sure, but there were also firm bits. There were signs of the life it had led – stretch marks, the staining on my forearm from bad sunburn in 1996, my mother's bunions, the odd scar or two – but overall, OK. A Skoda sort of body. That wouldn't be the most coveted by the thieves in the car park, but not the least either.

I began to dither about the bra. Perhaps it was fine after all? Thought I'd better get a second opinion, and called through to Hugh in the bathroom to ask did he think I needed a new bra? He didn't hear me, so I went in and repeated the question. He picked up his toothbrush before he glanced at me, and I realised with a small jolt of sadness that not only was his attention polite at most, but that I didn't really mind, and didn't even really mind that I didn't really mind.

We are taught to anticipate this. In the all-consuming early days, when Hugh would not have been able to see me in my bra without instantly getting me out of it, and we were constantly tripping over our own lust, and elated by its uncompromising demands and inconveniences, I remember thinking smugly that – no matter what the magazines in the doctor's surgery said – ours could not diminish by so much as a kiss. Very often, that's what the interviewees themselves would say too – that they'd *known* themselves to be the exception to the waning passion rule and were surprised to discover, a few years in, that they followed it just as closely as everyone else. I'd read all that, then dismissed it as gaily as I did all the other inevitables they try to warn you about – grey hair, cholesterol, death.

But here we were, my husband and me, in a bathroom with a squeaky tap and a frozen waterfall of rust running down beneath it, me in an elderly bra and him with an elderly toothbrush, with about as much heat between us as that of a damp match.

As if to cruelly reinforce this black hole of romance, my eye was caught through the window at that moment by Aristide, our resident cock pheasant, named for a flamboyant friend of Hugh's. As is their custom at this time of day, he and his lady wife were taking the air, Mrs Aristide pecking musingly at some titbit while her husband watched over her, ever alert, scanning the environs for danger. They reminded me of nothing so much as a courtly couple strolling the avenues of Versailles, Mrs Aristide admiring the view while her beau, his plumage alight in the morning sun, kept one hand round her waist and the other ever ready on the hilt of his sword...

'What did you want to know?' Hugh asked.

'This bra,' I said, rather wishing I hadn't bothered to ask him in the first place, 'is it a bit grotty? Should I get some new ones?'

He glanced at it, shrugged, and said he applied the same rules to me as to himself: once married, there is absolutely no need for either partner to make any effort with their appearance whatsoever. I looked at him, not really sure what to think about this. On one hand, I was very pleased to be accepted just as I am, but on the other I felt a lurking disquiet that you shouldn't let yourself go – even if you weren't really sure you'd ever been holding yourself in the first place, so to speak, or if your spouse didn't care – but couldn't pinpoint exactly why. Self-respect, perhaps? Or maybe because, without some periodic and critical self-examination, you begin on a slippery slope that starts with not minding the odd stain on your jumper and ends with complete indifference to warts, hairy chins and halitosis?

It was a conundrum. I put bras on my shopping list just to be safe.

Took boys straight from school to the optician to pick up Pete's new glasses. There was a bit of a wait – always a worry when the boys have nothing to occupy them – so I had to do the usual balancing between boy entertainment and authority annoyance. We all tried on the funkier glasses (benevolent smiles from optical staff). The boys sat on adjacent spinny chairs and span them up and down and up and down (rather less benevolent smiles from optical staff). Then I had a brainwave and we all gathered round a mirror to compare things our faces could do, such as nostril flaring (boys, not me), ear waggling (all of us), independent moving of eyeballs (none of us, no matter what Pete thinks), and incredible twisting of tongue into weird three pronged shape (Billy alone amongst us, and very possibly the rest of humankind). Specs at last arrived, Pete made the poor optical lady show him their entire selection of glasses cases, before eventually settling on the very first one she took out, and as we emerged onto the pavement declared that he didn't think he really needed specs at all. Looked at him, then heavenward, and prayed – hard.

28TH JUNE

Bit of a drama with Rose today. I've been increasingly worried about her recently and wasn't surprised, really, that it should all come to a head.

When she was first here, with the rediscovery of the piano and, I think, just being with us and all our family chaos, she was OK; but then the novelty wore off, and she started to sink again. She began to follow me around like some sort of beautiful, mournful greyhound, sighing and asking me what I was doing as if the bag of potatoes/woodworm spray/strimmer I was holding at the time were purely for decorative purposes. Then she'd say right, I must help, and I'd thank her and hand over aforementioned potatoes, etc, but as soon as they were in her hands she'd sigh again and say she couldn't understand why she was so tired all the time, and put everything down. Ashamed to say I was finding this whole routine absolutely maddening and it was increasingly difficult not to shout that *I* couldn't bloody well understand why she was so tired either.

Hugh didn't help. After his initial softness with her (did they *really* sit down at the piano together?) he seemed to become as irritated with her as I was, despite the fact he barely saw her all day (deeply wrapped up with Mrs Noble in the workshop at the moment), and kept turning into some sort of 1950s patriarch every suppertime, asking her sternly What Have You Done Today? and What Are You Going To Do Tomorrow? Which turned Rose either sulky or shouty, depending on how much wine she'd had, and pushed me and the boys into glum silence.

Worse still, I had a sneaking suspicion that she'd got her eyes on Tony, as I caught her in his workshop the other day when I took him a cup of tea, mournful greyhound utterly transformed into sleek feline hunter, purring, 'Oh, how *interesting*, you're *so* talented,' at him, come-hither cleavage carefully angled into his line of sight at all times. Poor Tony looked half-impatient and half-embarrassed by her attentions, so that I felt it wise to say to Rose, as if to a small child, come on now – I'm sure Tony wants to get on with his work – and haul her and her bubbling lust out of the door.

Then this morning, I went onto the terrace to pick up two million rubber bands from the boys' rubber band guns (Father Christmas not really focusing last year) to discover Rose draped on a sunbed flicking through *Vogue* in an exaggeratedly desultory manner, and found myself standing up, putting my hands on my hips and barking, 'Right! Rose! Come and pick some elderflowers with me.' Why, why to pick elderflowers? Must wild nature hound my subconscious hunting-gathering guilt as much as the domestic variety does? I felt, though, it was important to maintain an air of decisive assertiveness and that I couldn't backtrack from the elderflower suggestion, and so off we went through the back gate and over the stile into the track, Rose with a bag for life and me with a tiny pair of rounded child-safe scissors, all grown-up sensible ones having – as usual – been stolen by thoughtless family members and presumably distributed – as usual – in random and inaccessible places throughout the house and garden.

But calm and compassion returned to me, thank goodness, after a couple of minutes cutting. The sun was so warm and delicious, and I could hear skylarks in the distance, and I found when I opened my mouth the right words miraculously just came out. Rose took a big breath, and the next thing I knew we were both knocked sidewise by the great teary sob that came out of her, followed by everything unhappy in her heart, of which there was a great deal. We sat down on the verge and I found a dock leaf for her to (rather unsuccessfully) blow her nose on, then out of nowhere Toby – Juliet Morris's vast soppy golden Labrador – appeared. Delighted as all vast soppy golden Labradors are by happening upon humans at their own head height, he fell upon us with licks and great happy whacks of his tail, completely disregarding the angry calls to come here now, Toby, TOBY NOW! by Juliet herself, who had broken into a trot up the track towards us. She apologised profusely on reaching us, then turned to Toby and gave him a huge telling off, which clearly neither he nor she expected for one moment he would take seriously. I like Juliet Morris, and I didn't want to do either her or Rose the discourtesy of ignoring Rose's tear and green dock leaf streaked face, so introduced them and said we were grateful to Toby rather than cross with him, as he'd given Rose something to laugh about after a really massive cry. Juliet looked surprised and pleased at this, and thanked me – the compliment to Toby clearly reaching her brain before the news of Rose's distress. As soon as the latter registered, however, she acted quickly, pulling from her pocket an immaculate packet of tissues and handing them to Rose.

I thought then, as I often do, that Juliet is a funny old thing. While I genuinely don't expect everyone's coat pockets to contain the same mess of acorns/lollipop sticks/furry sweets as mine, I do think a brand new, uncreased packet of tissues is unusual. I'd put money on my guess that other than her phone and two or three poo bags folded with origami-like precision, there was nothing else in those pockets: no fluff, no crushed autumn leaf, no loose thread or alarming sticky patch. Either banned from entry in the first place or scrubbed out with the slightly scary discipline I see so much in her, which always makes me wonder what made her like that. Not that I could ask. A clam has nothing on this woman's protection of her privacy. The first time I met her she was reluctant even to tell me where she lived. I know she's divorced, with no kids, but I learned this from the village, and even though the accuracy of information from this source is shaky at best, I'd rather burn myself on my curiosity than offer it up to her for dousing.

I suspect that, in all the world, only Toby has her confidence. She does her best to disguise this, almost always remembering to keep him sternly in the background in public, but as not even her most brusque command can stop his tail wagging for more than a second, you can only assume that this is a dog who, at home, has been long lavished with just the sort of comfort, indulgence, and love that Juliet takes such pains to deny when away from it.

Not long ago, I went for a walk with her and the boys, and when Pete shocked himself on an electric fence (twice – once by accident, and then again "to make sure") it suddenly occurred to me what Juliet was like: an electric fence. Taut. Charged. Ever vigilant of entry and exit. It made me feel so sad for her, and weary too.

'Come *on*, Toby,' she was saying crossly now, heaving him back onto the track. 'Well, see you soon, no doubt,' she added to us, and then, when her eyes landed on the bag for life, 'what will you do with the elderflowers?'

'God knows,' I said gloomily.

'I've got an excellent recipe for fritters,' she said, moving off. 'I'll e-mail it to you when I get back.'

Once Juliet was out of sight, Rose and I found ourselves suddenly both ravenous and demob happy, so often the case after a big cry, so went home to demolish a packet of Bourbons washed down with a handful of custard creams, and decided to go to Hereford to buy something extravagant (Rose) and tackle bra crisis (me).

We found the something extravagant first – a pair of suede, raspberry pink, sky-high heels secured by long satin ribbons. As she was paying, Rose noticed a small selection of exquisite lingerie at the back of the shop and determined to steer me towards it, but I point blank refused, appealing eventually to the shop-lady to confirm that while her boutique (for it was, without doubt, a boutique) was absolutely the natural habitat of my sister-in-law, it simply wasn't mine. No offence to anyone, including myself, intended, but I would be much happier tackling the bra crisis in a High Street Store. The shop owner, having just secured a £120 sale (I *know*), and with therefore no need to flatter me into a fancy bra purchase, said silkily, 'It's *so* important to feel comfortable in a retail establishment,' and Rose nodded quietly and we left the shop with me thinking actually just a *tiny* bit of encouragement from one or other of them wouldn't have gone amiss.

But *this* was more like it, I thought when we got to the underwear department of the High Street Store. Unlike the fragile and delicate scraps of lace in the boutique, floating beneath their hangers, the merchandise here was robust and no-nonsense. As were the customers, whose interest in the look of the items they were perusing was most definitely secondary; the main question being were they fit for purpose? I watched with great approval and warmth as a couple of women discussed – in loud and unabashed voices – the merits of a bra so gargantuan (each cup providing ample room for a litter of puppies at least, held up by straps that seemed more harness than garment) that I wondered briefly whether its creators were clothes designers or structural engineers.

This was underwear to get your teeth into, I thought happily, as Rose stared at the King Kong bra in horror. It may not win a beauty competition, but if it came to a bare-knuckle fight it would crush the lingerie lightweights like an ox would a butterfly.

Just then a slightly ferocious shop assistant passed and I asked if she could possibly measure me for a new bra. She frowned, clearly busy, but did eventually usher me into a cubicle – albeit with such briskness that I wasn't entirely certain if I was about to be fitted for a bra or a contraceptive. After much flicking about with a tape measure, and some rather vigorous manhandling of my boobs in different bras by the shop-lady (had to tell Rose off for sniggering as she watched all this), the perfect bra was discovered (a 30C indeed!) and was so comfortable, so unlike any other bra I'd ever had, that I was surprised a celestial chorus did not at once sing out in celebration. Completely over-excited, I threw financial caution to the winds and said I'd take not one, but *two*.

29th June

Slept badly. Things kept popping into my head, and I felt overwhelmed by them, like that fairground game where the little rats pop out of their holes and just when you've whacked one with a mallet another one appears:

- Billy's year's cake bake for charity tomorrow – must make batch of rocky road. What is rocky road? Is there any Tupperware in the house that is not full of aged conkers/feathers/nails/mysterious powdered chemicals that I've allowed Peter to purchase online with great parental irresponsibility and no risk assessment whatsoever??
- Where *are* all my scissors??
- Ridiculous to keep worrying about Tree House and not doing anything about it. Must resolve.
- Still haven't defrosted freezer, removed ivy from inside of cellar, asked Ian about Charles I, checked boys for nits (*very* shouty letter from school this time), sourced cause of vile smell in Pete's room, replied to week's worth of e-mails from beloved people let alone the non-beloved ones...

On top of all this, I kept returning to the most surprising thing Rose had said on the verge yesterday – that not only did she still love Nick but that she *wanted him back*. I could not be more astonished about this, as she's been neither too nice nor too nasty about him to give any hint of this in the two years since she left him. There was the initial exhilaration to be free, but once the divorce was finalised she can't have mentioned him once – so I assumed that was that and we shouldn't mention him either. Which I was very sad about, as both Hugh and I liked him a great deal.

Surely you *could* get him back, I said excitedly to Rose, remembering his quiet devotion to her and already 100% convinced that Happily Ever After was merely a phone call away, but Rose said it didn't matter even if she could – she *wouldn't* get him back, she'd decided, because of the baby business.

The baby business. Rose's preferred euphemism for the fertility issues that Greer had managed to bequeath with one hand and renounce with the other, so that a condition which had been difficult enough for the mother was lavishly poisoned and sharpened for the daughter.

Three babies Greer had lost between Hugh and Rose. A fact that, though ever present in the household, was never discussed. 'It's too, too painful for her,' Grandpa would say, in hushed tones, if someone mentioned the "lost ones" by mistake and Greer, having lightly touched the pearls at her neck, withdrew quietly from the room. And this official explanation for Greer's silence on the matter was wonderfully versatile. It lent her a very flattering air of the grief-stricken mother. And if someone was audacious enough to ask about the lost ones – a fifteen-year-old daughter, for example, distraught at diagnosis and desperate enough for support and information to appeal to her mother – Greer's refusal to engage seemed entirely justified, to her husband at least. Rose the selfish one. Rose the insensitive one.

I'm sure the loss of Greer's babies caused her pain, I am, but what *really* got to her, I'm convinced, was the failure of her body to meet her demands. How dare her uterus let her down? She was disgusted by the triumph of a weakness in a world she otherwise so mercilessly and successfully controlled. People pointing and frowning at the nine years between her children, Narwhals too – it was demeaning, outrageous...

Not a badly-wounded heart that kept her from consoling her daughter, therefore, but anger and loathing, so that it seemed to Rose she'd laid at her mother's feet not a pure and aching plea but some grotesque, gruesome, stinking thing. Get it away from me! Greer effectively said. It's got nothing to do with me – do you hear? It didn't matter how hard Hugh and I tried to counterbalance this rejection, or how hard Rose tried to let us; Greer's opinion – as ever where her daughter was concerned – defied all laws of emotional physics and could not be shifted through any kindness, love or logic that came from anyone other than the dreadful woman herself.

It's been seventeen years since Rose found out that her chances of motherhood are as good as zero, and she's as unable to carry this knowledge comfortably now as she was then, shifting it awkwardly from shoulder to shoulder, bursting into tears (angrily wiped) when we told her I was pregnant with Pete, claiming proudly that four months of intensive counselling had brought her to terms with it, and then, at a party that very night, standing on a chair and shouting that she was barren and therefore an ideal shag if anyone was up for it...

'Dearest girl,' I told her, back on the verge, 'Nick never cared about the baby business – it was *you* he wanted.'

'Well, I care,' she said. 'It's not fair, no babies. He deserves babies and he needs to find someone who can give them to him.'

What to do?? I knew very well there was no point in me trying to persuade her that Nick had always, would always, want her exactly as she was; she was fully aware of that already. It was believing it that was the trouble, and that – if you ask me – was the real reason she left him in the first place ("I don't love him anymore", my arse). Was there not a way, though? There had to be a way.

'Could we not...' I began, but trailed off at her vigorous head-shaking.

'Promise me,' she said. 'I know you. You must promise me that you won't contact him or *anything*.'

I've read that if you ask your subconscious to solve a problem on going to sleep, it'll have the answer for you when you wake up, and I was hoping very much therefore to be presented this morning with a cunning plan to enable Happily Ever After without breaking my promise to Rose. But alas I woke up thinking about marshmallows, my lazy subconscious having clearly skipped the tricky questions and gone for a quick stab at the recipe for rocky road instead.

30TH JUNE

Most of what we ever knew about Nick we learned via Rose rather than from the man himself. He was an architect, and a successful one. Ambitious. Canny. Renowned as much for his unshakeable composure as for the fearsome temper that allegedly lay sleeping beneath it, and that had once long ago – it was whispered – put a man in a coma. Whether or not this was true (and none of us, not even Rose, ever found out for certain), it wasn't hard to forgive, because any fearsomeness in his character now was dedicated to the love of Rose. I don't mean he was possessive or controlling or anything – Lord, no; just that *nothing* was as important to him as her. I was about to say he'd do anything for her, but that's not right either; he was never a fawner. Just that if it came down to his life or hers, he'd have offered his up in a heartbeat.

Nick's background was unusual to say the least. He was born into one of the East End's most notorious families, part of the criminal aristocracy, if you like. Had fate not intervened, he would have dutifully carried forward the time-honoured Lambert family traditions of armed robbery and a little light extortion. But sometime in 1982 his father had an epiphany, the result of a mysterious conversation with a stranger in the back of a stolen car, after which the Lamberts swerved abruptly onto the path of righteousness. Education became the mantra in a household that may have respected it in others, but never thought to appropriate it before. Three of the five Lambert boys, Nick being one of them, trained for professions, and the Metropolitan Police found in time they no longer knew by heart all Lambert first names.

But a short-lived move to a semi in Ashford showed the family that life as a law-abiding citizen required rather more than abiding the law. They were culturally lost. No matter how hard they tried to learn it, the language spoken by the good Ashfordians remained incomprehensible. They returned to London barely six months later, and Nick and his brothers grew up straddling two worlds. The crooked and the straight. Which meant that Nick and Rose's wedding was... interesting. Though everyone's manners were impeccable, I'd have been much more surprised to learn there *weren't* weapons at the reception than that there *were*. I remember a lot of male guests on Nick's side had names like "Bull" and "Lightning", and sported the sort of scars rarely seen outside Wormwood Scrubs...

But our Nick was kind, and good, with a wry wit and a steady gaze. Who always knew instinctively how to love a girl who needed loving a great deal more than most.

It'll come to me – a way to get them back together. It *has* to.

3RD JULY

I was having a happy breakfast with Rose and the boys this morning, and was looking forward to a quiet day ahead, when Billy asked casually what time we were going to the fete, and how many sweetie jars had I made for the sweetie jar stall? I told him with calm confidence that the fete was next Saturday, not today, only to have my diary fetched and to be shown today's date with FETE – SWEETIE JARS scrawled across it in, there was no doubt, my own handwriting.

I swallowed a great mouthful of expletives. Rose was swiftly commandeered to find any empty jam jars or, if absolutely necessary, encourage the emptying of slightly full ones, while the boys and I ransacked the darkest depths of the back larder for forgotten sweets and, heavens be praised, struck lucky. Billy assisted by reading out the sell-by dates and putting aside the expired ones, at which point I sent him on as long an errand as I could think of (finding some ribbon; hens' teeth literally more likely to be unearthed in this house) while Pete and I hastily stuffed half a dozen jars with the out of date sweets and I told myself it was all sugar and therefore definitely *fine*. I felt far more guilty about lying to Billy's little face when he returned with what looked like some ancient curtain fringing, mumbling, 'Oh yes, we found some fresh ones after all,' which evil lie he swallowed with heart-breaking innocence.

It was out of politeness that I asked Rose if she wanted to come with us, as I could only think a village school fete would bore her stiff, but I was delighted, albeit mystified, to discover that she did. (No point even asking Hugh, as all school events where there is the threat of Having to Talk to People are apparently my department.) We got there just in time to catch the end of the headmistress's opening speech.

There's something rather timeless about a good school fete. Bunting waving in the breeze, wonky stalls with hand-written signs, much anxious conversation about the weather if it looks uncertain, or happy relief if it looks fine... The mothers too, I suspect, have fallen into the same two broad school fete camps since the dawn of time. On one side there are the active supporters, comprising one terrifying silverback and some lesser assistants, who will view their leader with awe, fear, resentment, or a combination of all three. On the other side are the passives. They do not volunteer to help, and work hard to escape conscription by careful avoidance of the silverback for at least six months prior to the event. It couldn't be easier to spot which group each mother belongs to. Anyone from the former will either be behind a stall or loitering fretfully within sight of it. Anyone from the latter will be in front of the stall, dripping in guilt that they try to assuage by over-spending or bitching energetically about the silverback.

I was shocked to see Rachel *behind* the second-hand stall, as she's definitely a passive like me, and my first question when I went up to her was how she'd found herself there. She explained ruefully how Penny (our silverback) had caught her only two days ago.

‘So close!’ I commiserated. ‘What happened?’

‘I was late for pickup and thought I’d be safe,’ said Rachel. ‘You know how early she is.’ I nodded vigorously. ‘But just as I pulled up I saw her. I hid in the footwell straightaway, obviously, but it was no good...’

I reached across and rubbed her arm. Told her how well she’d done, that a lot of mothers never made it as far as she had. That she should be proud.

The second-hand items for sale were the usual collection of sad strays and rejects, and I wondered if the quantity of things donated would be a little less, and their quality a little greater, if the donors’ names were attached. I recognised a packet of doilies from last year, its cellophane yellow and brittle with age, and the creepy doll with the weird hair had appeared with such regularity that she was practically a mascot. A small girl arrived beside me then, and spent a good ten minutes in solemn study, picking up and carefully examining each item. When she reached an elderly stuffed elephant, she suddenly exclaimed in great joy that she used to have an elephant just like this one and how much was it? Rachel and I exchanged glances, both of us certain of the cause of this amazing coincidence, and, as Rachel sold it to her for five pence, I thought of the poor parent who was shortly going to have to feign equal delight in the serendipitous arrival of the doppelganger elephant.

I went off to do the fete circuit. I secured a slightly lopsided but well-filled Victoria sponge for Hugh, then found myself in front of the sweetie jar stall where I was horrified to see our own contributions, labels poorly removed, dusty sweets bizarrely obscured by crimson curtain fringing, amongst an array of beautifully clean beribboned jars, like a bunch of Miss Havishams in a crowd of young brides. A mother at my shoulder leaned forwards, pointed in the direction of the Miss Havishams, and laughingly observed that she'd eat her hat if *any* of those sold. I could only agree sadly. I comforted myself with the purchase of a cup of tea, which I drank while lurking under a nearby tree so as to avoid the boys, who I knew from experience would have long run out of money, and would be looking for me with fretful, sugar-fuelled pleadings for more.

When I returned to the second-hand stall, I was surprised to see not Rachel but Rose in charge. (It turned out Rachel had been required for an emergency, to cut a toffee apple out of her middle daughter's hair.) Rose was waving aloft a Jackie Collins and apparently encouraging a bidding war between the two elderly ladies who seemed desperate to possess it. Of all the surprising aspects of this scene, by far the most was Rose herself. It wasn't just the focus and motivation on her face, though it had been a long time since I'd seen either there, but her proficiency at the task at hand and, above all, the naturalness that accompanied it. The girl had always had multiple talents, but none that seemed actually to engage her. She'd play at being interested in her own skills for a while, but couldn't sustain this for long, just as she couldn't her serial passions (both romantic and occupational). Fulfil my potential? I could practically hear her saying; where on earth is the fun in that? But here she was, at a humble second-hand stall, her aptitude and her enthusiasm entirely hand in hand, like the magnificent love child of Alan Sugar.

The moment Jackie was sold (£1.50), she turned her attention back to the crowd, swiftly assessing any poor punter who strayed within earshot and reeling them in with perfectly pitched manipulation, flirting with the dads and flattering the mums, while simply coercing sales from the children. I don't know how long I would have stood there with my mouth hanging open if Lucasz, Billy's little friend, hadn't then arrived, clutching the same sweaty pound I'd seen him with the entire afternoon. I saw Rose, cobra-like, turn towards him, and felt compelled to intervene.

'Thinking about the storm trooper, Lucasz?' I asked, picking up the little scratched Lego man he was staring it.

'Yes,' said Lucasz anxiously, looking at the coin in his palm. 'Is it more than a pound?'

Rose opened her mouth, but I stopped her with a look.

'Well, Lucasz,' I said, 'it's fifty pence, but I tell you what – why don't we haggle a bit?'

'OK,' said Lucasz, 'wait a minute.' And the sweet boy then put the pound carefully in his pocket in order to have all ten fingers and thumbs available for agonies of mathematical calculation.

'Would seventy-five pence be OK?' he wanted to know at last. I explained very gently that this wasn't quite the way it worked, and why didn't he try twenty-five pence instead?

Doubt I will ever make anyone happier in my entire life.

4TH JULY

I'd promised my old friend Helen a while ago that we would host some friends of hers who'd just moved up from London, and they came for Sunday lunch today. Usual pre-meal panic stations, me wrestling with the roast in a hot kitchen, the boys maddeningly underfoot and Hugh nowhere to be seen. I was very grateful for Rose. She picked some flowers for the table, cut the runner beans on a fancy angle and delumped the gravy so that, I thought with relief, we might just pass as civilised and competent human beings. However, when the Harts arrived on the dot of one o'clock, I took one look at them and realised instantly that even had we hand-carved the beans into little London landmarks and placed an entire and award-winning Chelsea Flower Show garden on the table, we were not going to get anywhere near waving at their expectations from a distance, let alone meeting them.

Olivia Hart, impossibly smooth and shiny, was dressed in brilliant white from top to toe. I was so befuddled by this that my eyes could not take in the detail of the husband or daughters, only a general alarming sense of glossy cleanliness and good teeth, as if I'd opened the door to four expensive thoroughbreds. I turned blankly to Rose, as she alone – young, fashionable, and, crucially, *from London* – could save us now. With airy grace, she sashayed past me to clasp the manicured hands of James and Olivia Hart, and steered them deftly past the hall detritus into the kitchen, where – after a quick and panicked survey of their surroundings – the Harts huddled together by the French windows.

I called for Hugh and the boys in my very best family-summoning voice, shortly after which the three of them arrived – Hugh in his workshop trousers and frayed shirt, the boys barefoot and grubby. Looking at them through Olivia's eyes, it was quite clear the whole lot of them were riddled with lice and germs, and had probably been raised by wolves.

Ignoring the instantly obvious and primal dislike between my boys and the two Hart girls, I said to Pete brightly that perhaps Brontë and Portia would like to see the trampoline? Nobody moved. Olivia and James exchanged "what a shame" glances then Olivia explained apologetically that – so silly really – but they weren't very keen on trampolines; so dangerous when you thought about it, and Portia's best friend had lost a front tooth on one, hadn't she, darling? Though Hugh was behind me I could quite clearly see what his face was doing at this point and suggested hurriedly that maybe they could go and have a look at the lake instead? But once it was established that the lake was unfenced, this too was struck off as a possible activity, and, failing the speedy invention of excitements involving solely rose petals and cotton wool, I was completely at a loss. When Rose proposed a nice drink, therefore, Hugh practically bellowed his wish for a stiff gin – at just the same moment as the Harts wondered if we had any elderflower pressé?

I can't deny that the meal was challenging. Rose and I dug hard for common ground with the Harts, and then, when this proved fruitless, headed to the fail-safe social harbour of Elaborate Interest in Offspring. The parents perked up no end at this, and most of the main course was filled with lengthy and detailed descriptions of Portia's latest ballet recital and Brontë's hilarious portrayal of the eldest ugly sister in the recent school production of *Cinderella*, for which achievements Rose and I expressed enthusiastic, if (looking at the girls' sullen faces) rather unconvinced, admiration. Perhaps wanting a little admiration of his own, Billy interrupted at this point to say he too had a remarkable skill, laying down his knife and fork with a clatter and proudly proceeding through his full range of tongue contortions. The Harts stared in horror. Hugh, who'd parked a bottle of red beside his plate when we sat down and had become increasingly sharp and glittery throughout the meal, shouted, 'Excellent work, Bill! Do it again!' Then wondered out loud if anyone could fart with their armpit?

Before the boys could erupt into the cacophony of bodily noises that Hugh was unhelpfully encouraging, I had just enough presence of mind to send all three of them outside, on the pretext of cutting some courgettes for the Harts. (No really, said Olivia; Oh no, I insist, said I.) With me and Rose the only remaining Narwhal representatives at the table, pudding and coffee were worked through tolerably, if with unseemly speed, then Pete returned, looking hot and excited, saying he had something to show us at the Tree House. I was instantly suspicious, but had no opportunity to investigate as the Harts – their keenness to leave by now quite unashamed – had jumped up. There would just be time, said James, to see the Tree House before they left. Rose and I expressed great sadness that they had to go so soon (it was 2.13 p.m.), the Harts said how sad they were too, and, with these ludicrous but necessary falsehoods exchanged, we went through the French windows and walked across the lawn towards the Tree House.

My anxiety grew stronger as we approached. I could see Hugh and the boys on the Tree House balcony, looking busy and whispery.

'Not too close, girls,' said Olivia.

'Can you come a bit closer?' yelled Pete. 'You won't be able to see it properly from there.'

'How exciting,' said Olivia, looking pale. 'That's close enough now, Brontë.'

'Ready, Bill?' shouted Pete.

'Ready!' called Billy, from inside the Tree House.

'On the count of three!'

As the bell tolled the first time, Pete scooped up what looked like bubbles from a dish beneath him. On the second toll, I dimly recalled his requests earlier for unlikely items – butane and washing-up liquid amongst them – which, being too distracted by lunch preparations, as he would well have known, I had foolishly, *foolishly* not questioned...

There was no third toll. With a lit match, Hugh touched the bubbles Pete was holding, and then, as if stage directed by Satan himself, Pete's hands erupted into a ball of flame at just the second that the bell – breaking free from its rotten supports at last – plummeted joyfully through the Tree House to land, with an almighty clang, at the feet of the most risk-averse family on the planet.

Once it was clear that no one was hurt, Portia had stopped crying, and all four Harts – still clutching one another – had disappeared round the house towards their car, I asked Rose calmly if she would take the boys inside. I turned to Hugh but found to my astonishment when I opened my mouth that what came out were not the calm words gently questioning the wisdom of recent behaviour that I'd anticipated, but a tsunami of anger that made my outburst on the Jamboree night look like a light shower. It knew no thought or pause; it was as ravenous for its own gratification as all long-dammed passions are, and just as inarticulate – at first, anyway.

'Enough!' I kept shouting. 'Enough, enough, enough! What is *wrong* with you? Drunk, sneering, rude to the Harts, humiliating me, leaving me scrabbling to show that family we do not treat people poorly in this house, not even those we don't much like or understand, scrabbling and failing and then *this*,' I said, thrusting my palm towards the Tree House then bringing it down so hard against my thigh that I winced at its sting. Hugh clasped his hands behind his head and forced his elbows together, as if to stop his brain from exploding, and, just like the sight of him pushing against the kitchen counter the other day, this brought a pang of compassion despite myself. I walked up to him and felt, in his laboured breathing and the vice-like grip of his forearms around his head, the crackle of his distress. 'Listen to me, Hugh,' I said. 'I'm not about to leave you, but I'm beginning to see that one day I might. I won't know till it happens, but there'll be some straw – not a row even, but some tiny last look or word that'll break my back. And you know what? You've been such a shit in so many ways, but actually that isn't the problem. It's watching you writhing around in yourself and not being able to help you. That's what'll finish me.'

I had to pause then, more to recover from my own words than to study their impact on Hugh. *Leave* him? Where had that come from? I wasn't a leaver – I was a sticker and a stayer; I didn't know if I was more frightened or stunned to discover such mutiny within me, attacking our unsuspecting marriage with its roar and raised cutlass. Hugh looked as shell-shocked as I felt.

At that moment a small oak branch, damaged by the bell's descent but presumably only now relinquishing its last connecting fibres, fell to the ground behind Hugh. We both watched as the leaves first bounced then whispered into stillness. Hugh released his hands and dropped them heavily to his sides, and I too felt a weary resignation of some kind.

'If you're going to say you're sorry, or promise to change, please don't,' I said. 'Just show me, OK?' He gave a long sigh, and cast his eyes to the ground. I waited to find out if I had any more words for him, but there were none. 'I'm going back to the house now,' I said, and began to walk towards the terrace, noting how long it seemed since the Harts had gone, and how tired I suddenly felt. I was half-way across the lawn when Hugh called to me and I turned.

'Don't give up,' he said, separating the words and articulating them so carefully that not a drop of meaning was spilled.

I looked at him, his expression fierce and expectant and hollow all at the same time. 'Don't let me,' I replied.

5TH JULY

Breakfast was subdued this morning. Ever since yesterday afternoon, Hugh has been stiff and quiet and overly helpful to us all, so that it's rather like having a butler in the house, and one much better suited to ironing newspapers than passing out Rice Krispies. He's arrowed his attentions to those areas where his usual lack of them is most exasperating: putting the children to bed last night instead of leaving me to do it, tucking his boots under his bedroom chair where I can't trip over them on my way to the loo; and my phone charger, possibly for the first time in living memory, has remained where I left it and not been pinched. But just as with his apology after the Jamboree, this attentiveness is at once exactly what I wanted and not what I wanted at all. Too effortful. Too laden with a sort of self-directed fury, as if one part of him had a stranglehold on the neck of the other. The boys are finding all this very confusing; not just their father's behaviour, but their own, which has mirrored his, in a way. I've never known them so polite or biddable. When Hugh stood up and circled the table with the juice jug, filling everyone's glasses, they were surprised into thank yous that were practically genteel.

This is him trying. It's as painful as watching a man with withered legs try to walk – the futility of those gritted teeth, that beaded brow. Having never thought about leaving him before yesterday I find I can't now think about much else. Do I actually want to leave? Was it an actual wish? Or a threat? Or a sort of verbal shaking of his shoulders – the last call of desperate concern? There's no doubt he heard me. He wants to make things right, but the question is, *can* he?

The room was silent save for the clink of spoons on bowls, and goodness knows what we would have found to talk about if Rose hadn't marched into the kitchen, sat down at the table with an air of iron purpose and said, 'Now. What are we going to do about this Tree House?'

I was so relieved to have the awkwardness at the table broken that I jumped straight in with my reply, saying that I knew everyone loved the Tree House, and that – yes, Pete – it *is* great to drop water bombs off, but the fact was that it would cost thousands and thousands to repair it, which (avoiding Hugh's eyes determinedly at this point) we just could not afford.

'You can have what I've got in my money box,' said Billy.

'And mine,' said Pete. 'I *like* the Tree House.'

'No one's taking the contents of your money boxes,' said Rose. 'They're for you to spend on your usual nonsense. No. I made a decision last night. I'm going to use *my* money box.'

When Hugh and I simultaneously burst forth with protestations, the synchronicity of both our speech and opinions gave me a flash of hope that there was some common ground still between us. It might have been the size of a postage stamp, but it was *something*. It wasn't right that Rose should pay, we said, the Tree House was our responsibility, she needed her money from Nick to live off, we're talking tens of thousands probably…

But Rose put up her hand and told us to shush, listen, the Tree House was important to her too and as for the cost of it, well, she could *more* than afford it.

'Yay!' said Billy.

'No,' said Hugh. 'It's very generous of you, but I can't allow it.'

'Yes!' said Rose. 'It makes perfect sense! Don't I need a project anyway? I could stay here and oversee things – if that was OK with you two? And we'd get the Tree House back. The Tree House would be *back*, Hugh.'

'No,' said Hugh.

'*Yes*,' said Rose.

As they squared up to each other across the table, I thought we'd be more likely to reach an equitable outcome between a pair of raging hippopotamuses than those two, and was glad it was time to take the boys to school. In the quiet of the car on the way home I replayed the breakfast scene. Rose did need a project, it was true, but in a way it was curious that she should have chosen the Tree House because she's never cared about the preservation of anything here before, whether property or practice. Maybe part of this is because she's not officially responsible for it – everything was left to Hugh, after all – but I think mostly it's just her nature. There's a sort of deference in unquestioned conservation, in bowing to the past just for the sake of it, and Rose doesn't do deference very well. Particularly if she's told to. She's got to see the *point*. It's nigh on impossible to impress her, as many a past suitor, smug in their fame or wealth, has soon learned.

You'd think the house itself would resent this indifference to its age and history but, on the contrary, it reserves its most special embrace for Rose. No room seems happier, more its best self, than when she's within it – especially on her own. An artist would cry out to capture it. How I wish the same could be said of the heir himself! But how can it? When he feels every Narwhal past and future hanging round his neck, demanding allegiance: preserve, protect. Pay. No wonder he skulks about like some half-starved fox. As I turned into the yard, a memory pinged into my head of Hugh and Rose – years ago; Rose can't have been more than seventeen – when we were sitting with a bunch of other people on the bridge over the neck of the lake, drinking, in the dark, in December, after some party, and Hugh had said to Rose (or Rose had said to Hugh), 'Dare you,' and the other one said, 'Dare you back', which none of the rest of us had understood, though there was no doubting from their tone the weight of the gauntlet nor the certainty that it had been tossed between them many times before. And the next thing we knew there were two loud splashes in quick succession, followed by a pause, and then triumphant spluttering as the two of them broke the surface of the icy lake.

I wondered what the memory was trying to tell me. Not that they were reckless, as I'd always known that. Nor wilful, stubborn and proud – Lord knows I was only too aware of that too. No. It was their *bond,* long loosened, but – I realised now, thinking of them locking horns so readily at the breakfast table – perhaps not irreparably broken after all.

The house seemed very empty when I came inside. Hugh was obviously in the workshop, but there was no sign of Rose. I was collecting up the weekend washing from the boys' rooms (Billy's folded in his laundry basket, Pete's variously on floor, bed, and lampshade), when I heard a bang above from the attics, which I was able to identify from weary experience was caused not by sparrow, mouse, squirrel, bat, rat, pigeon, distressed small boy or meddlesome small boy, but definitely adult human.

To all but the most jaded visitor, the attics here are dusty treasure troves of delight, like vast cabinets of curiosities, where each generation of eccentric Narwhals has deposited the eccentricities of the generation before. Natural history features prominently – not the modern, politically correct kind, but the justly frowned upon Victorian version, involving the cheerful and conscience-free slaughter of any creature that caught the Narwhal eye – from trays and trays of poor pinned butterflies, through the mounted heads of a couple of stags, a boar, three kudus, and a zebra, to – most shameful of all – two stuffed polar bears, well over nine feet tall on their hind legs. Their jaws are agape, and front paws outstretched, presumably to give the terrifying impression of imminent attack, but one of the ancestral Hughs had an interest in taxidermy and had clearly been in the early stages of learning this art when he'd boldly tackled the polar bears. They don't look remotely frightening. On the contrary, you could swear they were smiling, not growling, their arms more ready to greet you warmly than knock you to the ground, and about to say at any minute something like, "OMG! It's been ages! *Love* your frock."

When Grandpa Hugh died, and Hugh and I moved in, I was so full of eager ambition to sweep a broom of modernity and organisation through the house. I remember going into the attics and thinking I'd have them sorted in no time, but I completely under-estimated the impossibility of this. In the first trunk I opened, I found dozens and dozens of ancient wills, was instantly seduced by the swirly writing and the seals, and a whole afternoon vanished in learning of Narwhal fixations on having their veins opened after death and the detailed bequeathals of their feather beds. On my second visit, I was fiercely determined to resist the attics' charms, but then opened a large oak linen press to discover a number of magnificent (though mouldering) feather headdresses, as well as a clutch of hideous shrunken heads (explorer ancestral Hugh) and knew myself to be defeated. History had won. Giving everything a sort of solemn, hollow value that made any course of action, other than just admiring then leaving well alone, practically sacrilegious. And what could be done with it all anyway? It couldn't be thrown away – Hugh would kill me. Too aged and decayed to be sold, surely, and when was the last time you saw, on those lists they put in the charity shop windows, *We need your yellowing collection of marine bird skulls?*

I pushed open the attic door to find Rose on her knees beside an opened tea-chest, papers spread all around her. She was wearing Hugh's head torch, and I just had time before she spoke to note that, as ever, an item that would have diminished a lesser beauty only made Rose look lovelier still – much more Cleopatra than Dalek.

'Look,' she said excitedly, waving something at me in the gloom. 'I knew they'd be up here – the original plans for the Tree House.'

'Oh. Great,' I said, noting with not a little shame my sinking heart at her enthusiasm. I'd never admit it, but if it had been left to me I'd have encouraged the death of the Tree House over its resurrection any day. It would have meant one less thing to worry about, serendipitously erased like the cherries were by the birds.

You should be pleased, I said to myself sternly as I made interested noises at the Tree House design; aren't you always complaining about how you're the only one who bothers with the maintenance of everything? Well, here's Rose getting stuck in – let her, be *glad*, for goodness' sake.

I cleared my throat. 'Gosh,' I said, 'doesn't it look immaculate in the picture? I didn't realise there used to be another balcony bit. Is this what you're thinking, then? To restore it to how it was?'

Rose bobbed her head from side to side. 'Not sure yet. I need to think about it. And it's not just up to me anyway, is it? Everyone needs to agree.'

'What happened with Hugh in the end – about the paying for it all?'

'Oh,' said Rose, waving her hand dismissively, 'it's *fine*.'

'He said that you can pay for it? Really?'

'Well, as good as.'

'Oh. How as?'

'He's insisting he pays me back at some point,' she said. 'You know how he can be when his Big Brother syndrome kicks in – overprotective, completely illogical. I agreed, but I didn't mean it. You know, like when he'd make me promise to take a taxi rather than walk back to the flat, always use a condom etc, etc...'

I found myself suppressing a smile at the affection that glowed through her exasperation, and that had been so absent in the early rows I'd witnessed between her and her brother:

Hugh: You're not going out like that!
Rose: I bloody well am!

Or:

Hugh: Eat some cake!
Rose: It's called slim, Hugh, not anorexic, *slim!*

Ah, the slammed doors, the sulks, the histrionics – it felt like they went on for years. And then, perhaps as he realised she was growing up, and she realised that his dictates were about love and not control, the fights softened and lightened and ripened into rich parodies of themselves: teasing exchanges about curfews and sun hats that were almost as much a delight to observe as they surely were to perform.

When Grandpa died, these communications were severed by the same great guillotine that sliced apart everything else between them, but, I wondered for the second time this morning, could they come back? It was like the first caught glimpse, in May, of something swooping in the sky – was that a swallow? Were the swallows coming back?

But there wasn't time to dwell on this, because just then Rose slapped her palms on her thighs, raising a great cloud of ancient dust, gave me the hugest of smiles and said how she couldn't *wait* to get started.

8TH JULY

I think I may have been reckless and stupid. Part of me feels defiant but another part is shaking its head, lips pressed.

It began at dawn, when I woke up with the most incredibly cunning plan already perfectly formulated in my brain, all shiny and insistent. Rose had received a rather shouty phone call yesterday evening from her downstairs London neighbour, saying a large pot of thyme had fallen off her balcony and shattered on his brand new, polished sandstone paving, and that it was the bay tree the year before, and it was getting so neither he nor his cat felt safe being outside for fear of further herb bombardment and what *was* she going to do about it?

Rose quite clearly gave not one fig for either neighbour or cat, and told him, in the sort of snooty tone that Nick would never have let her get away with, that she wasn't there, and was incredibly busy, and it would just have to wait till she got back. Unsurprisingly, this anti-apology proved rather inflammatory, but if the poor man thought a good dollop of rage was the way to make his point, he was sadly mistaken. Rose rolled her eyes in boredom, then suddenly called out, 'What's that, Billy? You think you're on fire?' and with a breeziness that completely negated the veracity of the apparent emergency, she told the neighbour she had to go and then hung up.

At breakfast this morning, I explained the non-devious part of my cunning plan to Rose.

'With you so involved in the Tree House,' I said, 'and probably staying here a while, how would it be if I went to London for you today? I could appease the cross neighbour, solve the herb bombardment issues, and surely you'd be glad of some more of your stuff?'

Rose frowned at me. 'That's crazy,' she said. 'There's absolutely no need – besides, you've got far too much on your plate to go tramping off to London on my behalf.'

'Oh, but Rose, I'd love it! I'm sure Hugh wouldn't mind doing the school runs,' I said, noticing as I have done ever since my outburst on the day the Harts came, the slight straightening of myself that happens every time I speak about, or even think about, Hugh. If I'm actually with him, it only becomes more pronounced, manifesting itself as a stiff politeness almost as careful as his butleresque own, so that ours feels oddly like a relationship that's over, or that hasn't yet begun. 'Come on, Rose,' I continued, pushing these thoughts away hurriedly, 'I'd get a bit of peace and quiet, staying overnight, perhaps some window shopping… And it's the least I can do with you taking on the Tree House.'

She looked at me hard. 'I can't deny I could do with some things from the flat, but do you really–?'

'Great!' I said, and ran upstairs before she could change her mind, half-horrified and half-thrilled that the first stage of the plan was in place.

Before I knew it, I was on the train.

I felt very peculiar as far as Newport. Lord knows how many years it's been since I was on a train on my own, and I found myself acutely conscious of the absence of the boys, Hugh, and home, appalled to recognise a sort of panicky homesickness rising in my throat. My brain started clawing away at all sorts of possible disasters that it would usually nonchalantly flick aside – the house burning down, the children drowning in the lake – and then filled up with weepy and ridiculous regret that I'd neglected to stock up on double albatrosses and choclat biskits before departure. I hadn't even told the boys I was going! Despite the reserve between us, I was very tempted to call Hugh anyway, to hear his voice, pour out my stupid plan, and tell him I felt like a wife out of water and wanted to come home.

How was it possible, I thought, blowing my nose loudly, that the people in the carriage hadn't noticed I didn't belong there? They were almost all tapping away at their phones, or laptops, or tablets, apparently oblivious to a scruffy, teary woman with a seed catalogue she'd hoped to drool over (gardeners' porn) but instead found herself clutching as a small child might the hand of its mother.

By the time the train left Newport, I'd pulled myself together to an extent, but no matter how many times I repeated the mantra that it was London I was going to, not Mars, and that I'd lived there for eleven years, and that I was completely at ease in the urban landscape, my heart continued to beat much faster than it should have done. What's more, I realised when I fell over as soon as I got out onto the platform, I was going to have to combat the clumsiness that always comes over me when I'm nervous. Thankfully, however, I reached Rose's flat with no further mishap other than tripping over my suitcase and hitting my head on her front door.

Once I'd got my breath back, I was rather shocked at the state of the flat; not because it was a tip (which it most definitely was), but because the cheerful Rose I'd left that morning was so far removed from the one who'd left here a fortnight or so ago. Most of the lights were on. The window onto the square was open, the sill sticky with sap from the huge lime tree beyond. There was a crumpled duvet and a pillow on the sofa in front of the TV, with a liberal sprinkling of tissues, Diet Coke cans and empty Monster Munch packets on the floor around it, and there must have been eight or nine mugs languishing unwashed in the sink. The whole place looked like the "before" part of an advert for a flu remedy, just missing the red-nosed and coughing sufferer herself, who, mere seconds after taking the wonderful and clinically proven medicine, bounces up from the sofa and grabs her keys in order to get on with her fascinating and busy life, pausing only to breathe deeply through her nose to camera.

I spent the next couple of hours restoring order to the flat, learning in the process that cleaning other people's houses is much easier than cleaning one's own, and that hoovering is excellent therapy for wife out of water nerves and lack of confidence. By the time I finished, it was nearing five o'clock – just two hours to go. I quickly realised that if I stayed in the flat till then, all the benefits of the hoovering would vanish in rising anxiety at the mission ahead, so I decided to go for a walk. I checked my bag for my trusty A-Z (essential accessory in my London days but now, judging by what I'd seen on the Tube, anachronistic embarrassment), my phone and Rose's keys, checked it all again – twice (damn you, nerves), then took a deep breath and left the flat.

I wandered slowly along Westbourne Grove, peering into the shops and wondering what Hugh would make of their contents. Ladies' lycra sporty things (shrug); cashmere baby clothes (snort); entire shop apparently dedicated to fancy kitchen knives (either paroxysm of snorting or, contrarily, intense interest); bespoke furniture (sad silence). I was quite tempted by the fancy kitchen knife shop myself, but felt I'd fail the London credentials passport control at the entrance and sheepishly moved on.

By the time I emerged into Notting Hill it was just after six, and I decided that a drink was essential. I found the small pub I'd been to with Rose once or twice, ordered a double gin and tonic, managed not to faint at the price, and sat down at a corner table. As the gin began its work, I stopped frowning at my watch every five minutes and began to look around, my eyes eventually settling on a couple near the bar. They looked familiar, but I couldn't place them.

Late twenties (did I know *anyone* in their twenties anymore?), both in jeans, both drinking beer from the bottle. The man was talking, trying to describe something by the look of his hands shaping the air, while the girl listened patiently – twisting her head the better to see the sketch he then drew on a beer mat. It's funny how much you can tell about someone from a distance. I knew that the man was accustomed to sketching, and to doing so skilfully, spontaneously, with vigour, and I knew that the girl enjoyed this about him. I also knew that this couple were not calibrating themselves surreptitiously against their surroundings, unlike so many of the people around them; the man by nature and the girl by association with the man. You could have put them anywhere and they'd have sat, spoken, smiled, in exactly the same way.

I was just asking myself yet again where I could possibly remember them from, when I realised it was Hugh and me.

At that age, living in Crouch End, Hugh working at Vaughan's, and me with Amanda in the smart gardens of Hampstead, both of us underpaid but thriving, believing ourselves to be so much better off than the stressed and fretful wealthy clients we both served. We could more than afford such smugness then.

I was saved further unhelpful reminiscing by a text from Rose, adding *green Whistles dress too pls* to the list of things she wanted me to bring back for her. I texted back, then checked my watch. Oh Lord. Time to go.

I was in position by six-fifty, hiding behind a corner where I had a clear view of Nick's office, which, if anything, looked even shinier and more impressive than the last time I'd seen it. He'd had huge double glass doors fitted, the handles of which were thick steel ropes that stretched from top to bottom. "Nick Lambert" was etched on the glass; no mention of the fact he was an architect, which absence I took to suggest he'd reached such heights of success there was simply no need.

My mouth had gone dry. What if he'd changed his routine? What was I even going to say to him? The whole thing was clearly a disaster. In a panic, I decided to retreat, and would have succeeded in this if I hadn't been edging away backwards, unaware of the uneven paving slab behind me that caught the back of my shoe and sent me tumbling onto my arse. The next thing I knew a hand was reaching down to help me up, and soon after that I noticed that the hand was attached to Nick himself.

In retrospect I should be grateful for this falling over, as it made the whole "Fancy seeing you!" and "What are you doing here?" bit that I'd particularly dreaded much less demanding of my equally poor acting and lying skills than if I'd had to pretend to bump into him as planned. What's more, I found myself hugely pleased to see him; and looking so well too. He had a bit of grey in his hair now, but it suited him – as of course it would – and he was still just the right side of being over-groomed, nails neat but not manicured, clothes expensive but not showy, smile warmly understated. I glanced at his hands to see if his dad's ring – a splendidly hideous fake gold sovereign number – had survived, and was quietly pleased to see that it had. Rose had always alleged that she hated it, endlessly complaining at Nick's refusal to take it off, but I was certain that, had he actually done as she asked, her respect for him would have slammed into a brick wall. Too many of her boyfriends had been biddable; she just liked to test the fact that Nick was not.

If the ring was a rather sacred totem to his past, he was more than capable of exploiting and even embellishing other aspects of it if this would help him hook a client. A little added rasp to his accent here, a wall of "authentic" graffiti in his office there, a hinted intimacy with back-streets and dark alleys designed to intrigue or deliciously unsettle those clients who were tired of the nice boys and were looking for a bit of rough...

It was at this point I noticed he was also wearing his wedding ring.

Whether or not he saw me looking, I don't know, but with pleasantries barely dealt with, Nick looked at me hard and said, 'How is she?'

So I told him. I hadn't planned to do this at all – the aim was just a bit of fishing to see how he felt about Rose, and to get him to visit – but I'd forgotten how his directness means somehow you can only be direct in turn. So it all came out – just standing there on the pavement – that I hadn't really come to London to sort out her flat (as I'd only just said) but to talk to him, that she was sort of OK, staying with us, taking on the Tree House, but also that she wasn't and that she missed him, but that she wouldn't do anything about that because of the baby business.

He listened to everything in silence, standing stock still, then looked at his watch.

'I've gotta go,' he said, not moving.

'Off to the gym as usual?' I said, remembering how much I'd always admired his exacting time management, though of course this was something else Rose had claimed to despise.

'No. Meeting.'

He still didn't move, his eyes following a taxi that was passing.

'Nick?' I said. 'I should point out that she will eat me alive – quite justifiably, I might add – if she knows I've told you.'

He nodded slowly, then seemed suddenly to snap out of his reverie.

'Fair enough,' he said. 'Leave it with me. I'll be in touch. Gotta go.'

And that – very confusingly – was that. He kissed me on the cheek, then simply strode off.

9TH JULY

I had been looking forward to a lovely lazy lie in this morning, but woke up early with the whole Nick episode going round and round in my head. It was like being a teenager again – when you've met a boy at a party, shared a handful of words and perhaps a snog, then spend day after weary day afterwards replaying every second, trying desperately to extract the crucial information Does He Like Me and What Sort of Wedding Dress Should I Get?

Did he mean he'd be in touch because he wanted to see Rose, or was he just being polite? Why didn't he ask anything about her? Leave *what* with him? I was cross with myself for not getting some sort of answer from him at the time, and also a signed affidavit saying he was *not* going to drop me in it with Rose.

I felt too antsy with all this to stay in bed, so got up, packed, checked train times, then went to have a look at the plants on Rose's little balcony. I was very relieved to discover that all were quite dead, meaning I could abandon them with impunity, rather than somehow haul the living ones home via Tube and train as Nature Neglect Guilt would, of course, have dictated. I pulled them right up to the wall therefore, where they couldn't cause any more damage to the neighbour below, and popped downstairs to see the neighbour himself.

I wasn't sure what sort of reception I was going to get, but actually he was far more reasonable than Rose deserved and I was even asked in to meet the cat – an enormously fat white Persian called Gladstone – around whom the neighbour's entire world clearly revolved. The ratio of the size of the cat to that of the tiny courtyard was such that I considered it nothing less than a miracle that Gladstone had survived not one, but two, falling plant pots and that, whatever happened with Nick, the trip to London had been worth it for the avoidance of future cat pot death if nothing else.

I caught the ten past ten train home, and found that my journey back took a rather mirrored shape to that of the journey down. Up to Newport, my thoughts mainly wandered over the events of the past twenty-four hours, but after that I began to look homeward, visualising such a fond reunion with the boys (who knew – perhaps even with Hugh too?) and planning such a special supper that anyone would think I'd been alone in the Arctic for a good six months, eking out my survival with raw fish and seal blubber.

As I turned into the yard, I thought the house had never looked more beautiful, and felt sure, when Hugh emerged from the workshop just as I parked, that he was coming to welcome me home. This foolish notion was quickly dispatched, however, when – after a brief enquiry as to how my trip had been – he told me Pete had superglued his fingers together, we'd run out of nit shampoo, and had I seen the foam template for Mrs Sadler's box cushions?

24TH JULY

Dear Diary! Found at last! I really thought I'd looked everywhere – not just in the sensible places, but all the possible crazy ones too, like in the fridge and the veg drawer. But it was sandwiched between two sheets in the airing cupboard – scooped up during washing sorting presumably – and I was so overjoyed to come upon it that I involuntarily declared my happy discovery to Jo, who was passing at the time. She gave me one of those suspicious upward nods that people do when they're warily acknowledging an excitement they clearly think insane, as if it was not a lost diary I'd long sought and now found, but a much beloved jar of pickled ferrets or somesuch. But I didn't care. I haven't been as relieved to find anything since I lost my wedding ring in the compost heap. It's become important, this diary. I usually write it in bed, before Hugh comes up, and never fail to think that the relationship I have with this pen and paper is rather better than the one I have with him. It's not unlike an affair, in fact.

But so be it. There's no harm done, is there? Whatever it takes.

There's not much to catch up on, other than that war seems to have broken out between Rose and Ian over the Tree House. I was on the loo when I heard Rose calling for me in the sort of impatient tone that suggested I was unlikely to be able to finish my wee in peace.

'Rose? What's going on?' I asked, reaching over to open the bathroom door.

She was so brimming with frustration when she saw me that there was no acknowledgement whatsoever of my undignified position – she just launched straight in.

'Who the hell does he think he is?'

'Who?'

'*Ian*,' she said, as if this should have been perfectly obvious. 'I *know* he's been here since forever, and I *know* this place is important to him, but that does *not* give him any rights to dictate what we do with it.'

I sighed. Ian and Rose's dislike of each other was legendary even when I first met them. I'd never come across two people whose characters were so exquisitely mismatched; that fate had doomed them to a lifetime of frequent contact seemed almost malicious. In Ian's eyes, Rose was frivolous, spoilt, an embarrassment to her ancestry, her home, and above all her mother, whom Ian worshipped. He disapproved of her beauty – as if she were doing it on purpose, to show off – and the wiles she tried on him once or twice only caused him to condemn her further. To Rose, on the other hand, Ian was like a recalcitrant donkey, only doing what he was told if he chose to, otherwise cementing his hooves into the ground.

It was a relationship the rest of us found variously funny, bewildering, exhausting, and maddening beyond belief.

'So, there I am,' said Rose, as I wondered if my peacekeeping hat would be needed straightaway, or if I'd at least be able to make the beds first, 'at the Tree House with the architect, and Ian's just – *hovering*. You know how he does? Allegedly clearing the last bits of debris away but really just *earwigging* on our conversation, although of course he'd never admit it, and then I go and get the old plans from the kitchen and I can *see* him – when I come back – ahead of me, talking to the architect – like he'd just been waiting for his chance – and then when he catches sight of me he just sort of slopes back to the yard. And the architect says who was that, and I say just Ian, and the architect says he seems to have a lot of emotion invested in the Tree House for someone who's just Ian. And I say *what* emotion, and the architect looks a bit shifty and says Ian's very concerned about "the integrity of the Tree House being preserved".' She paused to fling her arms up in exasperation. 'Integrity of the fucking Tree House! Again – who does he bloody well think he is?'

'Well—' I began, but there was no stopping her.

'So afterwards I went to Ian, and I told him the integrity of the bloody Tree House had nothing whatsoever to do with him, and in fact I was thinking about re-designing the whole thing so that it looked like a squirrel nest made of bits of pointy sticks and cow shit or whatever and that I was taking the bell to the tip.'

'You did *not*!'

'Yes I did.'

'Rose!' I said, washing my hands over-vigorously. 'For goodness' sake. Would it be so difficult once in a while to just – just *humour* him a bit? Try and see things from his point of view? Honestly, there'll be an enormous kerfuffle now – you *know* there will.'

She shrugged sulkily, and I was amazed, as I always am on such occasions, that someone I was so fond of could be exactly as Ian believed her to be at times. Reached crossly for peacekeeping hat and went to find Ian.

26TH JULY

All quiet – for now at least – on the Western Front. I *think* Appeasement of Ian went well, but you can never be too sure, as the stronger he feels about something the less he likes to discuss it, preferring a semaphore of silences and small adjustments of personal space. I learned this during our first Christmas here, when I came down the main stairs one morning to find him at the bottom of them – hands clasped and expectant in such a way that I immediately thought I was late for something.

'Oh! Hello, Ian – did you want me?'

'I've brought the Christmas tree...' he said, with the usual little hesitation at the end where my name should have been. (Despite warm and repeated offers to use our Christian names – the first being made by Grandpa Hugh in around 1980 – Ian has simply never been able to bring himself to do so. As he knows he's not supposed to address us formally either, every time a name of some sort is required he's therefore caught in an agony of paralysis that he can only resolve by not using any names at all.)

'Oh, right,' I said. 'I didn't realise we'd asked for one yet.'

'It always comes on the eleventh of December,' said Ian, as surprised at my ignorance as if I'd been unaware of the date of the Baby Jesus's birth itself.

'Oh. OK. We'd better decide where to put it,' I said, looking around the hall.

'It goes over there,' said Ian, pointing to its usual spot just beside the front door, where the draught ensured the needles dropped in perfect position to be tramped through the rest of the house.

'You know what, Ian,' I said, 'I was wondering about further back – by the stairs – don't you think?'

Silence.

'It would be out of the way of the front door then, and the presents wouldn't get sprayed with mud every time we come in.'

Silence, and a *very* small step back.

'And the wind wouldn't blow the whole thing over like it did that time? Don't you think? No? Ian?'

The tree went up by the door.

With regard to the row with Rose, I suggested to Ian with an inward sigh that he humour her a bit, and perhaps try to see things from her point of view.

I was in the middle of some rather depressing budgeting this afternoon when I heard the doorbell clang. I went downstairs and opened the door to find a very smart man standing there, his broad grin causing me great alarm as I feared he was going to try and sell me something that no doubt I wouldn't want, or couldn't afford, or both. But my fears were allayed and my interest considerably piqued when he said, in the most wonderful American accent, 'Ma'am, mah name is Calvin Montague Narwhal. Is this a convenient tahme?'

I told him warmly that there could not *be* a more convenient time, and did he want to come in? To which he replied that that was mighty kind of me and he would be much obliged.

I felt distinctly fluttery by this time, as I've always had a weakness for men with elaborate manners, particularly when accompanied by "ma'ams" and "mighty kinds". How I ended up with a husband who enjoys nothing more than farting at the dinner table, preferably in company, has always been a mystery to me.

'Well, ah declare!' Calvin said, the minute he was in the hall, which I always forget *does* look impressive if you squint hard enough to cut out the Acrow prop, the damp patch on the west wall, the crumbling plasterwork on the ceiling, and the absence of two staircase spindles thanks to Peter's unsuccessful tightrope construction earlier in the year. 'What a place! You must just *love* living here!'

I was struggling to form an appropriately enthusiastic and positive response in the face of my deep ambivalence when the boys suddenly appeared. Though afflicted by profound deafness when their presence is requested for meals/school/telling off, they have an uncanny ability to sprout bat-like hearing in the following circumstances:

- When any adult within a fifty-yard radius begins to whisper.
- When the post arrives.
- When an adult bedroom door closes in daylight hours.
- When anything breaks/smashes.
- When a packet of crisps/biscuits/confectionery is opened.
- When anyone unusual arrives at the door.

So reliable is this metamorphosis that I have often thought, should the ancient wiring at last spontaneously combust and the house burst into flames, the most successful way of ensuring the escape of my offspring would not be with a fire alarm but the simple opening of a packet of Haribos at the best exit point.

Despite urgent telepathic pleading with the boys to – just for once – greet the unusual visitor as instructed by Hugh and me many, *many* times, they stuck to their preferred etiquette of loitering by the door frame and eyeing the stranger with equal parts curiosity and suspicion.

'Peter, Billy,' I said, with a fine edge of threat that I hoped would avoid Calvin's head but penetrate the boys' like a dagger, 'this is Mr Narwhal. Come and say hello, please.'

Far more sensitive to nuances of tone than his brother, Billy responded even better than I could have hoped – advancing towards Calvin with his hand outstretched, and Looking Him in the Eye so fixedly that he could have just as easily been about to comment on some unfortunate deformity as introduce himself. Calvin was clearly very impressed by this – so much so that he seemed barely to notice the contrast between Billy's near perfect greeting and Pete's rather grudging, 'Lo.'

'It is,' said Calvin, grinning at them both, 'a great honour to meet you. Do you know who ah am?'

Billy, who is going through a phase of assuming he is in a classroom at all times, thrust his arm in the air.

'Yes, Billy,' said Calvin, with very generous charm.

'An American!' said Billy.

Calvin received this reply with awed astonishment, looking from Billy to me, and back to Billy again, as if it was not his nationality that had just been correctly identified but rather the complete sequencing of his DNA. Billy beamed, and I was tipped over by gratitude so powerful it felt almost like falling in love. How kind this man was! How *kind* this man.

'Ah can see,' said Calvin to Billy, 'that you are a very intelligent young man. Ah am indeed American, but ah am also, ah believe, your fifth cousin three times removed.'

The four of us then moved to the kitchen table the better to grapple with this concept, and Calvin described to us our respective positions on the Narwhal family tree, which absolutely none of us could grasp. I gave Calvin a piece of paper so he could draw it out for us, but if anything this only confused us even more – everything made much harder by the great herds of Hughs that tramped across each generation.

I could not help but imagine Ian's embarrassed disappointment with me had he been present, an encyclopaedic knowledge of Narwhal ancestry being the most fundamental attribute required of Narwhal chatelaines in his opinion, but as I've long realised I will never reach even the lower slopes of cloud-topped Greer-ness Ian admires, I remained relatively unscathed by this thought. In truth, very little of me was in the here and now at all. I was exploring elsewhere, daydreaming about me and Calvin in one of those lovely antebellum houses, sipping mint juleps on a porch foaming with bougainvillea...

Just then, I heard Billy saying, 'Do you want to look round our house?'

'Well,' said Calvin, looking at me half-hesitantly, half-expectantly, 'that depends entirely on your mama. Ah can't deny ah would dearly love to see the home of mah ancestors, but ah do not want to intrude or offend... Perhaps just the public rooms?'

Pete, Billy and I exchanged frowns.

'Public rooms?' I said. 'What – rooms open to the public?'

'Whah, yes,' said Calvin, surprised. 'Surely a house of this age and historical stature is open to visitors? At least from tahme to tahme?'

'Oh, no,' said Pete. 'We haven't got any of those red ropes, so we definitely couldn't be open to the public.'

Thinking that our lack of red ropes was perhaps not the predominant obstacle of the six or seven hundred I could think of before drawing breath, but that I couldn't possibly deny myself the pleasure of giving Calvin anything he wanted, I said brightly that of *course* he must see the house – as much of it as he liked – and that we'd all take him round.

It turned out to be a rather unconventional tour, in that the information we were able to give Calvin was either self-evident (me: lovely view from our room; awful smell in Pete's room – investigations ongoing) or perhaps not what he was hoping for (boys: respective best hiding places for sardines and capture the flag; which bathroom Never to Visit after Dark and Why). But by means of a (rather stressful) combination of blagging, distraction techniques and selective hearing, I managed to parry most of Calvin's questions, while fervently hoping that it wouldn't be until he left that he realised he had learned nothing of any value whatsoever.

Though he was far too polite to voice his surprise at many of the rooms, I could hear it loud and clear all the same, not least because I recognised it from my own in the early days. The inconsistencies between fittings and furnishings are so many and so extreme that one's eyes jolt over each in turn as one's car might over successive and acutely angled humpbacked bridges. Look at Hugh's and my bedroom, for example. The ceiling is high and ornately plastered, and yes, the bed is large and four poster, and there is even a bedside table for each side, but mine is a faded Lloyd Loom laundry basket, and Hugh's an early creation of his own – a wildly impractical and lumpy driftwood design. A glance at the floor reveals not burnished floorboards and beautiful rugs, but a piece of carpet of the bargain-basement, beige, highly flammable kind, which doesn't quite reach wall to wall. Upon this sits a 1970s melamine wardrobe, once white but now an attractive shade of old nicotine. Like some kind of vine, or thread fungus, pipes and wires run up and down the corners of the room and along the edges of floor and cornicing. From the ceiling rose hangs a small chandelier made of antlers, and from various cracks in the wreaths and fat putti legs of the plasterwork, like bizarre stalactites, are strung pieces of thick and ancient twine – Grandpa's triumphant invention – to train leaks into the buckets that sit in readiness at all times under the bed.

'This place,' my mother had said on her first visit, with the half-hunger/half-reproach of a woman who likes nothing more than to roll up her sleeves, 'needs taking in hand.' Which was all very well for her to say. She may have had the scalps of several tired houses tucked into her belt, but none was ever on this scale...

'It's probably not quite what you were expecting,' I said to Calvin, trying to keep the despair out of my voice as I caught his eye lingering on the stack of pre-war *Horse and Hound* that has long served as a support for Billy's three-legged bed.

'Not at all,' said Calvin, in thoughtful tones. 'Not at all.'

We ended the tour in the drawing room. I'd orchestrated this partly because I hoped its impressiveness would supplant the oddness of the rest of the house in Calvin's mind, and partly because I knew its features would elicit all sorts of questions from him for which I needed time to prepare. But just as Calvin pointed at the fireplace and opened his mouth, Jo suddenly appeared in the doorway, hoover at her heels, cleaning belt – bristling with trigger sprays – low on her hips. My usual apprehension at the sight of her was conquered by relief for the timely interruption, and I greeted her with reckless effusiveness.

'Jo! How *are* you? Completely forgot you were coming today. This is Mr Narwhal, who has come all the way from the States, and is our fourth… he's our twice… he's our distant relation. From America.'

With quite magnificent disregard for social niceties, Jo merely scowled at Calvin, then said threateningly, 'Need to clean in here.'

'Forgive me, ma'am,' said Calvin to Jo, 'ah have been holding up this charming household and ah must let you all get on with the business of the day.'

'Oh, Calvin, must you?' I said, all self-restraint abandoned to the wind. 'Won't you stay for supper? Or a drink at least?'

'You are most kind,' he said, 'but ah have already stayed longer than ah planned. Ah need to get back to London to catch mah flahght tonahght.'

'Will you come back again?' asked Billy sadly.

'Ah would lahke that very much, Billy,' said Calvin, ruffling Billy's hair.

So we walked him to the door, and goodbyes were exchanged with more fondness than could ever have been guessed at from the mere politeness of the hellos only a couple of hours earlier. As we watched Calvin get into his car, and I was thinking how perfectly obvious it was that Americans should always be the ones to save the world in the films, Pete said quietly, 'He was nice.'

'*Wasn't* he,' I sighed.

27TH JULY

I was inspired for some reason this morning to make pancakes with maple syrup, which put everyone in a good mood. The boys gorged themselves, Hugh sat peaceably reading the paper, and I told Rose all about Calvin's visit yesterday.

She was only mildly interested at first.

'We've had a lot of them over the years,' she said, licking lemon juice off her fingers. 'Distant relatives from wherever, usually somewhere in that direction. There was a pair of Narwhal twins – 1780 or something? – who went over to Nantucket. One of them came back, but the other one stayed... for the equally rich whaling and shagging opportunities, as far as I can remember.'

'It's all right, Billy,' I said, seeing his distraught face. 'Our side didn't do any whaling.'

'No. They were too busy slaughtering things with four legs to bother with those without any at all,' muttered Rose.

'He thought we were open to the public,' said Peter.

'Yes. Well,' I said, protectively, 'I think that was a perfectly reasonable expectation. How was he to know?'

'No,' said Pete, rolling his eyes at me. 'I didn't mean that. What I meant was I think we *should* be open to the public.'

Hugh emitted something from behind his paper that was half-laugh/half-snort.

'Shush, Hugh,' said Rose, frowning at her nephew. 'Why do you think that, Pete?'

'Look. Everyone's always going on about not having any money, right?' said Pete. 'We could get some from showing people round.'

Feeling rather shifty and ashamed at the realisation that I had not disguised our financial concerns from him as successfully as I'd thought, I was particularly gentle in my reply.

'Pete. It's a wonderful idea, in theory. But, look, do you remember when we went to Warwick Castle?'

'I think we all remember when we went to Warwick Castle,' said Hugh darkly.

'Not the business in the dungeons,' I said patiently, 'but the main castle bit. Do you remember, Pete? How immaculate everything was, and all the armour, and the little signs and everything?'

'I didn't know it was going to be so scary!' cried Billy.

'It's OK, darling,' I said, 'we don't need to go back there.'

'They won't *let* us go back there,' muttered Hugh.

'Shut *up*, Hugh,' said Rose.

'So what?' said Pete. 'Calvin didn't care that there wasn't any armour, or any signs. He was interested in *everything*. He would definitely have paid if we'd asked him.'

'Would he now,' said Rose thoughtfully.

'You're not seriously considering…' I began.

'Why not? Maybe we're not seeing the wood for the trees because we live here. Maybe people *would* pay to come and see it.'

'Yeah,' said Pete, triumphant.

'But. The *work*,' I said, horrified. 'The *state* of the place.'

Rose leaned across the table towards me. 'The *money*,' she said.

All this was weighing very heavily on me when I went to the supermarket later. Don't get me wrong – any extra income would be a godsend – but why on earth would anyone want to see our mouldering old place?

I was so absorbed in these gloomy ponderings that I didn't notice, as I got into the queue at Louise's till, that I was behind the woman least aware of checkout etiquette in probably a hundred-mile radius and, more surprising still, I didn't even care. I just watched blankly as she took her usual three hours to put her items on the conveyor belt and then transfer them to bags, with another four being spent in finding her purse, finding card within purse, peering at card, replacing card in purse, selecting different card, peering at card machine, inserting card wrong way round in card machine, removing card, peering at card, turning card right way and re-inserting.

'Cheer up,' said Louise, when I eventually made it to the till. 'It might never happen.'

I told her that I very much feared it already had; would *she* hand over her hard-earned cash to see a mouldy house with missing spindles and strange smells?

'Your mouldy house?' she said. 'Narwhal Hall, isn't it?'

I was astonished that she knew this, but became even more so when I learned that she'd actually *been* there, carol singing, years ago, and they'd been asked into the hall and there were two great polar bears on either side of the stairs – one with a tray of mince pies on his paws and the other with some sherry.

'Oh, yes,' she said, in between beeps, 'I'd pay just for another look at those bears.'

I told her this was *extremely* heartening, and thank you, and now, how was the wrist?

My spirits were further lifted as a result of some additional market research conducted on Juliet Morris, who I spotted and swiftly accosted – in possibly a rather needy way – in the car park. For someone who seems to be forever on her way to somewhere else, always onward, she has a surprising and touching ability to recognise and to respond to calls on her time. As I launched into the whole house opening business, she first stopped loading her bags into the back of her car, then turned to lean against the boot the better to absorb the flurry of words and wild hand movements I was throwing at her. She didn't say anything until I'd finished, then asked a series of brief, intelligent questions that told me she'd grasped every aspect of the situation.

'What do you think?' I said. 'It sounds like you might have some experience of this sort of thing?'

'Not of opening up houses,' she replied, 'but hospitality yes, business yes, project management yes.'

'Gosh,' I said, raising my eyebrows as I wondered if her CV was innocuous enough for me to ask about. 'Gosh,' I said again, deciding it wasn't.

'Look,' said Juliet, 'would it help if I came over? Talked it through? Tomorrow afternoon is clear if that's any good?'

'Oh, Juliet, would you?' I said. 'That would be fantastic. Just another opinion – are you sure you can spare the time?'

'Of course,' she said. 'And listen, don't despair. I think it's an exciting idea. Whether it's viable or not is another matter, but exciting is a great start.'

I found myself so grateful for this vote of hope, if not exactly confidence, that I had to hug her, which I haven't done before and which, received with stiffness as it was, it may be best not to do again. But even this slight faux pas couldn't dampen my heart. Is it possible that everything's actually going to be all right??

28TH JULY

As promised, Juliet arrived on the dot of two this afternoon, and Rose and I took her on a tour of the house. Bearing in mind that this had been arranged in a supermarket car park, and that Juliet was coming as – well, maybe not as close friend exactly but certainly not professional person either – I suppose I imagined that it would all be quite low key, but it wasn't like that at all. For a start, Rose and Juliet greeted each other with a clear gaze and a firm handshake; you'd never believe the last time they'd met one of them was weeping on a grass verge and the other handing out immaculate packs of tissues.

'Thank you so much for coming over,' said Rose warmly. 'I really value your input.'

Input, I noted, feeling somehow underdressed.

'It's not a problem,' said Juliet, whose eyes were already skim-reading her surroundings. 'Tell me all.'

Rose outstretched her hands as if putting a box firmly on a table. 'So,' she said. 'Picture your perfect National Heritage property. Public space, private space,' she continued, chopping her imaginary box in half, 'polished, prescriptive, *presented*. Are you with me?'

'Ye-es...' said Juliet, who was clearly thinking what I'd been thinking all along – that Narwhal Hall could as soon be a National Heritage property as a grapefruit.

'OK,' said Rose. 'Now take your picture and *tear it up.*'

Juliet cocked her head slightly at this, angling her attention more acutely.

Then, 'Show me,' she said. 'Lead on.'

But this is ridiculous, I kept thinking as I followed the two of them around. It was as if each room was a tangled jewellery box tipped out by Rose for Juliet, the rare diamond ring given no more than a passing word while the paste and the plastic beads and the scratched brass bangle were lovingly laid out. The value was all the wrong way round, surely?

'Isn't that from the Crimea or something?' I said, pointing at the cannon ball that serves as a door stop in Rose's room. 'Shouldn't we be mentioning that?'

'Maybe,' said Rose, 'but personally I'd be more interested in this,' she went on, lifting the foot of the ancient crewel curtains to show Juliet where her goat, Matilda, had chewed them circa 1999.

It seemed best to stay quiet after that, even when the tour was over and we were in the kitchen, Juliet and Rose intent on their conversation at the table, while I put the kettle on. If I say I felt rather detached from it all, I don't mean it in a feeling excluded sort of way. I think maybe, when Rose said we weren't seeing the wood for the trees, that's particularly true of me. Brain too full of housework and what's for supper to fit much else in. And it didn't make any sense to me either – people *paying* to see goat-eaten curtains and 1960s bathroom suites? But it made sense to Juliet – I could hear that. And with her brutal competence on one side, and Alan Sugar's lovechild on the other, were we not in excellent hands? So, with only the slightest of effort, I abdicated all responsibility. I suppose it's a bit like when they built the bypass at Monkfield (not Juliet and Rose obviously – though quite sure they would have had a good crack at it if asked). You're half anxious that they're going to make a balls-up of it, and half hopeful that your traffic frustrations will at long last be over, and you could decide to get in a flap about it, or just lazily, deliciously, surrender your concerns.

As I was showing Juliet out, I caught sight of Tony in the yard – hammering at a wooden crate with his back to us – and said to her that she should meet him. She frowned slightly as we went over, and as I called to Tony and he turned around, each looked at the other in such a fierce manner that my first thought was that they knew each other already, and not as friends.

'Oh,' I said anxiously, 'do you two…?'

But, 'No,' said Tony, nodding an acknowledgement at Juliet. 'No, we don't.'

And Juliet stretched out her hand, and everyone appeared superficially to behave exactly as they were supposed to – trotting through the weather and the usual standard niceties. Only I had this overwhelming sense that the two of them were having an entirely different conversation between themselves. *Most* peculiar. And then, quite abruptly, Juliet said she needed to get going, and I took one look at her face and said I'd walk with her back to the village. She didn't want me to – I could see that quite clearly – but concern made me bolder than I would otherwise have been, and I set off at her side regardless.

'Juliet,' I said then, 'is anything the matter?'

'No,' she said. 'I just need to get on.'

'But you're upset,' I said. 'What's happened? Has Tony done something?'

But she pressed her lips together and shook her head

vigorously, enough for her smooth blonde bob to break free from its silky straightness for nearly a whole second. I thought then that her eyes let her down; not in the sense that they spoilt an otherwise attractive face, but rather as a weak Achilles tendon lets down an athlete – a cruel self-betrayal. They were too big and too clear to be filled in or frozen over no matter how hard she tried; open season for any Tom, Dick or Harry who questioned them with even the lightest glance…

'I told you,' she said, 'it's nothing. Toby'll just need his walk. You go back,' she added.

'But Juliet…'

She stopped suddenly, and looked at me.

'Go back,' she said again.

We had the strangest sort of stand-off then. She wasn't going to move until I did, but it took a second or two for me to relinquish defeat. I blinked at her.

'I…'

Correctly recognising surrender in my hesitation, Juliet relaxed her stance, and reached over to briefly squeeze my arm.

'I really think it could be great,' she said. 'The house. Truly exciting. She's got a lot of vision, your sister-in-law, and drive. You're in good hands.'

'I… Thank you…'

'No problem at all,' she said, moving off, 'anytime. See you soon.'

I watched her striding down the lane, back straight and gait brisk. There was something brave and sorry and ridiculous about the sight of her, marching through the soft dapples, like a lone soldier defiant despite disaster behind him and likely doom up ahead.

I wandered slowly and sadly back towards the house, thinking grimly as I did so that I would Have A Word with Tony, but realised as soon as I saw him that this was an absurd idea. What was I going to say? How dare he upset Juliet with his, "Supposed to rain later in the week"? Or the deep insensitivity of his, "Private commissions mostly"?

I put the puzzle to Rose when I arrived back in the kitchen, and was appalled to hear her say, 'Menopausal?'

'She is *not* menopausal, Rose,' I said, most of my bristling, if I'm honest, due to the fact that I'm much nearer in age to Juliet than Rose, and therefore presumably in the same category of demented aged person as far as Rose is concerned. 'You'll be telling me it's PMT next. Honestly, Rose, it's like talking to Hugh.'

'Just saying,' she shrugged, as Hugh himself appeared.

'Like talking to Hugh what?' he said, making his way to the larder.

'Women and hormones,' I said, finding myself actually embarrassed that he'd heard me, as one always is when caught referring to jokes that are no longer shared. He is still being "good". My days are punctuated with little surprises like finding the loo roll replaced, or the bins already out – always practical tasks completed or pre-empted, so that it still feels like I've got a butler rather than a husband. I'm not sure what I think about this. I'm grateful for the help, I am, and for the intent behind it, but is this as good as it's ever going to get? Not so much a marriage as a contract? Hugh not a husband but rather a debentured colleague with a valuable skill set? But it's best not to think too far ahead. A butler is better than a bastard. 'Anyway,' I continued, 'look, Hugh, while you're here, could you possibly have a look at the washing machine? It's been making such a funny noise – I daren't use it really and there's such a pile to do.'

I noted my formal courtesy, awaited his in return.

'Of course,' he said.

We went into the scullery, and I sat on the stool and watched him as he settled to the task in hand. He assessed the issue, identified the cause, and proceeded with the solution – so smoothly you sort of knew even as he started that he would succeed. Like an accomplished walker whose pace and breathing stays precisely the same no matter how challenging or unknown the terrain. I think we all love to see our partners doing things they're talented at, particularly if we're useless at them ourselves, and watching Hugh mend things has always been a joy to me. I felt nostalgic suddenly; found myself thinking about that couple in the pub the evening I went to find Nick. Hoped they knew how lucky they were.

'Hugh,' I said, for something to say, to break the silence. 'What do you think about this whole opening up to the public thing?'

He was lying on the floor, scraping bits of limescale off the exit flow tube with a screwdriver.

'She's not serious about it,' he said. 'The Tree House is one thing – we'll pay her back – but it's just talk about opening. You know what she's like.'

'I don't think it is just talk, you know,' I said, and told him about Juliet's visit and how the whole thing seemed already to be under way.

He looked up to stare at me then – not at me so much as on me, his attention so weighty it needed to rest somewhere, my face being the nearest spot. It went on and on and on, this look, as if in response to news far more serious than that which I thought I'd just given him.

'You're looking like this is a bad thing,' I said. 'Are you worried Rose has bitten off more than she can chew? Or... But this *could* be good, Hugh. Maybe she'll make it work. Maybe,' I said, growing excited, 'this'll mean you won't have to sell the field after all!' I waited for his face to brighten at this, but it only darkened even more, looking almost panicked in fact. 'Hugh?' I prompted. 'What's the matter? What are you thinking?'

He sniffed sharply and sent his attention back to the washing machine. 'I think,' he said, shifting the screwdriver to his other hand, 'that no one wants the furniture and that upholstery's not going to sustain us. But it's not Rose's job either – she should know that. Not her responsibility.'

Realisation dawned on me. It was the Narwhal pride that was the problem. Not doubts about Rose's abilities or an altruistic wish to save her from effort, but alarm at the threat she presented to his sense of duty and identity. I stared at the back of his head in despair. *Why* can't we change other people? Why isn't there some sort of antidote to their toxic beliefs that we can slip surreptitiously into their tea? That would set Hugh free from all his Narwhal chains and show him that this place is just a house, and he is just a man, and a better life *is* possible.

He'd spun the drum, satisfied himself that the grating had gone, and was washing his hands at the sink. I had something to say, hardly knowing if exasperation or entreaty was behind it. But, startled by the vigour of his scrubbing, the breadth of his back, it vanished before I could catch it.

'I...' I said.

'You...' I said.

'Never mind,' I said.

30TH JULY

I had a massive pang of guilt yesterday that I had yet to invite any of the boys' friends over to play this holiday, to which I reacted with my usual (and invariably deeply regretted) overcompensation. The result of this was the arrival of thirteen children this morning. I'd foolishly told the mothers they were very welcome to stay or go after drop off, which of course meant the yard was entirely empty seconds after their respective offspring had been deposited at the front door. As the children, delirious with freedom and overexcitement, scattered almost instantly, I felt a horrible mounting panic at the multiple calamities that were inescapably to befall them all. I saw the headlines with absolute clarity:

PLAYDATE TRAGEDY: 13 DEAD

'I hadn't really thought it through,' says mother *"in charge"*.

'ROSE!' I yelled, and continued to yell, until she burst out of the house with all her blue lights flashing.

When the nature of the emergency was explained to her, she immediately took matters in hand.

'Right,' she said grimly. 'Let's show the little bastards who's boss.'

Within half an hour, everyone had been gathered, and

rules, threats and bribes had been issued. Rose and I threw everything that could possibly be needed into the wheelbarrow, and established a sort of watchtower in the middle of the lawn, where the lake, garden and house were best visible. By the time the parasol was up and the deckchairs opened, I could almost believe I was about to enjoy a pleasant few hours chatting with my sister-in-law rather than engage in hawk-like observation of deeply damage-susceptible small visitors. Rose too was clearly under this impression, fishing around in the wheelbarrow for a couple of cans of Diet Coke, and giving a deep sigh as she opened hers. It was a beautiful day. I was amazed to find that behind the birdsong and the shouts of the children, I could hear the bees in the lavender all the way over by the house. I felt a deep glow at this, as I always do when I see wildlife (of the considerate and outdoor variety) take advantage of our hospitality.

Rose had her eyes closed and her face tilted towards the sun, and looked as content as it was possible to be.

'Don't feel like I've seen you properly in ages, favourite sister-in-law,' I said to her fondly. 'How is everything?'

She launched straightaway into how her plans were going regarding opening up the house, from which I understood how much at the forefront of her mind they were. I wondered briefly what had happened to all the other things that had held that privileged position over the years – the plight of the manatee, the evils of gluten/capitalism/pesticides – and whether or not the new passion might actually last this time?

At that moment, my eye was caught by a blinding, flashing light just by the gate into the orchard. I fetched the binoculars out of the wheelbarrow, peered through them, then reached for the megaphone.

'Josh and Jamie,' I called. 'Put the mirror *down* please. Definite fire hazard.'

'Oh, well spotted,' said Rose, twisting in her deckchair towards the boys.

We watched as they clocked us clocking them, exchanged a few words, clocked us still clocking them, then slumped their shoulders and sloped away in defeat.

'Anyway?' I said to Rose.

'Yes. So,' she said, 'definitely a good start made, and I'd say we could be open by Christmas.'

'Wow,' I said. 'You don't hang around, do you? What about the Tree House?' I added, looking across to the oak which had held it and now seemed so bereft.

'Still in hand,' said Rose, not missing a beat, 'although to be honest I'm struggling with the architect a bit.'

I queried the reason for this, and was told he lacked imagination; that she'd shown him the original plans she'd found in the attic, and he'd just pretty much reproduced them when what she was after was something – you know – *different*. Had she showed him the sort of different she meant, I asked, to which she looked astonished and replied that of course she hadn't – that was *his* job, not hers.

'Right,' I said. 'So what you want is for him to magically interpret what you want when not even *you* know what you want?'

'Well, obviously,' she said, frowning. 'That's what they're supposed to do.'

'The really good ones maybe,' I said; then, before I quite realised what I was saying, 'I mean if it was *Nick* we were talking about…'

'We are *not* talking about Nick,' she snapped, flapping

her hands angrily at a bee that had been showing only the slightest interest in her Diet Coke. 'Sorry,' she said, more quietly now. 'But we're not. Anyway, shouldn't we be thinking about feeding the children?'

'I suppose so,' I sighed, inwardly kicking myself for the Nick comment. 'You stand guard, I'll go and get the sausages on.'

It never ceases to amaze me how obedient children are when they're hungry. It only took one shout through the megaphone to say the food was ready, and seconds later they were all crowding into the kitchen in a jostling, sweaty little mass. We got them in a line, and Rose dished out the hot dogs while I conducted a brief check on each child as it passed, prising a jumper off one beetroot-faced boy, pressing a tissue into the reluctant hand of another, and successfully applying cream to the nettle stings of Rachel's smallest daughter despite her fidgeting. I was gratified to see that all limbs of all children were present and correct, and was just trying simultaneously to inform Matty that yes, there was ketchup, but no wholegrain rolls I'm afraid, Rory, when I heard the front door clang with impeccably bad timing. I told Billy to go and see who it was so I could get the cones ready for pudding, thinking at the same time that didn't someone have a lactose intolerance? And did that cause vomiting or actual death? And I had just seen a half-eaten sausage fly through the air – almost certainly at Peter's hand – when Billy ran into the kitchen, beaming from ear to ear, shouting, 'It's Uncle Nick!'

I very nearly dropped the tub of vanilla onto a nearby head.

How could that be possible? Had I somehow summoned him to us with the mere mention of his name?

Would my own head shortly spin round and round on my body as a result of my mysteriously acquired witchy powers? Or – dear Lord – more likely be separated from my neck entirely courtesy of Rose-rage at my meddling...?

There he stood on the kitchen threshold, as cool and fresh against our lunchtime chaos as a fountain in some hot and dusty bazaar. It was at once the most astonishing and familiar of sights.

I'd got as far as an expletive and a big breaking smile when a flicker on Nick's face made me turn, just in time to see the back of Rose as she fled into the garden, hair streaming behind her like some sort of awful banner of distress.

'Oh dear...' I began, but Nick quietly walked over to me, kissed me on the cheek with his usual, 'Hello, sweetheart,' and set off through the French windows after her.

I had not the faintest idea, as I watched them for a second, what would happen next, and was extremely glad that I didn't then have the time to consider it further. The momentary lull that had opened up around the kitchen table as the children, sensing Something Interesting going on, had paused to watch, closed abruptly the instant Nick had left the room, and the clamour seemed to be double what it had been before. I felt a rush of heroic determination as I realised that I must now cope with the children on my own, a lone, beleaguered captain against a horde of sticky-fingered insurgents. I held the vanilla aloft to attract their attention, and reiterated firmly all the instructions from that morning, with the addition that they were to leave That Man and That Lady alone – particularly you two, I said, frowning at Pete and Billy. Once solemn oaths of obedience had been extracted from everyone, I finished the cones and released the children back into the wild.

The E numbers and sugar now rampaging through their bloodstreams meant that the next half hour was fairly interesting. There were two injuries, and three lots of tears, and it became increasingly difficult to ignore the proximity of Josh and/or Jamie when each of these occurred. The last straw was when I discovered Lucasz weeping piteously inside the Tree House bell (still lying like a great bronze mushroom at the foot of the oak), which he had chosen as his hiding place for a round of capture the flag. Someone, he sobbed, had banged on it while he was inside and now his ears and his head hurt and everything was all ringy. I'm not surprised, I said grimly, glaring at Josh, who was standing a few feet away – the large stick clearly visible behind his back completely cancelling out the wide-eyed expression of innocence he had swiftly cast over his wicked little face.

As every mother knows, you approach the decision to tell off someone else's children with all the caution of a president with a big red button at his fingertips. The risks are many and varied, as even the most rational of parents can be transformed into crazed fiends if they suspect their offspring have been wrongly judged, as the naughtiest ones take great care to imply. But lone and beleaguered captains do not have the luxury of caution, I told myself, when protecting the good insurgents from the bad ones – particularly when the good insurgent in question was Lucasz, for whom I have had huge affection since the storm trooper purchase at the fete. I wiped his tears, gave him a sweet, and told him to go and sit quietly under the parasol at the watchtower until he felt better. Then I beckoned Josh and Jamie (hiding inefficiently behind a very slim tree), and told them in no uncertain terms that if there was any more trouble I would be phoning their parents to come and collect them immediately. With further crises (hopefully) averted, my mind turned to Nick and Rose and anxious wonderings as to how they were getting on. I'd only glimpsed them once since lunch, Rose bolting across the terrace with Nick strolling calmly behind her in so similar a manner as before that I wondered vaguely if they were going to keep circling the house like that until the end of time.

As four o'clock and the arrival of everyone's mothers drew near, I herded the children into the kitchen for a wash, squash and biscuits, and decided a nice quiet game of wink murder would keep them occupied for the last half hour. The moment silence descended, however, it became clear that Nick and Rose were having a fearsome row nearby; the sort where each party is so maddened by the need to get their rage out that nothing will stop them doing so, not hell or high water, and certainly not the risk of adult insults soiling small and delicate ears.

'OK!' I shouted, as we all learned the exact number of sexual partners Rose had had since leaving Nick.

'What's a fug?' said Matty.

'Hug, Matty,' I said desperately, 'she said *hug*. RIGHT, EVERYONE, WE'RE GOING TO SING A SONG. WHAT ABOUT ROW, ROW, ROW YOUR BOAT. I'LL START. LOUD AS YOU CAN!'

In what I hoped was a passable representation of a highly experienced primary school teacher, I now leapt to my feet, singing heartily and clapping in time, simultaneously signalling that they were to follow me outside. To my utter astonishment and relief, every single one of them took the bait – even Josh and Jamie, albeit with an entirely ironic enthusiasm – and we marched in single file around the garden, orchard and lake, taking turns to lead and choose the songs. We rounded the corner of the house and arrived in the yard bellowing, "We are the Champions", much to the admiration of the awaiting mothers who clearly and wholly erroneously thought we had spent the entire day as the von Trapps. My conscience could not let this impression stand, and I did try to correct it, but with no immediate supporting evidence available (physical wounds long since patched, and psychological ones presumably repressed) I eventually had to give up.

With belongings collected, thank yous ordered by the mothers and received by me, the children were thrust into their respective vehicles and – dear Lord, how grateful I was to see it – driven away. Only Rachel remained. I asked her if she wanted a cup of tea, and she said no, she should get home, but neither of us made any attempt to end the conversation and I was able to relieve myself of at least a synopsis of a very full-on day. I'd just called her daughter Sophie over so as to point out her nettle injury to her mother, when I thought I heard something through Rose's open bedroom window above us. I did not quite trust my ears, however, as the information they were passing to me seemed rather improbable against a backdrop of the comparative benefits of Germolene and Anthisan, so I asked Rachel if she could hear what I could hear.

'Oh, yes,' she said, nodding slowly.

I understood as a result of this confirmation that the source of the sound was indeed the exuberant coupling of Nick and Rose that my ears had initially suggested, and was so filled with hope that this might be the first step towards them getting back together that I told Sophie and the boys to go and play for a minute, and began to tell the whole story to Rachel.

'I thought you said she told you not to say anything?' said Rachel, when I got to the bit about me going to London.

'She did,' I said, 'but she's never known what's good for her where her love life is concerned.' Rachel pursed her lips doubtfully. 'Yes, but listen to that,' I said, pointing towards Rose's window, knowing very well even as I did so that Rose's reasons for shagging have never been reliable indicators of how she feels about a man, or indeed herself. We all have quicksand in our souls. Some people fence it, or strive to find the tools to breach it, but Rose's is too broad for either strategy. Instead she finds a man and pulls him in; for the company if nothing else, I always think.

Rachel and I fell into quiet contemplation for a moment, as Rose's bedsprings began to complain vociferously above us.

'Mark and I used to go at it like rabbits,' said Rachel after a while, a little mistily.

'Didn't we all?' I agreed.

'But honestly – now – children, life...'

'Oh, definitely,' I said.

'In fact... Christ,' said Rachel, looking at her watch, 'we need to go. Mark's mother's coming and there's still something's vomit on the front door.'

With the special tone of voice she uses for telling dogs not to eat cowpats, Rachel now called for Sophie. I was deeply impressed by the latter's arrival mere seconds later, though not remotely surprised. In fact, the only wonder was why any other Sophies within a thirty-mile radius did not also immediately appear, clueless as to why they had come but compelled to nonetheless.

With everyone at last gone, I felt a wave of exhaustion – permission now granted – rush over me. The multiple events of the day tumbled through my mind in such a tangle that I felt the need to lay them out in front of someone, to order them through telling, as I hadn't had time to do this properly with Rachel. Rose would have been my first choice of ear, but clearly she could not have been less available, and most of what I wanted to get off my chest had her at its centre anyway. Who else was there to talk to? Not the boys, obviously. Not Tony, and certainly not Hugh... No one then? No one. Right. Never mind – the kitchen wasn't going to clear itself anyway.

I'd finished the washing-up, and was beginning to tackle the ketchup/ice cream splatters on the walls, when Nick and Rose arrived in the kitchen. I looked at Rose first, sharply, hungry for information, and gleaned from her exaggerated post-shag languor that the message she wished to press upon both Nick and me – that a comprehensive reconciliation had taken place – could not have been further from the truth. Nick knew it too. Despite each of them trying their hardest – Nick slipping his arm around Rose's shoulders as they sank, sighing extravagantly, onto the sofa – they were somehow misaligned. Arm and shoulders seemed to have no idea how they'd got there.

'Cuppa?' I said, no other words forthcoming.

As if released by this, Rose sprang from the sofa and said, nodding at the kitchen clock, 'What are you talking about? It's well after six.'

She moved swiftly to the dresser to fetch glasses, saying

as she did so that she hoped I'd been all right with the children on my own, and weren't some of them poppets, but she could never be a teacher, and did we have any ice in the back freezer as there wasn't any in this one, and then disappearing into the scullery without waiting for a reply.

Nick rose and came over to me in the silence that opened up behind her.

'Hello again,' he said gently. 'Haven't said that properly to you yet.'

'Oh, Nick,' I found myself saying, looking up at him anxiously. I couldn't help it. He's just got one of those faces that draws out one's latent pleas for reassurance.

'Don't you worry, sweetheart,' he said, 'it'll be all right. We've got the ball rolling.'

I was about to press further, but couldn't as–

'Those two – what were they called? Josh and someone? Their parents need to take them in hand if you ask me,' said Rose, coming back into the kitchen. 'Got the ice. Now where's Hugh?'

This was a good point, I realised, seeing that it wasn't just past six but nearing half past. He would usually be well into his second gin by now. As Nick took the glasses off Rose and headed for the drinks table, I went to text Hugh, only to discover a message from him already there.

Gone off, it said. *Don't phone*.

I stared at this while my brain worked so hard to resist instant understanding that it could not spare even an inch of effort to reply to Nick's repeated query as to what I'd like to drink. And when he came over to squeeze my arm, and look at me with great kindness and concern, I found – to my equal astonishment and horror – that I was bursting into tears.

1ST AUGUST

Have rather had to wade through the last couple of days. Can't seem to focus on anything, and keep getting stuck staring at things. An upcoming event guide from the Assembly Rooms came through the post today, and could I decide what to do with it? To keep (perhaps we'll go to something), or not to keep (we'll never get around to going to something). It felt like I debated for hours, appalled at my brain's incapacity to manage such a tiny decision, eventually hiding the wretched thing from myself between my least used recipe books.

I'm still surprised at my own reaction to that text. If you'd told me beforehand that Hugh was about to leave I'd have scoffed mightily – it wouldn't have made any *sense*. Not because he wasn't unhappy, of course he was unhappy – more than ever with the top field at risk and Rose's unwitting threats of cruel emasculation – but leaving would have sounded like the wrong outcome for him, too shouty for the man I knew. When faced with a problem, his standard methodology is firstly to try to solve it by any means possible, doggedly, to the point where those of us around him think for goodness' sake why doesn't he just give it up? Beyond that point, in fact. We give up telling him to give up whatever he's trying to do, and usually it's about then that he succeeds in doing it. But on those few occasions when he doesn't, he won't stride away in plain sight but rather shut down any acknowledgement of the issue he's previously been unable to leave alone and enter a period of hyper-condemnation of other people's weaknesses. That's the traditional Hugh approach. If he has to admit failure and retreat he does so with a rather touching sidestep, like an actor who, realising he's on stage when he shouldn't be, tries to sidle off it unseen, perhaps creating a small distraction first. There's never any hand-to-brow wailing, or soggy soliloquy, or dramatic exit – he'd be mortified at the very thought.

So what I should have felt at the news of his leaving was denial and disbelief. Only I didn't. On the contrary. The shock, the tears, they came not because I couldn't understand his actions but rather because on some inarticulate level I *could*. And in one way this was frightening. Why the sense of recognition, even of relief? Was I *glad* he'd gone? Glad he'd looked at our marriage, wounded on the side of the road, and had the guts I hadn't? To put it out of its misery? But when I tried on this reasoning I just couldn't make it fit. Neither of us thought we were beyond saving – I knew that. All I did know was that I had to trust his request to leave him be, as Hugh, more than anyone I know, must fight his hardest battles alone if he's to win them.

Not that this has been easy. I'd give anything to know what's going on in his head. Later on that first evening, I went over to the workshop to look at his work diary. I turned first to the 30th July, sneering at my own expectations even as I did so. What on earth did I think I'd see? "Deliver Mrs Sadler, order calico, leave home"? Presumably with a long explanation as to *why*? How was "Perkins bun feet" supposed to help me? I moved onwards – a dentist appointment (should I cancel it?), a fabric rep, Ramsay-Smith drop end sofa with a question mark, stock check, Lewis chase… the entries getting fewer and finally petering out, like the last roses, in the autumn.

Hugh puts such pressure on his pen when he writes that as soon as he's touched a page it can no longer lie smooth on its neighbour, the indentations from his notes swelling out the pages so that you can *hear*, as well as see, where he's been as you flick through – a sort of soft, irregular crackle instead of the purr of the untouched months – and this brought a lump to my throat that I had to fight. Look, I said to myself, *look*, this means he didn't plan to go. If there's no abrupt halt in the entries that means his leaving was impulsive, perhaps already regretted – doesn't it? Who knows what made him go? Maybe he'll be back tomorrow?

But he wasn't.

Nick and Rose have been very sweet. After her initial outrage ('What does he mean, "gone off"?' Rose had said on reading Hugh's text. 'What does he think he is – a fucking *cheese?*') she's settled on an awkward, stiff upper lip support manifested mainly as school ma'am briskness, with the occasional vigorous rubbing of my upper arm. She's always struggled a bit with sympathy – both giving and receiving. The signals get scrambled at some synapse she can't find, let alone reach, which frustrates her into impatience and irritation so that you're not always entirely clear if you're being consoled or given a massive telling off. On this occasion, I couldn't be happier with this approach. It's Nick's I need to watch out for. He's got compassion taped, the bastard. Neither too gloopy nor too gritty, neither too smothering nor too absent, but just the sort of Goldilocks kindness that would quite undo me if I let it. I find I'm often on the edge of tears. It's as if I've sprung a leak somewhere, which confuses me as I'm usually pretty watertight. It's not as if I miss Hugh exactly; maybe it's just the shock? Like going to put the kettle on and discovering the kitchen's disappeared into a sinkhole. Whatever the reason, I'm working hard to keep myself together, not least because Nick and Rose have their own troubles to worry about.

The sex is exhausting, and it's not even me who's having it. They think they're being discreet, the abject failure of this belief very touching – like that of the boys when they were younger, "hiding" in near plain sight, boy-shaped bulges behind the curtain – and just as I did in those days with the boys, I collude warmly in Nick and Rose's self-deception. Thank God Rose is so noisy. Without that warning I'd have stumbled upon them a dozen times: the airing cupboard, the scullery, the glasshouse, the snug, the orchard... If it was "We've just got back together, hooray!" sex, I wouldn't mind, but of course it isn't – this is Rose we're talking about. Poor Nick; you can see how even he's wearied by it, not the sex itself so much as all her thrashing around behind it.

I need to hold it together for them, and, above all, the boys. So far so good on this front. I've told them their father's gone to London for work. This has happened before – just frequently enough to be believed – but if he's away longer than a week or two I've no idea what I'll say to them other than that I must lie, cheat, steal, kill to keep them safe from the truth.

I think – really – I'm fine. Confused, yes; upset, yes; anxious, yes; insecure, yes; leaky, yes; but basically fine.

2nd August

Normal day.

4TH AUGUST

Went to town. Billy bought a Lego man. Did some dead-heading. Had small cry.

7TH AUGUST

I had the house to myself last night. Thanks to hosting millions of children the other day, the boys have received millions of invitations in reply, and both were on sleep-overs. Nick had an awards do in London, and Rose refused to go with him at first, spouting some nonsense about needing to get her car serviced. She is a hopeless liar. I don't think that car has ever had a service in its life, and I'd be as likely to believe her insistence that it needed one now (particularly as we all know there's nothing she likes more than the chance to dress up and waft about with a glass of champagne) as I would if she were to declare her imminent departure to the nearest nunnery. I pointed this out to her, and watched her blink fiercely as she wondered whether to pursue her rapidly dissolving line of deception or not.

'I'm not leaving you on your fucking own,' she shouted then, clearly having decided it was a not.

'Dearest girl,' I said, 'look at me. I'm *fine*. I *want* you to go and have a lovely time.'

'I don't give a fuck what you want,' she bawled. 'You shouldn't be on your own. What if something happens, or you get really sad? You're probably really sad right now, and just being fucking stubborn about it.'

I took her hands off her hips and held them.

'Rose,' I said gently, just as Nick came in, 'I'm not letting you win this one. You're going to London.'

'No,' she said, pulling her arms away and folding them.

'*Yes*,' I said. 'Nick, will you please take her away right now?'

'Come on, girl,' said Nick. 'Time to go. Who's going to lord it over all the other women if you're not there to do it?'

Rose considered this with interest.

'I've got nothing to wear, Nick,' she said, this being somehow much more query than statement.

'So get a move on and we'll have time to sort it,' said Nick. 'A night like tonight – best get you something new.'

That did it.

Putting her excitement to one side, she grasped my shoulders and frowned at me.

'We'll come back as soon as, OK?'

'No rush,' I said. 'Take your time.'

She stared at me for a moment longer, then gave me the sort of choked, solemn nod that, in films, usually precedes words like farewell, or – my personal favourite – godspeed.

'It's not ET, for fuck's sake,' said Nick, exasperated. 'You're not leaving the fucking planet. Go and get your stuff, and let Elliott here have her shoulders back.'

I stood at the door to wave them off, smiling as they went through their old routine at the car: Rose opening all the doors to put things in and take them out again, Nick shutting them behind her, muttering about why she couldn't ever get in a car like a normal bloody person, with Rose saying it was his own fault for keeping his car so tidy that she couldn't find anything in it. Then at last she got in, and Nick called out pointedly to me that I wasn't going anywhere was I as she'd probably want to phone home at some point, and was amply rewarded for this with an abstracted, 'Fuck off. Where's the lever for the seat?'

The smile stayed on my face long after they'd turned out of the yard, still rabbiting on at each other as they went. It seemed impossible that they'd ever split up – past or future tense. Maybe they'd make use of the car journey to talk, rather than shag, their way through their problems and come back as complete and as committed as they were so clearly meant to be?

I got a lot done that afternoon: mended the puncture in the wheelbarrow, pressure-washed the memorial column, pushed over that very dead laburnum by the workshop and – with such outstanding skill that I almost wished everyone was back in the house so I could crow about it – fashioned the trunk into a basic prop for the pagoda roof, sorted out my desk, cancelled Hugh's dentist appointment, and the rep; and was therefore feeling pretty smug by early evening.

I made my way to the kitchen, and its silence at once reminded me how much delicious solitude still remained before I had to get the boys. When was the last time that had happened? I wondered luxuriously. No supper to cook unless I wanted to. No one to nag to have a bath/stop hitting their brother. No distractions, interruptions, demands, complications… I rolled around in these riches for a while, then sat up and considered how best to spend them. My first thought, obviously, was to eke out my afternoon's productivity, and press on with long-buried jobs like defrosting the fridge and lifting the floorboards in Pete's room to determine once and for all if something had died down there, but my motivation proved strangely pathetic. I opened the fridge, ready for battle, but one look at its contents was enough to defeat any enthusiasm for the task, and I found myself reaching for a bottle of wine and pouring a large glass instead. This slipped down my throat like silk, so I immediately poured another one. I went outside with the glass and the bottle and a vague plan to sit on the terrace in the remaining sun, but I got distracted by a large patch of nettles – thriving below a leaking downpipe in the corner between the drawing room and the kitchen. Some sort of switch clicked in my brain as I glared at them and the next thing I knew I was scrambling through the hydrangeas and descending upon them, pulling and yanking and hungering for the sight of the soft yielding of their yellow roots from the soil. Every now and then I paused to slurp/top up/slurp, then plunged again to rip and tear and toss the limp stems onto the lawn, and could well have carried on like that forever if I hadn't come across a newt, dislodged from its hiding place and looking (to my eyes at least) horribly lost and confused.

It seemed imperative to take the newt to the safety of the lake immediately. I scooped him up with infinite gentleness and managed to keep him in my hands even as I tripped and fell heavily on a cotoneaster, cutting my ankle and swearing at the drunkenness I'd been so ferociously pursuing up to that point. I made it across the lawn successfully, if not exactly in a straight line, and had just crouched in search of a suitable new residence for the rescued newt, when a cluster of bulrushes to my left called out hello and nearly scared the life out of me.

'All right?' said Tony, from within the undergrowth. 'Didn't mean to give you a shock. *Are* you *all right*?'

'Yes,' I said, rising carefully and going towards his voice. 'Got a newt. You need to see my newt.'

He was sitting on an old tarp, eating a sandwich, his fishing rod beside him. I sat down and proffered up my cupped hands with such hushed reverence a bystander could only have thought they held baby dragons. 'Look,' I whispered, opening up my fingers slowly. 'SSSSsshhhhhh. Don't frighten him.'

If the newt was aware of the intense expectation that preceded his revealing, he did not show it. He merely stirred as the light hit him, and blinked.

'That's a female, that is,' said Tony, bending his head over my hands. 'See? The markings aren't dark enough for a male. She'll need somewhere cool.'

I peered at him gravely.

'I hear you. We need to put her somewhere *cool,*' I whispered. 'Quick. Where? Where does she like, Tony?'

'Down there. Look,' he said. 'At the bottom of those stones. That's it. There she goes.' We watched in silence as the newt paused, assessed her new surroundings, then crawled slowly into a mossy crevice, bit by bit, until the tip of her tail had vanished.

'Hugh's left me,' I said then, nothing like as surprised at myself at this announcement as I could have been.

Tony looked at his feet, but not from embarrassment at this news; more a heartfelt acknowledgement of it. He didn't say a word, and he didn't look at me, and somehow through this shook out a stillness at my feet that I could, at last, step upon.

So I did – starting right from the very first day that Hugh and I had met (those trousers...) – hesitantly at first, then with increasing speed and volume, through the early days and then marriage and moving here, and the boys, and the pressures of the bloody house, and money, and no one wanting the furniture, and everything getting a little worse every day, though so slowly you hardly noticed it let alone focused on it or tried to do something about it, which I hadn't, I cried, seeing with sudden and painful clarity the graph of our marriage in its steady decline from together forever to gone off and don't phone.

Just as I'd finished, a soft whirring alerted me to a dragonfly swooping towards us over the lake, and at the sight of it I came abruptly back to the bank.

'Lord, Tony,' I said, suddenly as horrified at my outburst as if I'd thrown up all over him. 'I'm so sorry. You don't want to hear all that.'

But Tony pressed his lips together and shook his head gently.

'Don't mind me,' he said. 'I'm just sorry about it, is all.'

The dragonfly landed on a sun-faded football that has been floating aimlessly around the lake for a year or more, allowing us a moment to admire its iridescence before taking off again.

'I'd better go in,' I said.

'Yeah. All right,' said Tony. 'Will you – your hands...' he added, nodding at them.

Confused, I glanced down and wondered how I could not have noticed the state of them before. They were black with soil, bloodied from goodness knows what injury, and mottled all the way up the forearms with angry red nettle stings. It was only then I realised how much they hurt.

I could not have felt more rough this morning, therefore, when setting off to collect the boys, nor less prepared for polite pickup chit-chat as I turned into Rory's lane. I felt heavy with hangover, with tingling benettled arms, and with guilt, as clearly it was all my fault that Hugh had left. This awful truth had only sprung into existence overnight but was already enormous. You'd think (or I'd thought) that one of the central tenets of marriage, one of its greatest appeals, in fact, was that you could trust it to its own devices. Any ministrations would be for love, for pleasure, but never for duty – as with a cat that enjoys the strokes you give it when you want to but would not dream of demanding them. Of all the couples I knew this assumption would apply to none of them more than Hugh and me, so proud we were of each other's self-sufficiency. If our relationship was built on anything, it was in the ostentatious dismissiveness of need, never need itself. We competed in understatement, affectionate insults, displays of independence; that was the way we loved.

But now it looked as though I'd been wrong about this all along. It looked as though our marriage was less like a cat and more like the wretched vegetable patch. Certainly it could be left alone, if it was nettles and docks and tiny scabby potatoes you wanted, but any sort of proper crop? Then you'd better put your back into it.

I hadn't really supported him, had I? I hadn't *really* tried. Just because he was resistant to comfort, criticism, conversation, company full stop, did not mean I should have given up trying. Which I had. Not being able to change other people, I had.

No wonder I was teary all the time – it was *me* he'd left.

I remembered reading an article (thank God for doctors' surgeries – would I know anything about anything without the magazines I'd been through there?) about the need to "nurture your relationship", with little thoughtful gestures, date nights, gifts, and how I'd laughed out loud at the thought of Hugh's face on receipt of any of these solemn offerings. Should I have...? No, I thought, shaking my head at the windscreen with a shudder, that would never be the way, but maybe just asking more, just listening more, just bloody well paying attention – *that* was what I should have done. How could I have thought that neglect was the privilege, the *entitlement* granted by marriage?

The misery this train of thought had brought me to was only exacerbated when I reached Rory's gates. Despite telling myself that the Mortimers had lots of cash, and a gardener, and that therefore comparisons with our own weed-ridden and potholey drive were not only destructive but unfair, I could not help but take the perfectly maintained topiary, lawn and gravel before me as further indications of my own pitiful inadequacy. The gleaming front door was opened by a housekeeper, who glanced with confusion at the Skoda, as if it were not a functioning motor vehicle but rather a tyre-less wreck propped up on bricks, and full of chickens. Having given me a brief but identical look, she told me Emma and Guy were in the kitchen and led the way across some sort of incredibly shiny floor while I tried to distract myself by guessing what sort of soap they had in their cloakroom (definitely pumpy and beautiful-smelling, unlike the coal tar slab insisted upon by Hugh in ours).

I arrived in the kitchen at an unfortunate moment of tender exchange between Emma and Guy, just as she was setting a coffee cup and saucer carefully on the kitchen table in front of him, rotating it so that the handle was exactly positioned for his right hand, while he raised his head to give her a loving smile.

As my eyes started to ache warningly (never once had I given Hugh his coffee in a proper cup, let alone turned the handle for him), that this was too touching a scene for me today, and I had to cough loudly so as to try and break the shimmer around it. This objective was achieved, but respite wasn't, as their greetings were first warm, then both warm and laced with concern – a most deadly combination. Hayfever, I told them firmly, giving the same excuse to Billy when he arrived and asked me what was wrong, and to Pete when I collected him afterwards, though this latter was purely for continuity purposes – I doubt he even noticed the tears, let alone thought to question them.

We were about to set off home when a text arrived from Rose, telling me with great forests of exclamation marks that Nick had won the top architect award. You'd think this wonderful news would have cured the hayfever at once, but bizarrely it just seemed to make it worse.

8TH AUGUST

Brain bouncing around like ball in a bucket. Just some of the thoughts it's pinged at me today are:

- Am going to phone Hugh right away and sort things out.
- Should we go to counselling?
- What if he doesn't pick up when I call?
- Is he eating properly?
- What the hell am I supposed to tell the boys if he's away much longer?
- Phone him? You must be joking.
- Did Calvin leave his number?
- I'd *never* get him to counselling.
- Where *is* he?
- How much is a face lift?
- I'm going to be on my own forever.
- Where are we going to get any money without the upholstery?
- Fine. Forever is absolutely *fine* by me.
- Looking forward to it, actually.
- Someone else can pick up after him.
- I'm going to get us some *pumpy* soap.
- I never wanted anyone else.

It's all very tiring, and I can completely understand why people talk about keeping busy when they're upset. Without backfilling all that emotion with some hard work you'd simply topple over.

It hasn't escaped my notice either that my oozing guilt and sadness where Hugh is concerned has turned into something grittier, like a surprise mouthful of sand at the beach. Little grains of anger and resentment that catch one's teeth and must be ground upon. Who says it's all my fault? And never mind the impact on me – what about the boys? What about money? Of course we're not on the breadline, but it's rather like trying to keep a vast horde of zombies at bay with a kitchen knife – you can dispatch the ones just about to eat you but you haven't a hope of reaching the ones behind, pressing forward, licking their mouldy lips... Tony's rent helps a bit, but without the upholstery I'll have only my fists to rely on, and Lord knows I've never been much good with them.

I haven't *neglected* our marriage. How could I have thought that? Haven't I tried to talk to him, help him, support him? Verbally sometimes, but silently always, keeping his feet free from bindweed and brambles, staking his limbs and mulching and watering as a good gardener does without even thinking, so that all he had to do was get on with his growing? And wasn't he grateful for this too? But that was then. When the soil was rich and right. Here, it's as if he's waterlogged or diseased, not just resistant to my tending, but seeming to sicken further at the lightest touch, so that I wonder if I actually encourage it. Maybe my sort of love – busy, background, patient, forgiving – isn't as OK as I thought it was. Not kind, but indulgent. Not accepting, but weak. The sort of love that a proper feminist would burn aloft with her bra. What, no thought for the money? No thought for the kids? You're not a wife, you're a *doormat*. Maybe the self-reliance I've smugly seen as strength is just cowardice in disguise.

I was itching for some sort of action but had not the first clue what it should be. So I did what all sensible people do under these circumstances and turned to Google. Even though I knew it wasn't infallible. ("What is the hottest thing on Earth?", I typed in once, when Pete wanted to know if it was magma or something else. The online discussion was lively, but everyone seemed agreed that the essential components were two girls, blonde, busty, preferably twins.)

I'd only got as far as "What to do when your husband—" before the miseries of a million wives sprang up for me to choose my own from. What to do when your husband says you're fat, dies, calls you names... For a minute I saw them all, these unhappy women, poring over the pages that the algorithms spat out for them, desperate for a little hope and solidarity. It was with some trepidation I added, "leaves you", which turned out to be wise. Keep every text! I was immediately commanded. Print every e-mail! Get the best attorney you can afford! *Oh*, this was American advice. I amended the search for UK results only, but the only difference was fewer exclamation marks.

No no no, I thought. I didn't know quite what information I'd hoped to find, but it certainly wasn't this. Hugh and I weren't splitting up. Yet? Ever? I could only push the whole problem out of sight, like a shirt with a stubborn grass stain shoved into the bottom of the laundry basket, and get on with other things.

Which I did. Before the boys were even up, I'd made a

rather satisfactory celebratory cake for Nick for when he and Rose came back. Then I went upstairs with hammer, crowbar and nails, and turfed Pete out of bed to help me sniff methodically along his floor until the epicentre of the stench was located. It turned out there was no need for any of the tools, as the floorboard in question simply lifted off. Pete produced a torch and shone it into the darkness while we held our breaths against the smell and peered gingerly inside. Then, 'Ohhh,' said Pete, 'I forgot about that.'

"That" was an open egg box, inside which sat six apparently perfect eggs. Pete reached for it eagerly, explaining as he did so that they were homemade stink bombs.

'They've really worked,' he exclaimed proudly. 'You only have to put little holes in them then leave them – see?'

'Any reason,' I asked lightly, backing away from the proffered egg box, 'why you chose your bedroom to store them? Rather than – say – the scullery, or perhaps an outbuilding far, far away?'

'I wasn't *storing* them,' said Pete, rolling his eyes, 'I was *cooking* them. You have to leave them until they *really* smell.'

'Well,' I assured him, 'no one can say the experiment hasn't been a magnificent success, and perhaps we can dispose of it now?'

He considered this for a bit.

'Can't I hold onto it until Dad comes back? When *is* he coming back, anyway?'

Of the two boys, Pete has always looked more like his father. Same unrelenting eyebrows, same frown.

It's been over a week.

'Meant to tell you,' I said, patting his leg, 'Dad called last night. He's... doing some work for Ravi – remember Ravi?'

'Motorbike Ravi?'

'That's it – motorbike Ravi. He's going to make him a kitchen and... some shelves and maybe some tables and stuff. So it'll be a while longer yet, I'm afraid. He said to give you this,' and I took hold of his head and blew a raspberry into his ear. Pete squirmed happily.

'OK,' he said. 'Well, I'll just do some more stink bombs when he's home. Can I go back to bed now?'

Told him he most certainly could not and that I wanted him dressed in ten minutes, then went downstairs with my teeth clenched in grim acknowledgement of the ease with which I'd lied, and the awful necessity of it.

Nick and Rose arrived at tea time, Rose bursting into the kitchen and exclaiming, 'He took the top prize, no less. Absolutely *best* in show and officially brilliant in every way,' she added, taking Nick's face in her hands when he appeared behind her, and kissing him extravagantly.

'Behave,' said Nick fondly, removing her hands and turning to me. 'You all right?' he said.

'Never better,' I said firmly, 'and just thrilled for you – *what* an achievement! I made you a cake – glacé cherries for the conquering hero – come and have some.'

It took only about thirty seconds for the low frequency sound waves from the opening of the cake tin, inaudible to all but cetaceans and young children, to penetrate the ears of offspring and drive them at speed to the kitchen table.

'Lo, Aunty Rose. Lo, Uncle Nick,' they said, eyes glued to the cake, and it struck me how unquestioning they had been over Nick's two-year absence and recent reintroduction to the household. Adult behaviour – unless it impacted on areas of high importance such as food or bedtimes – was just accepted, and I thought how consoling this somehow was. Why wrestle with the whats and whys? It was as it was and it was fine. It certainly looked fine, Rose with her hand on Nick's knee, complaining happily about how it was all very interesting having slates for plates at the awards do, but it did put your teeth on edge when your fork scraped against it, and Nick munching on his cake while engaged in a highly competitive staring competition with Pete. It was all exactly as it used to be, I thought, and was about to cut myself a big slice when, with a lurch, I remembered of course it wasn't – *there was no Hugh* – and dropped the knife with a clatter on the table.

'Whoopsie,' said Billy, as Nick glanced at me sharply.

'OK?' he said.

'Whoopsie indeed!' I said brightly, springing from the table to get a cloth. 'Boys, did you know Nick has won a very important award for his work? Isn't it wonderful? I'm surprised you didn't stay in London, though. Isn't the phone ringing off the hook with clients desperate to get you to design things for them?'

'We wanted to talk to you about that, actually,' said Rose. 'I was too excited to wait. It's the Tree House.'

It didn't take a genius to work out what was coming next, and I had my 'Absolutely yes!' ready before Rose had even asked how I'd feel about Nick helping with it.

'Not just a rebuild of the same, though,' said Nick, clasping his hands on the table. 'You don't go backwards.'

'Quite right,' said Rose, picking a cherry off the cake.

Recognising that no further entertainment would be forthcoming from Nick, or from Rose and me, the boys left the table, while I did my best to tell my brain to concentrate on what Nick was saying. Honestly, it's as if Hugh took all my focus with him when he left. I could only blink a lot and hope for the best.

13TH AUGUST

Woke up with a start, as I'd completely forgotten it was Anna and Steve's dinner party this evening. Every fibre in my being wanted to phone and cancel, but this was the third time she'd invited us and I'd already used up the ill child and flooded kitchen excuses (neither of these true, but conscience slightly eased by the fact that both *had* been true – albeit on entirely different dates). Any excuse presented today, therefore, would have to be escalated to a quite ridiculous urgency and severity to be believed – such as my own death – news of which, I had to admit, would be challenging for me to impart.

'Why on earth are you so set against going?' Rose wanted to know when I said to her this morning there was no getting out of it and would she mind babysitting. I thought for a moment, then directed her to a horror film we'd watched (mostly between fingers) a while ago, in which an evil alien fed on human life forces, hoovering them up and leaving the poor victims all dead and completely desiccated. Other than the poor teeth and green slime, I said, Anna Jenkins was a lot like that.

I realised at that point that I was going to have to call Anna anyway, to let her know Hugh wasn't coming, and decided to pick up the phone straightaway while Rose's cheerful presence could hopefully act as a shield against the inevitable onslaught of negativity from Anna. My cowardly hopes that the phone would go through to the answer machine were dashed when Anna picked up with a typically exhausted-sounding and melancholy 'Hellaaaaaahhh?' In my best and brightest voice, I told her I was very sorry but Hugh wouldn't be able to come this evening as he'd unexpectedly received a large commission from a friend in London (ashamed to say this quite trilled off my tongue).

A profound sigh blew out of the receiver and into my ear, instantly bringing with it an assortment of depressing images: snowy Siberian wastes, weeping orphans, lonely old women abandoned by their husbands...

The day had already been, said Anna, just one thing after another, on top of a terrible night's sleep too, and she wondered if she should actually cancel the whole evening. Hurriedly suppressing my surging heart at this possibility, I said I was sure it would all be wonderful, and apologised again for the inconvenience of an absent Hugh. Was there anything I could do to help? But no, said Anna, maybe her headache *wouldn't* turn into the migraine she was fully expecting it to, and if she didn't rest (as the doctor had specifically ordered), and if she began plucking the quails straightaway, on her own, she should just be ready by eight o'clock, though we'd all have to forgive her exhaustion when we arrived.

I was already beginning to acknowledge, by this point, the certainty that all life was futile and meaningless, and even though I knew very well that any sympathy or concern I offered up to her stretching tentacles would merely draw me ever faster towards them, I was too weakened to resist her, and so succumbed to commiseration with her plight.

'You're sweet,' she said, coughing feebly, 'but you know me – I never complain. Steve's always said so. Anna, he says, if only everyone had the same soldiering-on attitude as you, the world would be a better place.'

I doubted very much that anyone had ever referred to Anna and soldiering-on in the same breath, but I merely expressed the hope that her day would improve, and although I would have leapt at the opportunity to have pins inserted in my eyeballs rather than see her at supper, I dutifully expressed keen anticipation of the latter, and hung up.

I took unusual care in getting ready to go out, as I knew that every lick of mascara and brush of hair would help me – armour-like – to survive the evening. I even put on foundation, after locating it inexplicably in the medicine cupboard, dusty and smelling slightly of Calpol and Wasp-Eze. I stood for a moment looking at myself in the mirror when I'd finished, wondering who I saw before me. I'd always be a mother, but was I still a wife? And if I wasn't going to be a wife anymore, what was going to fill that space? As if heaving great weighty piles of blankets off myself, I tried to lift the wife off my face and work out if there was anyone else underneath. I thought of the photos my father had kept on his bedside table: me in dungarees and wellies grinning through one front tooth; me and my friend Lizzie off Interrailing with shades pushed up on our heads and rucksacks the size of small cars on our backs; or the one Hugh kept in his wallet, me cross-legged in Hyde Park, with fag and can of lager...

I squinted at my reflection, lingered on my wrinkles, and tried to see the photos of the future, but the pages of the album were stubbornly blank.

It was all very curious. On one hand, it made me panicky – like feeling so confident you know where your passport is that you don't even bother to check, and then, when you go to fetch it just before your holiday, discover it isn't there. But this was countered by the tiniest flutter of something I dimly remembered as possibility, followed shortly afterwards by the genius idea that I should cut all my hair off. Was just beginning to get excited about this when Billy came in and asked why my face was orange, which meant the immediate end of further ponderings in my frantic haste to reapply non-orange make-up without being late for dinner.

In the car on the way to Anna's, I recklessly twizzled the stereo knob away from Radio 4 until I found a young person's radio channel – identified as such by the raucous laughter between the two presenters – and decided to dye my hair as well as cut it all off. Why the hell not? Maybe I could start smoking again too. I bet the presenters did. Ah! Lovely fags! How I miss them! Not the hacking cough and foul-smelling clothes so much as the fun of taunting early death...

I would no doubt have arrived at Anna's with my new hair settled upon, twenty Marlboro Lights in my bag and an appointment with a tattoo parlour in my diary, had it not been for the realisation in swift succession that I didn't actually understand a word the trendy radio presenters were saying, how could I have ever *expected* to understand a word the trendy radio presenters were saying, and what I'd thought of as possibility earlier was clearly nothing more than your common or garden midlife crisis. If sense was not immediately talked into myself I would surely end up gate-crashing the boys' future teenage parties in boob tube and miniskirt, handing out hash cookies and calling everyone dude.

I twizzled back to Radio 4 and listened sheepishly for the rest of the journey.

Despite my best efforts to cast an optimistic spin on the evening ahead, a first glance at the guests assembled in Anna's sitting room was not encouraging. Perched side by side on the very edge of the sofa was a couple I recognised vaguely from school, looking rather reedy and earnest. Opposite them was a ruddy-faced man with unusual hair, and next to him, moulded utterly into the contours of his armchair, was Steve. The conversation, thrillingly, seemed to be about creosote.

Introductions were made, I was handed a small glass of wine, and had barely taken a sip before Paul (ruddy-faced man) appeared at my side offering a top-up, whispering conspiratorially that us singletons needed to stick together. I explained that actually I was only a temporary singleton, Hugh being in London, to which Paul responded with a sympathetic, though extremely confusing, 'Course he is.'

'No,' I said, 'he really *is* in London.'

'I understand,' said Paul, nodding maddeningly. 'When my wife went off, my own line was that she'd gone to stay with her sister. I'm not judging here,' he added, lifting his hands into the well-recognised "I surrender" position, 'we've all got to find our own way through.'

I stared at him for a moment, thinking what on earth was I going to have to do to persuade him that Hugh had *not* left me, and then confusing myself with the realisation that there was still no evidence as to whether he had really left me or not, and perhaps Paul was not being obtuse but on the contrary had rather psychically penetrated my brain and extracted this truth without me noticing. Luckily, no further action was required on my part, as Paul had already launched into the story of his divorce – how he couldn't deny he'd been devastated at first, particularly as she'd got custody of the children, but the only word for how he felt about it now was relieved.

'Between you and me,' he said, bending closer, 'I'm having the time of my life. Fighting them off with a stick.'

I did wonder at this point, rather cruelly, if he'd got the stick fighting bit the right way around, but then again, it never ceases to impress me how imaginative women are in what they find attractive in a man – perhaps there was a greater market for red-faced men with unusual hair than I appreciated?

Anna arrived beside us then, wincing loudly as she did so.

'Something up?' asked Paul.

It was really nothing, Anna said. She had hoped no one would notice, but if he was asking then she supposed she should confess that she *was* in agony – her bad ankle – all the standing up she'd been doing that day. Not that she was complaining. She was so glad to have everyone to dinner; well, nearly everyone, she added pointedly in my direction – she was known for nothing if not her hostessing – and there was no amount of pain she could not withstand if it meant giving others a happy evening.

She paused to give us a brave smile, and I found to my great surprise that my usual tolerance towards her – reluctant, but still robust – had suddenly vanished in a flash of frustration.

'How awful for you,' I said coolly. 'How long have you had it?'

'My bad ankle?' said Anna happily. 'Oh – years and years. And years. After a while, you just get used to the constant pain.'

'What does the doctor say?'

'Oh, totally incurable. Absolutely nothing to be done.'

'But what *is* it, exactly?'

'Can never remember the name,' said Anna, 'it's terribly rare. A syndrome. Totally incurable.'

I was shocked to hear myself say at that point that I had studied orthopaedics extensively in my youth and perhaps I could help?

'Orthopaedics, you say?' said Anna uneasily.

'Oh, yes,' I said, 'with – strangely enough – a particular interest in feet and ankles. Tell me,' I added, peering down at her shoes, 'where is the *precise* location of the pain?'

'Well...'

'Whereabouts *exactly* in the joint?'

'It's hard to...'

'The obvious possibility is *Taraxacum officinale*, of course, but – from what I can see from here at least – you're not presenting the inflammation one would expect with that condition. Which leads us to consider *Urtica dioica* – are you experiencing much *stiffness?*'

Paul and I looked at her expectantly, while I wondered if she knew her Latin plant names and hoped rather guiltily that she didn't.

'So sorry,' said Anna, blinking rapidly. 'Really must... the beans.'

And off she sped from the room, as light on her feet as a young mountain goat.

It wasn't long after this that we were summoned to the table ('Government orders,' said Steve, with an infuriating, complacent jolliness), where I was placed between him and Leon – the husband of the earnest couple – who opened the conversation with the query as to whether *I* used creosote in my garden? He had been very surprised to discover that Anna and Steve still did, having thought the dangers to both health and environment had been more than adequately detailed in the specialist press. Not the popular press, obviously, but we all had a responsibility these days to inform ourselves about those subjects that are so often suppressed by capitalist lobbying. Didn't I think?

He spoke so quickly that the pause I left before replying was taken up entirely with waiting for my brain to finish digesting the words that had poured into my ears, and nothing whatsoever to do with careful consideration of the final question itself, though I tried very hard to disguise this with slow frowning nods.

My initial elation at the certain knowledge that we had *never* used creosote soon dissipated with the realisation that this was purely as a result of luck, not judgement, and that a single glance at the contents of even *one* of Jo's trigger sprays would betray the fact that ours was a woefully ecologically illiterate household. I glanced at Leon's grave expression and could practically hear him saying sadly that I'd let him, my family, my country and my planet down, but worst of all I'd let *myself* down.

I told him feebly that we were pretty good at recycling, and that my sister-in-law *always* bought organic, at which Anna – opposite Leon – said how lucky my sister-in-law was to have the choice between organic and non-organic. She, on the other hand, had no such luxury, as she was *extremely* sensitive to chemicals and if so much as a single factory farmed sprout touched her lips she would suffer for *days* afterwards.

'Honestly,' she said, shaking her head, 'you wouldn't believe the cost of it all. You'd think there would be some sort of government support for sufferers like me; I can't buy anything that isn't entirely made from 100% natural ingredients and I don't think any reasonable person would deny that I have a disability – *just* like being blind or in a wheelchair, or whatever. But is there an allowance for me? Is there any financial support?' She trailed off, quite overcome.

I found myself instinctively reaching out a hand to restrain Hugh from his inevitable outrage at this astonishing speech, only to remember just too late that he wasn't sitting beside me. But Steve, who has never to my knowledge deviated from a flatline of equability, merely responded to my grasping of his knee with an unsurprised 'Hmmm?' Though partly exasperated by this (did the man *ever* wake up?) I was extremely grateful for it too, as I was able to turn my attention to him and away from his wife.

About half-way through pudding, it came to my attention that Paul was well down the road of roaring drunkenness. He'd already passed reckless outspokenness (the law was a bitch and so was his wife), and judging by the fact that, when I moved my foot away from the table leg, the table leg moved back to my foot, he'd hurtled through light flirting and had just arrived at inappropriate and unwelcome romantic advances. I felt rather sorry for him, but that did not negate the need for action, so I tucked both feet briskly under my chair and asked Marsha (wife of Leon) about her children.

As she spread her fingers across her upper chest, which only ever signals great emotion, it became immediately clear that Marsha was one of those mothers who adore their children in private as well as in public. As someone who struggles to muster more than a confused sort of affection for mine in either sphere for much of the time, I always view mothers like Marsha with a mixture of awe, envy, and deep depression. They were her absolute world, she said. She lived for the holidays, when they were home every day and she could spend every waking moment with them.

'I expect,' I said to her faintly, 'you do lots of lovely activities together? Gluing and baking, etc?'

'Oh, yes!' she exclaimed. 'There just aren't enough hours in the day!' On a roll of masochism now, already certain of the answer I would receive, I asked if they had a TV. 'Oh, no!' she laughed. When the world was so full of opportunity and adventure, why would they need a TV?

An image of Billy popped into my head then, when I'd gone to get him off the telly one night and found him clinging, gibbon-like, to the arm of the sofa in resistance, remote control stuck down the front of his pants. But I was saved from more miserable perusal of this by the extraordinary sight of Paul bursting into tears.

'I *miss* them,' he wailed. 'I miss them so much, and the bitch won't let me see them more than what I do, and that smug fucker Simon gets to do *my* fucking job. *My* job! *My* kids!'

It was like pushing your trolley around a corner in the supermarket and stumbling upon hell's gaping maw. We all stared at him aghast, until Marsha said, distraught, 'Oh, you poor man. You poor, poor man!' And put her arms around him. Then I went to find some kitchen roll and Leon went to squat beside Paul's chair, while Steve and Anna gazed at each other in bewilderment.

I would have been mortified at such distress in *anyone*, but in a man, a near stranger, in the middle of a dinner party? It ripped the heart right out of me.

His drunkenness was such that, not only could he do no more than weep and say over and over, in the most pitiful way, my kids, *my* kids, but he got stuck in the loop of it. And as it became clear that he would probably continue in this way forever, the three of us who had been trying to comfort him had no choice but to look at one another slightly awkwardly with the unspoken question as to what on earth we were going to do now? But I am nothing if not an expert in alcoholic excess – other people's and, less infrequently than I'd like to admit, my own – and I turned to Anna and said I really thought I'd better drive him home and where did he live?

'Next door,' said Anna crossly. 'I only invited him this morning, to make up the numbers after you called about Hugh.'

So Marsha, Leon and I got poor Paul to his feet and, between us, half-carried him out of the Jenkins's house and into his own, Marsha and I exchanging sorrowful glances at the bare and grubby rooms we passed through on our way upstairs.

Paul had stopped crying by this time, and was actually not far from passing out as we heaved him onto his bed. Leon stood quietly in the doorway while Marsha and I took off Paul's shoes, covered him with a blanket, and generally busied ourselves with his comfort, as mothers just do. I went to find a bucket and a glass of water to put beside him, and Marsha took off his watch and laid it carefully on his bedside table, then we each sat on a side of the bed for a moment looking at him.

'Do you think we should put him in the recovery position?' whispered Marsha. We both thought that was a good idea, and were about to turn him over when he suddenly sat bolt upright and stared at each of us, blurry-eyed, in turn.

'You the marry one?' he slurred at Marsha.

'Yes, I'm the married one,' said Marsha.

Paul considered this, swaying slightly. 'You stay married then. OK? Stay married to the creosote man. OK? Don't do what I got done to.'

'OK, Paul,' said Marsha. 'Yes. Don't worry. I'll stay married.'

He then blinked at me.

'You the single one?' he said.

Had the strangest desire at that point to shout *I don't know!*, but luckily recognised it was not quite the time.

'Not single, no,' I said.

His eyelids were drooping now.

'No chance of a snog, then?'

'It's a lovely offer,' I said, 'but no snogs, I'm afraid.'

'Worth a try,' he said, and promptly fell asleep.

We arrived back at Anna and Steve's to find the table completely cleared. Steve had returned to his armchair and was reading the paper, and we discovered Anna in the kitchen – elbow-deep in the sink, not washing-up so much as banging pots and pans together under the water.

Marsha was just beginning to say why didn't we give her a hand, when Anna cut her off.

'You'd better all go,' she said coldly, her back resolutely turned to us. 'It's all completely ruined and I'm too upset to say another word about it.'

With quite astonishing generosity, Marsha rushed over

to Anna, put a gentle hand on her shoulder, and was again about to speak when Anna shook her off, and, having apparently changed her mind about not saying another word, launched into a tirade against Paul.

'You try and do something *kind*,' she said, 'and invite someone into your home, and they repay you with that sort of behaviour! It's rude, and what's more it's selfish, *desperately* selfish. Does he think he's the only one with problems? What about me? I can't begin to tell you how much I've got on my plate at the moment! I'm permanently exhausted, and Steve doesn't lift a finger, but do I complain? Do I indulge in the sort of drunken attention-seeking that Paul does? My kids, my kids,' she said in a horrible sing-song voice. 'He needs to pull himself together and get on with it like the rest of us!'

Felt suddenly that I couldn't bear to stay in that house a moment longer.

'Marsha, Leon,' I said, 'it's been a real pleasure. Anna,' I added in a much, much frostier tone, 'thank you for a ... an evening.'

I collected my bag from the sitting room, and said goodbye to Steve, who responded affably with a thank you for coming. Could not work out if he was unaware of his wife's outburst in the kitchen, or simply untouched by it; either way it propelled me even faster out of the door.

Once back in the car, I wound down all the windows and drove faster than I should have done. I felt homesick, desperately wanting to be back amongst my own things, with two little boys whose sleeping heads I could not wait to kiss, and the house all lit up with the glow of Nick and Rose's refound relationship, or what I *hoped* was their refound relationship.

It's as if, I thought, every couple is a planet, each with its own atmosphere and ecology – some so lush and rich in nutrients that a visit can only leave you warmed, nourished and uplifted, while others are barren and airless, or swept by toxic winds, or blackened with pitch and ashes...

To my surprise, I felt a rush of sympathy towards Anna. Wouldn't anyone be driven to hypochondria and chronic complaining with a partner that... that *absent*? As for Paul, cast out from his planet, adrift and alone in deep, deep space, was that where I was heading? I felt a wave of panic that persisted despite the rational part of my brain telling me not to be so melodramatic. Wasn't I pretty sure Hugh and I were *not* splitting up? And even if we did, weren't there plenty of people I knew who had survived a separation successfully – some of them positively *thriving*? Look at Juliet, for example. There was that strange business with Tony (*must* ask her about that), but otherwise wasn't she happy? Or OK? Ish?

But it was no good – I could feel my heart pounding.

By the time I turned into the drive, I was utterly resolved. Never mind "Don't phone" – I bloody well would.

14TH AUGUST

In a minute. That's what I kept saying for most of the morning. I'd call in a minute, when I'd worked out exactly what I was going to say. I needed a clear head, and could only achieve that once I'd got the boys to tidy their rooms, phoned the chimney sweep, mended Pete's trousers, cleaned the oven, refilled the birdbath, and lopped back the buddleia. I was just thinking there was no better time to have a look at the U-bend under the kitchen sink, the leak from which I've been ignoring for a fortnight at least, when I happened to glance out of the window to see Pete and Billy collapsed in laughter on the trampoline, their hair all gilded by sunlight, and something about this sight set off a very firm voice in my head, telling me to *get on with it*. Went to find my phone.

The only thing I was certain of was that I wasn't going to play games. I wasn't going to play nonchalant, or amend my responses according to his, or employ any other self-protective contrivance. We were too old and too married for that sort of teenage skittishness; besides, I'd never been much good at it. It was crunch time.

It seemed very strange that my phone made no acknowledgement of the altered circumstances between myself and the primary contact within it. I felt bizarrely hurt that it offered up Hugh's number exactly as it would were I about to phone with a request to pick the boys up from school, or pop to the post office. It could at least, I thought foolishly, have sympathised with a sad face emoji, or that "Oh dear" sound it makes when a text fails to send. I was frankly disappointed. I thought we were closer than that.

When a text pinged in from Hugh just as I was about to dial him, it caught me so off guard that my first thought was what was he bothering me for when I had an important call to make?

Can we talk? it said.

It hadn't occurred to me once that he would make contact first. I stared at the screen, thinking of him staring at his screen, a great echoing space between us.

Now's a good time, I replied, and moved instinctively to the French windows, as if I needed the best light possible for the call that was coming.

'Hi,' said Hugh.

'Hi.'

'Are you OK?' he said. He sounded calm, controlled, concerned; like a well-trained paramedic.

'I've been better, Hugh. Are you going to tell me what's going on?'

'Yes,' he said firmly. 'I need to apologise first – you've had enough of apologies, but I've got to say it anyway. It can't go unsaid, no matter how you hear it. It was a shit thing to do, and a cowardly one, to go off like that. I just lost it. First the field, then Rose bouncing in with her bright ideas – what sort of man am I? What sort of father? What sort of husband? What sort of provider? I couldn't stand it. And I couldn't stand the fact that I couldn't stand it. What a *prick*.'

He'd gone from nought to sixty in about five seconds.

It was like watching a supercharged centrifuge at work, turning faster and faster until such speed was reached that Hugh's feelings about himself – chemically sealed inside his brain – got spun right out of him.

'I don't think it was cowardly,' I said quietly. 'Not exactly ideal, but not cowardly either. You didn't know what else to do.'

'So what?' he said. 'That's no excuse. I ran away. I *ran away.*'

The repetition was clearly designed to persuade me of the dreadfulness of this crime, but he was sabotaged by the force of his own vitriol, which washed my own clean away. He as good as reprieved himself.

'Put that aside if you can, Hugh,' I said. 'Let's just look forwards. What are we going to do? Where actually are you for a start?'

'I'm at Ravi's,' he said. Just as I'd said to Peter, I thought. An inadvertent truth. But really, where else would he go? A welcoming face and a free bed – wasn't that exactly what best friends were for? 'I can stay as long as I want.'

'OK,' I said. 'Do you know how long that will be?'

He paused quite a while before answering, and his voice was altered when he did. Calm again, and concentrated, but jerky, as if his throat kept putting obstacles in the way of his words.

'It's not a time,' he said. 'It's a purpose. I won't come back as I am. I've only realised since I left. You put your shoulder to the wheel and get stuck there – *I've* been stuck there. Keep the wheel moving, that's all you think about. That's the only thing that matters, keep it moving no matter what. And because your head is down all you see is your feet trudging. It always feels like now but it isn't.

Years pass. Your kids are growing up and out and into themselves but they're stuck as background chatter, just mess on the stairs to you. Your wife's slipping out of focus but you don't notice because everything else is slipping out of focus too, and even if – very, very occasionally – you recognise this, you dismiss it as an unavoidable cost, just another overhead. You never understand that it's a *loss*. You honestly believe you're doing your very best for those around you. It wouldn't matter what they felt even if you made the effort to ask yourself, let alone them; all they're allowed to be is grateful, considerate, quiet.'

Had I written this speech myself, it could not have been more exactly what – for seven years – I'd wanted to hear. Realising what he was like to live with, or rather without. Acknowledging his accountability, and even recognising the need for change; it was all there. The full road to Damascus, scales-falling-from-his eyes miracle. But I didn't feel one bit as I had assumed I would. No surge of love or relief, no whoops of joy. I simply heard the words and was glad. That was it.

Hugh mistook my silence for distress.

'Fuck – you're not crying, are you?' he said. 'Please don't tell me you're crying.'

'No, I'm just thinking. It's a lot to take in. Well, not take in exactly. It's hearing you say it that's the surprise. Don't get me wrong, Hugh – it's a good shock. I'd have you leave all over again if I knew this was what would come out of it.'

I heard him sigh. Across the lawn, a squirrel scampered through the canopy of the Tree House oak then paused, confused, expecting a branch that was no longer there. He crouched to jump, turned around, approached and paused again.

'I've stopped drinking,' Hugh said then. There was a quiet pride in this statement, and a gift too, because wasn't this, for the first time, real proof that he *meant* what he said? That change had actually begun?

'Hugh, that's – *thank* you. Genuinely. And well done. But – so, what comes after that?'

'First off I need your permission,' said Hugh. 'If I stay away for a while, can you hold the fort? I'll send money, but – I know it's a lot I'm asking.'

I found myself raising my eyebrows, and nearly let loose a small snort. 'No offence, Hugh, but that's my speciality. Holding the fort. It's all I feel I ever do. I've already told Pete that you're working for Ravi, luckily, so we can stick with that line where the boys are concerned. For the moment, at least. I suppose it all depends how long you're gone...'

The squirrel was trying a new tactic. He'd retreated into the depth of the oak but was now pelting towards the end of the snapped branch, as if recklessness would make the missing parts of it reappear. He stopped abruptly, just in time, then stood up on his back legs in total bewilderment.

I'd stung Hugh with my comment about holding the fort – I could feel it somehow down the line. I found I wasn't all that sorry. He may have had an epiphany about himself, but it was still muddy around the edges, I realised. Still some painful details about life here that needed pointing out to him.

'Understood,' he said, clearing his throat.

'Yes to the money, though,' I continued. 'We'll need that. Your MOT's due, by the way. And I'll tell any customers you're away till further notice, shall I?' I seemed to have turned into some sort of sniffy secretary. 'Carry on with what you were saying. How you're not coming back as you are?'

‘Right,’ said Hugh uncertainly, perhaps sensing my sudden pince-nez and shorthand pad at the ready. ‘Look. You said you might leave – I understand that. You want a better man. I want to *be* a better man, OK? I’ve just got to work out how to do it and I can only do that on my own. Get money, save house, stop being a prick – that’s the goal.’

‘Get money, save house, stop being a prick… That’s quite a list, Hugh.’

‘Don’t you agree?’

‘Yes, but it’s the how…’

‘That’s for me to worry about. All I need from you is what you’re giving me already – time and space. It’ll be worth it – I promise you. And if I can’t make it work, I’ll divorce you, OK?’

‘OK. Great.’

‘I don’t mean it like that,’ he said. ‘I mean if I can’t give you and the boys the life you deserve I’ll let you find one elsewhere. I’ll insist on it, in fact.’

The squirrel had given up. He sloped sadly back up to the canopy.

‘Hugh?’ I said. ‘Two things. Firstly, just so we’re clear, I don’t want you back as you’ve been either. You can have the time and the space – I don’t know how much of it, but I give it willingly for now. I’d very much like a better man. But it would help to know,’ I said, remembering the night of the Jamboree, and my outpouring to Tony, and the doubt that kept on niggling, ‘if you do still actually love me. That is to say, is it love that’s driving all this, or just duty?’

‘Wife,’ said Hugh, instantly and decisively, ‘this is love. Do you hear me? This is love.’

I heard.

15TH AUGUST

I did. And I was relieved. Again, not jumping for joy, but pleased and relieved. The problem I had wasn't with the motivation behind the challenge Hugh had set himself, but the challenge itself. Get money, save house, stop being a prick – in my eyes this could not be a more inherently contradictory combination. Like get dressed, get undressed. Or have children, refrain from drinking. The primary reason Hugh is a prick is precisely *because* of trying to get money and save the house. As long as the latter two are key to his plans, I can't see how he'd ever change the former. With the lottery odds so unkind, and bank robbery still illegal as far as I am aware. How much would we actually need? Lord – hundreds of thousands, millions if we were really going to get the place in order.

No. There's only one real solution. That I've long known, but never dared suggest. Sell the house, Hugh, I've said over and over in my head. There's no other way – sell the house.

To be fair to him, he made it clear very early on that he would never sell, but though I thought at the time I understood, I didn't. I had no idea.

It was one of my first weekend visits up here – I remember it exactly – and we were driving back to London in the rain. Before leaving, Hugh's father had wanted

Hugh's advice; not on his tax return, or a possible birthday present for Rose, or any other sane subject, but the possible purchase of some wallabies. Still fresh-faced and surprised by Narwhal eccentricities at that time, I was curious, and asked Hugh about it when we were on the motorway. He said the wallabies were the last in a list of utterly useless ideas his father had come up with to save money, the equally useless ones he'd had to *make* money having long since been exhausted.

'What are they going to do?' I asked, wondering at unknown wallaby skills; perhaps you could put them in a big wheel to generate electricity?

'They're excellent grazers, apparently,' said Hugh. 'He thinks we can use them to keep the grass down. Never mind that they're about a £150 a pop, or that they don't like dogs, or that they escape at the drop of a hat and seem hell-bent on getting run over, or that we'd have to feed them in the winter.'

'Did you tell him all that?'

'Absolutely no point,' said Hugh, checking his mirror and pulling into the fast lane. 'I stopped bothering with that way back, with the mushrooms I think it was. He's like Jack with his bloody beanstalk – you put in the magic seed, go to bed, wake up in the morning, and abracadabra, you have a thriving mushroom farm slash campsite slash flock of wallaby lawnmowers. It doesn't even occur to him that these things won't work. He thinks he wants me to "discuss" them with, but really it's just a pair of ears to splurge into.'

'But if they keep going wrong… doesn't he realise perhaps it's not the best way forward?'

'Fuck, no,' said Hugh, with a short laugh that he seemed instantly to regret. 'I suppose you could say it's not his fault. They've all been like that, the Narwhals. Because before the money went it really was like planting a bean – they'd have an idea, present it to some poor bastard below stairs who'd have to put it into action, then crow about its success over the port. He's just stuck around 1908.'

I was quiet for a moment, listening to the unbalanced squeak squeeeaak, squeak squeeeaak of the windscreen wipers.

'He certainly doesn't act like a man who's worried about money,' I said, thinking about his appreciative sighs of satisfaction after Sunday lunch, the way his specs seemed to snooze gently at the end of their cord on his stomach.

'That's because he's not,' said Hugh. 'There's still just about enough sand for him to stick his head into. Most of the land and property went while his father was alive, but there was still stuff in the house. A small Stubbs. Porcelain. You'd go to school one day and come back to find a space where something used to be, although you couldn't always remember what that something was. Neither of them would say a word about it, but there'd be workmen around for a while, and we'd get steak.'

It sounded rather like he'd been repeatedly burgled by his own parents.

'Does it piss you off?' I said. 'All the heirlooms and whatever getting sold?'

'I don't give a shit about the heirlooms,' he said. 'It's what happens when they've all gone that bothers me. Do me a fag, will you.'

I lit two and passed one over to him, studying his profile as I did. I saw the anxiety there, but was surprised he hadn't mentioned the blindingly obvious way to get rid of it.

'But Hugh,' I said, 'at the end of the day, it's just a house. If there's not enough money to look after it, then, well, you just sell.'

At this, he began a slow head shake – stretching the ligaments of his neck so far that I thought for a second he was taking the opportunity to do some exercises, his face blank in concentration. Then he stopped, rolled his hands forward on the steering wheel and said, 'You do not sell the house. You never sell the house.'

The penny dropped, and I fell silent. Sometimes people make statements, but sometimes statements make people, and in the case of the latter there's absolutely nothing anyone can do. I'd seen it before, of course, as we all have – owners squeezing the last drops of life from already wrung out pets, my widowed aunt and her dead husband's beloved double bass... It does so often involve the trouble with letting things go.

'You might want to think about that,' said Hugh, frowning through the windscreen, 'looking forward.'

In those early days, a certain proportion of my brain was a finely tuned radar – sweeping all boyfriend words/actions for relationship status updates. I considered this a disability and an embarrassment, as one might a colostomy bag. Even as a bit of me therefore clasped the "looking forward" part of his words to my leaping heart (because *clearly* this was as good as a proposal), another bit tapped its finger briskly at "you might want to think about that". But pah, how hard could it be, I thought happily, kicking off my shoes and resting my feet on the dashboard. I was capable, wasn't I? I could learn how to get the feathers and the beaks off pheasants. I could run that house. I could live anywhere, do anything, I thought, skipping through the soft focus shampoo advert meadows of my girlishness, as long as I was with him.

So naive! Had I been able to take this girl to one side and explain to her the true nature of what she was so eager to take on – the work of it, the constant lack of money and any sense of security, the withering of the man she adored into a husk of his former self – she'd still have laughed in my face.

I had an awful thought in the night. Maybe that's exactly why Hugh chose me – because he knew I was a coper. A cheerful person. Someone who'd stand by him no matter what life with him turned out to be. *He* knew what was ahead of us. *He* knew what to expect. While I was wondering dreamily if our future children would have his hair, he was assessing my stoicism, measuring me up for work. The house came first then, and I can only think it always will. Look at his list, after all – save house, stop being a prick. *It's the wrong order, Hugh.*

No. You can take the man out of the house, but I just don't think you can take the house out of the man. Which doesn't bode well for any of us. Doesn't bode well at all.

16TH AUGUST

'So,' said Nick, once he'd finished explaining the plans on the table before us, 'what do you think?'

'It's extraordinary,' I said, shaking my head. 'I haven't even got the words...'

'A lot of it's been in his head for years,' said Rose. 'He's always hankered after having a go at it.'

As well as the plans, Nick had done some of those very helpful computer-generated pictures to show what it would look like when finished, and I picked these up to study them more closely.

There was our lovely Tree House oak, Photoshopped in somehow, but there seemed to be only clouds where the Tree House itself had been – clouds on the west side, the orchard on the east, fields and hills on the south and, most astonishingly of all, a tiny doll's house version of the house on the north. All reflected in the mirrored surface of a giant cube that was at once there, and not there at all, like some sort of vast and bewildering trompe l'oeil.

I blinked at it, then felt that rare and thrilling dislocation everyone feels when their brains envelop something unwieldy, like a snake swallowing a suckling pig. I love it when this happens. My imagination started out spectacularly beige, laid out by my mother with a set square when I was a child. New things, different things: they didn't horrify or frighten her – she was never a book-burning sort – she just didn't see the point. Change was untidy. Novelty was illogical. Experiment and exploration were a waste of time. Why bother with the scenic route when you could take the motorway instead? Four Brighton townhouses she renovated around us, and each was a perfect facsimile of the other. Even the paint colours were the same, so that these houses – particularly the last one – felt as if their windows had not been opened for a hundred years.

If it wasn't for Hugh, my vision might have stayed as magnolia, as resolutely meat and two veg, as hers. But his arrival in my life was like that of some great shaggy dog leaping into small stagnant waters, whipping the still strata of mud and slime and weed into broiling whirlpools, trampling the reeds, lapping noisily, sniffing furiously, snapping at the flies – a glorious, fearsome shaking-awake for a girl like me. The set square snapped. The world widened. If it wasn't for him I'd have looked at those plans with exactly the same suspicion a great many people showed for his furniture.

'I just wish it was already built,' I said to Nick earnestly. 'I just want to get at it, and walk around it and – oh! It's going to look different at different times of day, with the light and the seasons! It's always going to be new. Oh, Nick, when will it be done?'

He smiled at me, not triumphantly, not smugly, but as if he'd just proposed the trip of a lifetime and was thrilled to have me along. Self-made men, in my vast experience of knowing hardly any of them, tend to follow a common path that begins with ferocious hard work, ambition and self-belief, and then, when sustained success is achieved, diverges. Some fatten themselves on overconfidence, tossing out opinions us commoners should be honoured to receive, like alms to a bunch of peasants. Others, on the contrary, grow leaner. How lucky we all were, I thought, that Nick was one of the latter. The more he accomplished, the more modest, the more generous he became.

'*And*,' said Rose, 'people will be able to stay there. Just think! You'd come to visit Narwhal Hall, and you could actually *stay the night* in the Tree House. A Tree House designed by award-winning architect Nick Lambert. We reckon £100 per night at least. Very simple inside but cutting edge – everything the latest and the best – you know the sort of thing.'

'£100...' I breathed. Did this gift never stop giving? But something occurred to me. 'It's Hugh's house though. We can't just decide on it without him.'

Rose folded her arms abruptly and glared at Nick, who received this so equably it was clear her annoyance had nothing to do with him. She increasingly reacts like this whenever Hugh is mentioned, instantly aflame with outrage at his leaving – allegedly on my behalf. It worries me for all sorts of reasons I haven't even begun to unpick yet...

'I've had the all clear,' said Nick.

Really? When Hugh was so protective about decisions concerning the house – had he really handed over permission just like that? And for such a wild design too? He was so conservative about everything here, all his shaggy dogness so brutally trimmed and tamed; could he really be in support?

'Did you actually speak to him?' I asked.

Nick shook his head. 'Text, e-mail.'

'But you're sure he's in favour?'

'He didn't say,' said Nick. 'He said to do what we want as his views shouldn't count if he's not here; he said not even to ask him for them. About anything, not just the Tree House.'

Not permission then, but abdication. A fair decision on Hugh's part, I thought, but a costly one. It would have pained him a great deal, and just for a second I felt for him, this unhappy king forced for now at least to throw down his crown.

'Right,' I said, wondering if Nick had noticed any distress in Hugh. 'Did he say anything else at all? About... anything else?'

I searched Nick's face for any crumb of news he may have picked up, possibly without even noticing, like the police do to witnesses in TV dramas – anything at all, however small, that might help us? But unlike the witness, who always ends up passing some apparently trivial, but actually crucial, gem to the detective, Nick could only shake his head again.

'Look,' he said. 'You and me, we've not talked about what's going on with him, and I've not talked about it with her much either,' he nodded at Rose, 'because she just flies off the fucking handle. You don't talk, she doesn't talk, and he doesn't talk either. He's got his head down somewhere, on walkabout if you like, that's what I'm thinking. And the more space he gets, the quicker he sorts his fucking head out.'

'Does that mean,' I said, 'that you think he's going to come back?'

Nick considered this. 'Yeah,' he said. 'Yeah, I do, if you're asking. It's not a fucking walkabout if you don't come home at the end of it, is it?'

Just then, the front door clanged.

'Shit,' said Rose, eyes wide. 'That'll be Ian. I asked him to come over. We've got to tell him about all this,' she said, pointing at the Tree House plans, 'and try and get him onside. Come in, Ian!' she yelled.

Such was the conspiratorial urgency of her tone that it completely swamped all thoughts of Hugh. She and I began trying hastily to rearrange ourselves into positions of "nothing to see here" nonchalance, while Nick watched us in amusement. But it was clear from the way Ian hovered in the kitchen doorway that, not so much despite our efforts but no doubt because of them, we looked as guilty as hell.

'Ian!' I said brightly. 'Lovely to see you. You remember Nick? Come on in and have a seat.'

'Morning,' he said cagily, edging forwards, frowning at each of us in turn. 'I'm better standing, if it's all the same.'

He'd been in the room for less than ten seconds, but had already managed to irritate Rose.

'No one's going to *bite* you, Ian,' she said. 'We just want to show you our plans for the Tree House, so that you know what's going on. Out of *courtesy*,' she added threateningly.

Nick shot her a quick glance, then stood and put his hand on Ian's stiff shoulder.

'We want to know what you think,' he said, looking at him steadily. 'You've known this place longer than anyone in this room – it's important.'

The alarm which crossed Ian's face when Nick touched him had softened slightly at this weighty appeal to his importance in the household, but I didn't think for a second that we were out of the woods yet – nowhere near.

'I'll talk you through the plans, Ian,' said Nick, applying

just enough pressure to Ian's shoulder to move him over to the table. 'Rose, shift over, please.'

The man was masterful! Ian gave a self-congratulatory little blink as Rose's features darkened. She would not like being offered up to Ian like that, I thought, even if she knew very well the wisdom of the sacrifice. She moved her chair grudgingly, tight-lipped and silent.

Was I right in thinking, I wondered, as Nick began to talk, that he was describing the new Tree House in an ever so slightly different way to Ian than he had to me? He had stressed to me (I was flattered to note) the innovation of the design, had lingered on the juxtaposition between the permanence of the structure and the transience of the images reflected in each surface, had even nodded to my inevitable anxieties about wildlife by explaining how he was working on a way to stop birds flying into those same surfaces. But Ian was hearing a different story.

'...aluminium,' Nick was saying. 'Strong but lightweight, easy to install on site. And the bell will be here, higher up in the canopy, with a crossbeam here.'

I looked at Ian, eager to see if Nick's focus on the structure of the Tree House would distract him from the radical look of the thing, as Nick had no doubt intended, but he was inscrutable, merely nodding as Nick spoke.

'Got any questions?' Nick said then. 'Anything unclear?'

Ian shook his head. 'No,' he said. 'No, it's all clear to me, thank you.'

We stared at him expectantly.

'So,' said Nick, for the second time that morning, 'what do you think?'

Ian cleared his throat, and I winced as he then took a very, very small step away from the table.

'What does Mr Hugh say about it?' he asked eventually.

'Oh, he's *very* keen,' said Rose quickly. 'Loves it.'

'Right,' said Ian. 'That's what matters, then. If he and you all like the...' he gestured weakly at the plans, '...the big glass... box, then that's all that matters.' And he lifted his chin and straightened himself heroically, like a captain staring fixedly at the horizon as onrushing waters wrap around his legs.

Nick ran his hand through his hair briskly, in ill-disguised frustration. I saw this with some alarm; if *he* didn't know what to do now, then we were lost, as Lord knows I was clueless and Rose was too busy simmering to be of any help whatsoever. Talk about a rock and a hard place – if Ian had taken against the Tree House design, there was no force on earth that could make him change his mind, so what were we to do? Yes, his views were important, but surely we couldn't abandon the whole thing just because he didn't like it? But then if we went ahead without his support, he'd never let us forget it – not maliciously, or even deliberately, but simply because his obstinacy would not permit him to draw even the finest veil over the steel slab of his objection. It was just like when we told him our decision to call our firstborn Peter, not Hugh – a liberating breaking of a heavy chain of tradition from our point of view (one that Hugh would never have agreed to had we been living here at the time), but for Ian a brutal and ignorant severing, his horror at which not only kept him from Pete's christening but has led him ever since to look upon the poor child with a mixture of pity and embarrassment.

But with a short cough, Nick had regained his composure.

'Fantastic!' he said, as if quite overwhelmed by Ian's enthusiasm. 'Thanks for your support – it means a lot,' he added, reaching out his hand to shake Ian's limply proffered fingers.

'Yes, thank you so much, Ian,' I said feebly.

Nick enveloped us all in a broad inclusive smile designed to seal our apparently unanimous agreement, and said to Ian, 'We'll keep you posted. Thanks again.'

We waited until poor Ian had gone with slow, stiff steps out of the kitchen, and we'd heard the front door shut before we each released the stress of the past half hour in our own manner – with sighs, head shakings and, in Rose's case, a short volley of expletives.

'We shouldn't be surprised, Rose,' I said in response. 'You didn't honestly think he'd like it, did you?'

Rose flung her head back and addressed the ceiling rather than me.

'I know, I *know*,' she said, 'it just drives me crazy: the stubbornness, the looking *backwards* all the time, this idea that something can only have value if it's been done before.'

'You've got to hand it to him, though,' said Nick, with a faint smile, 'he's one hell of a nut to crack.'

'But what do we *do*?' I said. 'Do we just go ahead despite him? Poor Ian…'

'Look. Contrary to what you might think, even *I* care about his views,' said Rose with a sigh, 'and if we were unsure about the design then, yes, maybe we'd reconsider, but we're *not* unsure. We couldn't be *more* sure, in fact. So yes, I say we go ahead.'

Nick looked at each of us in turn.

'Agreed?' he said.

'Agreed,' said Rose firmly.

'Oh, Lord… agreed,' said I.

20TH AUGUST

Nick went back to London on Wednesday, but seems to have spent most of his time since then texting Rose. It feels like every ten minutes or so; first you hear the little ping, then you see her beaming at the screen – sometimes dreamily, sometimes mischievously, running her thumb over her lips – and then her fingers start to fly as she replies.

Have to say I've been struggling with this a bit. It's a very intimate sight somehow, and though I try to steer clear when I hear the ping, it often seems to happen when I'm in the room. I go out for fear of intruding, but when I come back I see her, say, standing at the French windows, gazing at the view, or drifting to the sink with a mug, every move slowed by the misty floatiness of one drunk on love. You'd think it would be easier without Nick here, but his presence actually strengthened the dams of the courtship, kept it contained, stopped it surging through the house and soaking everyone right through to the skin.

I genuinely could not be more pleased that they've found each other again, and in one way Rose's wafting about is a delight to see, but in another it feels rather like I'm drowning in their bliss. So much so that I can only think about getting to dry land, not a thought to spare to worry about their relationship, or to ask Rose if she really feels as reunited as she appears to. Not that her answer could be in any way relied upon, of course.

When I first got to know her, it took a while for me to realise she has a phenomenal capacity for lying to herself. Particularly when she wants to feel something more strongly than she actually does. She betrays herself with just a touch of defensiveness, or over-eagerness to persuade *you*, at least, that she truly means what she says. It's never a good idea to confront her, as I've mentioned before. Best to be patient as it passes over, and kind when it comes to an end.

But as I say, I did not have the energy for any close observations this morning. When it took three repetitions to call Rose back from her daydreaming to discover if she wanted any eggs for breakfast, and I noticed my irritation increasing exponentially each time, I thought I'd better get out of the house as soon as possible. I decided to call Juliet, who said yes, she'd love a walk, and we agreed to meet at Ditton in an hour.

Was rather pleased with myself as I put the phone down, as I always am when I realise a decision made hurriedly turns out to tick all sorts of boxes I hadn't spotted before. A walk, I thought, would be the perfect opportunity to see how Juliet was after the strange business with Tony, and to get the boys to have some proper exercise. Millions of birds with one stone!

I went to look for my offspring and found them in the yard. Pete was standing on Tony's sack truck, yelling, 'Come on, child!' as Billy, red-faced but happy, pushed him back and forth between the two workshops.

'Boys,' I said sternly, 'did you ask Tony if you could borrow that?'

With totally unwarranted indignation, they immediately began to clamour that of *course* they had, just as Tony himself came out of his workshop.

I realised as he did so that this was the first time I'd really seen him since my drunken outpouring by the lake, but also that, astonishingly, I felt no embarrassment whatsoever at this recollection. No internal cringing at the newt or even the wailing about Hugh, just a rush of gratitude for his past kindness, and pleasure at seeing him.

'Yup,' he said, smiling at the boys, 'no problem at all. They did ask.'

'You're very kind,' I said, 'thank you. And how are you?'

'Good, yeah, thanks,' he said. 'You?'

The sun was behind him, and I shielded my eyes to see him better as he said this, but his face was just as open as ever – no tilted head or frown of concern, thank God.

'I'm fine,' I replied in kind.

We smiled at each other for a brief moment, then I turned to the boys and said, in a tone designed to brook not a word of dissent, 'Right. We're going for a walk. Go and get your wellies now, please.'

One day, I thought grimly, as they began a vociferous litany of complaint, I really would get them to do what I wanted them to do when I wanted them to do it. No doubt not long after hell had frozen over.

'Not listening,' I said. 'Wellies, please. Now, please,' over and over again until at long last they moped off to the house to fetch them.

'They're keen,' said Tony, with a grin.

'But you know what,' I said, 'they'll be happy as Larry the minute we get there. It's always the same. And they like Juliet, and they *love* Toby, so if I can just get them in the car we'll be home and dry.'

There was a pause, just long enough for Tony to fold his arms and for me to think he wasn't going to reply, when he said, pushing at a stone with his boot, 'If you're seeing Juliet, could you give something to her for me?'

I looked at him in surprise. 'For Juliet? Yes, of course. Have you got it here?'

'Inside,' he said, jerking his thumb towards his workshop. 'Have you got time if I just go and get it?'

'Go for it,' I said, opening up my hands to show the extent of my willingness.

I wouldn't have been nosy enough actually to ask what he was fetching for her, but while waiting for him to come out I couldn't help but be curious as to what it might be, part of me even wondering if it might explain the weirdness between him and Juliet, though I couldn't for the life of me imagine how. A present? An official apology of some sort? With no clue as to the issue it was impossible to guess at what the peace offering was – and who said it was going to be a peace offering anyway?

'It's just this,' he said when he reappeared, handing over a dusty slip of paper with one hand and rubbing the back of his neck with the other.

I didn't want to look at it (nosiness worries again), but it seemed somehow rude to put it in my pocket *without* looking. Luckily, Tony began to explain what it was. I say luckily, but I was distracted by the sound of the boys coming towards us across the yard bickering, so Tony's words were cloudy. I just about grasped that it was to do with the commission he'd been packing up in the crate when I took Juliet to meet him. A coat on a slab? A *quote* on a slab. A Persian poet. For someone's garden. That Juliet had liked.

I didn't remember us talking about his work at all, but

that wasn't as surprising as it might have been, bearing in mind how I'd been focusing so hard on the *unspoken* conversation rather than the spoken one.

He gestured at the piece of paper, encouraging me to look at the words he'd written.

If there is a Paradise on earth, it is this, it is this, it is this.

I looked up at him in wonder, as all at once, like footage of a smashed glass reversed, all the shards of information I'd been puzzling over flew together into a single shimmering fact.

Bloody hell, I thought. They're *in love*.

Juliet was waiting for us when we arrived at Ditton, tapping at her phone with the car door open, and I studied her through the windscreen as I approached. The certainty I'd felt only minutes earlier about her and Tony didn't feel like certainty anymore. My instinct still told me I was right, but now that I re-examined the facts, wasn't it all rather improbable? As far as I knew, they'd only met once. And of course love at first sight is possible, but when you try to imagine the Hollywood pitch for these two – nice but normal middle-aged man meets rather strict and uptight singleton in workshop yard in Herefordshire – well, what *was* I thinking?

Oh, Lord, I thought then, maybe it was all because of the me and Hugh situation, or because of Rose's mooning about? Maybe my brain was just so overwhelmed by the great wave of the latter, and the drought of the former, that I was seeing romance, romance, romance everywhere I bloody well looked? By the time we'd got our wellies on, and gone over to Juliet's car, I'd quite convinced myself this was the case.

Once effusive greetings had been exchanged between Toby and the boys, and the inevitable pleading for a dog of their own had been parried in the traditional fashion (Who's going to look after it? We will! That's what you said about the stick insect. But he was boring. Well how do you know a dog won't be boring too after a while? But he wouldn't be! What about picking up his poo? *Silence*), we'd reached the gate that marked the start of the walk, and I was surprised, as I am every time we go there, by my deep internal sigh of pleasure.

It's a public footpath and bridleway, but it follows the private road within an estate. You walk through an avenue of ancient sweet chestnuts, each one of which could entertain the eye for hours, but, should you have a restless gaze, there is a rising slope and mixed woodland to your right, while to your left the land drops gently away into the most generous of views: houses and church spires, fields and woods and far off peaks you can never remember the names of, and even, right on the brim of the horizon, the tiny high-rise blocks of the distant city. What's more, there are streams for clambering in, or damming up, and best of all as far as the boys are concerned, an old rusty oil drum half hidden behind a lone oak just beyond the second cattle grid.

'You don't mind, do you, Juliet?' I asked, as I tilted the drum onto the ground so that the boys could get into it.

'*Shush,* Toby,' she said, possibly to disguise a certain amount of disapproval of this idea, as he began to bark in confusion at the two pairs of wellies, which were soon all that were visible of the boys in the drum.

Since Hugh left, I feel as if my maternal skills, like just about everything else, have deteriorated. I seem to ricochet between impatience and an overeager attentiveness, snapping at the boys to get out from under my feet one minute and insisting they explain every detail of their Lego creations to me the next. They are too young, and – thank God – too well-balanced for this see-saw to affect them, but it will. If I carry on like this, it will.

It was essential, therefore, that we followed the drum routine as it gave a strong affirmative nod to normality.

'Ready?' I called, peering into the gloom of the drum.

'Ready!' came the muffled reply.

I straightened up and gave the drum a hard push with my foot to set it in motion.

'Aaarrgghh!' screamed the boys happily as they began to roll over each other, Toby barking furiously at – presumably – the monster that was devouring his friends.

'Toby, for goodness' sake, be *quiet*,' said Juliet, snapping a lead onto his collar as Toby sneezed in defeat and darted his eyes up at her sheepishly. 'Stupid dog,' she added softly, stroking him with her free hand.

'Are you dizzy yet?' I called to the tangled wellies, and, on receiving a definite Noooo, continued to push them along the tarmac.

Conversation was not easy with the noise of the drum and the effort it took to push it, and I have to admit I was quite relieved when I heard a weak little voice say, 'Mum, I feel sick.'

Although Pete insisted that he was fine and it was only Billy who wasn't, it was clear from the khaki hue of his face that we'd done enough drum rolling for one day, so I got them to return it to its position behind the oak, and, after a few minutes of dragging their feet, both boys picked up and ran on.

If I wanted to *talk* to Juliet, I thought then, as she let Toby off the lead and he raced off after the boys, now was the time. But this seemed like a spectacularly bad idea. It was as if she'd somehow heard all my thinking about her that morning, as if her forcefield had sensed an intruder and strengthened itself in anticipation. I felt certain that my head would get well and truly bitten off if I so much as whispered a word. But I also knew that either boys or dog could be demanding our attention at any moment, and perhaps because my mouth seemed unable to seize a threatened opportunity, my hand reacted instead, reaching into my pocket and pulling out Tony's piece of paper.

'I nearly forgot,' I said. 'Tony wanted me to give you this. It's what he'd carved on that slab.'

Oh, Juliet! You'd really think that someone who works so hard to hide their feelings would have become skilled at it by now.

She made a noble pretence of taking the paper with impatient disinterest – the sort you feel when accepting a flyer from a determined hand in the street – but her eyes had gripped the paper the moment I produced it. And again, as she read it, I had the strongest sense that the dismissiveness with which she did so, and the brutish way she shoved it, crumpled, into her pocket, were entirely for my benefit, and that, had she been alone, she would have pored and lingered over every stroke and curl of every word.

Just as I realised I was right about her and Tony, I wished with all my heart that I wasn't. For whatever reason, she was clearly as open to the prospect of love as she would have been to a hefty dose of salmonella. She gave a little shake of her head and said briskly, 'Nice of him to write it down for me. It's a lovely quote – don't you think?'

'Lovely,' I said, 'and *very* nice of him to write it down.'

We carried on walking in silence for a while, Juliet squinting hard at the boys in the distance to try and persuade me her interest was very much with them. Then: 'Do you know much about him?' she asked.

We've all been there. Desperate for information about someone we've fallen for, but even more desperate not to let this show. Knowing I had to be doubly careful in my reply, I thought it best to stick to the facts. I told her what I knew, but tried to keep from my voice the warmth I felt for Tony, which would have poured out of me if I'd been talking about him to anyone else. Juliet listened intently, though took great care to look anywhere other than at me, and I found I didn't trust myself to tell her the very thing she'd most want to know. My face is always doing things I don't want it to, and I couldn't risk it misbehaving then.

I really thought I'd got away with it, and was about to change the subject in relief, when Juliet said, with quite excruciating nonchalance, 'Married?'

Immediate panic stations. 'Oh, yes,' I said brightly. 'Completely forgot to say. Yes. Tony's married.'

Hopeless. I knew at once that she knew I knew her feelings for Tony. And she knew I knew. So we did what all sensible English people do when engulfed by the awkwardness of everyone knowing what everyone else knows and started talking urgently about the weather.

23RD AUGUST

Went out after supper to bring the washing in and found that the little bit of sheltered wall between the scullery and the End Room was so covered with daddy-long-legs that I had to put the basket down to further examine this astonishing phenomenon. There must have been two or three hundred of them, manifesting the full but minuscule spectrum of standard daddy-long-legs behaviours: butting aimlessly against the brickwork, shedding legs wildly (they should never have been entrusted with so many limbs, or certainly not such spindly ones, if they were going to be so careless with them), and dying – caught in spider webs or bits of leaf or just exhausted by their ridiculously poor suitability to a long and happy life. They can't even move about sensibly. Other winged creatures are imbued with the innate knowledge of what to do with their legs when flying – usually tucking them neatly beneath their bodies – but a daddy-long-legs will flail through the air in the most untidy, somehow panicky fashion, so that I always think if you listen very carefully you'll hear them making just the sort of noise I would if someone launched me unexpectedly on a zip wire.

A few of them were mating, I saw, or at least presumed from the way their bottoms were stuck together. Their front ends seemed completely uninterested in what their rear ends were up to – they had that joyless, trance-like look of people in a long post office queue – but then what would you expect from a daddy-long-legs? It was a miracle they could stay alive long enough to reproduce at all.

What an awful lot of work human relationships seemed in comparison, I thought, starting on the unpegging. All the angst and uncertainty, the peaks and troughs, the startling immediacy and the long drudgery... How infinite the heart's contortions where love is concerned! Look at poor Juliet. Look at Hugh and me – where we are now, where we began.

The trousers were made of such thick brown tweed that my first thought when I saw them was if they would actually stand up on their own without anyone's legs inside them. They were high-waisted, and secured not with a belt but a pair of old-fashioned button braces that hung from a perfect set of shoulders – straight and strong in a tie-dye T-shirt. I couldn't have described in advance what sort of face I was hoping for above those shoulders, but the one I saw was somehow exactly it – open and fully engaged in the conversation it was having, but with just a touch of something restless underneath. The girl Hugh was talking to was looking up at him, curling her plastic cup of wine to her neck in a strangely coy fashion, and I realised with interest that I was rather jealous of her.

It was one of the last of those house parties your early twenties are full of. No one cared that the wine was rank, or that it took an age to cross a room because of the crush within it, or that you could barely hear a word anyone said because of the volume of the music. It would all change in a couple of years, but at that time there was nothing any of us wanted more than to emerge from someone's front door at three or four in the morning, more than a little drunk, marvelling that a cool, fresh, quiet, peaceful world still existed after the sort of night that had preceded it.

Who was that lovely girl from work? Hair the most gorgeous mass of dark corkscrew curls... Josefina! It was her and her housemates' party, and I remember it was Stoke Newington – one of those Victorian terraces that's probably all bay trees on the doorstep now, but was dustbins, weeds and fag butts back then. Hugh was in the pocket-sized front garden, with the plastic cup girl and a couple of others. I had no reason to stop – didn't know any of them – so went on into the roar and the blazing lights, unscrewing the lid of my bring-a-bottle as I did so.

The next few hours are hazy. I made a lot of drunken new friends whose names I never learned, and there was a lot of shouting, and Lord it was *hot* in there. Then someone ran out to be sick, and a bull terrier ran in and was greeted like a long-lost mascot though nobody knew whose he was. He stayed right through the shouting to the early hours when the guitar and the spliffs came out, and people started either drifting away or falling asleep on the floor. But I was still hyped – not remotely ready for Simon and Garfunkel, or for bed – and I was coming downstairs looking for trouble when I saw Hugh sitting on the bottom step with a full bottle of wine and the bull terrier curled up at his feet. He looked up as I came down, caught my hand, said he'd been waiting for me and what was my name...

We ticked every box. Insatiable in our gazing, obsessed by every inch of each other's skin, every thought, wish, fear, need... You can't live forever like that, of course – it's just not practical. You're too preoccupied to eat, let alone remember to do the church flowers or empty the dishwasher. It would be ridiculous to want that time back; I'm just saying it's sad to compare it with what I've got now.

I've realised over the last few days that I don't think I love Hugh anymore. Some part of me has probably known for years. What other explanation could there be for my tepid response to everything he said on the phone the other day? There he is, determined to become a better man for me and the boys, to plough up the scrub of the last seven years and plant something beautiful, and I receive this news with barely a flicker? It's as if all the millions of receptors I had in my head for Hugh in the old days, which lit up at every single word he said, have quietly died, like little bulbs on a string of fairy lights, broken one by one. I can want them to work all I like; it'll make no difference.

But I've also understood that this isn't as disastrous as it might sound. It's helpful, actually, when you think about it rationally. Not loving him is like being fireproof; I can walk through whatever blazes might be up ahead and not get burned.

25TH AUGUST

Heard the front door clang this morning, and found our postman, Graham, with a parcel that needed signing for. There are two certainties where Graham is concerned: firstly, that I will always think how much the wrinkles on his forehead look exactly like a fan trellis, and secondly, that he will talk – his desire to do so sometimes such that he will pull the bell in order to put a single postcard in my hand.

It has been one of the great surprises in life that not only are so many of the relationships one enjoys built entirely on frequent, brief, identical transactions, but that these flimsy foundations do not diminish by one iota the solidity of the friendship or the affection in which one holds the other party. Take Louise at the checkout. In the seven years I've known her, I've never seen her away from her till, or out of uniform. I've never even seen her legs – cannot in actual fact be certain that she's *got* any legs – but what on earth does this matter when I know very well that she's allergic to penicillin, suspicious of aubergines, quite sure her grandson has ADHD (but unwilling to mention this to her daughter), and that there's no one I'd approach before her for post-natal advice?

It isn't quite the same with Graham, as when I say talk, I do mean *talk* – not listen – but in my opinion knowing someone is invariably more rewarding than being known, and having received a great deal of information about his life, from his pride in his award-winning sheepdog Zip to his righteous disdain of the Internet ("I've got a washer dryer, and that's enough by me"), he's become a great deal more integral to mine than some of my own relatives.

But as he launched into his wife's sciatica today, I realised my attention was not what it should have been, or would have been if I hadn't glimpsed in the hand that wasn't holding the parcel an envelope with Hugh's unmistakably enormous handwriting rolling across it. I eyed it apprehensively. I thought he wanted to keep a distance; what was he writing to me for?

Just then there was a clattering on the stairs behind me, and I recognised both the cause and intent of it at once.

''Fraid not, boys,' said Graham, as Pete and Billy arrived on either side of me in the doorway. 'Not for you. It's for your mum.'

'What's in it, please, Graham?' Billy wanted to know, his interest in the parcel not the letter, of course.

Yes, what's *in* it, Graham?

'Not a clue, young man,' said Graham.

'Shake it,' said Pete to Billy.

It had only been a few days since Hugh and I had spoken – he couldn't have made any sort of decision already, could he? And even if he had, why write rather than ring?

'Not Lego,' said Billy, taking the parcel from Graham and shaking it with an expert ear.

'Open it,' said Pete.

'Boys...' I said, distractedly. 'I think it's just some scissors.'

He'd definitely ring if it was important. He'd think of a letter as the coward's way out.

'Ooh, scissors!' said Billy.

'Not for you, Billy,' I said.

'Can we open it?' said Pete.

'It's just *scissors*, Pete,' I said.

'Can we open it?' said Pete.

'Go on, then,' I said with a sigh, watching as they ripped the poor parcel asunder like a pair of lion cubs with a baby gazelle.

'Oh,' said Pete. 'It's just some scissors.'

On their way heavenwards, my eyes met Graham's, which were crinkled up with the sort of merry amusement that people whose own children have long grown up and fled the nest always display on such occasions. Their curiosity unrewarded, the boys scampered off, abandoning the cardboard carcass to the floor.

'Well,' I said to Graham disingenuously, 'we'd better let you get on.' I saw the "But I haven't finished my story" surprise on his face as I shut the door, but I'm ashamed to say I pretended not to. Marge and her sciatica would just have to wait till another time.

I opened the envelope. Inside there was a cheque for £500, and a note saying, *as promised*.

Nothing else.

Yes. Of course. He said he'd send money. I realised though, as I stood there blankly, that I'd expected more from the contents of the envelope. I didn't know what exactly, just *more*. The cheque was drawn from the account of someone I'd never heard of – presumably Hugh was doing some work for them? No way of knowing. Though *as promised* was clear enough. Only too clear actually. Would it have been so hard to pad it out a bit? Make it a bit – I don't know – friendlier? Anyone would think we were in the midst of some hideously acrimonious divorce, where any communication was bitterly resented, pared down by hate to its barest bones, while the children were shuffled back and forth between us like little lost parcels…

It was thinking about the boys that did it. All at once, much to my own mortification, I was blubbing like a baby, seeing them both bewildered, with all the bounce shaken out of them, looking up at Hugh and me on changeover days, hoping to see something to hang onto but finding nothing but hard stares and vicious accusations, their toys and their teddies and all the rest of their stuff split into two, their loyalties under constant, double-pronged attack…

Stop being ridiculous! I told myself. But it was like trying to haul back a bolting horse; Hugh already had a new wife – Mercedes Benz body, gracious smile, penchant for sleeveless polo necks – while I'd grown mad and grizzled, pointed at by small children in shops. And where would the boys and I *live*? Till they left me, that is – they'd be desperate to leave by then. No money, no friends; off the top of my head I couldn't even think of any half-decent bridges to live under.

In the end I let myself get on with it and sank to a heap for a good howl. I took my T-shirt off, blew my nose heartily upon it, and was just thinking with relief that at least there was no one around to see me when I heard the latch lift on the door and saw Jo come in. She took in the soggy, T-shirt-less creature sitting on the floor and for the first time ever, just for a second, I saw something soft flicker across the reinforced concrete of her face. But almost as soon as I'd noticed it, it had gone. She sniffed, nodded at the flagstones I was sitting on, and said, 'You'll get piles sitting on that damp floor. My mum always said so.'

I stopped crying at once, straightened my back and sought courage from my new bra. With what I hoped was enough pride to counteract the pitiful picture I no doubt displayed, I said, 'My mum said, actually, that it was radiators.'

'Suit yourself,' said Jo, in a "Don't come running to me" sort of voice. 'I'm doing windows today.'

'Right,' I said, just like someone fully-clothed and functional, 'good. Thank you.'

I waited until she'd stumped off into the scullery then looked again at the note in my hand. I'd had more than enough of self-pity for one day. You, I said to myself firmly, are going to pull yourself together. And you're going to start by getting yourself a sodding job.

26TH AUGUST

Despite yesterday's very real intention to find work, I never made it to the shop to get a paper or even to the computer to look on there, as – yet again – life got in the way.

I had just put on a clean T-shirt, wondering as I did so how long it might take to train as a plumber, and whether I could tie it in with school hours, when I heard the door go again. Though I knew Jo was in the kitchen, and therefore much nearer than I was, I also knew it would more readily occur to her to break into a rendition of "You are my Sunshine" than see who was ringing, so I had no choice but to go wearily all the way back to the position in which it felt I'd been in all morning, what with the talking to Graham and the weeping on the floor.

I opened the door to have my eyes instantly blinded by a great sheet of shimmering platinum blonde hair, sweeping through the air like the wings of archangels as the head beneath it turned towards me. The face I saw then did nothing to diminish this divine impression, but – if anything – merely enhanced it; it was the face for which all the clichés were designed. The girl's skin was indeed flawless. Her eyes could only be described as being like sapphires, and her teeth, now revealed to me through the widest of smiles, were like the rarest and most precious of pearls.

This was not the sort of beauty, I thought, realising my mouth was hanging open, that a woman could envy; it would have been as pointless as trying to touch the moon and all the stars at once. It was hard enough just to stop gawping.

The heavenly creature now offered up her slim, tanned fingers.

'Hi!' she said (and yes, her voice was like silver). 'Saskia. I'm looking for Nick – is he here?'

This is where you say something, I had to remind myself.

'Yes. No. Sorry! Nick's not here – can I help at all?'

From the way a flash of irritation crossed her face at this, two things became immediately clear. She had fully expected him to be here, and she was not accustomed to, or best pleased by, things not being as she expected.

But very swiftly, the beatific smile with which she'd greeted me returned.

'What a shame,' she said. 'I was *so* hoping to see him. Do you know when he'll be back?'

No wonder she was so used to things going her way, I thought a little crossly, recognising in myself a pressing urge to set Nick at her feet at once, preferably on a velvet cushion. If the goddess desired it, it must be done!

'Afraid I don't,' I said firmly, so as to stop myself from the ludicrous thought that I was letting her down. 'But Rose will. That's his...' What on earth was she? '...girlfriend,' I said uncertainly. 'She popped out earlier – do you want to wait until she gets back?'

'Oh, yes. Rose...' said Saskia with a faint smile, acknowledging her loftily as a lily might a dandelion. 'I don't think I'll wait – *thank you,*' she added, 'I was only passing. I'll catch up with Nick back in London.'

I narrowed my eyes, as all Narwhals do when someone tells them they were "just passing". We couldn't be less on the way to anywhere. The lane from the main road, three miles away, is forbiddingly narrow and twisting, lined by high hedges that try to hide the fingerpost signs and shadow the potholes and the tractor spoors of straw and mud, and the dogs you come across, often muzzled, run *at* the car rather than away from it. There's a flush of relief and surprise when the village opens up suddenly before you – bewilderingly large, astonishingly inhabited by people, not witches or pixies – but this soon fades as you turn into our own lane and see the crumbling tarmac, the weeds bursting through the central strip, and read from this the implausibility then impossibility of any habitation ahead, on and on and on until at last, just as you think you're lost forever, you reach the reward of the gates.

The house is so remote, so improbably located, that it has many of an island's attributes. Newcomers arrive like shipwrecked sailors on its shores, blinking at the natives and their shrugged acceptance of the mutations that time and isolation have wrought upon their surroundings. They look for the evolutionary rules and patterns of their own homelands and are variously confused, thrilled or frightened to find not a single one.

I was just thinking (with some relief) that I was well and truly going off Saskia, goddess or no goddess, when Rose's car pulled into the yard.

'Oh!' I said warmly. 'Here she is now!'

No doubt because of Saskia's ill-disguised condescension towards my beloved sister-in-law, I watched with fierce pride as the latter got out of her car. She was wearing her harem pants (it's lovely that you like them, darling, she'd said to me the day before, but "baggy trousers" they are not) with a tiny vest top and about twenty-eight necklaces – so much more *interesting*, I thought happily, than Saskia's immaculate linen sundress. And wasn't hair like the wings of archangels really a bit *obvious*?

As Rose made her way towards us across the yard, it was apparent that she too was comparing herself to Saskia, casting a cool appraising eye over her from top to toe, which Saskia – equally unabashed – returned. Neither of them was going to yield so much as an eyelash to the other, I saw with increasing fascination, as if watching a couple of heavyweights begin to circle each other in the ring.

'Rose,' I said as she arrived beside us, 'this is Saskia. She knows Nick.'

'Oh?' said Rose, beginning to swing her key ring slowly back and forth on her finger, with all the dangerous dispassion of a leopard's tail. 'In what way?'

'He's a *very* good friend,' laughed Saskia, shaking back her hair, but the only impact this opening punch had upon Rose was a tiny darkening of her brows.

'Really,' said Rose. 'That's strange. He's never mentioned you.'

'Well,' said Saskia, treating Rose to a conspiratorial, faux-humble smile, 'he probably *wouldn't* have.' Then, sighing deeply, as if she really didn't want to say what she was about to say, though clearly she could barely restrain herself, she pressed her lips together and said, 'We were *very* close, if you know what I mean. And what man wants to tell his new lover about his last one?'

There was a brief jangle, as Rose's fist closed abruptly over her keys. Saskia observed this with a little start of triumph.

'Oh my God!' she said, fluttering her beautiful lashes at Rose. 'Have I upset you? I'm *so* sorry. That's obviously the *last* thing I wanted to do,' she lied. 'And, you know, in normal circumstances I would never have mentioned it. *Obviously*,' she stressed, spreading her fingers out across her long and graceful neck. 'That's just not the sort of girl I am. But these are not normal circumstances, I'm afraid. You see, the thing is...'

Here we go, I thought. This is what it's all been building up to. Hold on to your hats.

'The thing is,' she continued, beginning to flap her fingers in front of her eyes, allegedly to stop herself from crying, 'oh, it's just so wonderful! The thing is... I'm *pregnant*.'

I turned to Rose in horror, as the possible consequences of this for her – all of them hideous – crowded into my brain. She herself could only stare at Saskia, the only defiance she now had the strength for, while Saskia laid upon her face the shy, modest bliss of a maiden newly With Child. At this final straw, Rose fled into the house.

Saskia watched her go, then turned to me with the sort of sympathetic, embarrassed look one mother gives another when the latter's child has just badly misbehaved.

'I can see it's hard,' she said, 'hearing that sort of news, but she's going to have to face up to it. We would have had to tell her at some point anyway.'

'We?' I said, frowning.

'Nick and I. You must know as well as I do what sort of man he is. He'd never let me have his baby on my *own*.'

'You don't know that,' I said, pushing my frown down as far as it would go. 'You haven't even told him yet!'

She laughed and laid a hand on my arm in a "You poor, misguided fool" kind of way.

'You just wait and see,' she said. 'And listen, I'll leave you to it. I expect she'll need you,' she added in a whisper with a patronising little nod towards the house.

I watched as she got into her snazzy little convertible. Watched her take her sunglasses out of a case and put them on delicately, then press a button that lowered the roof. She checked her lipstick in the mirror, tapped briefly at her phone, and only then started the engine, the time it took for her to do all this deeply offensive somehow, as if she didn't even have the grace to acknowledge with a speedy departure the bombshell she'd just dropped.

I took a deep breath and went in to look for Rose. I found her – or rather the mounded duvet I assumed was her – in her bedroom. I was instantly reminded of the early days, when she was a teenager, and her room was not so much a place to sleep but the canvas upon which she scrawled, and erased, and endlessly rewrote her identity. You could still see on the walls the little grey circles from the Blu Tack that had held up the swimming certificates and pop posters at first, then Che Guevara, a massive Rasta-coloured cannabis leaf, Edith Cavell, her own paintings of strange melancholy bean-like creatures, a piece of dusty batik with photos of her friends pinned to it... But her bed had been the immutable core of these swirling surroundings, serving as throne of her castle, bridge of her ship, and haven of her heart.

'Rose,' I said gently, sitting on the edge of it and laying my hand on the bump that was my best guess at a shoulder.

'Fuck off,' she said, but the vehemence of this was muffled by the duvet and the fact she didn't jolt off my hand.

'Look,' I said, 'we know nothing about her. How do we know this baby really is Nick's? In fact,' it occurred to me then, 'how do we know she's pregnant *at all*?'

At once, the duvet was thrown back and Rose's face – tear-stained and angry – reared up at me.

'It doesn't matter,' she said. 'It makes no difference if she's pregnant or not, with his child or whoever's. I don't ever want to know. All I do know is that I should never have got back with him. I was *weak*. I could've done it if I hadn't seen him, but then he goes and shows up here – *so* unexpectedly...'

The sarcasm of the *so* gave me the answer to the question I'd hoped I'd need never ask, and I hung my head, feeling Rose's eyes bore into the top of it.

'Do you know,' she said, 'how hard I'm trying here? When I told you not to say anything to him, made you promise *not* to say anything?'

'You were so unhappy,' I said feebly.

'And I'm so fucking ecstatic *now*?' she said, whacking the duvet for emphasis. 'For a while I thought I could do it – be with him again, and that I could make myself be fine about the baby business just by brute force, or brute forgetting, or brute something, but the minute there's even a whiff of a working womb in his vicinity and – it's ridiculous – can't do it. Can*not* do it. Won't do it.'

I couldn't look at her. Just listened to her rapid breathing.

'The only reason I'm even talking to you,' she said, eventually, 'is because Nick said, when I guessed you'd been involved, that he was glad you'd done it. Because he'd never stopped loving me.'

I lifted my head. 'What are you going to do?' I asked meekly.

'Tell him to fuck off,' she said, as though this could not have been more obvious. 'What else am I going to do? I'll tell him to fuck off, and then wait and wait and wait until I don't mind anymore.'

I looked at her drawn and defiant face. There he was, Prince Charming, hacking away at all those thorns on one side while Rose kept spinning them out on the other…

It was no good. I couldn't stop myself.

'I'm going to call him,' I said, jumping up from the bed.

Rose's mouth formed into a great, horrified NO, but I was already out of the door before the howl itself came out. Nearest phone and door with lock was my bedroom, and I hotfooted it there with Rose only a few metres behind me, hurling every possible threat and insult at my back in a most un-Sleeping Beauty-like way. Managed to slam and lock the door just as she reached it, and found I could actually manage quite well to ignore the thumping that then began.

Rang Nick. Told him about Saskia. Told him about Rose. He listened, and then he issued instructions while I listened. It was such a brief, smooth, controlled conversation I almost wanted to say copy that, over, at the end. I put the phone down, unlocked the door, and opened it to find Rose sitting on the floor with her knees drawn up and her head upon them, quiet now.

'Right,' I said. 'You're to pack and go down there at once.'

'No,' she said.

'It's not about yes or no, I'm afraid,' I said, folding my arms. 'Come on, please.'

'I'm not going,' she said.

'He said you'd be difficult. If you don't – right now – pack your stuff and get in your car and go straight to his office, I'm to get Ian to take you.'

She lifted her head to say angrily, 'I am *not* going anywhere with Ian.'

'Fine. Then you'd better do as you're told. Chop, chop, please.'

'For fuck's sake!'

'No, not for fuck's sake – for your sake. Give me your hand.'

She seemed to contemplate her obstinacy for a moment, whether to flex it a little further or not, but we both knew she was already at the point of petulance and where could she go after that? She took my hand and let me pull her up and lead her back to her bedroom to pack. I put her in her car barely half an hour later.

I could not quite believe, as I looked at my watch, that it wasn't yet even noon. Who would have thought so much could happen in a single morning? And all so emotional, too; though I'd been at the house the whole time it felt like I was only just arriving back there. I cast my eyes over the kitchen and let the chores within it crowd over to reintroduce themselves – washing-up, watering plants, somehow sewing up that long, ragged rip in the curtain by the fireplace – what else? Children. Oh yes, I had children. Where on earth were they?

I listened carefully for some indication of where they might be. Silence. And they hadn't even come to the door when Saskia arrived, which meant they must be thoroughly engrossed in something… With a sharp sigh of irritation I made my way to the End Room.

The floorboards are so squeaky that the boys were alerted to my approach with just enough time to turn off the telly before I arrived in the room. Despite myself, I had to repress a smile at the utter uselessness of their attempts to look innocent. They were sitting, very still, side by side on the sofa, blinking, in perfect imitation of the pigeon that's nesting in the wisteria outside my bedroom window when she doesn't want to be seen.

'Now,' I said gravely, 'we could talk about what you've just been doing. Or we *could* just remind ourselves that we do *not* watch telly in the daytime, and that we won't be doing it again, and then go and take a picnic lunch to have by the lake.'

From the long-forgotten taste of such an offer in my mouth, and the exuberant delight with which they accepted it, I realised with shame that it had been a long, long time since I'd spent any proper time with them. I took great effort with the picnic therefore, and with the rest of the afternoon, even going so far as to swim – something I loathe (I don't care what anyone says, there's *every* possibility that something with big teeth and tentacles lives amongst those weeds) and that, as the boys knew this, was the greatest gift I could give them.

We took Rose's little boat, the SS Boudicca, for a row to the fallen willow and back, then lay in the sun with a small pile of bulrush heads harvested by Billy for their strokeability, and I was just wondering how the newt was getting on, and hoping it was well and happy, when Billy said, 'I wish Dad was here.'

Pete propped himself up on his elbow at this and looked at me. 'Yeah. Hasn't he finished all that stuff for Ravi yet?'

I was at once consumed by guilt: there is no pain quite

like that felt when a maternal lie is relayed back so trustingly as truth by one's children. I find Father Christmas hard enough. But on top of this there was the awful thought that I'd underestimated how much they'd missed their father. I'd assumed, just because they hadn't said anything, that they hadn't *felt* anything either. What sort of mother was I?

'Does it feel like a very long time?' I asked them.

'Like... *forever*,' said Billy, arranging his bulrushes into a tidy line.

Realising I was about to say something rash, but, seeing their faces, quite unable to stop myself, I said, 'Maybe we can ask Dad if he'd come up for the weekend or something? I don't know when he'll... when he'll *finish* what he's doing, but I'm sure he could visit at least.' Yes, I thought, suddenly furious. I may not have focused enough on the impact of all this on the boys, but neither had Hugh.

Once we were back at the house, and the boys had helpfully dropped their muddy, sodden trunks on the kitchen floor and gone upstairs, I fetched my phone and, with lips firmly pressed together, texted:

Hugh – the boys miss you. None of this is fair on them, you know. We should have sorted something earlier. Can you please arrange to see them?

I pressed send, and stood, hand on hip, willing a speedy reply with a fierce glare at my poor phone that only deepened every minute, as if having no signal, or running out of juice, or any of the other myriad reasons for a belated response were quite impossible – the only true one clearly being a despicable lack of love from a father for his children.

But all my venom vanished when my phone pinged and I read:

I miss them. Can I have them this weekend? Will you bring them to that service station with the dinosaur? This Sat 10am?

I could picture the service station exactly, as we always stopped there on our way to Borth. Every regular journey holds its markers, whether honoured with an actual stop or not, and this was ours. It was where the first treat of the holiday was bestowed (chocolate frogs for the boys), where we heard the first Welsh accent, where I would always get distracted by the random selection of home-grown plants and Hugh by the walking maps, and the boys would always yell at us to hurry up. A holiday did not begin at Borth, but there, and had it closed or changed or otherwise put out the flame of its significance I'm not sure even the most blessed holiday would have survived it.

We changed each year though – or rather the boys did. When they were very tiny, no matter how hard we tried to reassure them that the fifteen-foot T-Rex was made of fibreglass and therefore fairly unlikely to eat them, they would dash from the car to the safety of the shop in real fear for their lives. A couple of years later, they would dare each other to touch him, and later still, to climb all the way to the top of his head.

I found myself smiling at the memory of this, and at the baffling but happy incongruity of finding an enormous dinosaur outside a provincial service station in Mid Wales, but this quickly turned to a frown as I realised that Hugh could only be planning to take the boys to Borth, and to take them without *me*. Could he not think of somewhere new, where there were no family memories and where I would not be able to picture with agonising clarity my absence on our favourite part of the beach? Who would remember to hang out the towels after swimming? Who would make sure the usual top/bottom bunk argument between Pete and Billy at the youth hostel would be resolved equably? It was a bit like being dead and having to watch everyone go on without you, possibly without even giving you a passing thought, and certainly without sun cream.

This is *not* about you, I had to tell myself firmly. It's about the boys spending time with their father. But even so, I had to keep a careful eye on my finger to make sure it texted back appropriately and not, as a great chunk of me wanted it to, with a prim refusal to let him see them.

OK, was the best that I could manage.

27TH AUGUST

When the boys came down this morning, I took a deep breath and told them they were going to spend the weekend with their father. Tried not to feel utterly bereft when they greeted this news with great excitement.

'Just to be clear, I won't be coming at *all*,' I said, in the vain hope they hadn't quite understood. 'Not for *any* of it. It'll just be you and Dad.' Pete nodded with a slow frown, not out of concern but rather in the manner of someone who realises they're *supposed* to be concerned but can't for the life of them work out why. 'Billy?' I said, appalled to find myself hoping to see some sign of distress, however small, in my softer second son.

He narrowed his eyes in deep concentration.

'Can I take Tat?' he asked, referring to his bedraggled but best beloved toy cat, his attachment to which Hugh increasingly discouraged.

'Of course you can take him,' I replied, a little sulkily.

His face instantly brightened, and he declared that he was going off to pack, leaving me to gloomily confront my maternal obsolescence.

No doubt looking for some distraction, my brain hopped back to its thinking about Nick and Rose, which it had been doing approximately every five minutes since Rose left, though not in a remotely productive way. It was like that dragonfly on the football on the lake, alighting for a second or two, just long enough to feel cracked leather at its feet, then flitting off before even stilling its wings. Each time it brought conviction with it – though, unhelpfully, this alternated between leaping expectation and deepest doom. Happily ever after or forever split… Nick is one of the most persuasive people I know, but prising trust out of Rose? It would be the greatest challenge of his life.

I found myself picking up my phone and texting her:

Just thinking about you. And hoping you're OK.

The one constant was that I didn't feel a single jot of guilt for phoning Nick, nor apprehension as to the consequences. I was as confident in my decision as I would have been in calling an ambulance despite Rose, bleeding out on the floor, insisting I didn't.

Please God, I thought, let it work out all right for Nick and Rose.

'Mum!' I heard just then from the top of the stairs. 'Should I take two pairs of shorts or just one?'

'Oh…' I said, trying and failing to picture Saskia's baby in Rose's arms, '… two!'

Would she ever be able to look at it and not see where it hadn't come from?

'Mum!' came Billy's voice again. 'Should I put my flippers at the *bottom* of my suitcase or at the *top*?'

'You're not going till tomorrow, Bill,' I called up. 'Maybe let's leave it till later, shall we?'

Because Saskia was wrong about Nick. A gentleman he was, but not a stupid one. There's no way he'd leave Rose to be with that woman, baby or no baby. I just–

'Mum!'

'WHAT?'

'Can you come and help me?'

With a deep sigh, I took off from the football once again, and dedicated the next half hour to helping my younger son negotiate the acute complexities of packing an overnight bag.

28TH AUGUST

Meet up day. I woke already heavy with dread, and could not seem to counter this no matter what tactics I tried, not least because I didn't know exactly what the dread was for. Seeing Hugh – the inevitable awkwardness of this – was definitely part of it, but worse was the thought of handing over my children when so much of me didn't want to. Out of jealousy? Fear? Panic that this was the start of the new, broken family life that I'd worked myself up in imagining when I'd got Hugh's cheque?

The boys' chatter and excitement in the car was exhausting – their bouncing about in the back felt like slaps on sunburned skin not just endured, but encouraged, because the mother is always stronger than the wife. Yes, yes – what a *lovely* time you're going to have! Chips! The beach, you lucky things! Just ten minutes now! So taut was I when I turned into the service station that, for a second, the shock of the sight of Hugh, leaning against the bonnet of the van, came as a divine relief, as the sound of a pistol might to a long blindfolded man.

'Dad!' yelled Billy, his head and most of his shoulders already out of the window. 'Dad!'

Hugh lifted his eyes from his phone and gave Billy a smile that began like that you'd give a loved one in their hospital bed, but then spread its wings into undiluted joy.

Both boys caught it and, as if only realising at that moment just how much they'd missed him, flew out of the car towards him before I'd even put on the handbrake.

I hope I will never again feel as lonely or as lost as I did then.

I'd deliberately parked facing away from the van, so as not to see the reunion that was going on there, but I could still hear it bubbling over itself behind me. How could it be, I thought, blinking at the fag butts on the verge, that something that would under any other circumstances bring me nothing but pleasure now plunge me into such despair? It seemed to make no difference that the boys were unaware of the fence that stood between their father and me; it still felt like they'd vaulted over it without a backward glance, as if every hug or laugh we'd ever shared was nothing but a sham. I'd never seen them on the far side of any fence before and would have given anything at that moment to have them back on mine.

I could not get out of the car. The lump in my throat was painful and I couldn't let go of the steering wheel. You *can't* just drive off, I said to the pleading voice in my head, you've still got all their stuff in the boot. No, the ground is not going to swallow you up, either. No. *No*, I said out loud. Looking wildly around me for *something* to help – emergency counsellor in the glove compartment, invisibility cloak, gin – my eyes lit on Rose's enormous sunglasses in the money tray, and fell upon them as one might a frying pan when all the proper shields have already been taken. I got out of the car and made my way as steadily as I could to the boot. I fetched the boys' bags, then walked towards Hugh.

He had both boys in headlocks and was somehow managing to tickle them at the same time, to wriggles of delight that drew warm smiles from a couple who were just coming out of the service station shop. At the sight of me, all the mischief on Hugh's face drained away, leaving a blankness that was impossible to interpret. Sensing a dip in his attention, the boys ducked out from his arms and ran off for a joyful reunion with the T-Rex, oblivious to the high-pitched tension that opened up behind them.

'Hi,' said Hugh quietly.

Think about the Queen, I told myself sternly. Mahatma Gandhi. Nelson Mandela. Helen Mirren.

'Hi,' I replied.

'Thank you for bringing the boys,' he said. Then, frowning at Rose's great black glasses, 'Are you OK?'

'Fine. Let's just get this over with, though.' It was as hard to look at him as not to. He'd cut his hair, shorter than I'd ever seen it, so that his hairline stood out sharply against his face. He was thinner, and also seemed somehow taller, more *grown up*. 'Boys!' I yelled. 'I'm going now! What about collecting them?' I added to Hugh, pushing the sunglasses up the bridge of my nose.

He stared at me hard for a moment and just this looking, without even any words, was almost unbearable.

'Five o'clock tomorrow? Here?'

'Right. It is Borth you're taking them to, I assume? Boys!'

They ran over, panting and grinning.

'I beat Pete,' said Billy, beaming. 'I got to his head first!'

'Whatevs,' said Pete coolly.

I hugged them, for about half the length of time and half the intensity that I wanted to, and gave them a short lecture on bunk bed etiquette, teeth brushing, and reasonable bed times – all of which was entirely for Hugh's benefit rather than theirs – then hugged them again, asked Pete if he'd remembered some clean pants, and reminded both boys that just because their watches were water resistant did *not* mean they would welcome drowning in salt water, and perhaps it would be...

'Mum,' said Pete.

... better to give them to me now for safekeeping? Because they'd only be...

'*Mum*,' said Pete.

So I hugged them one last time, as my kids, *my kids* began running on a loop through my brain, then walked stiffly to the car and drove off without looking back, as there would be equal pain whether they waved at me or not.

The journey back took longer than the one out, as I had to stop for yet another howl in a lay-by. (I'm getting quite used to this now.) Once this was flushed out of my system, it left me in a rather strange mood that I was just nudging nervously with the toe of my consciousness when I turned into the yard and saw Rose's car.

I found her at the kitchen table, frowning at her laptop. Her hair was all twisted up, secured by means of a fringed scarf and two pencils. She'd pushed all the table detritus to one side, and had laid out a notebook, a calculator and her phone neatly to her left. To her right, glinting deliciously in the sunshine, was a whisky so large I thought at first it was apple juice. The fact she was on a mission was clear – whether of world domination or prostrate drunkenness was not.

She looked up when I came in and blinked at me, her mind obviously elsewhere.

'I didn't expect to see you back so soon,' I said. 'Are you all right?'

There was a pause, and further blinking, but not the sort where someone is deliberating how to respond, whether or not to give their sister-in-law an earful for her bullying the day before, for example. She was still just coming back from wherever she was.

'Fine,' she said eventually.

'How did it go with Nick?'

'Fine,' she said again, idly aligning the edge of the calculator with the pine boards of the table.

It was as she did this that I noticed a large emerald had appeared on her finger – the fourth of her left hand. This caused me to gasp involuntarily, and then to hold my breath, as one might having spotted a knife in someone's handbag. Rose glanced at me, then at her hand, and seemed immediately to surrender to the pointlessness of trying to hide what flashed upon it.

'Is that what I think it is?' I said.

She looked at the ring gloomily.

'Apparently,' she said.

'What do you mean, "Apparently"? I assume you were involved in the engagement process, as is traditional?'

'Not exactly, no,' said Rose, and with a rueful sigh she explained how Nick had marched her to a little jewellers, stood her in front of the display, and told her to pick a bloody ring out. The poor shop assistant, sales patter swiftly turning to dust in his mouth, had responded to Nick's barked instructions with never a word, hands shaking slightly as he laid each glittering tray on the counter. He'd had enough, Nick told Rose, of her messing about, and they were none of them leaving the shop until she had a ring on her finger.

Too tired to fight, she said she'd watched Nick take her hand as if it belonged to someone else entirely. With all the impatience of a man at a locked door with too many keys to sift through, he'd tried ring after ring upon her finger, discarding all at last but the emerald – art deco, bezel set, platinum band – which had slipped onto her finger and instantly made itself at home. He'd nodded his acceptance to ring and to shop assistant, then turned to Rose, kissed her, and said, 'Do you get it now?' And she had found herself saying meekly that she did.

She fell silent then. With her thumb, she rolled the new ring around and around her finger, familiarising herself with it in the sort of glum, resigned way you might a tattoo that you'd obtained drunkenly and were seeing in sobriety for the first time.

The conventional squawks of excitement with which one receives news of an engagement seemed quite impossible, and when my brain failed to produce any useful alternative I decided to move off the subject altogether.

'What about Saskia?' I asked.

She took a big swig from her glass before replying.

'He says they only slept together once and that she said she was on the pill. He's properly angry. Says she was the most narcissistic person he's ever met and a dreadful lay, which is sweet, but as for the baby...' she tailed off into a shrug.

It was very hot in the kitchen, even with all the windows open, and breezeless. A cluster of tiny flies floated aimlessly over the fruit bowl.

'Where are the boys?' she said. She focused on me as I told her. 'No wonder you look a bit pale and twitchy,' she said when I'd finished. 'Can I help?'

'I have to get a job,' I said loudly. 'As soon as possible. It's very important.'

'But you've already got a job,' said Rose, frowning. 'Didn't I mention it? You're going to be Head Gardener, in charge of all the plants. For the tourists,' she added.

At once, with the joy you feel on throwing open the shutters on the first morning of a holiday, I saw my perfect garden – crisp-edged, glossy lawns, and great fulsome frothy beds of stocks, peonies and blush roses. A cutting garden; ranks of little seedlings, green and tender, in the potting shed; the glasshouse resurrected, thick with scent and steamy shade; water flashing through the grotto's lush ferns; agapanthus and alliums, white roses twining up the dovecot...

'Don't be ridiculous,' I said. 'Look at it. Half the pot plants are dead, your father's topiary has long since morphed into lumpenness, and the only things that are thriving are the greenfly and the valerian growing out of the chimneys.'

'Yes, yes, but that's *now*. When you've got everything else to look after,' said Rose. '*And* just you doing the gardening. We're going to do this "Friends" thing, and get you some helpers.'

'Friends?'

'Yes,' said Rose, 'there are these Friend people you can get, where they come and help you for free, just because they like the plants or dusting or whatever. I've already started the Facebook page.'

I don't think there's ever a precise moment when you realise a certain plan is not, in fact, a plan at all, but fantasy. It's more a slow settling of sediment, discovered only when you try to launch your boat and find it runs at once aground. The woman who wakes one day and knows not only that she'll never marry the man beside her, but that this knowledge has long been there; the retirees and their trip around the world; learning the violin, emigrating, being thinner, better, fitter, more productive, changing house/car/husband/curtains – a thousand times a day people are understanding that such things will never happen. My ambitions for the garden were no different. What began as solid achievable intent revealed itself as risible pipe dream long ago. So to learn that they might be possible after all...

'Oh, Rose,' I said. 'I think I'd like that very much. *Very* much.'

'Thought you would,' she said proudly.

'Is that what you're working on?' I asked, nodding at her laptop. 'The house planning stuff?'

'Yes,' she said. 'If I don't focus hard on something to get this Saskia business out of my head, I shall go insane.'

'You didn't want to stay down there?' I said. 'Until it was sorted out?'

She shook her head.

'We did try. He said we'd be together no matter what happens with her, and I believe him – I do – but it's the not knowing, you see. It's really very difficult to know what you feel when you don't know the facts.'

'Is there any way of getting some answers?'

'Nick's going to speak to one of his... mates,' said Rose.

We fixed each other with looks of mute alarm. Nick has mates, and he has... mates. The latter, never named, loiter in the last remaining shadowy, ungentrified corners of his old East End, fingertips resting on their complex webs of loyalties, tensed for a twitch. Rose and I regard these men rather like small children do the dark depths under their beds: one part of us terrified of what might lurk there, and another part ever so slightly disappointed in what might not.

The fact that Nick himself does nothing to either allay these fears or confirm them only adds to the frisson we feel. We know there's some sort of shared history there, but it's not the open, sunny one of school friends or colleagues. There's never been so much as a whole sentence from Nick about his... mates, let alone fond anecdotes. It's as if they've been hostages together, or lost at sea – bound by the kind of salt and suffering that demands the exclusion of outsiders.

'What are they going to do?' I asked Rose faintly.

'Sort it,' Rose replied.

We widened our eyes still further, Rose no doubt progressing through the same thoughts as I was; that "Sort it" could just as easily mean a sensible chat as a pair of concrete shoes, and anyway, weren't both Krays dead?

'*Fuck*, it's hot,' said Rose, fanning herself with her notebook.

It felt like it had been hot for years and years, and that the rain – tantalising in a big black cloud on the horizon – just would not come.

I jumped up. 'Let's plan everything,' I said. 'Let's do the whole house, *and* outside. Tell me what you and Juliet came up with the other day, tell me everything. And let's make some Pimms too, just in case.'

We started in the cellar, where it would be cool, and worked our way up through the house, following the route the visitors might take. The higher up we went, the more frequently we got stuck; perching on Pete's bed for a bitch about Saskia, a hair consultation in my room (Rose very much of the opinion that I *should* cut it), then an intense discussion as to how the innocent visitor might react to the aged photographs that line the Long Corridor – amused or aghast at the multiple transgressions of twenty-first century mores depicted in each, thick as they are with beaming, pith-helmeted ancestral Hughs and bemused indigenes. In a trunk in the back bedroom, that I don't think I've ever looked in before, we found a small collection of Edwardian evening dresses, and thought it a good idea to try them on, and an even better idea not to take them off again. Valiantly overcoming the twin impediments of satin frocks and our fourth Pimms, we then made our way into the attics, to be greeted silently, but still effusively, by the smiling stuffed polar bears.

I realised then that I'd never told Rose what Louise had said – about the mince pies and the sherry on their paws that Christmas – and the minute I did, she seemed quite overwhelmed by outrage that the bears had been stuck up in the attic for so long.

'Poor darlings!' she exclaimed, stroking the arm of the less mothy one. 'I'd forgotten you used to live downstairs. It's dreadful. How *could* we leave you to rot up here?'

The polar bear did not respond, but seemed pleased by the attention.

'Rose!' I said, breathless at the shining glory of my sudden idea. 'Rose! Let's release them! Let us take them back into the light!'

She squeezed my arm, and blinked rapidly, clearly moved.

We were both a little surprised to discover that enthusiasm alone – no matter how fresh or fierce – does not much help with the liberation of two nine-foot polar bears from a cramped attic. Ten minutes of ineffective grappling with different furry limbs, in different combinations, left us red-faced and sweaty, but the creatures themselves unmoved.

We began to eye them a little crossly, as their resistance to our eager rescue began to feel a tiny bit deliberate. Luckily, just then, I spotted a blanket tucked in between the horns of one of the kudus, and thought we might be able to topple the bears onto that and drag them thereafter. This new plan instantly rekindled our dwindling fervour for the task in hand, and somehow it actually worked. One by one we got the bears on their backs, and heaved them out of the attic, down the narrow stairs, along the back corridor, past Billy's room, across the landing and down the main stairs, until both were lying in the hall and we were standing over them – panting but triumphant.

'I know, poppets,' said Rose, smiling at them, 'you want to stand up,' which is exactly what it looked like they wanted to do, their outstretched paws reaching up towards us; 'but you'll have to wait till we get Ian or someone. You're *very* heavy,' she added, wagging a finger at them for this naughtiness.

They were not quite as intact at the end of their journey as they'd been at the beginning of it, but, as Rose said, with a mission as difficult as the one we'd just accomplished, some collateral damage was inevitable, and she was sure the arm that had snapped could be reset, and the ear stuck back on.

'Next!' I said, hands on my hips.

Words tumbling over one another as we stepped outside into the garden, I began to describe my vision for it, periodically bending to deadhead a rose here, pull out a bit of ragwort there, but without a pause in step or speech, because – with the Friends practically on the doorstep – I could afford such lightness of attention now.

'Hmmm,' said Rose, politely, from time to time. We both knew she was bored, but I wasn't ready to acknowledge it just yet. 'OK,' she said eventually (I say eventually, but it can't have been more than ten minutes), 'that's it, I'm afraid. Plants just not my thing. Do you mind?'

Told her that of course I didn't mind, that I had enough excitement for both of us, and with this particular road exhausted we had a brief consultation as to which to take next.

'Option A,' I said, counting it on my finger, 'we stop now. We have some food and some water. We feel shit for the rest of the day but come up shining in the morning.' Rose digested this thoughtfully. 'Or Option B,' I continued, 'is the sod it option. We get absolutely hammered, and take the hit tomorrow.'

It wasn't an easy choice, as each path had its own well-known seductions and penalties, but, 'Let's be sensible and go for A,' said Rose eventually. 'Though there's one thing we've got to do first.'

She took my hand, led me back to the house, and sat me on a chair. I heard her banging about in the kitchen drawers, and by the time she showed me the pair of scissors, I'd already worked out what she planned to do.

'Ready?' she said solemnly, as if about to push me out of an aeroplane.

'Go for it.'

She pulled my hair into a ponytail, and with one long, slow munching cut, removed it. There followed a handful of smaller snips, a bit of fluffing, and, 'Done!' she said. The whole thing took less than five minutes. She moved round to the front of the chair, and it quickly became clear from the way her beaming smile crumpled that she was not quite as pleased with her creation as she had anticipated.

'Obviously I'm not a *qualified* hairdresser,' she said, a little accusingly, pushing bits of hair behind my ears and pulling them out again.

'I know that,' I said. 'You haven't even asked where I'm going on holiday. Should I have a look now?'

She ignored me, picked up the scissors again, and snipped with great concentration.

'*Rose*.'

'Hmm,' she said, avoiding my eyes and clearly unwilling to let me go, 'I suppose so...'

I walked over to the mirror above the mantelpiece, raised my eyes to it, and was bewitched by the image I saw there. Not in the manner of the "Oh, I'm so beautiful now!" madeover ladies on the telly, but because the hacked and ragged head before me was my one true reflection, found at last. I recognised her instantly though I'd never seen her before. It was all I could do to stop myself lifting my hand to the mirror and laying my open palm against hers.

'Oh, God,' said Rose, appearing behind me in the mirror. 'You hate it.'

'You're wrong,' I said, turning to her. 'It's perfect.'

29TH AUGUST

Thanks to our selection of Option A yesterday, both Rose and I were feeling smug and efficient this morning, and I had the twin delights of new hair and new Head Gardener role to bolster me still further. Even so, I wasn't sure these pleasures would carry me through the trial of seeing Hugh this afternoon, so I asked Rose if she would collect the boys.

The speed and sharpness of her willingness to do so caused me some alarm.

'Rose,' I said, not quite sure I meant what I was about to say but saying it anyway, 'please don't give him a hard time.'

'How can you say that?' she said instantly, staring at me as if I was both imbecilic and insane. 'How can you, out of all of us, say that? The leaving as he did, practically silent ever since – in what way is that not the behaviour of an arsehole?'

There it was – that unassailable outrage regarding Hugh that I'd seen more and more frequently since he'd left – permitting not so much as a moment of hesitation on her face before she'd replied. You should have thought about that before asking her to collect the boys, I said to myself with irritation. There'll be all sorts of trouble now.

'Don't forget the money he sent,' I said carefully, 'and the seeing of the boys.'

'That's just window dressing!' she said, swatting away these mitigations. 'Where's the explanation? When's he coming back? *Is* he coming back? Where's the least bit of certainty?'

It was no good, I realised, metaphorically rolling my sleeves up. I was going to have to take her on.

'There's been more than the cheque and the Borth trip,' I said. 'I didn't tell you, because – I don't know – you've had so much of your own stuff to deal with, and if I'm honest I didn't think you'd take it too well.'

'What "more"?' she said sharply.

'He phoned,' I said. 'He said he was sorry – not just for leaving but for being such a shit for so long. He said he wanted to change, but he needed time and space to do it.'

'Time and space?' cried Rose, incredulous. 'What a fucking cop-out. You're right – I'm not going to take that well. Not when it's *you* who has to hold everything together while he's off contemplating the depths of his navel.'

I stared at her. How on earth to explain? Then inspiration struck me.

'Look. Do you remember your Honda?' I knew she would – who forgets their first car? But Rose's had been more special still. 'Remember how desperate you were for some independence, and how Hugh heard you when your dad didn't, and how he didn't just find the Honda and buy the Honda, but changed the seats and the stereo and put go-faster stripes on the side, and the furry dice and the trucker steering wheel?'

'Of course I remember Harriet,' said Rose, a little mistily. 'The best car a girl ever had.'

'Well, what you won't remember – because you were

back here and we were in London, and he never let on to you – is how hard he worked to buy that car and make it what it was. Got a second job, never sat down for a meal, up before me and not back when I went to bed... I barely saw him all that time, and even when I did he wasn't really there. It was like living with a ghost. But you know what? I didn't mind. Because he was doing it for you. It was just like when we looked after you when your mum died. He was all consumed, not for himself, but for you. And who couldn't forgive a man, who couldn't *celebrate* a man, who loves like that?'

Rose swallowed. Began pushing at the cuticle of one thumb with the nail of the other. 'What's your point?' she said.

'That's what he's doing now,' I said. 'He's trying to achieve something so hard that he needs every scrap of his resources.'

'What – he's being a self-obsessed arsehole out of love?' said Rose.

'I can't describe it properly, but somehow, yes.'

'Love of *who*?' said Rose. 'The boys? Me? You? By disappearing and leaving you in total limbo?'

'I know it doesn't sound very promising, but yes. For all of us. Somehow, yes. Please, Rose,' I added. 'We need to trust him. We need to give him this chance.'

She sighed, cocking her head to one side, as if to help herself see my point of view, while I watched anxiously. The roar of her loyalty to those she loves (me, ironically, on this occasion) can make her so deaf; how on earth could I get her to hear me? There was also the inconvenient fact that I'd ignored her wishes when I'd gone to see Nick; what was stopping her now quite justifiably ignoring mine?

'I'm sorry,' she said at last, shaking her head rapidly as if to remove a bee inside it, 'I'm not sure I care what you want at the moment. I'm too angry with him and too sure he needs to know that. I'll see what things are like when I get there – I can give you that – but nothing more.'

In the nicest possible way, I didn't want to be around Rose before she left to collect the boys. I wasn't cross with her, loved her more than ever in a way; but all that was difficult and painful had somehow settled upon her since we'd talked, like some sort of foul mediaeval miasma. She felt it too. So we peaceably avoided each other until it was time for her to leave, at which point we both found ourselves in the kitchen, giving each other a hug. A slightly forced and awkward hug, but a hug all the same. I saw her off at the door, then went out to the garden.

I was at the kitchen sink, scrubbing the dirt from my fingernails, when I heard the door bang back on its hinges, a bag thump down in the hall, and Billy shout, 'Mum! What's for supper?'

I forgot to reply in my hurry to re-appropriate my offspring, standing each boy in turn in front of me and submitting them to such a primal, proprietary examination of ears, teeth, etc, that if I'd progressed to actual gorilla-like grooming I don't think any of us would have been surprised. Oh, it was so good to have them back! Back with me, here, where they belonged, back with me, home.

'What happened to your hair?' said Pete then, alarmed, as if seeing it for the first time after a terrible accident. Which I suppose, arguably, wasn't far from the truth.

'Aunty Ro cut it for me,' I said, running my fingers through it proudly. 'Isn't it great?'

'No,' said Pete.

'I like it,' said Billy, his head on one side. 'You look like Shaggy off Scooby Doo.'

'Thank you, darling,' I said warmly. 'That's just the look I was hoping for. Now, you two. Bath in a bit. Go and watch some telly if you want to.'

I waited until they'd gone out of the room, then turned to Rose to see what, if anything, she'd brought back with her. She looked a bit shifty, but that didn't necessarily mean bad news. So many people enjoy the self-aggrandisement of the messenger role; the hungrier the parties to impart or receive the information, the better, as far as they're concerned, but Rose is the opposite of this. She is not comfortable with carrying things for others – whether messages, secrets, or bags of shopping. It isn't that she doesn't want to; I'd go so far as to say I think a part of her would very much welcome this skill. But it just doesn't suit her, and, like the purple beret I bought her optimistically one birthday, she's quietly, regretfully taken it to the charity shop.

'How was it?' I asked.

She shrugged breezily, beginning to scratch at a bit of solidified batter on the kitchen worktop.

'No. Really,' I said. 'How *was* it?'

'I'm sorry,' she said, with a defiant little toss of her head, 'but I did start with a bollocking.'

'Oh, Rose,' I said, sighing, 'what did he say?'

She swept her eyes across the ceiling in frustration. 'He wouldn't rise,' she said. 'I really wanted a rise, a good shouting, because that would have been *something*, you know? But he couldn't even give me that, just took everything I threw at him with this sort of quiet acceptance.

You've been a prick; yes. You've walked out on all your responsibilities; yes. You've been selfish and thoughtless and cruel; yes, yes, yes. What the hell can you do with that?' she said, so caught up in her words suddenly that she forgot to guard against the way she said them, and I saw with a pang the pain and appeal in her eyes.

Not once, I realised then, with awful shame, had I considered how Hugh's leaving had affected *her*. Of course she'd tried to whip up an argument between them; wasn't that exactly what she did at the Ringings? Because there's an intimacy in a good row. It wouldn't have been a patch on that which they'd shared in the old days, but it would have been – as she'd just said – *something*. There was every chance she felt worse than I did, after all. She'd had no contact with him to reassure her, and she'd have needed it more than I, because – to her – hadn't Hugh always been more hero than human? It wasn't indignation for me that had made her so furious with her brother since he'd left; she just thought it was. It was her own hurt. Involuntarily, I reached for her hand, but was not surprised when she shook it away.

'I don't know what you're feeling sorry for me for,' she said. 'I feel sorry for *you*. *Nothing* of use from him. Still think we should trust him now?' She glared at me.

I do, I thought, but did not think it wise to say so. 'Was there anything else I should know?' I asked instead.

'Don't give up,' she said, with rich contempt. 'At the end, he told me to tell you, don't give up.'

'Right,' I replied. I worked very hard to keep my face at least neutral, if I couldn't manage any of the companionable scorn Rose would have wanted, but it must have succumbed to her sharp scrutiny all the same, because –

'I know what you're thinking,' she said, with the sort of sad, soft smile a widow might give a bride. 'Always so trusting.'

'It's not necessarily a bad thing, Rose,' I said, thinking about her and Nick. 'Yes, there's risk, but the reward's so much the greater for it.'

She pondered this, but I could see it was more out of courtesy than true consideration. Then she looked at her watch, pursed her lips at me, and said, 'You do what you want with your heart. And I'll do what I want with mine.'

17TH SEPTEMBER

A long time of no writing – things have suddenly become busy round here. I wonder if it's something to do with the time of year? The end of the summer, when the change in the light and the adverts on the TV tell all of us, not just children, that it's time for school and the annual pruning of holiday hair, bedtimes, leisure, to their neat and structured term-time shape. Time for focus, time for work.

John and Shaun, father and son, arrived about ten days ago to start work on the Tree House, and have been happily embraced by the entire household thanks to the fact that the scales of trust and respect between us all are exactly balanced. There's no counting of hours, money, cups of tea – everyone is happily aligned in their expectations and equally sure of their just fulfilment.

First the scaffolding went up around the oak, then the work itself began. The frame of the new Tree House is in place, and although its lines are a bit confused by those of the scaffolding, its startling squareness is already doing exactly what it was designed to do: draw the eye again and again as the brain struggles to reconcile point and angle with sweeping branch and waving leaves.

Ian has been spending much more time here than usual, the true reasons for which have little to do with the ones he originally gave. I couldn't work out for the life of me at first why he appeared a day or so after the builders arrived, insisting on doing jobs about the place that I simply couldn't afford to pay him for.

'It all needs doing,' he said.

'There is not a single doubt in my mind that it all needs doing, Ian,' I said, 'but the only funds available are in Billy's coin collection, and I don't think pesetas or sovereigns are going to get you very far.'

Ian's face solidified into stubbornness.

'It all needs doing,' he said again, with the finality of a protester who's just padlocked himself to a tree and ostentatiously swallowed the key.

But it very soon became clear, from the fact that the jobs he chose to attend to were all at the back of the house, and from the number of times I spotted him peering suspiciously across the lawn, that his real intent was to keep an eye on the Tree House works. To begin with, he kept up the pretence quite well, but soon became completely unabashed, standing there frowning with his arms crossed, so that I couldn't ignore it, as would be the case if a nosy neighbour had suddenly thrown off his half-hidden peeping for a good clear view right in front of the window. You'd *have* to wave then, wouldn't you?

'Ian,' I said, 'would you like to come and meet them? John and Shaun? They're really doing a wonderful job.'

But no, no, thank you very much, he told me stiffly. It was nothing to do with him. He was quite sure, he said, in a tone that could not have counteracted his words more forcefully, that they knew what they were doing. And though I tried various means – cajolement, frustration, and even a little emotional blackmail – he would not change his mind, preferring to maintain the sort of sniffy, critical vigilance my mother used to employ whenever I did the roast potatoes.

On a more positive note, Juliet has been hired in a part-time capacity by Rose, to help plan the opening of the house to visitors, and is proving, Rose says, incredibly organised and efficient and just the right person for the job. She takes this hiring as a personal success, a validation of her excellent persuasive skills, as Juliet – citing a full schedule with her own work, and alluding to the poor pay Rose was offering – had originally, and emphatically, said no. Getting her on board is indeed a triumph, and I praised Rose fulsomely for it, but do not believe for one moment that either time or money had anything to do with Juliet's initial reluctance, nor with her eventual surrender. I feel desperately sorry for her, and completely at a loss how to help her; if her own heart and head are battling each other, how on earth should I know which to support?

She's tense enough at the best of times, but on the three days a week she's here I sometimes think she might actually snap from the strain she's imposed upon herself. She keeps as far away from the yard area as she can, but has chosen for her office a room that clearly overlooks it; this positive apparently overriding the multiple negatives of poor size, light, and Internet reception – her desk a card table from the attic, as nothing bigger would fit. Meanwhile Tony seems to find every excuse to visit the house when Juliet's within it, arriving in the kitchen and looking around vaguely as if for something he's not sure he's lost... I don't know what makes this thing between them so *loud* – the conflict? the concealment? – but I can hear it as clearly as you can the crackle and fizz of pylons when you walk between them, feel that same static prickle on the skin.

But it's not just those two – everything feels somehow charged at the moment – with a great deal of the electricity coming from Rose. She hasn't taken on a project this size before, but you'd never guess; she seems to know exactly where she's going, her effort solely in the push to get there, like an engine with a freight train, or Hugh fixing the washing machine. I've grown slightly in awe of her – have started to knock before going into her office – but do wish I could *understand* her vision as well as I can respect her determination to accomplish it. Other than the fact they'll have to pay, these visitors she's preparing for sound more like guests than tourists. No access denied anywhere. Red ropes, little directives saying *Private*, or *This way* would be positively rude, she says. There'll be tours and information if they want it, and a tea room, but otherwise what they do and where they go is entirely up to them.

It's not the "*mi casa es tu casa*" attitude I've got a problem with – on the contrary, I think it sounds rather lovely. What worries me, as it has all along, is the state of the *casa* in question. Surely, when you go to look around a house, half the point is to get away from your own? Why would you pay good money to see a place that – in its state of repair, in décor, coherence, tidiness, cleanliness, fragrance and resident wildlife – is almost certainly worse than yours? But Rose is adamant. Everything is to be shown as it is. We're not allowed to posh anything up – not even pumpy soap in the loo. It's all about being "honest", apparently. I can only hope with all my heart the visitors will think the same.

19TH SEPTEMBER

We watched *The X Factor* last night. It was an early round, and they picked out a handful of contestants to focus on – their back story, ambitions, etc – as they always do. One of them was a pale young man with not a lot of nose and a great deal of forehead, called Jackson. We first saw Jackson waiting for his audition in a large room vibrating with every possible strain of expectation. There were people sitting alone with their heads bowed, feet bouncing frantically on the floor; some were shaking their hands out, as if to dry them quickly, while others giggled in groups, or danced on the spot, or pecked at each other's make-up or hair, but Jackson's anticipation was quite different. He spoke very calmly, telling us how he'd only ever wanted to sing and how this was his chance to show the world what he could do. How supportive his mum had been. How he was ready.

And you could see quite clearly that he was. His conviction was such, in fact, that it freed him from the frenzy of the others in the room – he was like an albatross sailing high above a flock of squawking seagulls. We were all quite certain he would fly through to the next round. We held our breaths as he came out on stage. We watched him, our beloved friend, as he answered Simon's questions. We clasped each other's hands as the audience grew quiet and the music began, then felt our jaws drop as – at last – he began to sing.

Had a family of armadillos skidded altogether down a blackboard, the sound would have been celestial compared to what came out of Jackson's mouth.

It was every sort of awful – out of tune, out of time, squealing its way through the twists and turns of the melody, rocketing over the lifts, plummeting through the dips. Most excruciating of all, the singer himself seemed bewitched by his own voice, closing his eyes, swaying, bending tenderly towards the microphone...

We winced through Simon's verdict ("You said you were a delivery driver? Well, stick to that. Singing's never going to be for you"), and Jackson's exit offstage to where the camera awaited him.

'How do you feel?' he was asked.

Jackson was breathless and sweaty, but elated. 'I'm fine,' he said. 'It doesn't matter what they think. You can do anything if you want it enough, and I want to sing. I believe in myself. I'll keep going whatever. As long as it takes.'

I've been thinking a lot about this. About belief, mainly. I can't think of any emotion that's so susceptible to judgement from others, and such vehement judgement at that. Doesn't matter what the belief is in – the existence of aliens, God, one's possession of a stunning singing voice – the minute it's expressed it seems to be fair game for everyone else to rip apart. Unless you have actual evidence that you're right, what are you supposed to do? Keep on marching regardless of the ridicule, your banner aloft? Like Jackson? And what if, worse still, you're not even sure what that evidence might be? Because it's not Hugh coming home. That's not what I believe in. In fact, if I had to put my money anywhere at this point, I'd say he definitely won't. *Get money, save house, stop being prick* – it's still as impossible a combination in my mind as ever. No. What I believe is that Hugh is doing exactly what he said he would – trying to find a better version of himself for his family – and that he'll succeed. The only question is whether or not that includes actually living with us.

Jackson may have had an entire studio audience as well as Simon Cowell telling him he was wrong, but frankly I'd take them over Rose any day. She's relentless. We've had the same argument a hundred times:

Rose: Just explain it to me one more time.
Me: *Why*, Rose? We both know you're never going to change your mind.
Rose: No, go on. Maybe I haven't understood properly. I'll really listen this time.
Me (sighing): Hugh's trying to sort himself out.
Rose: Yes, I get that bit. Sort of. It's the next part I struggle with.
Me: Ideally, he'll work out a way of being back home with us while not being a bastard anymore.
Rose: OK...
Me: But if he finds he can't – that he can't find a way to be here and make enough money and not be a bastard, then he'll *stay away* and not be a bastard.
Rose (with exaggerated attempts to understand): So... There's a chance he'll actually leave you?
Me (more sighing): I don't know why you always have to put it like that. He wouldn't be leaving like *abandoning*, just–
Rose: Abandoning you here, alone, with the boys. Forever. And – I'm really trying here – you're OK with that?

Me: Yes, Rose! Because it'd be better than having him back as he is!

Rose: And what happens with the house in this scenario? Who looks after all that? Could it be you, by any chance? All alone?'

Me: You know I don't know how that bit would work!

Rose (screwing up her face as if trying desperately not to sneeze, then blowing all the air out of herself): Nope. Sorry. Still sounds like the work of a massive selfish arsehole to me.

Sometimes, after one of these little exchanges, I try and play devil's advocate with myself. Maybe it's *not* some noble quest Hugh's on, just a sly sloping off in disguise. What *would* happen with the house if he doesn't come back? How would he maintain it without being here? Would it really be better for the boys to have a good but absent father rather than a bad and present one? And look how much of my faith I've paid out already – even if he does come back, isn't it already too late? Can I reel myself back in safely? Never mind forgiving him – will I be able to forgive *myself*?

But it's no good. Any doubt I throw at myself just bounces off me. It *is* a noble quest Hugh's on, the outcome *will* be the best one for me and the boys, and I *will* keep on flying that flag regardless.

26TH SEPTEMBER

Any tiny hope I might have had that Rose was open to the idea of a more conventional experience for the future visitors was dashed yesterday.

Juliet had been saying for some time that we should really go and have a look at a National Heritage place, for research purposes, which Rose had, of course, been procrastinating about. She saw absolutely no value in such a visit, she said, as she was completely confident in her plans for Narwhal Hall – what was the point, therefore? I felt hugely ambivalent about this disdain, not least because I knew it sprang from a conviction just as clear, and just as unproven, as mine regarding Hugh. And hadn't I asked her to trust my trust in him? To believe in my belief? How hypocritical of me would it be then to withhold the very thing I'd begged for from her? I didn't want to doubt her – hopes for future financial security and a waterproof home being much lower down on the list of reasons for this than a wish to show my support of her – but at the same time no matter how impressed I was by her merciless sales skills at the school fete, or by the force with which she was driving towards the opening, no one could say either were really any solid proof of imminent success. Bankruptcy seemed just as likely.

So when Juliet popped over yesterday morning (it was

a Saturday) with some query for Rose, just as Pete and Billy had uttered the dread words, 'What are we doing today?', I found myself grabbing the bull by both horns and suggesting we all go to Grove Court. Surely it couldn't hurt, I told Rose. For fun, if nothing else? With varying levels of enthusiasm everyone agreed, and shortly afterwards we all squashed ourselves into the Skoda and set off.

As is so often the way with attractions on one's doorstep, none of us had ever been to Grove Court before. With the house set so far back from the road, we hadn't even glimpsed it, and as we went up the tree-lined drive there was a certain amount of surprise that such a substantial building, and such a popular one judging from the fullness of the car park, existed less than six miles from home.

Within moments of getting out of the car, everyone's attitudes to the hours ahead became abundantly clear: Pete began to chase Billy between the parked cars, Juliet took out a notepad and began to write in it, and Rose frowned with increasingly ill-disguised distaste at the other visitors, as they variously busied themselves with the putting-on of walking boots, baby carriers, hats, sun cream, binoculars, rucksacks and raincoats. She's always been old-fashioned like that, having apparently missed the memo from the Reasonable Behaviour department that specified, sometime in the sixties, the need to accept (or positively celebrate, if you were really going to enter into the spirit of the thing) any citizen's right to enjoy themselves, even in ways antithetical to your own.

I noted this, but thought I'd save any remonstrations, as I might need them later on.

'I make it fifty-eight cars,' said Juliet then. 'What did we think the paddock could cope with? Sixty?'

'Sixty-five,' said Rose vaguely, curling her lip at a couple who were just removing the Velcro fastenings from their identical, collapsible walking sticks.

The process of entry was rather more extended than we'd anticipated.

'Welcome to Grove Court!' said the lady at the counter, with a zeal that was part-welcome, part-congratulation, as if it was not tourist destination we'd just arrived at but pearly gates. 'Have you visited us before?'

'No, thank you,' said Rose firmly. 'Three adults, two children, please.'

The face of St Peter fell. 'Not members?' she said sadly; then, brightening, 'Would you like to *become* members?'

'No,' said Rose. 'Three adults, two children, please.'

'Because if you join today, it would cover your entrance now,' the other persisted, with admirable – if deeply unwise – determination to save Rose's soul. 'And you'd get in free to every other National Heritage property in the country for a whole year!'

Rose went very still, a clear danger sign, so I eased in front of her and said, 'Thank you for the suggestion, but it's just for today, please.'

The little sigh of relief I gave as the tickets were at last issued turned out to be misplaced, as first a map was pressed upon me, then the times of the tours of the house. And did the children want to do the Treasure Hunt? And did we know that the adventure area had just been refurbished and was very well worth a visit? And how lucky it was that we'd come today as there was a costumed interpretation team on site bringing History to Life, oh, and just before we went could we give our postcodes as they were collecting them for marketing purposes?

Other than Juliet, who had been busily scribbling notes throughout all this, we emerged into the sunlight variously bewildered, exhausted, and sore – as if after unexpected surgery – and it took a moment or two for everyone to compose themselves. The boys' energy levels swiftly regained their morning peak, however, and I suggested that we have a look around outside first, as the best means of ensuring good boy behaviour for the house tour. This was agreed, and we headed off to the adventure area.

It was immediately clear how much thought and effort had gone into this space. A section of woodland had been first cleared, then populated with various constructions to inform or entertain the children. There were wooden stepping stones, a willow tunnel, a pile of sticks and logs (*Bug Hotel*, said a little hand-carved sign, *Who do you think lives here?*) and a den-building section, also signposted, with wigwams of sticks already built. Here, I saw a young family: a father with a baby strapped on his back, and a mother peering out from one of the wigwams and beaming brightly at her small son, who stood gravely in front of her.

'Look, Nico!' she said. 'It's a lovely den! Why don't you come inside?'

He stared at her.

'Come on, darling! Help me put some of these other sticks up. You can pretend you're Robin Hood!'

I could only sigh sadly at this scene. So optimistic, this National Heritage team, this mother. I recognised their doomed enthusiasm exactly, as Lord knows I'd been through it enough times myself.

Why don't you have a nice carrot instead?

Let's play Old Maid!

Now. If the sweeties cost 70p and I've given the man £1, who can tell me what change I should get?

Children, I have learned, possess an almost predator-like ability to both spot, and pounce upon, opportunities for pleasure or diversion. Often, these are either invisible to the adult eye, or abhorrent to it, my own boys glazing over when, on walks, I point out primrose or breaking bud, but halted in awe by rancid squirrel corpse and inevitably pleading to take it home. But hand in hand with this comes another, even more bewildering skill. Because while a child is delighted to find their own means of entertainment, if something is presented to them as such by an adult – particularly if it's a thinly veiled attempt to instruct or improve – they become as instantly suspicious and resistant as a dog at the doors of the vet. They can sense the quotation marks around "fun" before the speaker's even opened their mouth; this acuity quite incredible in a human sub-group that will happily believe all grown-ups keep a ready stash of fifty pences behind their ears and that fibreglass dinosaurs *will* eat you.

In the far, dim corner of the adventure area, roped off roughly, was a patch of boggy mud – crusty on the top, squelchy underneath – and I could only watch, unsurprised and resigned, as first Pete and Billy, then the young boy Nico, oblivious to his mother's calls, spied this mud and jumped joyously into it.

'Are we having an adventure area?' I asked Rose then.

She'd been grinning at the boys, but turned to me straightaway when I spoke.

'No,' she said shortly. 'No adventure area. No "areas" at all.'

It took such an age to prise the boys out of their mud

bath that there was only time for a quick walk around the gardens before the house tour. This was possibly fortunate, as they brought forth nothing good in any of us. I grew wistful at the order and the pretty planting; no matter how many helpers I had, I doubted we could achieve a tenth of the splendour here. Rose meanwhile began a constant mutter of discontent – everything seemed to displease her, from the little blackboards with rhymed requests to pick up your dog's poo, to the ubiquity of willow (willow obelisks in the veg garden, another willow tunnel, a willow scarecrow in smocked shirt and flannel trousers... there *was* quite a lot of it, to be fair), to the artfully arranged and ancient tools in the potting shed – cheering up only when she stole a handful of figs from the trained tree in the walled garden and munched them brazenly as we walked. Juliet was either scribbling, or accosting other visitors with as many questions as they'd let her ask, while the boys trailed desultorily behind us, their mood as muddy as the stains their wellies left on the bowling green grass.

But if I'd thought things might improve on the tour, I was very much mistaken.

There were about a dozen of us in total, but no one could have called us a cohesive group. In fact, had we five been sporting sets of antlers, or dressed head to toe in bracken, we could not have been more different from the others, defined as such by our own behaviour and the frowns, tuts and determined distancing of everyone else. I did my absolute best to be normal despite my Shaggy hairstyle – following the gestures of the guide to nod and make interested noises at whatever she was pointing out, studiously ignoring the inappropriate interruptions made by Juliet ('And your annual turnover is...?') and Rose ('Is this going to take long?'), and Peter's ominous dawdling – but had no choice other than to throw off all such attempts when we reached the kitchen.

Until this point, members of the costumed interpretation team had been glimpsed rarely, and mercifully from afar – playing theatrical croquet outside, or weaving willow – so it came as quite a shock to discover the kitchen was full of them, mostly women, brandishing mob caps and rolling pins and ye olde dialects in every direction.

'Oh my God,' Rose whispered urgently, grabbing my arm, 'it's a nest. I've got to get out of here.'

But the only exit was the way we'd come in and was blocked by fellow tourists, laughing nervously in the manner of those who would offer up their own grandmothers before taking another step themselves.

'Don't be ridiculous,' I whispered back. 'Just stand close behind me.'

'Spread out, everyone!' called the guide at that point. 'Ask questions, discover for yourselves the workings of an actual Victorian kitchen!'

Middle-class reserve is a powerful force, but its obedience is greater still. People began to shuffle forward at the guide's invitation, though set their controls to "Repel, at all costs, repel" with rictus grins and desperate interest in either ceiling or floor. The kitchen ladies were not to miss their moment of glory, however, and began to pick off their audience one by one.

'I mean it,' said Rose. 'I won't be held responsible for my actions if one of them comes near me.'

'All right, all right,' I said irritably. 'You should be able to get out now, but for God's sake don't let them see you. We'll meet you in the car park.'

I heard her turn, then gasp.

I knew perfectly well what I'd see when I too turned around. Standing only a foot or so in front of Rose was a small, plump kitchen maid, her apron as well rounded as the pastry of a good pork pie, the smile on her face rooting Rose to the spot in horror.

'Now, now, my lovely,' said the maid, with a soothing chuckle, 'no need to be so bashful! Will you not try your fair hand at the churning?'

For reasons I really can't bear to go into, we had to leave the property shortly after the above, and at some speed. Everyone was silent in the car as we set off, and I noted this with grim satisfaction, thinking Rose must glean from it the magnitude of both her crime and the apology needed to atone for it. But–

'Just for the record,' said Rose from the back seat, 'if anyone's thinking I should be feeling ashamed of myself I'd like to point out that I'm not. Quite the opposite in fact. Fuck 'em.'

'How *can* you say that?' I found myself instantly bawling. 'You assaulted a member of the costumed interpretation team! What possible justification can you give for that?'

'It wasn't assault,' said Rose reasonably, 'it was self-defence. I did warn her.'

'Boys,' I said, fixing them with a glare in the rear-view mirror, 'it's very important you understand that what Aunty Rose did was *wrong*. If someone's trying to make you do something you don't want to do, you just say no – politely. Unless it's a teacher,' I added as an afterthought, 'or me. Or... well, you get the drift, don't you?'

Rose didn't give them the chance to reply.

'But that's exactly the problem,' she said. 'The whole *place* was trying to make us do what we didn't want to do, or sort of steering us – mind and body – like little white mice in a maze. It's *horrible*.'

'Rose, you're talking nonsense,' I said. 'You may have felt like that, but I don't think anyone else did. Look what a lovely time they were all having! Don't you think so, Juliet? Didn't you ask people?'

She glanced at me then flicked through her notebook for a moment.

'Yes,' she said simply. 'They were happy. The odd grumble about the queues in the tea room, but no serious complaints. It works for them,' she added over her shoulder to Rose. 'If we do what we're planning to do with Narwhal Hall, these people aren't your market.'

'Then who is?' I said, with sharply rising anxiety. 'You may not like the National Heritage way, Rose, but you can't deny that it works. And the way you're thinking of – well, I still can't get my head around it – no areas, whatever that means, and showing the rooms exactly as they are… Should we not be a bit more NH? At least hide the worst of our junk? Wouldn't that be wiser? Even just a bit?'

'I'm with Aunty Rose,' said Peter. 'They made it seem like you could do anything, but really you could do hardly anything at all.'

'*Thank* you, Pete,' said Rose, jubilant.

'Right. Great,' I said. 'So that's two customers. A woman who steals figs and slaps kitchen maids, and a boy who told me only yesterday that his favourite hobby was "fire". Neither of whom will even be paying. Fabulous. Billy, what do you think?'

'Hmmm?' said Billy.

'Do you think anyone will want to come and see our home?'

He thought hard, with furrowed brow. 'I'm not sure,' he said eventually. 'I haven't really been thinking about that.'

'Oh? What *have* you been thinking about?'

'Well, what I'm wondering is, why are you all so cross about the salt?'

'It's *as*sault, darling,' I said quickly, before Pete had time to jump in with inevitable ridicule for this mistake. 'It means attack, I'm afraid. Aunty Ro has been hitting people.'

Billy turned upon his aunt the child's devastating gaze of unsullied righteousness. 'That is very bad, Aunty Ro,' he whispered.

It may be very bad, I thought, as Rose batted away his disapproval with a sniff, but in the scheme of things I fear it's actually the least of our worries.

29TH SEPTEMBER

A rather discombobulating start to the day. I was shaken awake by Rose, waving her phone at me.

'Come on, come on. Are you with me yet?' she said, pushing me across the bed with her bottom so that she could sit down.

'What's going on?' I mumbled, not yet quite at the surface.

'Here,' she said, thrusting her phone at me, 'it's Nick. He's got news. He's told me already.'

'Nick?' I said blearily, my sleepy fingers struggling to hold the phone. 'Is everything OK?'

It can't have been much after six thirty, but his voice was that of a man who's already fully embarked on his day. I could hear his shower, his fresh clothes, his texts long since sent and answered. He was driving too; I could hear traffic behind his voice on the speaker phone.

'Morning, sweetheart. You OK?'

I tried to smooth my mop of hair with one hand.

'Yes, fine. Morning. Rose says you've got news?'

'Yeah. Your bloody husband. Hold on. Underpass.'

I widened my eyes at Rose as somewhere in west London an immaculate Audi drove through the longest tunnel in the world.

'You still there?' Nick said eventually.

'Yes, still here,' I said. 'What have you... about Hugh?'

'Yeah. He's working at porn.'

'He's what?' I cried, aghast. 'But he never even much liked porn – other than the retro kind, I suppose. How can...'

'Not porn, girl, *Vaughan's*. The furniture. Where he used to be.'

'Oh. *Oh...*' I said, needing two ohs – the first to let go of the last astonishment and the second to pick up the new one.

'Seems he showed up there, asked for work, got turned down, asked again, got turned down, then started making a proper nuisance of himself, harassing and banging on till they caved in and told him fine, but he wouldn't get a wage till he'd made something that sold.' He paused to check I was still alive, and then went on. 'First thing he made – lovely quality, shite design. Clever hands are ten a penny, they told him, when he started to kick off a bit. You've got to have the brain on top. You've got to hear it's shite and do something about it. So he shuts up, and he disappears for a while. Then back he comes and he doesn't leave for days. Or nights. Beavering away like a man possessed. Second thing he makes – it sells. It sells well. And he's in.'

'But, Nick,' I said, 'how do you know all this? Have you spoken to him?'

'No talking, no. Just fingers in pies. Mates. I've been making enquiries for a while. Look, I've got a call coming in – I've got to go. Give the old girl a squeeze from me, all right?'

I dropped the phone onto the bed. Rose had been watching me closely throughout my whole conversation with Nick, and didn't break her gaze now.

'So?' she prompted. 'What do you make of that?'

What did I make of that... I hardly knew. I felt elated, but in a strange, sharp, reckless way – as if surfing the crest of a wave I knew was way too big for me.

'He's back at Vaughan's,' I said.

'Yes, but what do you make of it?' said Rose, already impatient.

'Well, it's *fantastic* news,' I said. Of course it was.

In many ways a job is no different from any other obligatory surrender of one's time, like cooking or taking out the bins; the chances of you enjoying it are probably less than fair, while the chances of you thriving on it are practically negligible. But Hugh *did* thrive at Vaughan's. It was more vocation than work. He couldn't wait to get there each day, and was often more energised on his return than he was when he'd set off in the morning; his salary, though much needed, was the least part of his purpose. 'I can do my best work,' he'd kept saying in wonder when he'd started there, as that's precisely what his clients wanted, that's what they believed they'd get, and that was what they were more than willing to pay for. 'I can do my *best* work.' It was without question the happiest time of his life; how could I not be overjoyed to think he was back there? Stepping into the sunlight after so many years in his cell?

'Is that it?' said Rose. '"*It's fantastic news*"?'

Oh dear, I thought. Here we go again...

'Why?' I said wearily. 'What do you want me to say?'

'You do realise what this means, don't you?' said Rose, frowning at me. 'Because if he's working there he can't be here, can he? This means he's not coming home.'

I blinked at her for a moment while my ears absorbed the information my gut already knew.

'No,' I said. 'He's not coming home.'

At this, Rose's face fell abruptly. Even though she quickly propped it up again with a sharp tilt of her head, it was too late. She'd as good as told me that, despite all her bluster, and her fierce attempts to hide the fact both from me and from herself, more than anything she wanted her brother back.

'That's what you think, is it?' she said primly. 'Good. Yes. That's what I think too.'

I watched in dismay as she busied herself with sweeping her distress back under the carpet. She was wearing a sort of full circle gypsy skirt, black with bursts of embroidered roses, and had begun to smooth the fabric officiously, as a maître d' might the wrinkles on a tablecloth.

'And what do you... do you mind about that?' I asked gingerly.

'Mind?' she scoffed. 'Of course I don't mind. Not for *me*, anyway.' She got up from the bed and walked purposefully to the other side of the room. I didn't know the reason for this, and it turned out that neither did she; once she'd reached my chest of drawers she turned round and marched back again. 'It's just so *stupid* though,' she said. 'There's no need for him to stay away, just like there wasn't any need for him to go in the first place. So it's stressful looking after this place – *big deal*. I was helping, wasn't I? Didn't I take on the Tree House? Didn't I push for us to open up the house?'

'Oh, Rose,' I said, 'please don't tell me that's why you're doing all this – opening up the house and everything? Not specifically for Hugh?'

'Maybe!' she shouted defensively over her shoulder on her way back to my chest of drawers. Then she stopped, folded her arms and addressed her next, quieter, words to the ceiling. 'I thought I could help, take the pressure off. Show him I wasn't the waster he thinks I am.'

What I should have done then was console her. Not openly, obviously – this was Rose we were dealing with – but subtly, with a joke, or a compliment, or an offer to make her favourite eggs Benedict for breakfast. But maybe because it was still so early, and my head was in a muddle because of all it had had to deal with already, I didn't do any of those things.

'Rose,' I said, 'do you know what? It sounds awful, but everything you're doing here – all your wonderful work – makes it harder for him to come back than if you'd never tried at all.'

She turned, with ominous slowness, to face me.

'Sorry – *what*?' she said. 'I've made it harder for him? Shouldering some of his responsibility? Trying to get some money in? How can that not be just the sort of relief that would help him?'

Way too late for eggs Benedict now, I realised. I'd made my bed; I was just going to have to lie in it.

'Because you'd made it happen,' I said sadly. 'Not him.'

'What… because I'm a *girl*? You can't be serious.'

'Partly because you're a girl, yes. And second-born. He's not quite a modern man – you do know that, don't you? Half-modern, half-antique.'

It became clearer and clearer as I spoke. Of course we're all missing links between our ancestors and our descendants, I told her, carrying forwards some genes and bits of identity and discarding others as we go, but most people don't have that far to stretch. What if you're the first in your family – the first in a new land, or with new wealth or poverty? New freedom? New *chains*? What a chasm you'd have to breach! Let's think about Hugh, I went on, counting on my fingers. First-born. The first whose definition of making a living is earning money and not, as his forebears would have declared, finding amusing ways to spend the time until they died. The first to feel the ancient duties of his name and his sex and his property but not to have the ancient means to fulfil them. The first to pick up the Narwhal pride and feel it disintegrate in his fingers. The first to search in despair for a substitute...

'But that's ludicrous,' said Rose. 'He and I... I know Dad left it all to him, but he and I, we were always together, you know? We looked out for one another. We were a team. Just because this place is his – he can't think he's got to do it all on his own?'

'He can't help it,' I said. 'That's the ancient part. You think he had the same upbringing as you, but he didn't. He was trained for duty from the moment he was born. Oh, Rose – it's so sad and ridiculous and awful, isn't it, when you think. There he is at Vaughan's – doing so well, happy, free – then your dad dies and he's got no choice, as he sees it at least, but to come back and take on the burden of everything here. So first he tries his furniture – fail. Then he tries upholstery – fail. And then, just imagine, his little sister – who he's responsible for, by the way, like the house, and the garden and the lake, like the boys and me – waltzes in, waves her magic wand, and saves the day. He can't have the day saved for him, Rose. It's *his* job. He's got to be in charge of the saving.'

She went quiet then, as a train of thought set off from one side of her brain to the other and I watched the smoke rings it left upon her face. Exasperation first – of course. Then puzzlement. Concentration. Pity. A lingering stop at a sort of little-girl loneliness that pulled at my heart, and then–

'Who the fuck does he think he is?' she said. 'This is Narwhal Hall, not Windsor Castle, for Christ's sake. It's just a house. We're just a family. It's *conceited*, chauvinistic, "got to be in charge of the saving". For fuck's sake!' She flung her arms in the air and glared at me. 'For fuck's sake – aren't you angry?'

'No,' I said instantly. 'I know it's not what you want to hear, but no. Not remotely.'

'Unbelievable,' said Rose. 'Why's everything got to be about him? What do *you* want? Oh – don't tell me,' she went on, putting her palm up to me, 'you just want everyone to be happy, is that right?'

'And so what if I do? Why's that got to be such a bad thing?' I said sharply. 'I'm sorry, Rose. You boil up your fury if you want to; you're not going to get any out of me.'

She chewed on her lip, still glaring. 'Fine,' she said. 'But I'll tell you what I'm going to do. I'm going to get this place open. I'm going to make it work. And he can get his head around it or fuck off.'

And at that she grabbed her phone and swept out of the room, leaving me wrung out and wishing with every fibre of my being that I'd just got into bed and didn't right now have to get out of it. I was very aware that, in Rose's mind at least, I'd betrayed her. There she was, hurt and miserable, in desperate search of a comrade in arms to share the militancy of her anger, and I'd refused. Of course she'd dismiss the validity of my reasons for doing so; in her eyes I could only be a coward, a white-feathered fool. But the alternative to betraying her would have been to betray myself. *And* Hugh. I just couldn't do it.

So he isn't coming back – fine. It's what I've expected all along, isn't it? Of course it'll be weird at first, adjusting, but we've survived this far, haven't we? In fact, hasn't it already been better than before? He's sent more money since that first cheque. He speaks to the boys every Sunday and not just for a "How's school?" sort of chat, either. He FaceTimes them; helps Billy with his reading, gets each boy to hold the phone so he can watch while the other shows off their latest bike stunt (Pete) or word-perfect school song (Billy). I know this not from eavesdropping but because the boys themselves tell me. Dad watched them do such and such. Dad said this, Dad wanted to know about that. It's like they're waking up to him; their attention to him growing as his grows to them, gaining the sort of depth and detail it never had while he was here.

And when Hugh and I speak as we do, briefly, when he phones for the boys, there's attentiveness to me, too. Do I need anything, have I checked the oil in the Skoda, or asked Ian to cut some wood ready for winter? It wouldn't have occurred to him to ask any of that before. I feel more looked after than I have for years.

So I suppose it just needs formalising now. The official signing off of one chapter and the opening of another. Logistics. Where he's going to live – even Ravi wouldn't put up with him forever. How and when he'll see the boys. Money. Vaughan's never used to pay that well, but maybe that's changed? Or maybe it's just part of a bigger money-making plan. He'll tell me when he's ready, and I can use the time until he does in preparing myself. I don't mean that in a big dramatic sense, but in a practical one. He more or less extracted himself from my heart, but it's up to me to remove him from everywhere else, and that isn't going to be easy. Take his belongings for a start. In theory, almost everything in this house is his. Even if he wanted it all, he'd never afford the sort of place that could accommodate the tableware, let alone the polar bears. And what would the absence of all this stuff tell the boys, anyway? That their father hadn't just left but rather been purged from their home as well as their lives. Emphatically not the message I want them to hear.

And if the sorting of Hugh's possessions wasn't going to be difficult enough, what about those bits of him here that, despite feeling palpable, have no real physical presence at all? The sound of his radio drifting across the yard, the smell of his shaving soap in the morning, Wagon Wheels on the shopping list, cutlery the wrong way round in the dishwasher basket, doodles on the notepad by the phone... pancakes on Sunday, candlelight on Christmas Eve – and what about the Ringings? Do they go when he does? It's the boys I'm thinking about – so careful we must be with the disentangling of their father from their home... And people must be Told, and I'll need to find a form of words – amicable separation? Conscious uncoupling? That'll take some thinking, and the upholstery will need to be closed, and Hugh's workshop let – if we can – and and and –

I'm definitely going to need time to prepare.

3RD OCTOBER

There's no doubt that Rose meant what she said to me the other day – her motivation to get this place open has gone into overdrive. A couple of days ago she called a meeting in the dining room, insisting that everyone was there: Nick, Juliet, me, both boys, Ian, Jo, John and Shaun, with Rose sitting at the head of the table looking as if she were just waiting for an opportunity to bite our heads off. We were given an agenda, told she expected us to stick to it, and that we weren't allowed any tea until we were done.

She dropped the bombshell without any preamble: she'd decided, she said, that we were going to open with a big party on Bonfire Night. The only smiles that greeted this news were from Nick (half-amused, half-proud), and the boys: fireworks! John and Shaun exchanged raised eyebrows, Juliet slowly clasped her hands in her lap, Ian straightened his back – it seemed like I was going to be the only one who was going to say something, but I had to all the same.

'Please, please tell me you're joking,' I said. 'That's – what – about five weeks away! There's no *way* we—'

'Of course we can,' said Rose. 'There's absolutely no reason why not, if we're organised and we put our backs into it. There really isn't that much to do, remember, bearing in mind everything is to be kept pretty much as it is. Now. Listen carefully, everyone; here's what we have to do.'

With surgeon-like precision, she then dissected the work and allocated tasks to each one of us. John and Shaun were to press on with the Tree House – get the outside done at least, and prepare the oak for the lifting of the bell, which was to take place at the party itself. Nick was to help them when he wasn't in London. Juliet: website, legals, cash flow. Boys: Be Good. Ian: prepare parking, sort polar bears...

I should have been listening hard throughout all this, but found myself instead watching Rose. How proud her parents would be of her, I thought, before realising sadly that of course this was not the case. Praise, pride, positivity even, were always embarrassments to Greer, like faux flowers or heels higher than an inch, which were her duty to crush in her own home or observe coolly in other people's. Grandpa Hugh's warm affability, which could be mistaken by the casual observer as rich loam against Greer's stony ground, was, I suspect, only tolerated by her because it was respectably shallow. I could imagine them sitting there, Grandpa Hugh making enthusiastic and utterly irrelevant interjections, Greer intermittently sighing and openly checking her watch... But Nick was proud. He was trying not to show it; he'd have known well enough how close proud can be to patronising, but you could see the smile no matter how hard he pressed it down between his lips.

This of course led me to thinking about the two of them, one of the health checks I like to conduct when no one's watching. I really think their vitals are looking good. Nick has been coming up when he can – at least every weekend – and each time he does Rose eases a little more weight onto his constancy. She tempers her coquetry with tenderness. She no longer looks up every time he enters or leaves the room, and can even gaze back smoothly when gazed upon by him. But this is still so new a wonder that I can't help but observe it with my breath held, askance, as I would a bank balance in the black. How long it'll be before I take it for granted (and Lord knows I *want* to take it for granted), I have no idea. Maybe it *is* just a matter of time, or maybe it'll take a test of some kind – like the arrival of another Saskia – to prove itself.

Maybe too they need to remarry.

I've asked Rose once or twice about a wedding date and have barely got the question out before she shuts it down. She was evasive the first time, and told me irritably the second that she couldn't see why I kept going "on and on and on" about it. If it was any other couple I wouldn't care if they were married or not, as long as they were happy. But Rose *needs* marriage like a kite needs a string; she won't be able to fly properly without it.

Speaking of Saskia, Nick's… *mates* have indeed sorted it, though by means of such contemporary and relatively tame methods that I felt rather let down, as you might settling down to watch a nice violent film only to find it's been adapted into an episode of *Midsomer Murders*. They hacked into her e-mail account and discovered a long exchange with her sister in which Saskia, though fully aware of the identity of her baby's father, had offered up a selection of men who might be preferable in this role, as if paternity – like most other things in her life – could be bent to her wishes.

'He's all right,' she'd written about the true father, 'but

prospects dull. Zack would be first choice – *such* a gorgeous house – but not sure he'd leave his wife, which means Nick is probably best option. What do you think?'

Once Rose had got over the absurd indignation of Nick being second choice (she should have spent more time with him, she said crossly; there'd be no "probably best option" *then*) she hasn't mentioned Saskia again, and neither has Nick. It's as if their ship, which I've only ever known plunging and peaking in turbulent waters, has broken through to calm seas with, for the first time, horizons to plot from. There's been talk at the supper table of how, logistically, they can be together, with Nick's practice in London and Rose up here in charge of house opening and Tree House building. And *maybe* – but here I was disturbed by a familiar sandpaper voice in the background of my thoughts.

'...treading dog dirt and whatnot into my carpets, you've got another think coming,' said Jo. 'If I see them messing, they'll know about it.'

'I'd expect nothing less from you, Jo,' said Rose, unperturbed. (She and Jo have always had a certain understanding.)

'That's how it is in my house and that's how it'll be here – visitors or no visitors.'

'Completely understood, and I'm grateful,' Rose went on. 'It's not often you get both cleaning and security services in one package and we're lucky to have you.'

It was my turn next. I was told to sort the guest list for the opening party and set up the tea room. Oh, and get the garden ready.

'You can't just throw that in at the end, Rose,' I cried. 'That's the biggest thing of all! It's impossible – I'll barely make a dent in it by then, let alone get it presentable. We never found me any Friends!'

Rose glanced at her watch. 'Yes, we did,' she said calmly, 'and they should be waiting in the kitchen for you now.' Neither her words nor the look that accompanied them held anything that I pleaded with them to hold – no reassurance, or encouragement, or promise of further information or even the least bit of breathing time to get my head around any of it. Off you go, they seemed to say, chop chop.

I could feel my inner panic struggling to come out with pop-eyed, frantic whimperings, but I managed to push it back into its cupboard. Just because, I said to myself sternly, you've never been in charge of anyone older than ten before, does *not* mean you can't cope with this.

'Right,' I said, standing up and smoothing my jumper, 'excellent. I'll go and see them, then.'

There were six of them! And you'd think this would bring my panic quite bursting out, but what routed it was the fact that these were *gardeners*. Like me! People who liked plants! People who liked to be *in* their outdoors, not looking at it through a window; getting their hands chapped, pricked, muddied and callused, working to the seasons, watching from the corner of their eyes nests being built, filled, emptied, the dash of beetle or mouse, the not quite certain shush of a snake through the high, dry gold of the late summer orchard…

They were like *me*.

I could have kissed every last one of them.

8th October

Great progress being made! Juliet has finished first draft of website. I've started guest list. The mirrored panels for the Tree House are coming in about a fortnight, and we've even begun on the tea room. My main worry about this latter had been its proposed location – not because of its new role (near the kitchen, nice view of the garden, no smells, all ticks there), but rather because of its old one – as Greer's study.

It's been untouched since her death. While Grandpa Hugh was alive, this was at his insistence, though his reverence towards this room was not unlike that he showed for the war memorial in the village, pretty dormant until awoken by some threat. The only time I ever saw him angry was when Peter, aged two, was discovered in there, contentedly filling the wastepaper basket with items from Greer's desk. You'd think this shrine-like aura would have died when Grandpa did, but of course it didn't, sustained openly as it was by Ian and, furtively, resentfully, through pointed avoidance, by both Hugh and Rose. In a smaller house, there's no such thing as a surplus room. The minute its use is exhausted its memories get absorbed back into the whole and it's whitewashed ready for new ones; but things can linger here forever. Privilege or curse, I'm never sure.

It was always obvious that this was the perfect place for the tea room, but for the reasons above I've never mentioned this myself – just waited for Juliet first, then Rose belatedly, to articulate it. And before we knew it, there we were, Rose and I and a dozen flat packed boxes on Greer's rug in Greer's room, half-excited and half-fearful, as if about to plunder an enemy church.

'Well, look,' I began, thinking *someone* had to break the door down and it might be easier for Rose if that someone was me, 'shall I start on the books? They're always the easiest.'

Rose shook her head. 'No,' she said. 'We're not stripping it. It's the rule for everywhere, remember – leave what can be left. We just need to make room for the tables and so on.'

I'm still profoundly dubious about this plan for *any* of the rooms, but this was particularly true of Greer's. I wanted her swept out of the house, every last speck of her, and how could we manage that with half her stuff still peering at us from her shelves and her walls and her mantelpiece? But she wasn't my mother, it wasn't my house, and therefore it wasn't my call. 'Right you are,' I said, 'I'll follow your lead.'

We worked like spiders in reverse – starting at the outer edges of the room with the armchairs, the tapestried footstool, and working slowly inwards towards the centre, where sat Greer's vast mahogany desk, two lamps like sentries guarding the multiple items upon its leather surface. Her collection of glass paperweights, a tortoiseshell ink set with her fountain pen still in the little tray, a magnifying glass, paper knife, formal photos of her wedding, and of Hugh and Rose, and a small carriage clock, an old-fashioned phone with a dial… surely the woman herself would any second glide through the door and catch us in our dismantling of her? But no, of course she wouldn't. Her desk may have brought her life fizzing back to Rose and me, but it brought her death, too – in the big black 2000 diary in front of the phone and the little mechanical calendar beside it. July 10th, it read, blithely unaware that the fingers which had wound the date round that morning would be stiff and cold that very night.

We fell quiet as, one by one, each object was wrapped in newspaper and put in a box; I could only assume Rose was thinking about her mother, and I could only therefore think about Rose. Only Greer, a bad enough mother when alive, could have died in so spectacularly unhelpful a manner – too soon, too suddenly, too stupidly for a well-balanced adult to process competently, let alone a screwed-up fifteen-year-old girl. Rose stopped eating. She took to her bed. There was no drama to any of it – she seemed to open her arms and just fall from all reason, slipping like sand through her father's fingers, and those of her bewildered friends, till at last Hugh drove up, wrapped her in a blanket and brought her back to his flat…

'Annoyed,' said Rose then.

'… sorry?' I said, miles away.

She picked up the calendar and eyed it thoughtfully. 'That was the look on her face when they found her, apparently. Not frightened, or peaceful, or anything like that. Definitely annoyed.'

'No surprises there,' I said briskly. 'Annoyed was one of her two favourite faces after all. Annoyed or scornful. Both together if she was on really sparkling form.'

Rose didn't respond to this at first, rubbing her thumb back and forth over the little ivory July in the calendar. I watched her, feeling rather grateful for this task we were doing together. Ever since our – was it actually a row? – the other day, there's been a slight discord between us. Not a great chasm of distance or silence, more the discomfort you feel when a set of steps are not spaced as you expect them to be, the treads just a little too wide, so that you need to focus with a frown on your walking. I missed our rhythm, and was glad to see this shared purpose of packing up Greer's study was quietly bringing it back. As long as we didn't mention Hugh...

'Do you ever think about what actually happened?' she said eventually. 'Can you picture it?'

'Oh, yes,' I said. 'I can picture it. She sees the cows; she sees the calves. She knows, countrywoman born and bred, that the recommended advice here is to be careful – particularly as she's got Delilah with her – but then she remembers that she is above all that sort of nonsense and that the cows will graciously part before her. Only – the impertinence of it! – they don't. They run her over instead. No wonder she looked annoyed.'

Rose looked up at me with a dawning, wide-eyed expression that I thought at first was horror.

'Oh, God,' I said, mortified, 'I'm so sorry. That was awful – I shouldn't have said any of it. Let me wrap it away,' I added, reaching my hand out for the calendar.

But she didn't give it to me, instead taking it over to the mantelpiece and placing it right in the centre. Then she turned to me with a dark spark of mischief in her eyes and said, 'Her study turned over to the paying public? The "hoi polloi"? I'm going to put her here. She can watch.'

13TH OCTOBER

Just under a month to go until we open. Rose is confident we're on track, and not even remotely fazed by the news that the Tree House panels are delayed, but although everyone seems quite calm, there's a definite undercurrent of tension. In the adults, it's apparent in a trimming of ease: tea round the table, light chat, a spot of telly – all pared away like the fat on a lamb chop. Which makes for a very lean, but ever so slightly flavourless atmosphere. The boys, of course, could not be more thrilled, particularly Peter, who is never happier than when adult attention is elsewhere, like a small stealth bomber under the radar – in mismatched socks.

I'm not sure I've got the energy to worry too much about my mothering (or lack of it) at this point. It feels almost trivial to witter on about teeth and homework when 5th November is looming so large. It's not the work in the garden which takes up so much of my mind but rather the nature of that work – this whole business of "leave what can be left". Though Rose is nothing like as dictatorial about this rule outside as she is within the house, I'm still trying to obey it, but this is very difficult – as is always the case with directives one doesn't properly understand. I try and tell myself how lucky it is that all the Friends and I need to do is clear walkways, cut back brambles, and mow, and not worry for a moment about those fulsome, frothy flowerbeds. Lord knows the first tasks are more than enough to achieve by Bonfire Night, let alone the rest. But then I think about Grove Court, and its visitors, and how their faces – so full of delight at everything before them there – would crumple in horror here… But all our eggs are in this basket now. I've just got to keep smiling and push on.

19TH OCTOBER

A difficult day.

I was in Hugh's workshop looking for something I could use as gardening twine when I heard a car pull up in the yard. A quick glance through the door revealed that the driver of the car was Mrs Willis, and that she was getting out and heading in my direction. Her pleated skirt swung with such military rhythm and vigour that I could only watch her approach with dread. What on earth could the old witch want?

'Mrs Willis!' I waved brightly from the doorway, shocked to find my old obsequious customer service hat had landed on my head at the sight of her. 'I wasn't expecting to see you. What can I do for you?'

The impatient frown she'd been wearing before she saw me now hardened into a nasty, glinty glare, like that of a scorpion – who enjoys her work – as she raises her black and poisonous sting.

'I wish,' she said, 'to make a formal and serious complaint against your husband. Where is he?'

'Oh dear,' I replied. 'I'm afraid he's in London. Working. Can I help?'

'You'd better,' she said icily. 'Due to a rather distressing accident that is no concern of yours, I have just – not an hour since – had to remove the fabric from the sofa he upholstered.'

I nodded in solemn acknowledgement of this, though with not the first clue as to what she was about to say.

'This, Mrs Narwhal,' she hissed, pulling a square of lining fabric out of her bag and thrusting it in my face, 'is what I discovered tacked to the calico underneath. Read it. Go on – *read* it.'

Quite bewildered, I took it from her, and recognised at once Hugh's writing swooping across it. "Ode to Mrs Willis's arse", I read.

'Oh dear,' I said again, now squinting so hard in excruciation at the words before me that I could really only scan them. It appeared to be an actual poem – there were actual rhymes – and there was no escaping the fact that the subject was indubitably the arse of Mrs Willis. Its size. The many and varied ways in which it resembled its owner... It was appallingly offensive.

'Well?' snapped Mrs Willis.

I pressed my lips and shook my head.

Appallingly.

Horrifically.

Stupendously...

Prodigiously......

Accurately, exuberantly, *spectacularly*...... and before I knew it a great snort had escaped my nose, followed by a series of little staccato ones, and then came the laughter itself, pouring out all over me and quite soaking Mrs Willis, whose face – I didn't fail to note – was an Identikit of outrage.

'I'm sorry,' I smiled happily, wiping my eyes, 'but you've got to admit... maybe you haven't, but it *is* funny.'

She blew hard on the black flames in her eyes, but somehow I was untouched. I didn't care.

'How. *Dare*. You,' she said hoarsely. 'I'm going to turn your reputation to *dirt*. The minute I get home I shall phone everyone I know and tell them whatever I need to tell them to make sure you never get a day's work from any of them ever again.'

'Do your worst,' I shrugged. 'Hugh isn't doing upholstery anymore. He's back in London now. Bespoke furniture. *Sophisticated* clients. No one you'd know, of course.'

This felt marvellous! It was like being Rose!

'Bespoke furniture,' she sneered. 'I don't believe it for a moment. I've never known such a talentless clod as your husband.'

And suddenly I wasn't having fun. I stared at her for a moment, seeing *all* her kind lined up beside her.

'You wouldn't know talent if it came up and slapped you. You haven't got the imagination or the humility. You're pompous, rude and tight-fisted. You feed off those who do things for you – I bet you're an utter bitch to waiters – and I'd like you to leave now, please.'

'I...!' cried Mrs Willis. 'I...'

I took a step forward.

'Go home,' I said.

With a great deal of spluttering she marched back to her car, got in it with as much of a slam of the door as she could manage, and drove off. I went back into the workshop, sat down on the stool and took a moment to enjoy my righteous triumph over evil. I felt proud to have defended Hugh, proud to have seen a glimpse of his old spirit in his poem, proud to think of him thriving at Vaughan's once again. And what's more, for the first time, I felt a swell of confidence for the future. Hugh and I would have the best split ever. He was going to be a wonderful ex. A fantastic absent father. He and Rose could sort out the future of the house between them (there was no way I was getting involved in *that* argument) and I could actually *look forward* to the years ahead.

My eyes drifted around the workshop as I thought about all this. Everything was exactly as Hugh had left it – rolls of wadding stacked in the corners, bits of foam, his sewing machine, buckram and webbing and strips of brass studs, while the floor was strewn with a thousand snips of fabric, amongst which, I noticed, were little offcuts from Mrs Willis's own scarlet stags and whippets...

I stood up suddenly and, not questioning my motives, made the first of several journeys to the bonfire pile that has been growing steadily on the lawn, built from the garden detritus the Friends and I have been clearing. Bit by bit I emptied the workshop of all that was flammable and chucked it onto the yew clippings and browning branches of elder and hawthorn and ivy, then had to fetch an extra tarp to cover it all as the first one was now too small. It was very important to keep everything dry. On the night of the opening I wanted to stand there and watch every last scrap of it burn. Every bit of Hugh's hated old life, and every bit of mine.

Then my phone rang in my pocket and I answered it, my thoughts still on the bonfire and how I couldn't wait to see it blazing.

'Hello?' I said.

'Hello,' came a gentle voice. 'It's me.'

'*Hugh?* What do you mean it's you?'

'It's me. Calling you.'

'I know that. What I mean is, what for?'

'How are you?'

'I'm fine. What are you calling for?' Stop *saying* that, I told myself. You know why he's calling – time for him to tell you.

'I need to ask you something.'

What asking? Not *permission* to leave us officially, surely, because I'd given him that ages ago. 'Right. Go on, then.'

'I've been working back at Vaughan's.'

'I know. Nick told us. It's very good. I'm glad.'

Again I seemed to have turned into a sniffy secretary. What on earth was it about talking to Hugh that made me like that?

'Nick told you?' he said in surprise. 'How did he...? Never mind. Yes. Thank you.'

There was a pause. I noted a corner of one of the tarps was flapping in the wind and made a mental note to put a brick on it when I was off the phone.

'If you're worrying about actually saying it, you needn't, you know,' I said. 'I've been expecting you to ring ever since we heard about Vaughan's. We did agree, you and I, at the beginning of all this – remember? I completely get it. You staying permanently away. The only bit I don't get is about the house. You've got a plan, presumably? I haven't heard any more about the field – are you still going to sell? But maybe Vaughan's pays brilliantly now?'

'Hold on, hold on,' said Hugh. 'Who says I'm staying permanently away?'

'No one,' I said, surprised. 'But you're at Vaughan's. So you can't be here, can you?'

'What if I told you there was another way?' he said quietly. 'What if I told you I'd asked Vaughan's if I could work from home, and they'd said that wasn't a problem?'

My stomach flipped at these words, and not in a good way either. Why hadn't it occurred to me that he could work from home? Of course he could. He had a van, didn't he? Hadn't someone invented the Internet? All my careful mental preparation for being here alone with the boys, all the anticipation of a better life with a wonderful ex. I hadn't planned for this. Oh, Lord – I didn't think I *wanted* this.

'Are you still there?' said Hugh. 'Can I explain?' I mumbled some sort of affirmative and waited as he gathered himself down the line. 'I've done a lot of thinking over the last few weeks. A lot of talking with Ravi, as well. At first it was just obsessing about the house: how to afford to keep on living there, let alone save it from ruin. The responsibility – all that responsibility that I *had* to fulfil before anything else. What could I do? How could I earn? But then it all just... vanished. I don't even know how. I went to bed one man and woke up as another. Like it happened in my sleep. This realisation that it's not about the house, or the money, or the history or the fucking ancestors. It's about you – you and the boys.'

It was awful – I could actually feel myself recoiling more and more as he went on. But *why*? Why didn't I want this?

'That's great, Hugh. Obviously,' I found myself saying. 'But I'm afraid it's not as straightforward as that. Things have moved on a great deal. Rose is completely in charge now and we both know how much you'd struggle with that.'

'I don't give a shit,' said Hugh, quick as a flash. 'I'm *grateful* in fact. If anyone can make a success of Narwhal Hall, it's Rose – I'll support her in any way I can. And if it doesn't work out then I'll just sell the lot and we can all start over.'

Just sell the lot? Start over? Who *was* this man?

'It's not just Rose,' I said, feeling strangely like a rat being chased by a terrier, 'there are other things. The boys, me, we've all got used to you being away now. I don't think you can just suddenly come back – it'd be very confusing for them. And for me. So you think you've changed – well, we don't really know that, do we? What if you come back and we find that you haven't after all? You've never been OK here, Hugh. *Never*. Even before we lived here, even when you just *talked* about this place it was like a cloud coming over you. You can't just waltz back in when you feel like it, I'm afraid.'

There was a long silence. Good. He'd heard me. *You fucking old nag*. You can't forget something like that. You can't just welcome someone home with open arms – who did he think he was?

'I'd give anything to go back,' he said eventually. 'I look at myself... I'm more ashamed of what I've put you through than I'll ever be about anything else. I'm asking for the chance now to make it right. I know I've asked so much already – the space, the time, the silence – all the bullshit I asked for, you gave me, and if you weren't already my wife I wouldn't let you go until you were. This is the last of it and the biggest. Don't give up now. I promise you. I'll *show* you. Just let me come home.'

It was no good. It was too difficult. I had to get away, that was all I knew. I stuttered something to that effect, and hung up.

But his words rang in my ears for hours.

25TH OCTOBER

Things are getting rather frantic here, but I'm surprised (and, very secretly, a bit impressed) to discover that I'm clearly far more suited to a high-stress life than I ever thought I was. The more energy I use, the more I seem to have, while the less sleep or food I have the *less* I seem to need. It's extraordinary. I've never felt so productive. Not that anyone else in the household seems as happy about it as I am. They were to begin with, I suppose; there were a fair few claps on the back when they saw I'd finished the tea room way ahead of schedule, for example, but Nick didn't seem at all pleased when he found me re-laying that wobbly slab on the terrace that someone's *bound* to trip over at some point. I'd made up some mortar, got all the right tools, and was doing a very tidy job, so why he looked at me the way he did – as if I needed to be led gently to a darkened room – is beyond me. If you're lucky enough to own a high quality head torch, what's wrong with doing a job like that in the dark? Just because the lightweights are asleep at one in the morning doesn't mean us tough nuts have to be, surely? Work is good. The more of it I can get my hands on the better.

I will admit, though, that things might have got a little bit out of hand where the guest list is concerned. It began innocently enough, like all entry drugs, with me asking

Graham and Marge to the opening, but when I was rewarded with such effusive thanks and excitement, I found myself rather keen to repeat the experience, and thought it might be nice to ask just one or two of the families at school. Once the hit of their positive responses had died away, hunger for more meant that pretty soon anyone who so much as glanced at me – let alone smiled – would get an invitation thrust upon them.

I haven't really invited anyone to anything much for years. There's been so little time, and money, and spirit for generosity in our lives, or even for proper hospitality, and I have so missed that strange, heady mixture of giving and gratitude that it evokes. I do try to be disciplined. I took invites to the supermarket this morning with the firm intention of giving them only to Louise, and Stan if he was in. But it was hopeless. Before I knew it I'd asked all the staff, plus the little old couple who asked so charmingly if I could reach a tin of peaches for them, as well as a man I met by the broccoli who I recognised as a customer from the boys' barber. And the lady with the air ambulance charity tin. Watching this, Louise asked if there was going to be enough food for everyone. Thought about this and told her it might not be a bad idea to eat something before she came...

Like an alcoholic hiding bottles from her partner, I've taken great care to keep my addiction from Rose, and even from myself. I have assiduously stopped counting how many people will be coming on the 5th; I'm sure it will be *fine*.

Meanwhile, Ian has got the polar bears upright and looking magnificent on either side of the staircase, Juliet has finished the website and conquered the complexities of the new till, the Friends have dug up those damson saplings that sprang up at the back of the orchard when I wasn't looking, and Billy has made his own contribution to the visitor experience, with typical solemnity and conscientiousness, inviting me formally last night to a meeting in his room to discuss his progress thus far. It became apparent from the moment I walked in and was struck by the positive blizzard of Post-it notes everywhere that perhaps we had not explained sufficiently well that signs would not be required. Did I think, he asked anxiously, that he had provided enough information for the visitors?

'Oh, I think so, Billy,' I said, approaching a nearby shelf and reading the Post-its that were neatly lined up above it. 'Descriptions of every Lego model – that *is* thorough,' I said. 'And what does this one say – "Where I put my washing" – perfect! Just what people will be wanting to know. And – "A chair that is old" – good – well done.'

'Because people like to know the ages of stuff,' said Billy.

'You're absolutely right, darling,' I said. 'They do.'

I looked at his earnest little face and found myself giving him the biggest hug, and for some reason then finding it near impossible to let the poor child go.

1ST NOVEMBER

The Tree House panels arrived at last today. We've all been in such a pitch of anticipation that none of us was able to focus on anything other than what was going on outside.

The truck arrived early – its deep rumble, like some sort of hunting horn, drawing every man on site. One by one, the eight panels were unstrapped and lowered in concentrated silence. Each needed four men to carry it – Ian, John, Shaun and Nick taking the load with the synchronised solemnity of mourners with a coffin, and carrying it round the house, across the lawn and laying it oh so gently on the grass by the Tree House. Rose, Juliet and I watched anxiously from the kitchen, too jittery for the men and their fragile cargo to go anywhere near them – even to offer them a drink.

There was a lull of relief when all the panels had reached their destination safely, and this pitch and trough of stress became the pattern of the day, as each section of glass was lifted, painstakingly manoeuvred, then at last fixed into place. Nick felt it most of all; we didn't need to be with him to know this – it was more than apparent from our viewpoint in the kitchen. It was his pacing, arms folded, eyes pinned to the Tree House as the other three men worked; his motionless staring, then sudden point or shout, then the temporary easing of his shoulders until the whole process began again.

By the time I came back with the boys after school, there was only one panel left on the grass and one slice of wood waiting to be covered, and the men could afford a certain tolerance with the children's bouncing about at their feet that they could not have managed earlier in the day. We were all out at that point – Rose, Juliet, the boys and I – wrapped up in scarves and coats as we knew without saying that we'd stay out, now, until the end.

The boys immediately started to clamour to go into the Tree House, but Nick said it wasn't ready yet and would they help him get the grey plastic film off the glass? They responded just as they might if someone had laid out a whole roll of bubble wrap for them to stamp on, purely for the pleasure of the peeling rather than the revelation of the panels that the rest of us were so keen to see.

They began on the north face of the cube, Nick and John stripping the top corners and passing them down to the boys to rip off, and Rose, Juliet and I moved around to see – with the gasps of children – a perfect reflection of the house in the middle of the old oak. We pointed excitedly to tiny landmarks: the lit table lamp in Rose's office, the now neat line of the wisteria; while the boys, their excitement at the peeling utterly routed by this much greater one, ran back across the grass until they could see themselves within the mirror's frame, and waved frenziedly at their reflections.

It was the same with every panel. The minute the wrapping was off, another section of Narwhal space settled itself in amongst the darkening leaves of the oak: a square of little apple trees, the open bank of the lake and the water beyond it, the bridge just visible; and we would play with the doll's house image before us, bringing forth or banishing great swathes of view by means of a single step to the left or right, quite beside ourselves with delight.

Whether deliberate or not, Nick left the west facing panels till last. The land falls away here, and we always knew we'd get sky only reflected on that side, but what perhaps we hadn't predicted was the effect of this when the sun – and a great gold November sun at that – was caught fast by the glass and seemed to set the whole Tree House on fire.

'Fuck me,' breathed Rose.

'*Now* can we go in?' said Pete, just as I spotted Tony crossing the lawn towards us carrying a couple of six packs, his timing immaculate. We went on to toast first Nick, then John, Shaun, and Ian, and then the Tree House itself, while the boys christened it from the inside in their usual manner – with boisterous thumps and a quite bewildering amount of shouting. And maybe because of the camaraderie that any team triumph brings, or because of the Tree House itself and the way it seemed to shrink down to toy size not just the tangible features it reflected but the intangible ones too – all worries, even the ones too big for you to think about, suddenly small enough to be shrugged at – I had a moment of delicious light-headedness, like the one you get just between tipsy and drunk. If time had stopped right then I could have lain down and slept for a thousand years. But then Rose asked me where Juliet was, and I was brought back by her question, realising that I hadn't noticed Juliet since Tony arrived with the beer. Of course I hadn't. Of course she was now nowhere to be seen.

5TH NOVEMBER

I shouldn't be writing this now. I should be outside helping to serve food and drinks to the stream of people who started arriving at six o'clock and just keep on coming. I know the bonfire's burning beautifully because the light from it reaches through the closed curtains in my room, as does the noise – the unmistakable, slightly surprised pitch and din of people enjoying themselves rather more than they expected. They'll be raising the bell soon, then there'll be the fireworks, then everyone will be let loose inside the house... I'd love to be out there, I would, but there's not enough room in my head just yet.

I suppose it started with the Tree House. Ever since the panels went up, it seems to have been exerting some sort of tractor beam upon us all. Rose had to move her desk so as not to be distracted by it – the clouds appearing out of the oak, crossing above the house, and disappearing again into the leaves – and I've had a very similar problem myself. Once John and Shaun have left each day, one or other of us will slope off in the direction of the Tree House to moon our way around it. It was Ian yesterday. I caught sight of him through the landing window, just before he went home, and paused to watch him – the hope being, I suppose, that I could work out the opinions that he had taken great care not to express on the day the panels were fixed.

He walked around it slowly, with the crossed arms and silent scrutiny you might employ to show a second-hand car dealer you are *not* to be taken for a fool, and I found myself pleading out loud, 'Go on, Ian. You've got to love it – go on, go on, Ian.'

He moved back, undertaking a new, wider circle, then approached the shiny aluminium steps and climbed them, testing the strength of the handrail with a shake as he did so. He bent to look closely at the underside of the Tree House itself, running his hand along the joint between the base and the entrance face. He tried the door handle, which made me grimace, as it's been sticking – this flaw no doubt to be hoovered up triumphantly at once. But there was no sign of happy disapproval when it wouldn't open; he merely stood back, hesitated a moment, then walked slowly down the steps and across the lawn towards the yard, pausing from time to time to turn back and look at the Tree House, as if needing to clarify some detail in his head.

What to make of this? I wondered, as he disappeared out of my line of sight. But though I was no further ahead in understanding Ian's opinions, it turned out that my time spent watching him was not wasted after all.

With the opening so close, Juliet has been working much longer hours, and so when I passed her office early this morning and took in her coat on her chair and laptop open on the desk I thought little more of it than a sort of half-concern/half-respect for the time she was putting in – she herself presumably having just popped to the loo. But when I passed the open door again a little later, on my way to chivvy the boys for school, and there was still no sign of her, I was surprised enough to ask Pete – who was lying motionless on the floor in the corridor for reasons there'd be absolutely no point in pursuing – if he'd seen her? No, he said, he hadn't. I told him I wanted him in the car in five minutes, and went downstairs beginning to feel rather worried. I hoped that by the time I came back from drop-off she'd be sitting tapping away as usual, but she wasn't. I was standing by the French windows wondering where on earth she could be when the Tree House – its tractor beam, Ian, its dodgy handle – pinged into my head and I set off towards it at a run.

The knack, John had explained to me, was to slip a screwdriver into the edge of the door at the same time as turning the handle, to help the mechanism open properly. I didn't think he would mind under the circumstances if I therefore fished one out of his tool box, which he left under the Tree House at night, and with it in my hand I went up the steps, and managed – with the screwdriver's help – to open the door.

I don't know what I was expecting to find inside, but it would never have been the scene that actually greeted me. Standing just inside the door, looking drawn, distraught and exhausted was Juliet. I'd opened my mouth to cry out my apology for her having been stuck in there all night, as she clearly had been, but – before I'd got even a word out – she'd pushed past me and was half-running towards the house. There was no need to ask what had caused her such distress as the reason was right there in front of me, asleep on the floor. Tony.

I didn't know if it was the right thing to do, but I couldn't not follow her. So back to the house and up the stairs I went, round to her box room, where I found her packing up her things. And not packing them up in an end of day sort of way, but a that's-me-done-forever sort of way.

I knocked very gently on the open door.

'Are you OK?' I said, almost in a whisper.

Though I knew she'd heard me, she didn't respond in any way – not a word or a look or even a hesitation in her movements.

I tried again.

'Do you... Can I help?' I said.

But still there was nothing, and I was just thinking this was all rather difficult – Juliet like a bottle of coke after a thorough shaking but before the lid is unscrewed, and me biting my lip and hanging onto the door-frame – when Rose suddenly appeared at my side.

'Morning, both! Today's the day!' she said, the cheerfulness of her greeting so preposterous on this occasion that I found myself grimacing and clutching her arm to try and tone it down a bit.

'What's going on?' said Rose, sounding very loud, though she wasn't. She looked from Juliet to me and back to Juliet, and when no explanation was forthcoming from either of us, she said impatiently, 'I'm not psychic, you know. Is anyone going to say anything?'

Enough is enough, I thought then, with a sort of satisfying snap in my synapses. I pulled Rose into the room, shut the door, and manoeuvred both of us with difficulty to the far side of Juliet's tiny desk where we at least had a clear view of her fringe, her head still bent and busy, if not her actual face.

'So,' I said clearly and carefully, like a doctor to a crash team just before the ambulance arrives, 'Juliet and Tony are in love.'

Rose's eyebrows shot up, but she had the sense to stay

silent. Juliet gave a sharp exhalation through her nose.

'As far as I can tell,' I continued, 'each knows about the feelings of the other but neither has done anything about it. Last night, however, they were locked in the Tree House together. I don't know what happened in there, but as soon as I opened the door Juliet came up here and, well,' I said, nodding at her as she tried to stuff her mouse into a pocket on her laptop bag that was too small for it, 'that's where we're up to.'

We were all silent for a moment, Rose and I watching poor Juliet wrestle with the recalcitrant mouse with a sort of profoundly impotent sympathy.

'Juliet,' I said. 'Please. Talk to us. Maybe there's something we can do...?'

At this, she slammed the mouse on the desk, bent her head right to her chest, then let out what I thought at first was a great sob but turned out to be a bitter, joyless burst, almost a *hack*, of laughter. Rose and I looked at each other – appalled – as the laugh went on, dropping to a near silent shaking and then, when she ran out of air for any further laugh variations, culminating in a huge inhale and exhale of breath.

'Oh my God,' said Rose. 'I think she's having some sort of fit.'

'*Shush*,' I said. 'She is *not* having a fit. Juliet? Juliet? Can you hear me? *Shit*. Maybe she...'

But Juliet lifted her head, told us with great weariness that she was fine, then looked at us with heavy, knowing eyes that made me for one feel strangely like a child.

'I'm tired,' she said. 'Just tired of the lot of it. Tired of trying. Tired of hiding. Tired of being stronger than I really am. It's not complicated. Absurd if anything. I fell in love by mistake, without wanting to, without understanding, without even seeing his face. I fell in love with a man I can't have and that's the end of it.'

'Because he's married?' said Rose.

'Yes, Rose,' said Juliet, 'because he's married.'

I could feel Rose tussling with herself at this statement. The marital status of her own past partners has probably been about as much of a consideration in her pursuit of them as their choice of aftershave, and no doubt part of her wanted to recommend this blowsy disregard to Juliet as the answer to all her problems, but don't – I willed her – don't say it. Not to Juliet.

'But Juliet,' said Rose, 'these chances don't come up every day. True love and all that. It's a gift – you shouldn't waste it.'

I winced. Juliet considered Rose for a moment, then, 'You sound like a teenager,' she said. 'I'm sorry,' she continued, as Rose looked crestfallen in just the way her mother used to make her look, 'I know what you mean is that you want me to be happy. And I appreciate that. But this love that's come my way? It's no gift. You know that.'

As she said the last words, she slipped her laptop bag over her shoulder and picked up her coat.

'I'm going now,' she said, 'and I can't come back. I'm sorry to let you down.'

Feeling sad and strangely sheepish, Rose and I shuffled out behind her and followed her down the stairs and to the front door, where we halted abruptly, as if at some invisible line.

Juliet stepped down onto the gravel, paused, then turned to us and said, 'My ex left me for another woman. If you'd stood us side by side you wouldn't have understood why; she wasn't younger, prettier, thinner, cleverer. But he said that she was the one, and I wasn't. I thought I'd long stopped minding about that, but I probably never will. I won't do that to someone else. Do you see?'

We nodded silently, bludgeoned by her honesty, while she gazed fixedly at us.

'Learn from me at least,' she said then. 'Particularly you,' she added to Rose. 'Take your own advice.'

As we watched Juliet turn and walk quietly away, I wondered what impact – if any – her last words would have upon Rose.

'What do you think happened between them last night?' said Rose, eyes still on Juliet.

No impact then. Or not one I could see, anyway.

'I really don't know,' I replied, as we shut the door and made our way back to the kitchen, 'and I hope I never do. I just wish it hadn't happened today; there's so much to get on with. I won't be able to think about it all properly for ages.'

'There's worse to come yet,' said Rose, nodding at the French windows. 'Look.'

Tony was making his way towards the house, looking a little bedraggled but otherwise – it seemed to me with a pang – as innocent and light as a child in the moments before you tell them their gerbil's dead. I opened the door for him and, with no more than a murmured 'Morning,' he asked where Juliet was.

Rose and I looked at each other. I took a deep breath and jumped straight in.

'Tony,' I said, 'she's gone. She – I mean we don't know what happened last night – do we, Rose?'

'Oh, no,' said Rose, 'totally no idea.'

'But... OK... She loves you but she says she can't have you because you're married and she's had to go because it's all too difficult. I'm so sorry...'

Tony frowned at us – half-amused, half-bewildered.

'She's upstairs, you mean,' he said.

'No. Not upstairs. Gone. Don't-come-after-me-gone,' I said. 'She means it, Tony.' He stared at me then, fixing his gaze on one eye then the other in a way that told me I had to focus very hard on keeping them still. I thought Tony was a man who'd seen everything before, that he understood everything before it had even happened, but I realised now I'd been wrong. He hadn't seen this, and it showed most painfully. He put his hand on the back of his neck and pulled at it restlessly.

'Why not go home?' I said. 'Have a shower, maybe a sleep. What about something to eat – you must be starving.'

Tony frowned at this, as if he'd never heard of food before, then muttered something I couldn't hear and went back out, leaving Rose and I to watch him disappear just as we'd watched Juliet only a short time earlier.

'I'm sorry – I still think she's making a big mistake,' said Rose after a pause. 'Who would have thought it, Juliet and Tony... But I was right, wasn't I? Love is a gift – you should never turn it down. She should say yes. She could be happy. Right,' she said decisively, looking around the kitchen, 'I'm going to call her. Where's my bloody phone...'

'Rose, *don't*,' I said, in a voice that was sharper than I'd expected. 'Why do we always think the heart must have what it wants? Why this special, sentimental dispensation? No other emotion gets one. Hope, hate, jealousy – they've got to fend for themselves, but love? Well, we're supposed to do anything for love.' Rose opened her mouth to speak but, 'I know what you're going to say,' I continued. 'I know you think I'm a hypocrite, thinking it was fine to meddle with you and Nick but not with Juliet and Tony, but that's exactly my point. Sometimes it's right for the heart to win, but sometimes it just isn't. You heard what Juliet said; she will *not* let herself have Tony. We have to respect that. Anyone who thinks differently needs to do what she said – grow up.' The defiance on Rose's face stumbled, but seemed – maddeningly – about to find its feet. 'You should be pushing at yourself, not her,' I said then. 'Didn't you hear her? About taking your own advice?'

'That's different,' said Rose, instantly sullen.

'No, it isn't. She can't let herself have what she wants, poor woman, but you *can*. Happily ever after's just a deep breath away for you, Rose. It kills her, and me, and Lord knows it kills Nick. If you'd just take what's right there, just *waiting* for you.'

'We're engaged,' said Rose. 'What more do you want?'

'Engaged is a pretty ring and a promise. I want you to follow through. Have faith enough for forever.'

The room grew suddenly tight and hot as if in struggle with itself, so that when Ian arrived and broke whatever strain it was, I for one felt a sort of whiplash that was to continue throughout the day. We were all frantically getting ready for tonight. There wasn't time for lunch or the smallest pause to settle myself or do anything other than say a thousand times, 'Juliet? She's... not well,' or, 'There might be one in the scullery,' or, 'Can someone put the toad out', before I found myself back at school to collect the boys.

'What's for supper?' said Pete as he got in the car.

'It's the bonfire, remember? Where's your jumper?'

'In the classroom,' said Pete.

With a hundred and sixty identical sweatshirts in the school, and the majority of the children believing that ownership of these is dictated purely by proximity and not by any such nonsense as nametapes, it was essential to retrieve it straightaway – house opening or no house opening.

'Go and get it now, please,' I said.

Having first taken care to express his discontent at this unreasonableness with great groans and flapping about of his arms, Pete got out of the car and stumped back towards the school entrance. I twisted round in my seat to look at Billy, knowing without even a glance that all his belongings would be present and correct inside his school bag, possibly complete with full inventory.

'Hello, you,' I said. 'Anything good or bad happen today?'

And he was off, describing in great detail a game he, Lucasz and Rory had made up, and I took sneaky advantage of his chatter to let my eyes go over every detail of his face, like the kisses he wouldn't let me give him anymore. The impossible softness of his skin, his beautiful clear eyes, the front teeth that were still too big for him... What a balm your own child's face can be! I was just wondering whether he'd need a brace when he was older when I became aware from his expression rather than his words that he'd just asked me something.

'Hmmm?' I said.

'Are we?'

'Sorry, Billy. Are we what?'

'A single parent family?'

The speed of the segues between their subjects of conversation – would I ever keep up with it?

'A what?' I said, though I'd heard.

Billy rolled his eyes in exasperation at my apparent deafness. 'A single parent family. Is that what we are?'

There wasn't so much as a hint of distress in him, but still, but *still*...

'What makes you ask that?'

'What makes who ask what?' said Pete, who'd left the car door open and was now getting back in, jumper trailing from one hand.

'That we're a single parent family,' said Billy. 'Double parents are two of them, and a single parent family is a mum *or* a dad there, but not both. Like us.'

'What are you talking about, child?' said Pete, witheringly. 'Dad's just working, remember? He told us. Honestly. Single parent family. *Honestly*.'

A rather pointy silence opened up. I knew that it was up to me to soften it, and quickly.

I prayed desperately to all the maternal gods and gurus I could think of: Louise, Rachel, the Virgin Mary, Floella Benjamin, Mrs Weasley – what *could* I say?

'Mum,' said Pete, eyes fixed on me, 'isn't he? *Honestly*.'

'Well,' I said, in my best teacher voice, 'you're both right, aren't you, really? Dad and me aren't divorced (that's true, well done) but also he isn't living at home, so in a way we *are* a single parent family, and in another way we're *not*.'

I gave them my most valiant "See, it's all perfectly clear" smile, but – for the first time ever – this was not swallowed unquestioningly but held up somehow and examined. They will do this, children. Just when you think you've got to grips with the level of their maturity, they go and surpass it without warning you. I've no idea how it happens – while they're asleep? – but one night you're handing them their bedtime milk, and the next they announce they don't want it anymore. Or they spot the half-truths you spooned into them like aeroplanes just days, hours, before.

We looked at one another for a moment, while I prepared myself for what was coming next. But again, I underestimated them. They were not only suddenly old enough to question, it turned out, but also to resist the impulse to do so. Old enough to feel, if not to know, that some answers are like doors that are best kept shut.

'What *is* for supper at the bonfire, though?' said Pete, with a self-consciousness I don't think I've ever seen on his face before.

I was only too glad to tell him.

By the time we got home we were all working hard at normality, the boys getting out of the car in their usual tumble of noise and pushing, but I found my own pretence was thumping its fists against the edges of my brain as Pete and Billy disappeared upstairs. I went into the kitchen to find Nick and Rose at the table, putting tea lights into jam jars. They were working silently, peaceably, companionably, and somehow this felt like just the sort of vacuum I needed for the explosion that had been brewing in me, with increasing pressure, all day.

'Can someone tell me,' I shouted, 'how long I'm supposed to put up with this Hugh... this Hugh situation?'

'Ooh,' said Rose to Nick with relish, 'looks like she's found her angry hat.'

'I've had enough of it,' I said, 'I want it *off* me.'

'About time,' said Rose solidly.

'What *have* I been thinking? What a coward I've been, my head in the sand, how can I not have seen what I need to do?'

'I did try to tell you,' said Rose. 'You just weren't ready to hear it.'

'Hold your horses,' said Nick carefully. 'We're all of us knackered. We're opening in a couple of hours. Now's not the time for any decisions – not sensible ones at any rate. Let's just get through tonight and—'

'You're on his side!' cried Rose. 'I knew it! She realises *at last* she's got to divorce him, she finally grows a pair of balls, and you want to chop them off again. Back to sleep, wife,' she nodded at me, 'put up. Shut up.'

Nick took the long, deep, jagged breath of a man wrestling with his temper.

'Light of my life,' he said to her then, through gritted teeth, 'you need to get back in your bloody box. You think it's because of her that you're so angry with Hugh? Do you?'

'Of course,' scoffed Rose, 'why else would I be?'

Nick put his palms flat on the table and leaned in on her. 'Because your big brother doesn't love you anymore. So you think. He's been as bad a brother to you as he's been a husband to her, for just as long, and here's a nice bandwagon to jump on and hurt him with.'

Rose opened her mouth in outrage, then shut it again. 'I–' she said. 'He–' she tried again, her face hollowing out.

'That's it, girl,' said Nick, suddenly gentle, rubbing her back, 'get it down.'

'I didn't know,' she said to me then, her eyes wide and shiny in appeal.

'Darling Rose,' I said, 'it's all right. I did. And I wasn't talking about divorce. What sort of wife am I if I fall at the hardest hurdle? That's not the faith I've been spouting about. I can't divorce him, Rose. It's time to *take him back*.'

I went to give her a hug. Heard her saying tearily in my ear how much she missed Hugh. Found myself getting a bit teary too. Then Nick said had we both done with the histrionics as we had a party to lay on, and then we heard steps coming into the kitchen and when we looked up there in the doorway – there in the doorway was Hugh.

15TH MAY

I never questioned too much why I kept a diary as I didn't think I'd like the answer. I knew it wasn't a record, or even entertainment for myself when I was old, each entry like a deposit in a pension pot. I knew it was the writing of it that was important, not the future reading, and I remember how I felt each time I picked up my pen – full of a sort of covert excitement – as if about to share secrets in a den with my very first best friend. But sometimes you don't truly know why you do something until long after you stop.

In the dreadful clutter of my Lloyd Loom laundry basket bedside table, my diary always used to lie on the surface – floating atop the books, and the boys' stickman pictures, and the old birthday cards, like a sturdy little leather-bound boat. But at some point it lost its buoyancy, slipping deeper and deeper until it settled nearly at the bottom. Which is where I found it today when *determined*, after much half-hearted hunting, to find my nail scissors. And when I pulled it out, and flicked curiously through the pages, it didn't feel like meeting the me from a few months ago but one from many years before. I could sense the look on my own face as I read – the sort of soft, sentimental marvelling at times long past you get from old photos of yourself, clearly the bees' knees with your blue eyeshadow and your mullet.

I would have denied it fiercely, but the truth is I was lonely. And, frankly, scared. Neither my marriage nor my home were safe, after all – each a whisper away from collapse – and I needed a diary as the staircase needs its Acrow prop. Something to lean on. Something to hold my world up.

So this writing now, this is a letter to last year's self, a hand reaching down to her. Up you come now, I say. Brush yourself off. There's so much I want to tell you.

Rose was right. There *are* people willing to hand over a tenner for a few hours here, but I can't pretend there were a lot of them to begin with. Things looked *very* gloomy in the early days, in fact. There was the issue with Rose herself, who'd rather fancied herself as tour guide, but who'd had to be sacked after only a few days as a result of her Lilliputian patience with inevitable visitor irritations such as dawdling, asking questions, or – latterly – breathing. Nick also tried to have a word with Jo, who would take an abrupt and entirely arbitrary dislike to a particular visitor and stalk them, peering over their shoulders, rearranging anything they'd touched the second after they'd put it down, and generally hovering over them in a black cloud of bleach fumes and mal-intent. Now, of course, we understand from posts and reviews that she has become a key ingredient of the Narwhal Hall experience. Spotting her, receiving a glare from her, or – best of all – being half-blinded by one of her warning sprays of Pledge, seems to be a badge of honour for some visitors, boasted about like a particularly life-threatening bout of dysentery, or a comprehensive mugging. Once, I saw the male half of a rather trendy young couple go up to her and ask, 'Oh my God – are you Jo?', and quite swoon with delight when she replied with, 'And what the fuck is it to you?' But back then people were really not keen on this sort of behaviour at all.

But in the scheme of things, neither Rose nor Jo was the biggest problem at the beginning. Rather more concerning for a business that hoped to make its money from members of the public was the fact that they all seemed to hate us. Not just us, but the house, the garden, the Tree House – everything. After the success of our opening night, I was completely thrown by this – almost hurt. I can still remember some of the early comments in the visitors' book:

"The owners of this property do not seem to understand even the most basic requirements of the visiting public. Has any attempt whatsoever been made to curate the rooms? For ten pounds I do not wish to see amongst other things Minecraft posters on Jacobean panelling, mousetraps in the lavatory, nor an Acrow prop supporting the stairs in the main hall. I very much doubt the place is even safe. Will not be coming back."

"Brought my children specifically to see Master Narwhal's Combustible Conjurings and was horrified to find this involved a young boy, unsupervised, apparently setting fire to himself and other random objects. What sort of people are you??????????"

"I remember the old tree house it was lovely now ruined by that eyesore. It is not in keeping and if you are going to show people the scullery it should have some copper pans or old kitchen things and not your detergent and the floor was not even clean."

So many people asked for their money back that we even came up with an acronym for them – the MBs – and would tally them up gloomily at the end of each day, trying desperately not to let our spirits be hit as hard as the takings.

It was the Alternative Easter Egg Hunt, only a few weeks ago, that marked the change in our fortunes. It was our first large-scale children's event, and we knew almost at once – kicking ourselves – that we should have done one long before. Because of course it was the children, unfettered by expectations, eager little iconoclasts, who showed the parents the way. At first the adults stood uneasily at the edge of the lawn as their offspring tore back and forth across it (rules too complicated to explain, but they involved chocolate eggs, real eggs, and snipers in the Tree House), but bit by bit they seemed to relax; one or two of them even joined in. And they picked the daffodils we'd invited them to, and helped themselves from the tureens of Haribos that the polar bears held out for them on either side of the stairs, and didn't balk at the mismatched cups and saucers in the tea room, and even said they'd come again.

Word spread after that. Visitor numbers began to go up, as did the positivity of the comments they left behind, and – best of all – they began to understand what we were trying to do. That our dissimilarity from every National Heritage property they'd ever been to was due not to disrespect, but the opposite of this. We weren't about exhibiting, but simply showing. We wouldn't impose and we wouldn't demand, either. People started to take willingly the free plants I'd had to push on the early visitors. They stopped asking for maps, or tutting when told there weren't any. They allowed themselves to get lost, and used the whistles we handed out to call us when they did so. Some asked for tours, but others just sat in the drawing room with the papers, or played the piano, or helped us with the questions we asked on blackboards around the house – whether it was dry or wet rot in the tea room window frames, for example, or if anyone had come across a black school shoe, size 1.

I do get it now, Rose's vision. I see it exactly. Another suckling pig swallowed. Where the garden's concerned this means I wouldn't dream of trying to impose a Grove Court sort of order upon it, and am rather ashamed that I ever did – as if caught wrestling a mad, magnificent old woman out of her multicoloured rags and into a twin set. Awful! The Friends and I just keep her healthy, and only ever adorn her in ways that she herself sees fit.

Bookings for the Tree House go up day by day, and someone's even asked if they can get married in the glass-house. A country music group use the drawing room for practice every Monday night, there's a forest school here on a Wednesday... It's amazing how many opportunities for sharing or giving a place like this provides, and how delicious it feels when these are taken up, particularly as we always try to make them free of charge. Giving and gratitude – like when I was inviting all and sundry to the opening – such a *very* specific joy.

It's Ian who does the tours now. I'm ashamed to say I don't think any of us would have thought of him for the job if there simply hadn't been anyone else, but it's as if he's found his true vocation. There's his knowledge, of course, the fact that there's no question he can't answer, no piece of furniture whose provenance he can't provide, no Narwhal whose life story he doesn't know at least as well as his own. But it's much more than that. Until now there's never been any real convergence between what we wanted for Ian and what Ian wanted for himself. He didn't want the front door birthday fuss or seat at the Ringing suppers that I tried to push on him, and he didn't want Hugh and Rose's back door ajar option either. He wanted his own entrance, which is what the tours have given him – total autonomy over what he says and where he takes the visitors.

His notorious rigidity translates to a quiet authority when he's taking a group around, and carries no judgement. He appears to attribute just as much value to Pete's cluttered room ("Just like my boy's", the female visitors say to each other with a happy eye roll) as to the drawing room, and I do contemplate this mystery sometimes. Nowhere is this more of a conundrum than at the Tree House – his description of which seems almost to teeter on the edge of *proud*. Maybe he *has* changed? Maybe a great chunk of his resistance to the tiniest divergence from the old iron tracks of the past was because it was we who were suggesting it? The heirs of this place the biggest threats to his stewardship of it? Or perhaps he just needed his own authority all along? Certainly, the visitors' opinions reach part of him that his employers' can't, finding the gaps in his borders that we never could, smuggling their approbation through. I mustn't ask about this, or acknowledge his successes too openly, but I do smile a lot at him when he's not looking.

Tony still rents the workshop and welcomes visitors to come and watch him work. He's separated from his wife. He says it was dishonest to stay with her when he felt, when he *feels* the way he does about Juliet. To my knowledge he's made no attempt to contact her, but you can see her all the same like a heaviness behind his eyes that he weighs daily on some sort of secret scale. He won't let me tell her, on the walks she and I occasionally take, about the separation. For her sake. Not until it turns into a reconciliation, or a divorce. Juliet herself never says a word about him, although I must admit I do. It's a bit like trying to hide vegetables in the boys' food. I began with the tiniest morsel of information, not even mentioning his name, like a single pea hidden deep within a pie, and when this was swallowed without comment, I tucked in a little more, and a little more... She knows exactly what I'm doing, and she knows I know that too, but that's OK. I mustn't ever, ever suggest she sees him, or ask her how she feels; for now it's just about keeping the door open so that if, *when,* Tony gets divorced she can walk straight on through.

On a happier note, Rose and Nick remarried last month at a small ceremony in the village church. The bride wore oyster silk, held hands with the groom throughout, and was very gracious afterwards about the near constant nose-blowing I had no choice but to indulge in from the moment I saw her. It wasn't just the wedding part that made me cry; it was pride, joy, relief that – after so many tangled years – this gorgeous girl was straightening herself out. If I'm going to be deep and meaningful about it, I'd say what's helped her is the Tree House and the opening of everything to the public. The success of these on their own wouldn't have done it; she's had plenty of successes before, all of them sniffed at and tossed aside. No. I think it's because every idea of hers that we've adopted, and every non-Narwhal soul who's climbed the stairs or slept in the Tree House, has worn away a little of her parents' presence both here and in her heart, blurring first its fine details and then its very shape and form, grinding it into insignificance – just one more pebble on an empty beach. And she's created her own destination. All her mixed-up defiances, from her blue hair to her naked lake swimming, her banners, her promiscuity, made her future as incalculable to her as to the rest of us. What could become of such a girl? What map could possibly be made from such swoops and switchbacks, crossings out, replottings? But of course it was never about a place, but a time. The house knew this all along. It's just been waiting for her – its rightful mistress, its true next of kin...

You might think marrying Nick was another cause of her happiness, but it wasn't. It was a consequence. Only the fittest can accept the biggest gifts. 'You're like a Weeble now,' I said, clunky with emotion, at the reception. 'Weebles wobble but they don't fall down.'

'Absolutely no idea what you're talking about, darling,' she said, beaming, 'but thank you.'

And what, you'll be wanting to know, of Hugh?

Nick gave us not a second to talk that night before the opening. He took one look at my face, went over to Hugh, clapped him on the back, then told him welcome home and all that but he'd have to leave the heart-to-hearts till later. No time now, and not a bad idea anyway, he said. He was quite right on both counts; particularly the latter. A great multitude of emotions had begun jostling at the door of my brain at the sight of Hugh, like shoppers on the first day of a sale – all elbows and urgency. Lord knows what would have come out of my mouth if I'd spoken to him then. I needed the evening; single file, please, ladies and gentlemen, single file.

In many ways, once I'd crept down from my diary and into the garden, that night felt like being back at the Stoke Newington party all over again. Same happy heat and noise and seeing everything as snapshots rather than film. Same seeking-out of Hugh with swift scouting glances that reported back to me that he was not the same. As other men. As, now, himself. This was no scowling recluse; he was everywhere, and purposeful, present, in everything he did. He was there when he scraped the plates, and there laughing with Louise, and there with the boys, sitting on bales, their stillness and his measured movements as he spoke significant in silhouette against the bonfire's flames. He was there in the creaking of the upper branches of the oak as he and Ian secured the bell to the new beam, there in the absence of a harness, in the anxious anticipation of the crowd and in their whoops when he shimmied down scratched and shining and safe, and Nick let the bell ring out. He was there in a slow-dance sort of hug with Rose, chin resting on her head, there in the sparklers he handed out, in his hand shakes, and his smiles, and the certainty of every step he took. And he was conducting a fact-finding mission of his own throughout, looking for me as I looked for him, his scrutiny such that sometimes I actually heard it, as if called, and would turn to find his gaze upon me across the lawn or through the crowd; artless, direct, utterly uncompromising... It sounds like nothing really, just a few looks exchanged, but who would have thought? That was all it took. One by one those long-extinguished fairy lights lit up inside my head, stretching out further and further into the dark till everything was shimmering and spangled and new.

It wasn't until the early hours that the last stragglers

went home, and I found myself alone with Hugh in our room. We stood facing each other in silence for a moment or two.

'I just drove up,' he said eventually. 'I didn't know what else to do. I'm sorry for the shock. I tried to be patient but… I need to know if you meant what you said. About me coming home.'

I saw him set his jaw then, as all good men do when awaiting fair judgement. He smelled of smoke, and mulled wine and mustard, and I breathed this in for a while before I spoke.

'What we've been through,' I said, 'is a once in a marriage kind of thing. You only get one walkabout, no matter who you're doing it for. After that it's just running away.'

'Yes,' he said.

'One new start. One second chance.'

'Yes.'

'And it'll be hard work, you know. The boys, Rose; there's a great deal to be put right. More than they themselves probably realise.'

'I spoke to them this evening. I know an apology is only a first step, but I've begun.'

I nodded. He waited. We both already knew the decision I'd made, but it was a bit like arriving at a station in the dark. You're certain you know where you are, but you still want to see the sign – you need the naming.

Hugh said, 'What about you?'

I looked at him and smiled. 'If I've got a husband,' I said, 'you've got a wife.'

I read something interesting once about change. It said how whole industries are built on the irony that our eager will to change is often dwarfed by our incapacity to actually do so. We fling ourselves out into the pure air of peerless, new blue skies, only to find ourselves – whether hours, months or years later – nestled back in the comfort of our discontent… It's a strange kind of struggle. We always think it's about strength, or courage, or persistence, but that's where the problem lies. I think it's more about perception – a special sort of squint that lets you know you've just been reading the instructions upside down. Like Hugh, staggering about with four hundred years on his shoulders, understanding he could just lay them down.

One evening, not so long ago, we were having supper, and Hugh asked Rose – in a way at once a little startling but in another quite expected, like when the toast pops out of the toaster – if she wanted the house. 'It's you who's taken the poison out of the chalice,' he said. 'If you want it, you should have it.' Rose said there wasn't any point. Either way it would end up belonging to the boys, she said, so why change the route it would take to get there? She just wanted to run it, she said, and Hugh said thank God for that because he certainly didn't. She grew a bit shiny-eyed then; I wasn't surprised. Not just because of Hugh's offer – the significance of it – but because the baby business had reared its head in her reply. I looked at her with old anxiety, but there was no need. Nick took her hand under the table, and she let him, and smiled, and that was the end of that.

I should go to bed. It's the Ringing tomorrow. We'll be eight in the Tree House this time – Nick and Rose, Hugh and me and the boys, Ian and a piper (allegedly called Angus). It'll be Rose, not Hugh, making the speech. And there'll be no gloomy chewing of goose in the dining room in the evening, but a party at which the country music group will play. We'll wear what we want and it'll be willow pattern we eat off, and everyday glasses we drink from. And afterwards, Hugh and I might slip off to the lake, as we do sometimes. We take a bottle of wine and a couple of paraffin lamps and row out to the middle of the water to watch whatever the season and the space provide. We've been out there wrapped in blankets when it's snowing, and the glow of the lamps is like a hearth in the white and the stillness. We've watched the willows greening, and the moorhens, and the heron eyeing us from his favoured tree; heard coots, owls, foxes and even – we think – an otter. The boat drifts and the world rolls around like we're at its centre and we tend not to talk much – just a couple of souls in tune. I marvel at it, really. That its strength came from something so simple: the risk we thought we took in staying and in walking away, and the faith that showed us – in hindsight at least – there'd really been no risk at all.

ACKNOWLEDGEMENTS

My deepest thanks to Louise Walters, the one-woman marvel that is Louise Walters Books. Send her flowers, take her out for dinner, and please buy her books. All publishers should aspire to her standards, her energy, her warmth, and her unshakeable support of her authors. She deserves far more praise and gratitude than I can ever give her here. Thank you, Louise.

The Last Words of Madeleine Anderson

Helen Kitson

"Writing is like a love affair, or should be.
You get to know your story, it intrigues you,
if you're lucky it enthrals you, and ultimately
it ends, leaving you wretched and abandoned."

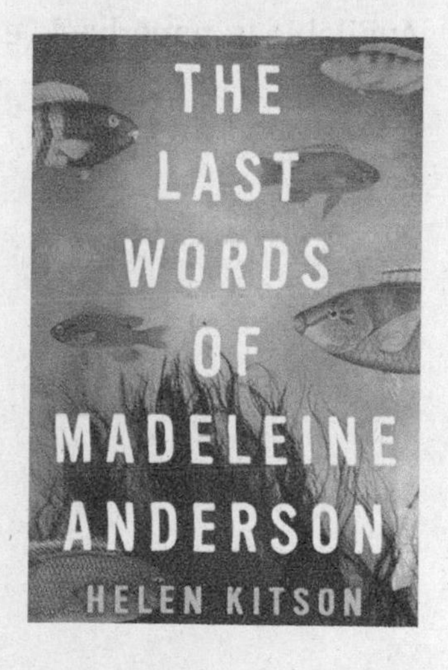

ONCE UPON A TIME Gabrielle Price wrote and published an extraordinary novel.

But twenty years on her literary star has dimmed, her "work of genius" is all but forgotten, and no further novels have materialized. She now lives an unremarkable life: middle-aged, living alone in the sleepy village she grew up in, and working as a housekeeper for the local vicar. Her lonely existence is dominated by memories of her best friend Madeleine, who died young, in tragic and mysterious circumstances.

Gabrielle's quiet world is turned upside down when she meets and befriends Simon – young, attractive, a would-be writer, and enthusiastic fan of the astonishing novel that Gabrielle published all those years ago. Charmed and flattered, she recklessly invites him into her home and her heart. But Simon is mysterious and manipulative, and it's not long before he forces Gabrielle to confront the demons in her past. Gabrielle's obsession begins to destroy her carefully cultivated life, and she comes to feel increasingly threatened by Simon's presence. Who is he? Why did he seek her out? And what does he really want?

The debut novel from acclaimed poet Helen Kitson is a joy to read: mysterious, reflective, and darkly humorous. Diana Cambridge describes it as "Barbara Pym noir".

Available in paperback, e-book, audio, and large print.

Don't Think a Single Thought

Diana Cambridge

"Hello? Hello? Emma, is that you?
Emma! It's only me... Hello? Are you there, Emma?"

1960S NEW YORK: Emma Bowden seems to have it all – a glamorous Manhattan apartment, a loving husband, a successful writing career. But while on vacation at the Hamptons, a child drowns in the sea, and suspicion falls on Emma. As her picture-perfect life spirals out of control, old wounds resurface, dark secrets are revealed, and that persistent voice in Emma's head that won't leave her alone threatens to destroy all that Emma has worked for...

Taut, mesmerising and atmospheric, *Don't Think a Single Thought* is a novel of dreams and nightmares, joy and despair, love and hate. It lays bare a marriage, and a woman, and examines the decisions – and mistakes – which shape all of our lives.

Diana Cambridge's debut novel is beautifully written, and tackles big themes in few words. Sophisticated and refreshingly short, this is the perfect holiday or handbag book.

Available in paperback, e-book, and audio.

The Naseby Horses

Dominic Brownlow

"I only know Charlotte is not dead. I feel it within me, her heartbeat the echo of my own. She is with me still. She is near. I have to save her, for that is all in life I have ever been required to do."

SEVENTEEN-YEAR-OLD Simon's sister Charlotte is missing. The lonely Fenland village the family recently moved to from London is odd, silent, and mysterious. Simon is epileptic and his seizures are increasing in severity, but when he discovers the local curse of the Naseby Horses, he is convinced it has something to do with Charlotte's disappearance. Despite resistance from the villagers, the police, and his own family, Simon is determined to uncover the truth behind the curse, and rescue his sister.

Under the oppressive Fenland skies and in the heat of a relentless June, Simon's bond with Charlotte is fierce, all-consuming, and unbreakable; but can he save his adored sister? And does she want to be saved?

Drawing on philosophy, science, and the natural world, *The Naseby Horses* is a moving exploration of the bond between a brother and his sister; of love; and of the meaning of life itself.

Literary, but gripping and readable, this was the first Louise Walters Books hardback.

Available in hardback, paperback, e-book, and audio.

In the Sweep of the Bay

Cath Barton

"They forgot the happiness. Or rather, pushed it away. But it was there, all their lives, waiting to surprise them."

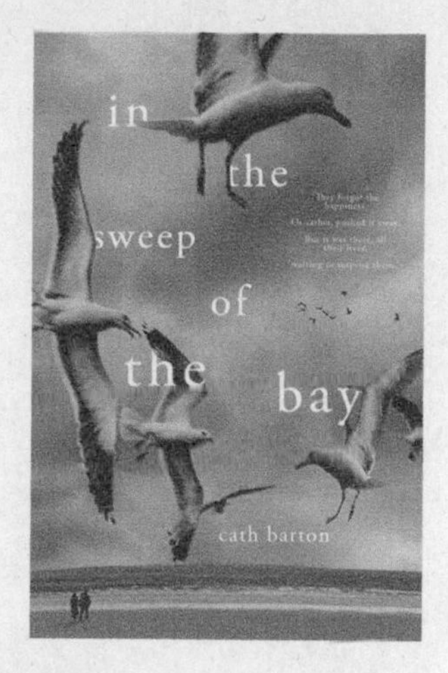

THIS WARM-HEARTED tale explores marriage, love, and longing, set against the majestic backdrop of Morecambe Bay, the Lakeland Fells, and the faded splendour of the Midland Hotel.

Ted Marshall meets Rene in the dance halls of Morecambe and they marry during the frail optimism of the 1950s. They adopt the roles expected of man and wife at the time: he the breadwinner at the family ceramics firm, and she the loyal housewife. But as the years go by, they find themselves wishing for more...

After Ted survives a heart attack, both see it as a new beginning... but can a faded love like theirs ever be rekindled?

A beautiful second novella from Cath Barton which, in just one hundred and four pages, takes the reader by the hand

and leads them through a long marriage, and several life-times. Magical stuff!

Available in paperback, e-book, and audio.

Old Bones

Helen Kitson

"So much of life is about pretending to be something other than what one is: prettier, cleverer, less ordinary."

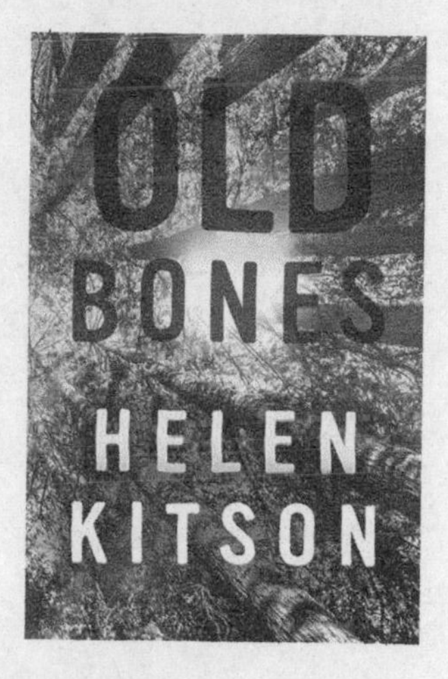

DIANA AND HER SISTER Antonia are house-sharing spinsters who have never got over their respective first loves. Diana owns a gift shop, but rarely works there; and Antonia is unemployed, having lost her teaching job at an all girls' school following a shocking outburst in the classroom after enduring years of torment. Antonia enjoys her "nice" magazines, Diana is a regular at the local library, and they treat themselves to coffee and cake once a week in the village café.

Naomi lives alone, haunted by the failure of her two marriages. She works in the library, doesn't get on with her younger colleagues, and rarely cooks herself a proper meal. Secretly she longs for a Boden frock.

When a body is discovered in the local quarry, all three women's lives are turned upside down. And when Diana's old flame Gill turns up unexpectedly, tensions finally spill over and threaten to destroy the outwardly peaceful lives all three women have carefully constructed around themselves.

Helen takes us back to the fictional Shropshire village of Morevale (first featured in *The Last Words of Madeleine Anderson*) in this, her brilliant second novel which exposes the fragilities and strengths of three remarkably unremarkable elderly women.

Available in paperback, e-book, and audio.

Louise Walters Books extends its gratitude to our Supporters. Supporter subscriptions are invaluable to a small publisher like us.

Please visit louisewaltersbooks/lwb-supporters if you would like to receive a year's worth of books, invitations to launch parties, exclusive newsletters, early glimpses of forthcoming covers, and many other nice bookish things.

Heartfelt thanks to:

Claire Allen
Edie Anderson
Karen Ankers
Francesca Bailey-Karel
Tricia Beckett
JEJ Bray
Melanie Brennan
Tom & Sue Carmichael
Liz Carr
Penny Carter-Francis
Pippa Chappell
Eric Clarke
Karen Cocking
Louise Cook
Deborah Cooper
Tina deBellegarde
Giselle Delsol
James Downs
Jill Doyle
Kathryn Eastman
Rowena Fishwick
Harriet Freeman
Diane Gardner
Ian Hagues
Andrea Harman
Stephanie Heimer
Debra Hills
Henrike Hirsch
Claire Hitch
Amanda Huggins
Cath Humphris
Christine Ince
Julie Irwin
Merith Jones
Seamus Keaveny
Moon Kestrel

Ania Kierczyńska
Anne Lindsay
Michael Lynes
Karen Mace
Anne Maguire
Marie-Anne Mancio
Karen May
Cheryl Mayo
Jennifer McNicol
MoMoBookDiary
Rosemary Morgan
Jackie Morrison
Louise Mumford
Trevor Newton
Aveline Perez de Vera
Mary Picken
Helen Poore
Helen Poyer
Clare Rhoden
Rebecca Shaw
Gillian Stern
John Taylor
Julie Teckman
Sarah Thomas
Sue Thomas
Mark Thornton
Penny Tofiluk
Mary Turner
Ian Walters
Steve Walters
Charles Waterhouse
Elizabeth Waugh
Alexis Wolfe
Finola Woodhouse
Louise Wykes